IN HIS IMAGE

IN HIS IMAGE

BOOK ONE OF THE CHRIST CLONE TRILOGY

JAMES BEAUSEIGNEUR

WARNER BOOKS

An AOL Time Warner Company

The author is represented by Jan P. Dennis Literary Agency, Monument, CO.

 An AOL Time Warner Company

Printed in the United States of America
First Warner Books printing: February 2003
10 9 8 7 6 5 4 3 2 1

Library of Congress Cataloging-in-Publication Data

BeauSeigneur, James.
  In his image / James BeauSeigneur.—Warner Books ed.
    p. cm. — (Christ clone trilogy ; bk. I)
  ISBN 0446-53125-1
    1. Second Advent—Fiction. 2. Holy Shroud—Fiction. 3. Cloning—Fiction. I. Title.

PS3552.E2319 I5 2003
813'.54—dc21

                               2002031122

Book design and text composition by L&G McRee

*For Gerilynne, Faith, and Abigail, who sacrificed so much
to allow this trilogy to become a reality.*

*But most of all for Shiloh, who sacrificed far more.
May it serve you well.*

Acknowledgments

While writing *The Christ Clone Trilogy*, I called upon the support of specialists in many fields of endeavor to ensure the accuracy and plausibility of my work. Others provided editorial direction, professional guidance, or moral sustenance. These include: John Jefferson, Ph.D.; Michael Haire, Ph.D.; James Russell, M.D.; Robert Seevers, Ph.D.; Peter Helt, J.D.; James Beadle, Ph.D.; Christy Beadle, M.D.; Ken Newberger, Th.M.; Eugene Walter, Ph.D.; Clement Walchshauser, D.Min.; Col. Arthur Winn; Elizabeth Winn, Ph.D.; Ian Wilson, Historian; Jeanne Gehret, M.A.; Linda Alexander; Bernadine Asher; Matthew Belsky; Wally & Betty Bishop; Roy & Jeannie Blocher; Scott Brown; Dale Brubaker; Curt & Phyllis Brudos; Dave & Deb Dibert; Estelle Ducharme; Tony Fantham; Georgia O'Dell; Mike Pinkston; Capt. Paul & Debbie Quinn; Doug & Beth Ross; Doris, Fred, & Bryan Seigneur; Mike Skinner; Gordy & Sue Stauffer; Doug & Susy Stites.

Sincere appreciation to poet Nguyen Chi Thien for his unfaltering spirit; and to the staff of the Library of Congress; the Jewish Publication Society of America; the Zondervan Corporation; Yale Southeast Asia Studies; and the hundreds of others whose work provided background for this book.

Important Note from the Author

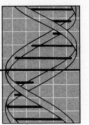

As with any suspense thriller, all is not as it appears in *The Christ Clone Trilogy*, and you should not assume you know what the story is all about until you've finished the entire series. I am not insensitive, however, to the fact that a story about cloning Jesus may not set well with some Christians. As you read, therefore, please consider the following: (1) Never assume that the characters—any of the characters—speak for the author. (2) I have taken the position of dispassionate reporter, telling the story and reporting the dialogue as it unfolds, and resisting all urges to judge or comment on the veracity of the story's participants. For readers who are Christians, I would ask your patience and remind you of the words of Ecclesiastes 7:8: "The end of a matter is better than its beginning."

Regardless of your religious persuasion, I now cordially invite you to experience *The Christ Clone Trilogy*.

IN HIS IMAGE

"Are these the shadows of things that will be, or are they the shadows of things that may be, only?"

CHARLES DICKENS, *A Christmas Carol*

The Right Place at the Right Time

1

Two decades ago
Knoxville, Tennessee

DECKER HAWTHORNE
He typed out the letters of his name and his hands paused on the keys. Quickly his eyes scanned the editorial for one last reassurance that he hadn't misspelled something, or that he couldn't say something just a little more convincingly, or perhaps improve the sentence structure. Finally he decided it would have to do. The deadline had passed, the newspaper was waiting to be put to bed, and Decker had a plane to catch.

As he left the offices of the *Knoxville Enterprise*, he stopped to straighten the hand-lettered placard that hung outside the door. It was a weekly paper, small by most standards, but it was growing. Decker had started the paper with a short supply of money and an abundance of naïveté, and it was still a struggle to survive financially. The upside was that with Decker's aggressive style, the *Enterprise* frequently scooped the two local dailies, including once with a story of national significance. Decker had always been an overachiever who wasn't afraid to take chances, and while he lost more often than he won, he liked to believe he had a knack for being in the right place at the right time. Right now he was supposed to be at the airport, but he wasn't.

"You're going to miss your plane," called Elizabeth, Decker's wife.

"I'm coming," he called back. "Start the car."

"It's already running. I know you too well."

They made it to the gate with three minutes to spare, but Decker didn't want to waste one second sitting on the plane when he could spend it with Elizabeth. After only three months of marriage, he wasn't looking forward to being away from his bride for two weeks, but finally he had to board the plane or be left behind.

As the plane left the runway, Decker looked out over the city of Alcoa on the southern outskirts of Knoxville. Below, he could pick out his small house on the edge of one of Alcoa's parks. The steadily receding sight recalled disquieting emotions. Decker had spent most of his life traveling. As a boy it was with his family, moving from one army post to another. After that he had spent a year and a half hitchhiking across the United States and Canada; then four years in the army. Partly he felt cheated: He had never really had a home. But partly he felt blessed. Decker hated leaving, but he loved going.

❑

Decker's flight arrived late into New York and he had to run to make his connecting flight to Milan, Italy. Nearing the gate, he looked for a familiar face but saw none. In fact, at first glance, there was no one at the gate at all. Decker looked out the window. There was the plane, but at that instant he heard the jet engines begin to whine. Thundering down the red-carpeted incline of the jetway, he almost collided with a ticket agent.

"I've got to get on that plane!" he told the woman, as he put on the sweetest "help me" look he could muster.

"You have your passport?" she asked.

"Right here," Decker answered, handing it to her along with his ticket.

"What about your luggage?"

"This is it," he answered, holding up an overstuffed and somewhat oversized carry-on bag.

The plane had not actually moved yet, so after notifying the pilot, it was an easy task to move the jetway back into place. After a quick but heartfelt thank you, Decker boarded the plane and headed to his seat. Now he saw a sea of friendly and familiar faces. On his right was John Jackson, the team's leader. A few seats back was Eric Jumper. Both were from the Air Force Academy in Colorado Springs. Jackson had his Ph.D. in physics and had worked extensively on lasers and particle beams. Jumper, also a Ph.D., was an engineer specializing in thermodynamics, aerodynamics, and heat exchange. In fact, almost everyone in this sea of faces had a Ph.D. of one sort or another. Altogether there were more than forty scientists, technicians, and support people. Though he knew most only by sight, many paused long enough from their conversations to offer a smile of welcome or to say they were glad he had not missed the flight.

Decker found his seat and sat down. There to greet him was Professor Harry Goodman, a sloppily dressed, short man with gray hair, reading glasses half-way down his nose, and thick bushy eyebrows that blazed helter-skelter across his brow and up onto his forehead like a brush fire. "I was beginning to think you'd stood me up," Professor Goodman said.

"I wouldn't have missed this for the world," Decker answered. "I just wanted to make a big entrance."

Professor Goodman was Decker's link to the rest of the team. Goodman had taught biochemistry at the University of Tennessee when Decker was in pre-med. During his sophomore year Decker had worked as Goodman's research assistant. They had many conversations, and though Goodman was not the type to get very close to anyone, Decker felt they were friends. Later that same year, though, Goodman had grown very depressed about something he refused to discuss. Through the rumor mill Decker discovered that Goodman was going to be refused tenure. Primarily this could be traced to his policy of "Do now, ask permission later," which had gotten him into hot water with the dean on more than one occasion. The next semester Goodman took a position at UCLA and Decker had not seen him since.

Decker, for unrelated reasons, had changed his major from

pre-med to journalism. He was still an avid reader of some of the better science journals, however. So it was that Decker read an article in *Science* magazine[1] about a team of American scientists going to examine the Shroud of Turin, a religious relic believed by many to be the burial shroud of Jesus Christ. He had heard of the Shroud but had always dismissed it as just another example of religious fraud designed to pick the pockets of gullible worshipers. But here was an article in one of the most widely read science journals reporting that credible American scientists were actually taking their time to examine this thing.

At first the article had aroused only amused disbelief, but among the list of the scientists involved, Decker found the name Dr. Harold Goodman. This made no sense at all. Goodman, as Decker knew from his frequent pronouncements, was an atheist. Well, not exactly an atheist. Goodman liked to talk about the uncertainty of everything. In his office at the university were two posters. The first was crudely hand-printed and stated: "*Goodman's First Law of Achievement: The shortest distance between any two points is around the rules*" (a philosophy which obviously had not set well with the dean). The second poster was done in a late 1960s-style psychedelic print and said: "*I think, therefore, I am. I think.*" Mixing the uncertainty of his own existence with his disbelief in God, Goodman had settled on referring to himself as "an atheist by inclination but an agnostic by practice." So why was a man like Goodman going off on some ridiculous expedition to study the Shroud of Turin?

Decker filed the information away in his memory and probably would have left it there had it not been for a phone call from an old friend, Tom Donafin. Tom was a reporter for the *Courier* in Waltham, Massachusetts, and had called about a story he was working on about corruption in banking—something that Knoxville had plenty of at that time. After discussing the banking story Tom asked Decker if he had seen the article in *Science*.

"Yeah, I saw it," Decker answered. "Why?"

---

[1]B. J. Culliton, "Mystery of the Shroud of Turin Challenges 20th Century Science," *Science*, 21 July 1978, 201:235-239.

"I just thought you'd be interested in what old Bushy Brows was up to," Tom laughed.

"Are you sure it's him? I didn't see him in any of the pictures."

"At first I didn't think it was possible, but I did a little checking, and it's him."

"You know," Decker said, thinking out loud, "there might be a story here. Religion sells."

"If you mean covering the expedition, I think you're right, but security is really tight. I tried to dig into the particulars a little, but hit a brick wall. They're limiting coverage of the expedition to one reporter: a guy from the *National Geographic*."[2]

"That sounds like a challenge to me," Decker said.

"Oh, I'm not saying it can't be done, but it won't be easy."

Decker began to muse how he might, if he wanted to, go about getting the story. He could take the direct approach of trying to reason with whoever was making the rules. After all, why should they have only one journalist? On the other hand, what possible reason could he give to convince them to take someone from a tiny unknown weekly in Knoxville, Tennessee? Clearly, his best bet was to work through Goodman.

Over the next three weeks Decker made several attempts to reach his old professor, but without success. Goodman was doing research somewhere in Japan and even his wife, Martha, wasn't sure exactly where he was. With little to depend on beyond luck and determination, Decker arranged to fly to Norwich, Connecticut, and booked a room in the hotel where the Shroud team was scheduled to meet over the Labor Day weekend. He arrived the day before to look things over.

The next morning Decker found that a private dining room in the hotel had been prepared for about fifty people. Checking with one of the waiters, he quickly confirmed that this was where the Shroud team was meeting. A few minutes later the first of the team members walked into the room. The eyebrows were unmistakable. "Professor Goodman," Decker said, as he approached

---

[2]For the resulting article see K. F. Weaver, "Mystery of the Shroud." *National Geographic*, June 1980, 157:729-753.

Goodman and extended his right hand. Goodman looked puzzled. "It's Hawthorne," Decker offered. It was obvious that
Goodman was struggling to place the face. "From the University
of Tennessee," he added.

A gleam of recognition began to show in the pale green eyes
beneath the massive clumps of hair. "Oh, yes, Hawthorne! Well,
how the heck are you? What are you doing here in Connecticut?"

Before Decker could answer, another person entered the room
and called out, "Harry Goodman!" and came over to where they
were standing. "So, where were you last night? I called your
room, hoping to have dinner with you."

Goodman did not respond but proceeded instead to formal
introductions. "Professor Don Stanley, allow me to introduce
Decker Hawthorne, a former student and research assistant of
mine from the University of Tennessee, Knoxville."

Professor Stanley shook Decker's hand, gave him a quick once-
over, and then looked back at Goodman. "So Hawthorne here
must be the research assistant that I heard you'd suckered into
helping out. What a shame," Stanley added, pausing and looking
back at Decker, "I'd have thought you looked too intelligent for
that."

"He is," responded Goodman, "and, unfortunately, so is the
young man you're referring to."

"Oh, so he jumped ship on you, did he?" responded Stanley
with a chuckle.

"Well, after all," Goodman shrugged, "it is quite a lot to expect
a young man to pay the cost of an airline ticket to Turin, Italy, just
to go on a wild goose chase."

Decker let none of this escape his attention. The possibility of
replacing the missing research assistant provided a much better
chance of getting onto the team than did the direct approach of
getting the team to accept a second reporter. Now it was just a
matter of waiting for the right opening.

"If you're so sure it's a goose chase, why do you insist on going
along?" Stanley asked.

"Somebody's got to keep the rest of you honest," Goodman
said, with a grin.

By now several other members of the team had filed into the dining room and were gathering in small groups for conversation. One of the men caught Professor Stanley's attention and Stanley walked over to greet the new arrival. Decker seized the opportunity to question Professor Goodman further about the missing assistant.

"What is it exactly that your research assistant was going to do on this trip?" Decker asked.

"Oh, everything from collection of data to general gofer work. We've got hundreds of different experiments planned and we may have as little as twelve hours to do them all. It's the kind of environment where an extra pair of trained hands can be very helpful."

"I don't suppose you'd be interested in a substitute?" Decker asked. He was counting on the fact that Goodman didn't know he had switched his major from pre-med to journalism after Goodman left the University of Tennessee. Decker felt a twinge of guilt, but this certainly wasn't the biggest omission of fact he had ever used to get a story. Besides, he was pretty sure he remembered enough to get by. And he could certainly qualify as a gofer.

"What?" Goodman responded. "After I just told Professor Stanley you were too smart for such a thing?"

"Really, I'd like to go," Decker insisted. "Actually, that's why I came here. I may be a little rusty, but I read the article in *Science* and I've got experience with most of the equipment you'll be using."

"What you read was just the beginning." Goodman paused long enough to frown and then continued, "Well, I'm not going to refuse help, but you know that you have to pay your own way: airfare, hotel, food, transportation?"

"Yeah, I know," Decker answered.

"But why?" asked Goodman. "You haven't gone and gotten religion, have you?"

"No, nothing like that. It just sounds like an interesting project." Decker realized it wasn't a very convincing answer, so he turned the question around. "Why are you going?" he asked. "You don't believe in any of this stuff."

"Of course not! I just want a chance to debunk this whole thing."

Decker refocused the conversation. "So, can I come along or not?"

"Yeah, well, I guess so; if you're sure about it. I'll just need to talk to Eric," he said, referring to one of the team's de facto leaders, Eric Jumper. "We'll have to get your name added to the list of team members. The security on this thing is really tight."

So, just that quickly, Decker was in. "The right place at the right time," he whispered to himself. It would take forty-eight years for him to realize it had been far more than that.

❑

After breakfast the team moved to a conference room. Decker stayed close to Goodman so that as they passed through the security check, Goodman could make sure Decker's name was added to the list of those allowed in.

Inside, team leader John Jackson called the meeting to order. "In order to get approval to work on the Shroud," Jackson began, "we've had to promise the authorities in Turin that we would maintain the strictest security. Obviously, our biggest problem is going to be the press." Decker struggled not to smile. "The best approach is simply not to even talk about the Shroud to anyone who's not on the team. As far as anyone outside of this room is concerned, we're still waiting for permission to do the testing."[3]

Eric Jumper took the floor when Jackson finished. "Ladies and Gentlemen, thank you for coming. It's really a thrill to have a chance to be associated with such a distinguished group of scientists. Now, we've gotten most of the protocols for the proposed experiments, but those we haven't received need to be in by the end of this coming weekend." Jumper turned on a slide projector in the middle of the room. The first slide was of a full-scale mock-up of the Shroud that had been manufactured by Tom D'Muhala,

[3]John Jackson's comments paraphrased. For actual words as recorded by Dr. John H. Heller, see *Report on the Shroud of Turin* (Boston: Houghton Mifflin Company, 1983), 76.

one of the scientists. Superimposed over this pseudo shroud was a grid. "Each of you will be given a copy of this," Jumper said. "The purpose of the grid is to help organize the experiments we'll be doing. Because of the time limitations, we'll want to do as much simultaneous work as possible. What we have attempted to do is to lay out the work to take the best advantage of the Shroud within the environmental, time, and space parameters required for each experiment."[4]

The slides that followed detailed the experiments that would be conducted. Most were designed to determine whether the Shroud was a forgery or possibly the result of some natural phenomenon. Every type of nondestructive test that Decker could imagine was included. One experiment that had been rejected was Carbon 14 dating, because the then-current method would have required that a large piece of the Shroud be destroyed to yield an accurate measurement.

When Jumper was finished, he introduced Father Peter Rinaldi, who had just returned from Turin. Rinaldi, Jumper said, had come to explain the politics involved in Shroud research. Decker wasn't sure what this meant, but it soon became clear that many fingers were wrapped very tightly around the ancient cloth.

Rinaldi was part of something called the Holy Shroud Guild, which had been formed in 1959 for the purpose of propagating knowledge about the Shroud and supporting learned investigation. He began with a brief history. The first verifiable ownership of the Shroud, Rinaldi said, was to a French knight named Geoffrey de Charney sometime prior to 1356. For reasons that have never been explained, the de Charney family gave the Shroud to the House of Savoy, in whose possession it remained for the next four hundred years. In the late sixteenth century the House of Savoy became the ruling family of Italy and in 1578 the Shroud was moved to Turin, where it has remained ever since in the Cathedral of San Giovanni Battista.

Additionally, Rinaldi explained, there is a group called the

---

[4]Eric Jumper's comments paraphrased. For actual words as recorded by Dr. John H. Heller, see ibid, 77.

Centro di Sindonologia, or the Center for Shroud Studies, which is itself part of another organization, the four-hundred-year-old Confraternity of the Holy Shroud. Neither of these groups has ever had any official standing in regard to the ownership of the Shroud, and neither of the groups really does anything. But after so many years, and with the names of so many bishops and priests attached to their rosters, no one dares question their right to exist.

The point of Father Rinaldi's talk was that many personalities, most of whom were quite impressed with their own importance, would have to be taken into account and many egos would have to be stroked in order to gain access to the Shroud.

When Rinaldi finished, Tom D'Muhala, the creator of the pseudo shroud, went over the logistical details. Immediately following the gathering, a trial run of the planned experiments was to begin in a warehouse at D'Muhala's plant in the nearby town of Amston. The next two days would be spent choreographing the entire sequence of experiments. All of the team's equipment would be taken out, tested, and replaced in crates, ready for shipment to Italy. It would be a full-scale attempt to debug the scientific procedures prior to going to Turin.

❏

As the team left the conference room they were swarmed by a dozen reporters. Ignoring shouted questions, the team members moved quickly to a bus waiting to take them to D'Muhala's plant. One reporter—a bearded man about twenty-five years old with a misshapen, protruding forehead—moved along the side of the bus, trying to get a closer look at one of the passengers. Decker watched his fellow members of the press. As far as he knew, it was just dumb luck he had gotten on the Shroud team. Still, he found it hard not to be a little smug.

His attention was drawn to the stare of the bearded man outside the bus. As their eyes met, Decker recognized his friend, Tom Donafin from the *Waltham Courier*. Tom's lower jaw dropped in a brief gaping stare that changed quickly to a friendly and congratulatory smile. Obviously impressed, he shook his head in what was only slightly exaggerated disbelief while Decker smiled back like the proverbial cat that had just swallowed the canary.

❑

Entering the warehouse at D'Muhala's plant where the team would work, Decker was impressed and a bit surprised at just how much planning, labor, and expense had gone into this effort. Around the room sat scores of wooden crates carefully packed with several million dollars' worth of cutting-edge scientific equipment on loan from research institutes around the country. In the center of the room, the pseudo shroud was spread out on a steel examination table that had been specially designed and constructed by D'Muhala's engineers to hold the Shroud firmly in place without damaging it. The surface of the table was constructed of more than a dozen removable panels to allow inspection of both sides of the Shroud at the same time. Each of the panels was covered with one-millimeter-thick gold Mylar to prevent even the tiniest of particles from being transferred from the table to the Shroud.

For a moment no one spoke. All eyes scanned the equipment and the pseudo shroud. Finally, Don Devan, a computer and image-enhancement scientist from Oceanographic Services, Inc., broke the silence, "Not bad!" he said. "This looks like real science!"[5]

The individual members of the team spread out to the crates and sought out equipment that each would be using in his experiments. Decker found ample opportunities to make himself useful. A few hours into their work, as he was helping to place a large microscope back into its crate, two scientists—Ray Rogers and John Heller—stood by an adjacent crate, discussing their experiment. Their work would involve the only true sampling from the Shroud, which would be done by placing strips of tape

[5]Don Devan's comments paraphrased. For actual words as recorded by Dr. John H. Heller, see ibid., 82.

onto the ancient cloth. When the tape was pulled up, small fibers would be removed with it.

Decker listened as Ray Rogers explained the plan to Heller. "To obtain samples for the chemical investigation, including your blood work, we'll be using a special Mylar tape with a chemically inert adhesive developed by the 3M Corporation. We'll apply the tape to the Shroud using a known amount of force—"[6]

"How will you do that?" Heller asked.

"Well," Rogers said as he reached into one of the packing crates, "our friends at Los Alamos have designed an ingenious little device that measures applied pressure." He unpacked the device and demonstrated it to Heller.

"Nice, but how will you know how much pressure to apply?" Heller asked.

"Well," said Rogers, "that's why we're here."

Decker followed the two men as they squeezed in around the crowded table. After the necessary preparations Rogers made some guesstimates. "We know the Shroud is at least six hundred years old," he said, "so it's probably quite a bit more fragile than this. I'd guess to be safe we should probably use, oh, about ten percent of the pressure we're using here." The decision, Decker realized, was a just a guess, but he wasn't about to utter a discouraging word at this point. "Next, I'll remove the tape from the Shroud," Rogers continued, "and mount each piece on a slide. Each slide will be numbered and photographed, and then it will be sealed in a plastic case to ensure it remains uncontaminated."

For the next two days the team continued to work, rehearsing their procedures. Decker tried to prove himself a useful member of the team, and at times he forgot all about being a reporter. He even began to wonder if choosing journalism over medicine hadn't been a mistake after all.

[6]Conversation between John Heller and Ray Rogers is paraphrased. For actual words as recorded by Dr. John H. Heller, see ibid., 86-87.

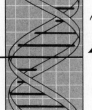

The Shroud

2

Northern Italy

BARELY MORE THAN MISPLACED STARLIGHT, the lights of Milan peeked dimly through the window as the jet flew over northern Italy. Decker studied the outline of this landlocked constellation as he considered the consequences of the job ahead. Like Professor Goodman, Decker was certain the team's research would prove that the Shroud was nothing more than a cheap medieval forgery. The problem was he knew there were a lot of people who would not appreciate having their bubble of faith burst by the truth, including Elizabeth's mother, a devout Catholic. So far his relationship with her had been pretty good. How would she take all of this? *I guess we'll be spending Christmas with my mom for the next few years*, he mused.

Father Rinaldi, who had gone directly from the meeting in Connecticut to Turin, had chartered a bus to take the team the 125 kilometers from Milan to Turin. By the time the bus pulled into their hotel it was midnight and though it was only 7:00 P.M. in New York and 4:00 P.M. on America's West Coast, everyone decided to go to their rooms to try to get some sleep.

The next morning Decker, who was never very good at adjusting to different time zones, got up before the sun. Because of the time difference going east, he should have wanted to sleep in. But it made no difference; he was ready to get up and logic was not involved. As the morning sky grew light, he looked out from his hotel window down Turin's long, straight streets, which inter-sect at nearly perfect ninety degree angles. On either side of the streets were homes and small stores occupying one- and two-story buildings, none of which appeared to be less than two centuries old. Beyond the city, to the north, east, and west, the Alps pierced the atmosphere and clouds on their way to the sky. *Elizabeth would love this*, he thought.

Decker left the hotel for some early morning sight-seeing. Despite the city's proximity to the mountains he encountered very few hills on his walk. About a quarter of a mile from the hotel he came to the Porta Palatina, an immense gateway through which in 218 B.C. Hannibal, after a siege of only three days, drove his soldiers and elephants into the Roman town of Augusta Taurinorum, or ancient Turin. As he walked, the wonderful smells of morning began to drift from the open windows of houses along his path. The sounds of children playing followed. And then, suddenly, the timeless atmosphere of the city was crowded into the present by the droning of a television in someone's kitchen. It was time to head back to the hotel.

◻

As he entered the hotel lobby, Decker heard the voices of team members. The breakfast meeting had already begun, and the conversation centered around a problem with the equipment that the team had brought from the United States. Without interrupting, Decker tried to piece together what was going on. Apparently the equipment had been sent in the name of Father Rinaldi with the intention of avoiding exactly the sort of problems with customs that the team was now experiencing. Unfortunately, though Rinaldi was an Italian citizen, he had been in the U.S. too long and back in Turin too short a time to be eligible to bring the equipment into the country without a sixty-day impoundment. Rinaldi and Tom D'Muhala had already been sent to the customs office in Milan for some face-to-face diplomacy and arm twisting.

❏

After breakfast, several members of the team decided to walk the half mile from the hotel to the royal palace of the House of Savoy, which for centuries had been the residence of the kings of Italy. It was in a suite of rooms in the palace that the team would be conducting its investigation of the Shroud. When they reached the palace they were stunned to find tens of thousands of people standing several abreast in lines that stretched for over a mile to the east and west. The lines converged at the Cathedral of San Giovanni Battista, which is adjacent to the palace. In the cathedral, in a sterling silver case sealed within a larger case of bullet proof glass filled with inert gasses, the Shroud is kept. Two or three times a century the Shroud is taken out and put on public display, drawing pilgrims from all over the world. The crowd that day represented only a small fraction of the three million people who over the past several weeks had traveled from all over the world to see what they believed to be the burial cloth of Christ.

The team was escorted through a courtyard into a restricted part of the palace. At every corner were guards armed with small European-made machine guns. The team paused as they entered, awestruck with the size and splendor of their surroundings. There was gold everywhere: on chandeliers, on picture frames, on vases, inlaid into carvings in the doors and other woodwork. Even the wallpaper was gold-gilt. And everywhere were paintings and marble statuary.

At the end of a long, opulently decorated hall was the entrance to the princes' suite, where the team would conduct their experiments. Beyond the ten-foot doors was a fifty-by-fifty-foot ballroom, the first of seven rooms that made up the suite. The second room, which is where the Shroud would be placed for examination, was as magnificent as the first. Crystal chandeliers hung from ceilings painted in classical frescos of angels and swans and biblical scenes.

Somewhere in the life of ancient buildings that remain in use comes a point at which time and progress can no longer be ignored. Whether it is the carriage house that becomes a garage or a closet that is converted to a phone room, some aesthetics ultimately yield to the demands of modern convenience. In the princes' suite the evidence of compromise was a bathroom and electricity. The bathroom was a strange arrangement of two toilets and five sinks. This would double as the team's photographic darkroom. The only electricity was provided by a wire just slightly thicker than a standard extension cord, which led to a single outlet about an inch away from the baseboard. The team's equipment would require far more power than that.

"We'll need to run electric cables up here from the basement," said Rudy Dichtl, the team member with the most hands-on electrical experience. "I'm going to see if I can find a hardware store."

Decker told Dichtl that he had noticed a hardware store while walking that morning. He wasn't entirely sure of the location, but thought he could find it again. "Great," said Dichtl. "If they have what we need, I could use some help lugging it back."

❑

For the next two days there was little to do but sightsee. Despite Father Rinaldi's best efforts, customs in Milan simply refused to release the team's equipment. Decker took advantage of the time to get to know some of the other team members. His intent was both to be friendly and to gather background information for the series of articles he planned to write. Everyone spoke freely of their thoughts about the Shroud and how each had become involved in the expedition. Decker was confident he'd be able to sell the story to the wire services. An exclusive like this could really boost his career.

All of this, of course, was based on the assumption that the team got their equipment. Finally, Decker decided they'd waited long enough. If Milan didn't release the equipment soon, this expedition really was going to end up as a wild goose chase. Wednesday morning, when Father Rinaldi came into the hotel lobby to report on his progress, Decker was waiting for him. "Any luck, Father?" Decker asked.

"None," responded the priest.

"Well," Decker said, "I think I know how we can break this logjam."

"Please, go on," Rinaldi encouraged.

"Now, this might not be the way you like to do things, but right now Turin is crawling with reporters covering the Shroud exhibit. If you held a press conference and announced that we can't do our research because a bunch of petty bureaucrats won't let us have our equipment, you could cause quite a bit of embarrassment for our friends in customs."

By now Eric Jumper and John Jackson had come into the hotel lobby where Decker and Father Rinaldi were talking. "Anyway," Decker said, "if you embarrass these guys a little, I bet they'll come through with the equipment."

After talking it over, Rinaldi, Jackson, and Jumper saw the merit in Decker's idea but modified it to be somewhat less confrontational. Rinaldi called the minister of commerce in Rome and pointedly explained that if the problem was not resolved and the equipment delivered immediately, the American scientists would not be able to begin their work. If that happened, Rinaldi continued, he felt it likely that the international press would be quite interested and would probably hold the minister of commerce personally responsible for preventing the scientific testing of the Shroud of Turin. Rinaldi was put on hold for about five minutes; obviously the threat had some effect. When he returned to the phone the minister agreed to have the equipment shipped to Turin.

❑

The truck carrying the equipment finally arrived at the palace on Friday afternoon, five days behind schedule. There were no forklifts available to unload the truck so the team's own brute strength was required to bring the eighty crates packed with some eight tons of equipment up the two long flights of stairs to the princes' suite. As soon as everyone caught their breath, they went to work opening crates and unpacking equipment. Soon the public viewing of the Shroud would end and it would be brought to the test room for examination late Sunday evening. There were seven days of preparation to be done in little more than two. For the next fifty-six hours the team worked nonstop.

Some of the tests required bright light, while others required total darkness. The first part would be easy but the latter required sealing off the eight-by-ten-foot windows with thick sheets of black plastic. Maze-like light baffles made of more black plastic also had to be built for the doorways. The testing table was set up in the Shroud room and the adjoining rooms were established as staging areas for testing and calibrating equipment. The bathroom, the only source of water, was converted into a darkroom for developing X rays and other photography. Equipment that malfunctioned had to be repaired on site with replacement parts the team had brought from the U.S. or by adapting locally available equipment. Quite a few square pegs would be forced into round holes over the next several days.

Finally, on Sunday night at about midnight, someone in the hall said, "Here it comes."

Monsignor Cottino, the representative of Turin's archbishop-cardinal, entered the Shroud testing room, followed by twelve men carrying a sheet of three-quarter inch plywood, four feet wide and sixteen feet long. Draped over the plywood was a piece of expensive red silk that covered and protected the Shroud. The men were accompanied by seven Poor Claire nuns, the senior of which began to slowly pull back the silk as the men lowered the plywood sheet to waist level. The testing table, which could be rotated ninety degrees to the right or left, sat parallel to the ground, awaiting the transfer of the Shroud.

Silence fell over the room as the silk was carefully pulled back, revealing a sheet of off-white herringbone linen. Decker waited for a moment for this second protective covering to be removed, until it slowly dawned on him that it was not a covering at all. It was the Shroud itself. He squinted and stared at the cloth, barely able to make out anything resembling an image of a crucified man. One of the unusual features of the Shroud is that when it is seen up close, the image seems to blend into the background. The same is true when you move several yards back. The optimum range for viewing the image is about six feet, and Decker was much closer than that. He had also expected the image to resemble the photos of the Shroud. But most of the Shroud photos are actually negative images, which, because the Shroud is itself a type of photographic negative, result in a much clearer image than can be seen with the naked eye.

Suddenly Decker felt drained. The anticlimax of seeing the Shroud, added to the weight of sleepless hours, rushed over him like the chill of cold water. The extent of his disappointment surprised him. Even though he believed the Shroud to be a fraud, he discovered that from a strictly emotional point of view he really wanted to feel something—closer to God, awe, perhaps just a twinge of the strangely religious excitement he used to feel when looking at a stained glass window. Instead he had just now mistaken the Shroud for nothing more than a protective drapery.

He moved back from the Shroud. To his amazement, the image became much more distinct. For a moment he rocked back and forth, watching the strange phenomenon of the Shroud's appearing and disappearing image. His curiosity went wild. Why, he wondered, would the artist who painted the image have painted it so that it was so hard to see? How could he have painted it at all, unless he used a paintbrush six feet long so he could see *what* he was painting?

Few, if any, of Decker's emotional drives were ever greater than his curiosity. The lack of sleep no longer seemed to bother him— he wanted to understand this puzzle. He watched as Monsignor Cottino walked around the Shroud, stopping every couple of feet to remove thumbtacks that held the Shroud to the plywood. Thumbtacks! Rusty and old, their stains rushed out in all directions to bear witness of their having been there. So much planning and effort had gone into keeping even the tiniest foreign particles away from the Shroud, only to find that the centuries, perhaps millennia, that preceded them had been far less careful.

❑

During the 120 hours allotted to the American team, three groups of scientists worked simultaneously, one at each end of the Shroud and one in the middle. The sound of camera shutters formed a constant background as nearly every action was recorded in photographs and on audio tape. Despite the sleep they had already lost, during the next five days few on the team would sleep more than two or three hours per day. Those who were not involved in a particular project stayed near to help those who were, or simply to watch.

❑

Thirty-six hours into the procedures, as husband-and-wife team members Roger and Marty Gilbert performed reflectance spectroscopy—a method of using reflected light to identify chemical structure—something very unusual happened. Starting at the feet and moving up the image, they began obtaining spectra. As they moved from the foot to the ankle, the spectra suddenly changed dramatically.

"How can the same image give different spectra?" Eric Jumper asked the Gilberts. No one had an answer, so they continued. As they moved the equipment up the legs, the reading remained constant. Everything was the same except the image of the feet, and more specifically, the heels.

Jumper left the Shroud room and found team member Sam Pellicori, who was trying to sleep on a cot in another room. "Sam! Wake up!" he said. "I need you and your macroscope in the Shroud room right away!"

Pellicori and Jumper positioned the macroscope over the Shroud and lowered it until it was just above the heel. Pellicori focused, changed lenses, focused again, and looked, without saying a word, at the heel image on the Shroud. After a long pause, he said dryly, "It's dirt."

"Dirt?" asked Jumper. "Let me look." Jumper looked through the macroscope and refocused. "It is dirt," he said. "But why?"

Decker watched as Professor Goodman, too, examined the heel and reached the same conclusion.

No one had an answer.

As the next shift of scientists came on everyone met for a review and brainstorming session to determine the direction and priorities for the next set of tests. "Okay," Jumper started. "Here's what we know. The body images are straw yellow, not sepia, as all previous accounts indicated. The color is only on the crowns of the microfibers of the threads and does not vary significantly anywhere on the Shroud in either shade or depth. Where one fiber crosses another the underlying fiber is unaffected by the color.

"The yellow microfibers show no sign of capillarity or blotting, which indicates that no liquid was used to create the image, which rules out paint. Further there is no adherence, meniscus effect, or matting between the threads, also ruling out any type of liquid paint. In the areas of the apparent blood stains, the fibers are clearly matted and there are signs of capillarity, as would be the case with blood."

"What about the feet?" asked one of the scientists. For those who had just come on duty, Jumper explained what had happened with the reflectance spectroscopy test.

"Of course there's dirt," one of the female team members said after Jumper's explanation. "What could be more natural than dirt on the bottom of the feet?"

"Yes," said Jumper, "but that assumes that this is indeed an authentic image of a crucified man, somehow transferred to the cloth." Personally, Jumper did not discount the possibility, but he knew that it was bad science to start from an assumption.

Still, the obvious was becoming harder and harder to deny, for not only was there dirt on the heel, but the amount of dirt was so minute that it was not visible to the naked eye. Why, they wondered, if the Shroud was a forgery, would the forger go to the trouble to put on the image dirt which no one could see? The question would remain unanswered.

As the meeting broke up, Goodman, who continued to be the greatest skeptic, remarked, "Well, if it is a forgery, it's a good one." Decker was struck by the tremendous allowance that Goodman had made in that little word *if*.

❑

It had now been three and a half days since Decker had slept and he resolved to return to the hotel. Before retiring, though, he sat in the lobby with team members Roger Harris, Susan Chon, and Joshua Rosen, unwinding with a slowly stirred cup of coffee heavily laced with Irish cream liqueur. Decker entertained little thought of interviewing anyone. Over the past three days, he had begun to see himself much less as a reporter and much more as a member of the team. Habitually, though, he continued making mental notes.

One of his companions, Dr. Joshua Rosen, was a nuclear physicist from Lawrence Livermore National Laboratory working on laser and particle-beam research for the Pentagon. Rosen was one of the four Jewish members of the team and Decker could not resist the opportunity to ask him about his feelings on examining a Christian relic.

Rosen smiled. "If I weren't so tired I'd lead you on a bit," he said. "But if you really want an answer on that you'll have to ask one of the other Jewish members of the team."

"You don't have an opinion?" Decker queried.

"I have an opinion, but I'm not qualified to answer your question." Rosen paused, and Decker's brow tightened in puzzlement.

"I'm Messianic," Rosen added in response. Decker didn't catch his meaning. "A Christian Jew," Rosen explained.

"Oh," said Decker. "This isn't something that happened in the last few days, is it?"

Rosen chuckled.

Roger Harris, too tired to even talk, barely managed to force down a mouthful of coffee as he began to laugh with Rosen. Decker's remark had not been that funny, but the pained look on Roger's face set Susan Chon to giggling and soon the four over-tired, punch-drunk team members were laughing uncontrollably, each member's inability to control himself fueling the others' merriment.

On the other side of the dining room, a woman had been sitting since before Decker and the others came in. On the table before her were the remnants of a long-finished cup of tea and a half-eaten hard roll. She held a red hotel napkin, pulling it in one direction and then the other. She had been watching Decker and the other team members as they talked, building up her courage to go over to their table. Their laughter made them seem somehow more approachable and human, while its infectious nature seemed to brighten her own dark mood. She rose from her seat and walked slowly but decisively toward them.

"You are Americans?" she asked when their laughter began to pass.

"Yes," Joshua Rosen responded.

"You're with the scientists examining the Shroud?"

On the woman's face Decker saw lines of worry; in her eyes, the evidence of recently blotted tears.

"Yes," he answered. "We're working with the Shroud. Is there something we can do for you?"

"My son—he's four—is very ill. The doctors say he may not live more than a few months. All that I ask is that you allow me to bring flowers to the Shroud as a gift to Jesus."

No one at the table had gotten more than twelve hours sleep in the previous four days and it seemed to Decker that the tears of laughter were joined by tears of sympathy for the woman's plight and her modest request. All agreed to help but Rosen was the first to offer a plan. It would be impossible for the woman to bring flowers to the Shroud herself. However, Rosen told her that if she would bring the flowers to the palace the next day around one o'clock, he would bring them to the Shroud himself.

❑

In his room, Decker fell quickly to sleep and felt totally rested when he awoke fourteen hours later, at noon the next day. When he arrived at the palace an hour later, Rosen was talking with the woman from the hotel. Decker noticed that the cloud of depression that had covered her the night before had been replaced by a peaceful look of hope. She smiled in recognition at Decker as she started to leave.

Rosen started up the stairs with the vase of cut flowers but, spotting Decker, turned and waited.

"Pretty neat, huh?" Rosen said.

"Pretty neat," Decker responded. But to himself he wondered what would happen to the woman if her son died.

3

Body of Christ

Ten years later
Knoxville, Tennessee

IT WAS COLD OUTSIDE. The usual warm autumn weather of East Tennessee had given way to a cold snap that sent the local residents scurrying to their wood piles for added warmth and atmosphere. Decker and his wife Elizabeth lay a bit more than half asleep, snuggled together before a waning fire, dreaming to the sounds of the crackling hardwood embers. The fire's warmth and glow offered more than enough reason for not getting up when the phone rang. One-year-old Hope Hawthorne lay sleeping soundly in her crib in the bedroom. Though he knew she wouldn't likely be awakened by it, on the third ring Decker finally lifted himself slowly from the floor and moved toward the offending instrument. On the eighth ring he answered.

"Hello."

"Decker Hawthorne?" responded the voice from the other end of the phone.

"Yes," Decker answered.

"This is Harry Goodman. I have something you'll want to see." Goodman's voice was excited but controlled. "It's a story for your newspaper. Can you come to Los Angeles right away?"

"Professor?" Decker said, a little dumbfounded and not yet fully awake. "This is quite a surprise. It's been . . ." Decker paused to count the years, "seven or eight years. How are you?"

"I'm fine," Goodman answered hastily, not the least bit interested in small talk. "Can you come to Los Angeles?" he asked again, insistently.

"I don't know, Professor. What exactly is the story about?"

"If I tell you over the phone you'll think I'm crazy."

"Maybe not. Try me."

"I can't. Not over the phone. All I can say is it has to do with the Shroud."

"The Shroud?" Decker asked in surprise. "Of Turin?"

"Of course the Shroud of Turin."

"Uh . . . Professor, I hate to bring this up, but I'm afraid the Shroud is old news. They did Carbon 14 dating of the Shroud and found out it wasn't old enough to be the burial cloth of Christ. Didn't you read about it in the newspapers last month? It was on the front page of *The New York Times*."[7]

"You think I live in a shell or something? I know all about the Carbon 14 dating," Goodman said, obviously not pleased at having to explain himself.

"Well, so what more is there to say about it?"

"I really don't think I can talk about this on the phone. Decker, this may be *the* most important discovery since Columbus discovered the New World. Please, just trust me on this one. I promise you won't be disappointed."

Decker knew that Goodman was not given to gross exaggeration. Obviously, whatever it was must be something pretty important. He did a quick mental check of his schedule and agreed to fly to Los Angeles two days later.

"Who was that?" Elizabeth asked after he'd hung up.

"Professor Goodman," Decker answered.

Elizabeth gave Decker a puzzled look. "Goodman?" she asked. "Henry Goodman, your old professor, the one you went with to Italy?"

"Yeah," said Decker without much enthusiasm. "Only it's Harry, not Henry. I'm afraid I'm going to have to skip the drive up

[7]Roberto Suro, "Church Says Shroud of Turin Isn't Authentic," *The New York Times*, 14 October 1988, sect. 1, p. 1.

to Cade's Cove on Saturday. I have to fly out to Los Angeles to see him about a story."

Elizabeth's disappointment showed on her face, but she didn't say anything.

❑

That night Decker and Elizabeth lay in bed talking about what it could be that Goodman had found. Decker had not even talked to Goodman since the fall three years after the Shroud team had formalized the findings of their 140,000 hours of work in a published report. In short, the report said that the image on the Shroud is clearly not the result of a painting or any other known method of image transfer. Based on thirteen different test measures and procedures, the scourge marks and blood around the nail holes and side wound are, indeed, the result of human blood. Fibrils beneath the blood show no evidence of oxidation, indicating that the blood was on the cloth prior to whatever process caused the image. Finally, the report said that while the material of the Shroud may be old enough to be the burial cloth of Jesus of Nazareth, it is impossible to even guess at its age without Carbon 14 dating, and that could not be done without destroying a large portion of the cloth.

But that was old technology. As science advanced it became possible to perform accurate Carbon 14 dating using a sample the size of a postage stamp. And soon afterward the Catholic Church announced that Pope John Paul II would permit the Shroud to be Carbon 14 dated by three laboratories. The Church announced the findings later that year. The labs found that, with a combined certainty of 95 percent, the Shroud was made of flax grown sometime between 1260 and 1390, and therefore, the cloth is simply not old enough to have been the burial cloth of Christ.

"What was it that Professor Goodman said?" Elizabeth asked. "That it was the most important discovery since Columbus discovered America?"

"Yeah," Decker responded, shaking his head.

"Well, if the Shroud has been proven a forgery, what else could he be talking about?"

"I don't know," Decker shrugged. "The only thing I can think of is that Goodman has discovered how the image was made. After all, even though we know it's a forgery, we still have no idea how the image was transferred to the cloth," he explained. "But if that's all he's found, he's blowing this way out of proportion. It could hardly be compared with Columbus discovering America."

"Well, then he must have discovered some way to prove that it's real," Elizabeth concluded.

Decker shook his head. "No, that's crazy," he concluded. "The Carbon 14 dating was conclusive. And besides, it's axiomatic that you can't prove the existence of God in the laboratory. So even if the dating was wrong, how could Goodman prove the authenticity of the Shroud? Proving the Shroud is a forgery is something science can do, but trying to prove it's authentic would be nuts." Decker paused and then added, "Not to mention totally out of character for someone like Goodman, who's not even sure of his *own* existence, much less the existence of God." Elizabeth and Decker laughed, kissed, and ended their conversation for the night.

Los Angeles, California

Harry Goodman met Decker at the Los Angeles airport. Once they reached his car, Goodman wasted no time getting to the subject at hand. "You remember, no doubt," Goodman said, "the effect it had on me when we discovered the minute particles of dirt in the heel area of the Shroud image." Goodman presumed too much—ten years had passed since Turin—but Decker politely nodded his recollection. "It made no sense," Goodman continued. "No medieval forger would have gone to the trouble of rubbing dirt into the Shroud unless it could be seen by the naked eye. It was *then* that I began to question my assumption that the Shroud was a forgery."

Decker shook his head, certain he must have misunderstood.

Could Goodman really be suggesting he thought the Shroud was real?

"You, of course, recall that some of the most conclusive work on the Shroud was done by Dr. John Heller using the samples gathered on the strips of Mylar tape." Decker did recall. Heller and Dr. Allan Adler had proven that the stains were human blood and had also determined that the images were the result of oxidation.[8]

"Yeah," Decker replied. "But how can any of that matter now that we know the Shroud's not old enough to be authentic?"

"I wanted to examine the tape samples taken from the heel and foot area more closely," Goodman continued, ignoring Decker's question, "so I arranged to have the samples sent here. You will recall that the samples were placed in a specially built case, and they took great care to guarantee that no foreign materials got onto the samples. Each sample was cataloged by where it had come from on the Shroud and then the case was sealed hermetically for shipping. Unfortunately, that was like closing the gate after the horses have already gone.

"In Turin, I personally counted more than a dozen different contaminated articles that came in contact with the Shroud. At least two team members and three priests kissed it. As far as kissing and touching the thing, it seems that's been going on for as long as it's been around. And don't forget the rust stains from those old thumbtacks. Even our procedures to prevent contamination introduced some contaminants. The cotton gloves we wore surely carried American pollen that, no doubt, got onto the Shroud material. And while we're talking about other materials, let's not forget the plywood, or the backing material, or the red silk covering.

"The point of all this is that the tape samples picked up all sorts of garbage that had nothing to do with the origin of the Shroud or the creation of the image. In his published report on the Shroud, Dr. Heller noted finding both natural and synthetic

[8]Heller, *Report on the Shroud of Turin*, 181-188, 197-200, 215-216.

fibers, fly ash, animal hairs, insect parts, beeswax from church candles, and a couple of dozen other assorted materials, not to mention spores and pollen.[9] Because of all this clutter, Heller decided that most of his examination should employ levels of magnification just powerful enough to examine substances that could have been used to create a visible image and to ignore the smaller, irrelevant materials.

"For his purposes, Heller did exactly what he should have done, but his procedures would have missed the kind of evidence I was looking for. That's why I decided to have a second look. I was interested in what might ordinarily have been missed among all the microscopic clutter.

"I believe that what I found will explain the whole Shroud mystery." Goodman paused. "But there's more."

Decker waited but Goodman was silent. "Well, what is it?" Decker asked.

"Where's your sense of drama, Hawthorne?" asked Goodman. "You'll see soon enough."

At the university, Goodman drove to the William G. Young Science building on the east side of the UCLA campus and parked in the tenured faculty parking lot. His office was on the fourth floor and looked out over a courtyard westward toward the Engineering building. It was arranged very much the same as the office he'd had at UT, including the ragged but now framed *"I think, therefore, I am. I think."* poster and a laser-printed version of *Goodman's First Law of Achievement.* "Before we go any farther," Goodman began, as they settled into his office, "I must confess that I have brought you here under slightly false pretenses." Decker didn't like the sound of that but he let Goodman continue. "What I am going to show you may not be revealed to anyone. At least not yet."

"Then why was it so important that I come out here right

[9]Ibid., 126, 163.

away?" Decker asked, both puzzled and a little perturbed at having been misled.

"Because," Goodman answered, "I need a witness. And the way I figure it, you owe me. You could have gotten me in a lot of trouble with my colleagues when you ran your story on the Turin project. The only reporter that was supposed to be there was Weaver from *National Geographic*. We weren't even supposed to talk to anyone from the press. And then a week after we got back, the whole world reads wire reports of a story in a Knoxville paper by some jerk reporter who managed to pass himself off as a member of the team. And that jerk reporter just happened to decide to pass himself off as my jerk assistant!

"I went through no end of scrutiny over that, but it could have been much worse. You could have cost me the trust of a lot of my professional colleagues. Fortunately you did make yourself useful while you were there and you made a good impression on the rest of the team members. But still, it might not have worked out so well. If anyone had thought that I knowingly helped a reporter get onto the team, I'd have been blackballed as a security risk on all kinds of future projects. So the way I figure it, you owe me, and you owe me big."

"Hey, I was just following *Goodman's First Law of Achievement*: 'The shortest distance between any two points is around the rules,'" Decker responded. But Goodman was right and Decker knew it. His conscience had always bothered him a little about the way he'd gotten onto the Shroud team. "Okay," he said at last, "it was a lousy thing to do. I do owe you. So what is it you want to show me that I can't tell anyone about?"

"You can tell anyone you like, but only when I say so. In fact, at the right time I'll want you to report it. Just not right away. Right now I need a witness and you know I can't stand most reporters. Truth is you're just barely tolerable," Goodman added with a grin, trying to lighten the mood. "I need someone I can trust to keep the story quiet until I'm ready to go public. You've covered the Shroud story from the beginning. People will believe you when you report what I'm going to show you, but if the story comes out too soon it could doom the whole project."

"But, Professor, if this is about some research you've done, why don't you just publish it yourself in a scholarly journal?"

"I will, of course, publish my work in detail later. But, well . . . I'm afraid I'll need to break the ice with the public before I reveal the exact nature of my research to my peers."

Decker frowned in confusion.

"It's just, I'm afraid I've applied a little of *Goodman's First Law* myself. There are those in the scientific community who, because of their narrow-mindedness, might condemn my methods. My hope is that once the benefits of my work are well known, public opinion will be too strong in my favor for my peers to condemn my methods. So, in exchange for confidentiality now, you get exclusivity later. As the story evolves you'll be the only reporter to have it. Certainly after you publish each part of the story, I'll have to talk to other press people, but I'll make sure you have the story a week or two before anyone else."

"What do you mean, 'as the story evolves'?" asked Decker.

"What I'm going to show you today is just the beginning. There will be several installments along the way before you report the overall story."

Decker still had no idea what Goodman had discovered, but he couldn't help but be interested.

"So it all comes down to five things," Goodman concluded. "First, I need a witness I can trust. Second, you owe me for Turin. Third, you've covered the Shroud story since the beginning. Fourth, if you provide me with confidentiality, I'll provide you with exclusivity."

"And fifth?" Decker asked.

"Fifth," Goodman answered, "is that if you report the story before I say to, I'll deny every word of it and you'll make a total fool of yourself. You'll never prove a thing."

"I thought you just said you thought that people would believe me."

"Yes, if I back you up and you back me up. But by yourself, and with my denial, they'll think you're crazy. Decker, I'm offering you the biggest exclusive of all time on the greatest discovery—scientific or otherwise—in the last five hundred years. But in some ways it's also the most bizarre."

"Okay," Decker said. "So let's hear it."

"Do we have a deal?" Goodman asked, extending his hand to seal the agreement.

"Sure," Decker said, leaning over the desk to shake Goodman's hand. "So what's this big scoop about the Shroud?"

Goodman leaned back in his chair, placed his fingertips together, his elbows on the arm rests, and gazed off into space, apparently considering his words. "Consider the following hypothesis," Goodman began. "The image of the man on the Shroud of Turin is the result of a sudden burst of heat and light energy from the body of a crucified man as his body went through an instantaneous regeneration or 'resurrection,' if you will."

Decker's mouth dropped open. There was silence for a long moment and then he began to laugh. "You're kidding me, right? This is all payback for Turin, isn't it?"

"I assure you, I am entirely serious," Goodman responded as Decker's laughter continued.

"But this is ridiculous," Decker said as he stopped laughing and tried to read Goodman's face for any hint that despite his denial, he was, in fact, playing a practical joke. Finding none, he continued. "Professor, that's not a scientific hypothesis; that's a statement of faith. And since the Shroud isn't old enough to be the burial cloth of Christ, it's not even blind faith—it's ignorant faith."

"It is not a statement of faith at all! It's based on sound scientific fact and reasoning. There *is* a way to test my hypothesis and to prove it."

Decker's eyes squinted, revealing the puzzlement behind them. "Okay, I'll bite," he said reluctantly. "How can you prove it?"

"By way of explanation," Goodman answered, "let me ask you what you know about Francis Crick."

Decker was a little resistant to Goodman's unexplained change of subject but decided to allow his old professor some flexibility and not argue the point. "I know he won the Nobel Prize in medicine back in the early sixties—"

"Sixty-two," Goodman interrupted.

"—for his codiscovery with James Watson of the double helix structure of DNA. And I know he published a book several years back . . ." Decker struggled to remember the name of the book.

"It was called *Life Itself*,"[10] Goodman said, finishing Decker's sentence.

"Yeah, that's it. *Life Itself*."

"Good!" Goodman said. "Then you're familiar with his book."

"I've read it." Decker tried to make it clear by his tone of voice that he didn't think much of Crick's book, but Goodman didn't seem to notice.

"All the better! You will recall that in the book Crick examines possible origins of life on this planet. He raises the question of why, with the exception of mitochondria, the basic genetic coding mechanism in all living things on earth is identical. Even in the case of mitochondria the differences are rather small. From what we know of earth's evolution, there's no obvious structural reason for the details of the coding mechanism being identical. Crick does not entirely discount the possibility that life originated and evolved naturally on earth, but he offers a second theory: that perhaps life was planted on this planet by a highly advanced civilization from somewhere else. If all life on earth had a common origin, that would explain the apparent bottleneck in genetic evolution.

"Crick calls his theory 'directed panspermia' and it's not unlike a theory propounded by the astronomer Sir Fred Hoyle.[11] Crick points out that the amount of time since the Big Bang easily allows for the development of life and evolution of intelligent beings on other planets as long as four billion years ago. And that's if we take a very conservative estimate of ten to twelve billion years for the age of the universe. What that means is that on one or more planets in our galaxy, there may exist intelligent life which is as much as four billion years more advanced than life on earth!

"Professor Crick goes on to suggest that if these intelligent

[10]Francis Crick, *Life Itself* (New York: Simon and Schuster, 1983).

[11]Sir Fred Hoyle and Chandra Wickramasinghe, *Diseases from Space* (London: Dent, 1979).

beings wanted to colonize other planets they wouldn't start by sending members of their own species. To colonize a planet, it would first be necessary to prepare that planet for habitation. Without plant life there wouldn't be sufficient oxygen for intelligent life, as we know it, to exist. And of course there wouldn't be food for the colonists either. To establish the needed plant life, they would have only to place some simple bacteria, such as blue-green algae, on the planet and let evolution and the eons of time do their work."

"Professor," Decker interrupted, "I've read the book. What's the point?"

"The point is, so what if Crick is right? What if life was planted on earth by an ancient race from another planet? Where are they now? Well," Goodman continued, answering his own questions, "Crick makes several suggestions: Maybe they all died. Maybe they lost interest in space travel. Maybe they didn't find the earth suitable for their particular needs.

"But there's another possibility Crick didn't mention." Goodman paused to emphasize his point. "Certainly earth wouldn't have been the only planet where they would have planted life. Probably they'd have seeded thousands of planets throughout the galaxy. So, what if when they finally got to this particular planet, they found that it was already populated, and not just by plants and animals. What if, through some strange set of parallel twists of evolution, they found that it was populated by beings not far different from themselves? Would they simply invade and colonize it anyway? Or might they instead decide to observe it and let it evolve naturally?"

"Professor," Decker interrupted again, "what has all this got to do with the Shroud of Turin?"

"Think about it, Decker. Somewhere in the galaxy there may be a civilization of beings, billions of years advanced to us, who are responsible for planting life throughout the galaxy, including earth. I believe that the man whose regeneration caused the image on the Shroud of Turin was a member of that parent race, sent here as an observer: a man from a race of humanlike beings, so far advanced to us that they are capable of regeneration, possibly even immortality. Not true gods—at least not in the way that term is normally used—but not too far from it."

"Haven't you heard what I've been saying?" Decker interrupted. "The Shroud of Turin is just not old enough to be the burial cloth of Christ!" Decker closed his eyes and took a long breath to gather his composure. "Professor, look," he said slowly. "This whole theory is ludicrous. And I think if you'll just stop for a second you'll realize how crazy it is. You're a scientist, and you're a good one. You know a reasonable hypothesis from a—"

"I am *not* crazy!" Goodman shot back. "So just cut the patronizing and hear me out!"

Decker stood up, ready to leave. "I'm sorry, Professor. You don't want me. You want someone from the *National Enquirer!*"

Goodman stood and placed himself between Decker and the door. "I'm not nuts. I fully expected your reaction, but I'm telling you I can test and prove both of these hypotheses. I know how crazy it all sounds, but when you see what I've found on the Shroud, you'll understand."

Finally, here was something solid Decker's curiosity could relate to. He no longer hoped to find the news story of the millennium, but he might at least find out what had made Goodman's conservative scientific mind turn to mush. He agreed to go to the laboratory. On the way there his thoughts turned to humor for relief. *I'll bet he found a mustard stain,* he decided, trying not to laugh at the whole ridiculous situation. *Elizabeth is never going to believe this.*

❑

In the lab Goodman opened a locked cabinet and pulled out a clear plastic case with several dozen slides in it. Decker recognized it as the case of tape samples taken from the Shroud of Turin. "As I told you earlier," Goodman began, "I borrowed the slides in order to examine further the dirt particles that were found in the left heel area of the image. I hadn't even thought about the Shroud for the last few years, but when it was announced they were going to do the Carbon 14 dating, it reminded me of something. I wondered if it might be possible to determine the specific makeup of the particles of dirt found on the Shroud and perhaps see if any unusual characteristics could rule in or rule out given points of origin. In other words, was there anything about the dirt that would indicate that it had originated in the Middle East or, conversely, was there anything that would instead indicate that the dirt was from either France or Italy or perhaps even somewhere else?

"If it was from the Middle East, or even from Jerusalem itself, it would not necessarily prove anything about the Shroud, of course. A forger who went to all the trouble of placing dirt on the Shroud in such minute amounts that it would take a twentieth-century macroscope to see it might just as well have thought to import the dirt from Jerusalem. It makes about as much sense, which is to say: none at all. I just wanted to get another look at it."

Goodman sat down in front of a microscope, turned on its lamp and placed a slide on the scope's stage. "In the car I told you that Dr. Heller had avoided using too much magnification because of what it was he was looking for." Goodman paused, looked through the eyepiece lens, and adjusted the scope's objectives and focus. "In my case," he continued as he looked up at Decker, "I used between a 600x and a 1000x." Goodman stood up and motioned for Decker to look through the scope. "This first slide is the sample taken from directly over the left heel."

Decker moved the slide around on the stage, refocusing as necessary. "There's not much there," he said, still scanning the slide.

"Exactly," Goodman said. "At first I was rather disappointed. I checked the grid, but the only other samples from the feet were from the nail wounds in the right foot." Goodman took the slide from the microscope and carefully placed it back in its designated slot.

"You remember that the right foot actually had two exit wounds, indicating that the feet had been nailed left over right. The right foot was nailed down first, with the nail exiting through the arch of the foot. The left foot was then nailed on top of the right with the nail passing through both feet, leaving an exit wound in the arch of the left foot and the heel of the right. Neither of these samples seemed very promising, though, because any dirt that had been in the wound areas would likely have been bonded to the cloth by the blood."

Goodman took a second slide from the plastic case. "This particular sample is from the blood stain of the right heel. I really didn't expect to find any dirt there, but I looked anyway." Goodman paused.

"That's when I found it."

Goodman reached around Decker, shut off the microscope's lamp, and handed him the slide. Decker took the slide and placed it on the microscope's stage. He adjusted the mirror to compensate for the loss of light from the lamp and focused the lens. Goodman rotated the objective to 800x. On the slide before him, Decker could see a group of several strangely familiar disk-shaped objects surrounded by and imbedded into crusty blackish-brown material that he assumed to be blood.

After a moment, he looked up at Goodman. His eyes had grown wide and his mind raced in disbelief and confusion. "Is that possible?" he asked finally.

Goodman opened a large medical text book to a well-marked page and pointed to an illustration in the upper left corner. What Decker saw there was an artist's representation of something very similar to what he had just seen through Goodman's microscope. The caption below the picture read, "human dermal skin cells."

Decker looked back through the microscope to be sure. Inexplicably, despite hundreds or even thousands of years, they appeared to be perfectly preserved. He felt Goodman reach around him again, this time to turn the lamp back on. The brighter light made the small disks appear transparent and Decker could clearly see the nucleus of each cell. Within a few seconds the lamp began to gently warm the slide. Decker looked away to rub his eyes and then looked back.

❑

In the warmth of the artificial light, the nuclei began to move.

Mother of God

4

DECKER'S CHEST FELT HEAVY and his head light. He struggled to catch his breath. Silently he watched the nuclei of the cells as they continued to undulate. His mind seemed to float in the sea of warm cytoplasm before him, void of points of reference except for the cells. A thousand questions rose and fell, fighting for his attention, but he was incapable of enough focus on anything outside of what he saw to even realize his confusion. It was only when he ceased his attempt to understand the full impact of what he was seeing that his senses began to reemerge from the ooze. Decker's ears slowly became aware of Goodman's voice.

"Decker . . . Decker . . ." Goodman touched him on the shoulder and he finally looked up. "Are you hungry?"

Decker hadn't eaten since breakfast, but right now he thought Goodman's question was insane.

"Believe me," said Goodman, "I know just how you feel. The same thing happened to me. I went looking for dirt and found live dermal skin cells. I nearly got religion! That's when I made the connection to Professor Crick's theory." Goodman took the slide from the microscope and carefully placed it back in the plastic case.

"What is it?" Decker asked finally.

"I showed you," said Goodman. "They're dermal cells—cells from just below the skin's surface. Oh, and as you've obviously noticed, they're alive." Goodman hid the excitement he felt in finally being able to share his discovery, and his calm, understated response simply served to accentuate Decker's confusion.

"But what? . . . How?" Decker pleaded.

"The cells were picked up on the Mylar tape along with some small flecks of blood. Apparently when the Shroud was laid over the crucified man, some of the exposed flesh of the wound was bonded to the cloth by the dried blood. When the man was regenerated and the Shroud was pulled away from his body, a small amount of dermal material was pulled away with it. The same thing can happen when bandages are removed from a large wound. I suspect the weight of the heel resting on the cloth helped some, too. What you have just seen are cells at least six hundred years old with absolutely no sign of degeneration. In short: They're alive."

"Six hundred years?" Decker asked, surprised that Professor Goodman had not said two thousand.

"Well, if the Carbon 14 dating is correct, yes. On the other hand, I think it is rather unlikely that anyone would have been crucified in the thirteenth or fourteenth century. I have no real evidence to dispute the Carbon 14 results, but my guess is that, in all likelihood, the Shroud does date to the first century and was, in fact, the burial cloth of Jesus. The historical evidence is rather conclusive that Jesus did exist. I've never doubted that any more than I've doubted the historical evidence of Alexander the Great or Julius Caesar. Actually, it all fits perfectly into my hypothesis."

"Professor, why weren't the blood cells alive?" Decker asked.

"That's an interesting question. I assume it's because the blood is from the body that died. The skin cells, on the other hand, are from the body *after* it was regenerated."

Goodman put his hand on Decker's shoulder and gently nudged him in the direction of the door. "I don't know about you, but I'm starved and my housekeeper was expecting us half an hour ago for lunch. My wife is visiting her mother in Kansas City."

❏

Goodman's house was an English Tudor with brown trim and stone on a quiet dead-end street about twenty minutes from the campus. The two men were greeted at the door by Goodman's housekeeper, a young Hispanic woman. "Maria, this is my guest, Mr. Hawthorne." Goodman spoke very slowly, enunciating every word. "We'll have our lunch now."

Decker looked around the house. Just about every wall had shelves full of books. A few shelves had additional books neatly stacked beside them. Decker had never met Goodman's wife, Martha, but she was obviously very tolerant of her husband's profession.

"Professor, we need to talk," Decker said as they sat down at the dining room table.

"Yes, I know," Goodman answered.

Decker's eyes glanced to the housekeeper and then back to Goodman.

"Oh, don't worry about her," Goodman said. "She hardly speaks any English. She's only been in this country about six months."

"We can't keep this to ourselves," Decker started.

"I have no intention of keeping it secret forever, but if we let the story out now there will be no end to the reporters. Not to mention the thousands of mindless religious kooks. You remember the crowds in Turin lined up to see the Shroud? What do you think would happen if word leaked out that live cells from the body of Jesus were in a laboratory in Los Angeles? Every sick or dying person in America would be here overnight hoping to touch the cells and be healed. I've touched the cells and they haven't done a thing for me. You may have touched them yourself, when you were handling the Shroud in Turin and I notice it hasn't stopped your hairline from receding," Goodman added in characteristic deadpan humor. "All that would result from releasing the story now is that a lot of people would be hurt. But if we wait until I've finished my research we may be able to offer some real healing power."

"What do you mean '*real* healing power'?"

"Decker, are you blind? You saw those cells. What do you think we've been talking about?"

"I'm not sure I know anymore."

"Those cells are hundreds or even thousands of years old. They have survived intense heat and freezing cold. As far as we can tell, they're immortal. Yet in most respects they're human. With time, we may be able to discover what makes them immortal. We may discover things that can lead to new vaccines, create powerful new life-saving drugs, extend life, perhaps even bring about our own immortality!"

Decker raised his eyebrows in surprise. "I hadn't even considered anything like that," he said.

"Actually, I'm already deeply involved in research on the cells. I began by inducing cell mitosis in the laboratory. The cells are extremely resilient and multiply rapidly. I've been able to grow a substantial culture. However, there is another area of research worthy of pursuit as well." Goodman paused to consider his words. "Decker, what do you know about cloning?"

It took Decker only an instant to guess what Goodman was getting at. Decker was not a religious person, but this idea rubbed him entirely the wrong way. "Hold it! You don't mean . . . You're talking about cloning Jesus?!" Decker's loud outburst startled Maria, who dropped a plate in the kitchen.

Goodman apparently had not anticipated Decker's opposition. "Just wait a minute!" he replied at a slightly lower and more controlled decibel level. "To begin with, we can't be certain that these are the cells of Jesus."

"Well, it's a pretty good guess!" Decker shot back, incredulously.

"But even if they are," Goodman continued, "I still find my hypothesis about his origin more reasonable than any silly religious notions you may have."

It was then that Decker put it all together. "That's what you were talking about before! That's how you plan to test your hypothesis that Jesus was from an advanced alien race! You're going to try to clone him!"

"Look, Decker, there's no need for a shouting match. And anyway, you're jumping to ridiculous conclusions based on insufficient data. All I meant was that you might *someday* be able to test my hypothesis of the man's origin in that manner." Goodman's clarification wasn't very convincing.

"Look, Professor," Decker said, "it's one thing to do lab research or grow cells in a petri dish, but you just can't go around cloning people, especially if the guy you want to clone might just be the son of God!"

"Decker, use your brain. If the image on the Shroud was from the son of God, then tell me this: Why would an all-knowing, all-wise, all-powerful creator allow the cells to get stuck to the Shroud in the first place?"

"Who knows? Maybe as a sign or something."

"And why would he allow me, a man who doesn't even believe in him, to find the cells? If it was some kind of sign, wouldn't God at least have chosen someone who believed in him?"

Decker didn't have an answer.

"But more important," continued Goodman, "even if you examine it from a religious point of view, you must ask how could a mere mortal manage to clone the son of God? Would the 'soul' of Jesus be in the clone?" Goodman struggled to hide the sarcasm in his voice. "Would God really allow himself to be so easily manipulated by men?"

Decker listened. As uncomfortable as it made him feel, what Goodman was saying made sense.

"Decker, I really expected you to be more open-minded about this. Where's your scientific curiosity? Surely you can see that if I did manage to clone the man on the Shroud, it would be proof positive that he was not the son of God. If, I repeat, *if* it was possible to clone the man, we still might never know his origin because he would not have the memory of the original. But we'd know one thing without a doubt, and it's that he was *not* the son of God, because if he was, I think you'll agree, it's a pretty safe assumption that God wouldn't allow us to clone his son."

Decker couldn't argue with Goodman's logic. An all-knowing, all-powerful God was not likely to just leave a bunch of his son's cells lying around. Besides, it was obvious that as far as Goodman was concerned, the discussion was over.

During their conversation the two men had taken only a few bites of their dinners. Goodman now focused his attention on the plate before him. Decker felt it wise to do the same. After the meal the conversation grew a little more amiable, but Goodman was clearly angered and avoided the subject of the Shroud entirely, except to say that he would call Decker when the next step in his research on the cells was under way.

As they stood to leave for the airport, Maria cleared the dishes and silver, stretching across the large table to reach Professor Goodman's saucer and cup. She carried them back to the kitchen, tugging lightly at her apron and adjusting her maternity dress.

5

Christopher

Twelve years later
Los Angeles, California

"IS IT VERY MUCH FARTHER?" Hope Hawthorne asked her father as they drove down the exit ramp of I-605 in Northern Los Angeles. "No, babe, just a few more miles," Decker answered.

Hope turned on the radio just in time to hear an announcer report the current temperature, "It's seventy-eight degrees—another beautiful day in Southern California."

"Seventy-eight degrees! Is this heaven or what? It was thirty-seven and raining when we left D.C.," Decker commented as Hope tried to find some music. They had flown in that morning from Washington, D.C., to visit Professor Harry Goodman, who was about to announce a major breakthrough that could prove to be a cure for several types of cancer. The discovery was a result of research with the C-cells (as Goodman had come to call the cells from the Shroud) and, in accordance with the agreement they had made twelve years earlier, Decker was to be given an exclusive report on any C-cell research two weeks prior to any formal announcement and press conference. To this point the research had not been nearly as successful as Goodman had hoped.

Decker had seen Goodman only once since their initial discussions about the origin of the cells. It had been in the summer four years ago, when Goodman believed he was close to developing an AIDS vaccine. What he found was a dead end. Most humiliating was that Goodman had discovered the error in his research two days *after* Decker's article reached the newsstands. The article had generated national attention for Goodman's work and Decker's newspaper, only to be followed the same week by embarrassment.

Decker turned the rented car down the narrow street and stopped in front of Goodman's house. They were greeted at the front door by Mrs. Goodman. Decker politely reintroduced himself from four years earlier to the woman who smiled warmly at her two guests. "Oh, I remember you," she said brightly. "And this must be Hope." She reached over to give Hope a grandmotherly hug. "Harry said you were bringing your daughter with you. Such a pretty girl! How old are you, dear?"

"Thirteen," Hope answered.

"We decided to mix pleasure with business," Decker said. "We're going to drive up to San Francisco this afternoon and visit my wife's sister for a few days. Elizabeth and our other daughter, Louisa, flew out there three days ago."

"Yeah, but I had to stay in Washington and take a math test," Hope interjected.

"In the news business things are very mercurial. It seems that our vacations have never worked out as we planned, so we just try to take a few days whenever we can. Sometimes that means the kids have to miss a few days of school," Decker explained.

Mrs. Goodman looked at Decker with disapproving puzzlement on her face. "Your daughter is in school in Washington? I thought you lived in Tennessee. Do you really think that a boarding school is appropriate for a girl Hope's age? Especially so far from—"

"Hope's not in a boarding school," Decker interrupted. "We moved to Washington two years ago after I sold my newspaper in Knoxville and went to work for *NewsWorld* magazine."

"Oh, forgive me. I didn't realize. It's just that, well, my parents sent me to a boarding school when I was twelve and I hated it. Anyway," she said, changing the subject and turning her attention again to Hope. "I'm glad you were able to come along, dear. Harry is out in the backyard playing with Christopher. They probably didn't hear you drive up. I'm afraid the professor's hearing is not what it used to be. I'll tell him you're here."

Decker and Hope waited as Mrs. Goodman went to call her husband. "He'll be right in, Mr. Hawthorne," she said as she returned and then excused herself to the kitchen.

A moment later Professor Goodman appeared. "How are you, Decker? How have you been?" He didn't wait for an answer. "You look like you've put on some weight and lost more hair." Decker cringed a little at Goodman's recognition of what was obvious to everyone but himself.

"And you must be Hope," the professor said, looking in her direction. "I'll bet you'd like to meet my grandnephew, Christopher." Goodman turned toward the back door where a young boy was standing with his nose pressed against the screen, looking in. "Christopher, come in here and meet Mr. Hawthorne and his daughter Hope."

Decker had never seen Goodman so animated or in such a good mood. "I'm very pleased to meet you, Mr. Hawthorne," Christopher said as he entered and extended his right hand.

"It's very nice to meet you as well," Decker responded, "but we actually met about four years ago when you were seven. You've grown quite a bit since then."

Martha Goodman emerged from the kitchen with a plate full of chocolate chip cookies. "Oh, good. I love chocolate-chip," said Professor Goodman.

"They're not for you," teased Martha. "They're for the children. Hope, would you and Christopher like to come out in the back-yard with me and have some cookies and milk?" Hope—who didn't like being thought of as a child but who did like chocolate-chip cookies—nodded and went with Christopher and Mrs. Goodman to the backyard.

Decker and Goodman settled in for a long conversation. "Professor, you look great," Decker began. "I swear, you look ten years younger than the last time I saw you."

"I feel great," Goodman answered. "I've lost twenty-four

pounds. My blood pressure is down. I'm even regular most of the time," he added with a chuckle.

"That's another thing," said Decker. "You seem . . . well, almost jolly. What's going on?"

Goodman looked toward the back door. Christopher was standing there with the screen door part way open, watching as Hope and Mrs. Goodman inspected some flowers. Certain he wouldn't be missed, Christopher ran to his granduncle. From his shirt pocket he pulled two chocolate-chip cookies. Goodman took the cookies and accepted the hug that came along with them. Christopher put the side of his index finger to his lips to signify a pact of silence and then went over to Decker and reached back into his shirt pocket. As he did, he saw the results the hug had on the two remaining cookies. Looking at the badly broken cookie remains he offered them apologetically to Decker. Decker accepted graciously as Christopher gave the same code-of-silence signal and ran out the back door before he could be missed.

" 'What's going on?' " Goodman said, repeating Decker's previous question. "That's what's going on." Goodman nodded toward where Christopher had made his exit. "I may look ten years younger, but I feel like I'm forty again."

Decker knew from his last visit with Goodman that Christopher's parents had been killed in an auto accident. His closest surviving relative was his grandfather, Goodman's older brother, who was unable to take care of him because of his failing health. So Christopher had moved in with Harry and Martha.

"Originally, I thought we were too old to take care of a child, but Martha insisted," Goodman continued. "We never had any children of our own, you know. Christopher has been the best thing to ever happen to Martha and me. But, I was right—we were too old. So we just got younger."

Decker smiled.

"Well, let's get down to business," said Goodman. "This time I think we've really got something. Let me go get my notes." Goodman left the room for a moment and returned with three overstuffed notebooks. Two hours later it was clear to Decker that Goodman was right. Goodman had developed a vaccine for treating many of the viruses that can cause cancer, such as Rous sarcoma and Epstein-Barr. Further testing was necessary to determine if the vaccine development process was universal, and there would have to be actual testing in humans, but all of the tests to date had been remarkable, proving as much as 93 percent effective in lab animals.

"So what you've done is to grow and support massive cultures of the C-cells, and then introduce the cancer virus in vitro," Decker said. "In that environment, the virus attacks the C-cells, which respond by producing antibodies, resulting in the complete arrest and ultimate elimination of the virus."

"In a nutshell, that's it," Goodman concluded. "And if the vaccine development process proves out, it will probably be just as successful with any other virus, including AIDS or even the common cold. Admittedly, those will be a little tougher because of all the mutations of the AIDS virus and all the varieties of cold viruses."

"This is fantastic! I think I can guarantee you a major story on this. I'd be surprised if my editor doesn't put your picture on next week's cover."

"So, we'll go with the same plan as before to explain the origin of the C-cells?" Decker asked.

"There's no reason to change it that I know of. I'll say that I developed the C-cells through genetic engineering and that I can't say more without revealing the process."

"Good," Decker responded. "I'd like to spend some more time looking over your notes, but I promised Elizabeth we wouldn't be late."

"I'm way ahead of you," interrupted Goodman. "I've already made copies. Just make sure you keep them under lock and key and call me if you have any questions."

Goodman gathered his papers and the conversation soon turned to small talk. Decker told Goodman that after visiting with Elizabeth's sister for a few days, he'd be going to Israel for six weeks to relieve the *NewsWorld* reporter covering the recent Palestinian protests. "By the way, do you remember Dr. Rosen from the Turin expedition?" Decker asked.

"Joshua Rosen?" Goodman asked. "Of course. Seems I read something about him somewhere a couple years back."

"That was my story in *NewsWorld*," Decker responded. "I sent you a copy."

"I remember it now. It was something about him leaving the U.S. and going to Israel after they cut his program from the defense budget."

"Right. Well, he's still there. They finally granted him citizenship. I'll be staying with him for a couple days."

"That's right, I had forgotten about that. He wanted to become an Israeli citizen but they wouldn't let him," Goodman recalled.

At that moment Martha Goodman, Hope, and Christopher came in the front door from a long walk. "Would you and Hope like to stay for supper?" she asked Decker.

"I'm sorry, we really can't," Decker answered.

"Are you sure? I know that Christopher would enjoy Hope's company for a while longer."

"Thanks, but Elizabeth and Louisa are expecting us," Decker explained. Soon they said their good-byes and Decker and Hope were on their way.

❑

As the miles rolled by and the highway scenery grew redundant, Hope told her father about her visit with Christopher and Martha Goodman. "We had a lot of fun," she said. "He's really a nice kid. It's a shame he'll be thirteen in a couple years."

"Why's that?" Decker asked.

"Because thirteen-year-old boys are so obnoxious," she answered.

"Obnoxious?" Decker said. "I thought you saved that term for your little sister."

Hope didn't answer but her father's comment reminded her of something. "Mrs. Goodman said that it's tough on Christopher because he doesn't have any brothers or sisters to play with and there's no one else his age in the neighborhood. She said that she and Professor Goodman were both only children, too, and that I was really lucky to have a little sister. I told her I didn't think so. So, anyway, if it's all right with you and Mom, I told her she could have Louisa to keep Christopher company."

Decker rolled his eyes. "Real funny."

"Yeah, Mrs. Goodman didn't think you'd go for it, either."

As they continued their trip Decker's thoughts went back and forth between his discussion with Goodman and his planned trip to Israel. He looked forward to visiting with the Rosens, and he especially looked forward to spending some time with his old friend Tom Donafin, who had joined *NewsWorld* magazine a few weeks earlier. He was not, however, looking forward to being away from Elizabeth, Hope, and Louisa for so long, although they would be joining him in Israel for Christmas.

They were now about a hundred and twenty miles from Los Angeles. The temperature was near perfect. The sun would be setting soon. Suddenly Decker took his foot off the gas pedal and let the car drift to a stop on the shoulder of the road.

"What's the matter, Dad?" Hope asked.

But Decker didn't answer. For a long moment he just stared as if in shock. "How could I have missed it?" he asked himself out loud.

"What?" Hope asked.

"We're going back," he said finally. Hope tried to object, but it was fruitless. Decker forgot all about his promise to Elizabeth not to be late. Two hours later they were back where they had started at Goodman's house, with Hope, who was still operating on Eastern time, asleep in the backseat. Decker went up to the front door and knocked.

Goodman and Christopher opened the door together. No one spoke for a moment; Goodman just stared at Decker in confusion. Christopher stood beside him dressed in pajamas, his hair still damp and freshly combed after his bath.

"Did you forget something?" Goodman asked finally. But Decker had already stooped down to Christopher's level and was closely examining his facial features.

"Hi, Mr. Hawthorne," Christopher said. "It's so nice to see you again. Can Hope come in and play some more?" The intensity in

Decker's eyes began to melt away, until he looked back up at Goodman, who was staring down at him.

"What on earth is the matter with you?" Goodman asked.

Decker stood up again. "You did it. Didn't you?"

"What are you talking about?" Goodman said, trying to appear calm and in control.

"You know very well what I'm talking about!" Decker answered without hesitation. Goodman felt like a rabbit in a snare. *Could Decker have meant something else?* he asked himself.

"The cloning!" Decker blurted.

"Christopher," Goodman said as calmly as he could, "Mr. Hawthorne and I need to talk for a while. Go back in the house. Tell your Aunt Martha I'm on the front porch."

Decker waited until Christopher closed the door before speaking again. "You cloned the cells from the Shroud!" Decker said in a whisper so loud and emphatic he may as well have been shouting. "Christopher isn't your brother's grandson! You don't even have a brother! You were an only child!" he blurted, abandoning any pretense of discretion.

The night was warm and the moonlight shone on Mrs. Goodman's flowers; their fragrance filled the air, but it went totally unnoticed by the two men. Goodman looked closely into Decker's eyes, examining his face for any sign of a twitch that might signal that Decker was bluffing. He found none.

Decker didn't flinch, but he *was* bluffing, at least a little. While he now knew that Christopher could not be Goodman's grand-nephew, that certainly was not conclusive evidence he was the clone of the man on the Shroud. The story about Goodman's brother might have been created for dozens of other reasons that had nothing at all to do with the Shroud.

"Decker, you can't tell anyone. You can't," Goodman pleaded. "They'll make him a zoo specimen. He's just a little boy!"

Decker shook his head, stunned that he had been right. "That's why you named him Christopher, isn't it?"

"Yes," Goodman answered, realizing that the damage had already been done and hoping to inspire a cooperative spirit in Decker.

"After Christ!"

For a moment Goodman honestly didn't understand what Decker meant, then it hit him. "Christ?! Don't be absurd!" he said, indignantly. "Columbus! I named him after Christopher Columbus."

"Why in the world would you name him after Columbus?"

The question surprised Goodman, who thought the answer was obvious.

"I told you I had made the greatest discovery since Columbus discovered the New World. I wasn't just talking about finding the cells or the possible medical benefits. I was talking about Christopher. I had already successfully implanted the cloned embryo in the surrogate mother, and she was several months into an otherwise normal pregnancy. I never expected it to work. It shouldn't have worked! Cloning a human is far more difficult than you can imagine. But the C-cells proved so resilient that transfer of the genetic material to the surrogate's egg worked the first time. I was going to tell you about it, but you got so bent out of shape when I mentioned cloning that I didn't dare.

"Don't you see, Decker? I've proven that somewhere out there in our galaxy there's life! The man on the Shroud may have come from the same race of people who first planted life on this planet four billion years ago. I thought if I could clone the man on the Shroud, I could learn more about them. I hoped it might lead us to that master race. I hoped that like Columbus, Christopher might help lead us to a new world—a better world.

"After Christopher was born I studied him. I watched him. I tested him. And you know what I found? Not an alien; not a god. What I found was a little boy."

"He's not just a little boy, though. He's the clone of a man who lived nearly two thousand years ago."

"But he has no memory of any of that. For all he knows, he's just a normal eleven-year-old."

"And you're saying that there's no difference between Christopher and any other kid?" Decker asked incredulously.

"Yes, all right, there are some differences. He's never been sick and when he gets a cut or scrape he heals quickly. But that's all."

"He seems awfully intelligent," Decker countered.

"He *is* intelligent," Goodman conceded, "but not exceptionally so. Besides, both Mrs. Goodman and I have spent many hours working with him at home in addition to his schoolwork."

"Mrs. Goodman?" Decker asked. "Does she know about Christopher?"

"Of course not. After he was born I paid the surrogate and dispatched her immediately back to Mexico to prevent any problems that might arise from bonding. I rented an apartment and hired a nurse to take care of him. I know it sounds terribly irresponsible now, but I had absolutely no plans about what I was going to do with him as he got older. I was so involved with the overall project that I didn't think about the child as a person. By the time I realized my responsibilities, he was nearly a year old. I couldn't just leave him on the doorstep of some orphanage, so I left him on my own doorstep. I put him in a basket, left a note, the whole nine yards. Martha had always wanted children, and after a few days of taking care of him while we 'considered what to do,' it wasn't very difficult to convince her that we should keep him in case the mother ever came back looking for him. Later we made up the story about him being our grandnephew and I had a birth certificate and some other papers forged to cover our tracks.

"Decker, maybe it was a mistake to go through with the cloning. If you'd like, you may say 'I told you so.' But I don't regret it. He's been like my own son. If you report that Christopher is a clone you'll destroy three lives: his, mine, and Martha's. Christopher will never have another normal day in his life. You can't do that to him. You have children. Can a story in some stupid magazine really be worth that much?"

Goodman waited for Decker to answer, but Decker didn't like the answer that came to mind. No, he didn't want to ruin Christopher's life, but there had to be some way to tell the story and still protect those involved. The standard promise of anonymity wouldn't work. It was too big a story. Someone would figure it out. And if he didn't use names and explain the circumstances, no one would believe the story anyway. There had to be some way around it. He needed time to think.

Goodman provided the answer. He had waited so long for Decker's response that he began to worry he wasn't going to get the answer he wanted. "Look," he said, "why don't you come back here next week and spend some time getting to know Christopher better?"

Goodman hoped that once Decker got to know Christopher he wouldn't want to risk hurting the boy no matter how big the story. It sounded like a good suggestion to Decker as well, but for a different reason. It would give him the time he needed to think, and if he *did* figure out something he would have a lot more information for the article.

Decker's answer was implied. "Can't do it next week. I'm going to Israel, remember?" Then a thought hit him. It was a long shot but Decker's career had been built on long shots and being at the right place at the right time. "How about if I take Christopher with me to Israel? Who knows? Maybe it will jog his memory a little."

Anger swept over Goodman's face. "Are you crazy! Absolutely not! How would I explain that to Martha?"

"Okay! Okay! I just thought it would be a neat idea."

"Well it's not!" Goodman shot back.

"Look," Decker said, preparing to strike a bargain, "I'll keep my mouth shut for the time being. I'll be back from Israel in January, so plan on having me around for at least a week or so."

Goodman swallowed hard. He was thinking more along the lines of a few hours, a day at most. He agreed anyway in hopes of arguing later for a compromise.

❏

Decker and Hope were soon on their way again, nearly six hours later than they had planned. Decker wondered how he was going to explain to Elizabeth why he was so late.

6

Secrets of the Lost Ark

Nablus, Israel

"TOM, HOW DO YOU TAKE YOURS?" Joshua Rosen asked as he poured coffee for himself, his wife, and his two American guests. Tom Donafin wanted his black. Decker started to answer but Joshua interrupted. "I don't need to ask you. I remember. You like yours with too much cream and too much sugar, just like you'd serve it to a baby."

In preparation for their assignment to cover the recent distur-bances in Israel, Decker and Tom had attempted to adjust to Israeli time but the coffee provided welcome assistance.

"So, Tom, tell us about yourself," Ilana Rosen asked. "How do you know our Decker?"

"Oh, we've been friends for a long time." Tom scratched his chin beneath his thick brown beard. "We met at a coffee house in Tullahoma, Tennessee. We were both interested in writing, so we hit it off right away." Tom looked off, as if through time, and added, "We were pretty weird looking back then. You know, long hair, love beads, the whole shtick."

Ilana Rosen looked across the table at Decker, now age forty-seven, trying to picture him as a hippie, and laughed. "Anyway," Tom continued, "we lost track of each other. Decker went into the army and I went to work on a construction crew. After a few years I decided I was tired of sweating for a living and went to college.

Well, one day I was sitting in a microbiology class the school computer had mistakenly assigned me to, and I looked up, and in walks Decker, as droopy eyed as you see him today."

Decker had taken advantage of Tom's story to 'rest his eyes,' but now gave his head a shake and forced down some coffee to try to restore consciousness. "I guess I really should try to stay more alert during Tom's stories," he said. "There's no telling what he'll make up about me while I'm asleep."

Satisfied that his friend was listening, Tom continued his story. "For the next few years we stayed in pretty close contact at school. After college, I got a job with a newspaper in Massachusetts, and I thought Decker was planning to go to grad school. But the next thing I knew he was publishing a weekly newspaper in Knoxville. After a few years I left Massachusetts and went to work for UPI in Chicago. Then about two and a half months ago Decker got me an interview with *NewsWorld* magazine."

Despite his best efforts Decker was again drifting off to sleep, but as Tom finished speaking he felt three pairs of eyes staring at him. Giving his head another quick shake and a roll, he tried to act as though he had been listening intently. Tom ignored Decker's latest infraction of good manners and asked the Rosens about themselves. "Decker told me a little about you during the trip over, but there's still a lot I don't know."

"Well, in a nutshell," Joshua Rosen began, "Ilana and I were both born in Austria a few years before World War II. When I was six years old my family left Austria when it became clear that there would be no place for Jews in Hitler's world. Fortunately my whole family was allowed to leave. Ilana's family tried to leave just two weeks later and were refused passports. They were smuggled out later by Lutheran missionaries.

"In America, my father was one of more than thirty Jewish scientists who worked in atomic research for the Manhattan Project. At home, he was a very strict taskmaster and insisted that my two sisters and I excel in our schoolwork. I went on to study nuclear physics and then became involved in laser and particle beam research."

Rosen paused to sip some coffee.

"That's how you got involved in strategic defense," Tom said, filling the brief silence.

"Right," Rosen responded. "Then a few years ago the president decided to cut back on nearly all directed energy research."

"And that's when you decided to come to Israel."

"Well, not right away, but soon after. My father helped build the first atomic bomb to try to end World War II; I wanted to help build a defense against missiles carrying atomic bombs to *prevent* World War III. When it seemed clear that the United States no longer had the resolve to build such a defense, I decided to come to Israel to continue my work here."

"Decker said something about your son turning you in to Israeli immigration authorities so that you couldn't become citizens," Tom probed.

At this Mrs. Rosen responded in defense of her son. "Scott is a good boy. He was just a little confused."

"Yes," Joshua said. "You see, Scott and I have not seen eye-to-eye on most things for quite some time. Our family was never Orthodox in our practice of Judaism: we kept the feast days, but only out of tradition. They didn't really carry much meaning. Then, just to understand our Jewish roots, Ilana and I began studying the Scriptures. After about a year and a half of study we began talking with some Messianic friends and, to make a long story short, Ilana and I accepted Yeshua as the Jewish Messiah.

"Three months after that my father died. Scott took his grandfather's death very badly." Ilana patted Joshua's hand and gave a supportive look. "At one time, Scott actually blamed us for his grandfather's death. He believed that my father died as punishment from God for Ilana and I accepting Yeshua and 'abandoning' our religion."

Tom nodded sympathetically, though he didn't entirely follow what Joshua was saying.

"As a result—perhaps he felt that he was punishing us—Scott left the United States and came to Israel, where he became involved with some of the most Orthodox and militant groups. He was only eighteen at the time.

"When we came to Israel three years ago we had not heard

from Scott in more than fifteen years. But when we went to complete the paperwork for our Israeli citizenship—which is granted to most Jews almost automatically by right of *aliyah*—it was denied. Later we learned that Scott had told the authorities we had renounced our faith, and he insisted we be denied citizenship.

"After discussing it for a few days, Ilana and I decided to fight the charge. We have never renounced our faith!" Rosen's voice grew both defensive and dogmatic. "Many Jews are agnostics or atheists; and Israel grants *them* citizenship. But because we believe the prophecies about the promised Jewish Messiah, they say *we're* the ones who have denied our faith! Accepting Yeshua is not a matter of denying our faith but rather of completing it! Do you know that over the centuries there have been more than forty different men who have claimed to be the messiah, and no one ever accused the followers of *those* men of denying their faith!"

It was obvious that Rosen had delivered this defense on numerous occasions, each time becoming firmer in his convictions. Ilana placed her hand on his as if to reassure him he was among friends. Joshua paused and smiled to lighten the mood and to offer silent apology for any hint of virulence.

"I had already talked with a number of officials in the Israeli Defense Ministry," Rosen began again, getting back to his story. "They were very interested in putting me to work on the Israeli strategic defense program. That's when Decker called me from America." They looked across the table at Decker, who was now sound asleep. Ilana softly brushed her fingers through his hair. Joshua continued, speaking more quietly to keep from disturbing their guest. "He was doing a story about the decline of American strategic defense research and had heard about my decision to move to Israel. He called me and I agreed to talk to him about it and suggested that he compare the strategic defense capabilities and goals of the U.S. to those of Israel."

"So you must have known Decker before that."

"Oh, yes," answered Rosen. "We met on the Shroud of Turin expedition in Italy."

"No kidding? I didn't realize you were a part of that project," Tom said. "I'd like to talk to you about that sometime."

"Please," said Ilana, "don't get him started."

Joshua pretended not to hear his wife's last remark, but went on with his story. "Anyway," he said, "where was I? Oh, yes, when Decker arrived I convinced him there were really two stories to be told here. First was the story about the United States' decision to scrap lasers and particle beams, which is what he had called me about; and second was about Israel's policy to deny citizenship to Messianic Jews."

"Decker wrote about what happened to us and how we had been refused citizenship," Ilana interjected. "He really put his heart into that story. But in the end the editors at your magazine cut huge pieces from our story and ran it as a sidebar article."

"While Decker was preparing the story he interviewed several members of the Knesset, who are very staunch supporters of an Israeli missile defense," Joshua added, retaking control of the conversation. "When they became aware of our situation they demanded that the bureaucrats grant us Israeli citizenship immediately. Within two weeks we were given a hearing that went so quickly we were not even given a chance to speak. Before we knew what was going on, the judge found in our favor and soon after we became citizens. You see," Rosen explained, "without Israeli citizenship, I would not have been allowed to work on classified defense programs. We were trying to draw attention to the law against Messianic Jews. That became moot when we became the exception to that law."

"So have you seen your son since then?" Tom asked.

"Yes, at the hearing," Ilana answered. "He was very upset about the way the case was rushed through. But apparently, seeing us there, fifteen years older, made him think. He called us two days after the hearing and asked to see us. He has never exactly apologized, but he has learned to accept us. And it turns out that, at least in one way, he has followed in his father's footsteps."

"Yes," Joshua said, continuing Ilana's thought, "Scott has proven himself to be a first rate physicist. That's how he found out that we were in Israel and seeking citizenship: he too is involved in strategic defense research."

"Now we see him every few weeks," Ilana interjected.

"We've even worked together on a couple of projects," Joshua added.

Each paused and took another sip of coffee, signaling the apparent close of the subject. Tom had one other thing he wanted to clear up, and so took advantage of the silence. "Joshua and Ilana, you've mentioned 'Yeshua' several times. I'm afraid I'm not familiar with who or what it is you're talking about."

"*Yeshua ha Mashiach*," Joshua Rosen answered in Hebrew. "You are probably more familiar with the Anglicized pronunciation of the Greek form of his name: Jesus, the Messiah."

Tom raised an eyebrow in puzzlement. "You mean that Yeshua is the Jewish word for Jesus?"

Joshua and Ilana both nodded.

"But how can you be Jewish and Christian at the same time?"

"Well, there are a great many people here in Israel who would ask the same question," Joshua answered. "But surely you know that *all* of the earliest Christians were Jewish. For most of the first century, Christians—who at the time were called 'Followers of the Way'—continued to live among their Jewish brothers as equals and became a rather large sect within Judaism. In fact, the first real disagreement among the followers of Yeshua was whether or not Gentiles had to convert to Judaism before they could become Christians."

"I guess I never really thought about that," Tom said. "So the reason that your son turned you in is because you're Christians."

"We prefer the name 'Messianic Jews,'" Joshua answered. "But to answer your question: yes."

Tom nodded thoughtfully as he considered the Rosens' story. The conversation seemed to have reached a conclusion, the coffee had all been drunk, and the bagels had all been eaten. Tom reached over and shook Decker from his sleep. Joshua had taken the day off so he could take Tom and Decker into Jerusalem for some sightseeing. Decker drank the last of his coffee, which was by now quite cold, and the three men left for the city.

❑

Joshua took his guests on a whirlwind tour of some standard tourist stops, all of which shared one thing in common: Israeli police and military. Jerusalem is a city where the people have grown accustomed to such things.

Tom Donafin was particularly interested in the Wailing Wall, which was the western wall—and all that remains standing—of the ancient Jewish Temple. As they approached the wall, they were handed black paper *yarmulkes* to place on their heads. The Israeli government allows tourists to visit the wall but requires men to wear the traditional covering for their head. Near the wall, dozens of darkly clad men formed a constantly moving mass as they rocked back and forth, in a practice called dovening, while they prayed or read from their prayer books. Some of the men had ropes or cording tied around their arms and wore small boxes called phylacteries tied to their foreheads like headbands. Inside the boxes, Joshua explained, were pages from the Torah, the first five books of the Old Testament.

As he had at their other stops, Joshua gave a brief history of the site. "The original Temple," Joshua began, "was built by King Solomon and was destroyed during the Babylonian captivity. It was rebuilt beginning in 521 B.C. and later went through major renovations under King Herod. In about 27 A.D. Yeshua prophesied that the Temple would be destroyed again before all of those listening to him died. Just as he predicted, the Temple was destroyed in 70 A.D. when Titus invaded Jerusalem to put down a Jewish revolt against Rome.

"An interesting point of disagreement exists among biblical scholars on the extent of the destruction Yeshua was prophesying. What he told his disciples was that the entire Temple would be destroyed before the last of them died. But, as you can see, this portion of the wall is still standing. Some say that he meant only to include the structures within the walls of the Temple. Others say that the western wall was merely part of the foundation and therefore, by their reasoning, was not included in Yeshua's prophecy. But according to Josephus, who was present at the

Roman siege of Jerusalem, Titus ordered that parts of the city be left standing as a monument to his accomplishments.[12] He wanted everyone to be able to see the kind of fortification he had to overcome to defeat the Jews."

"So, which interpretation do you hold?" asked Tom.

"I am reluctantly forced to side with those who say the prophecy only included the buildings of the Temple and not necessarily all of the walls."

"Why do you say reluctantly?" Tom asked.

"Because Yeshua seems to have gone out of his way to make the prophecy all-inclusive, saying that 'not one stone will be left standing upon another.'[13] Since the wall is still standing, there are only two other possibilities that I can think of: Either Yeshua was wrong—a hypothesis which I cannot accept—or," Joshua concluded with a strained chuckle, "at least one of those who was with Yeshua when he prophesied about the Temple two thousand years ago is still alive."

"Joshua, forgive my ignorance of such things," Tom said, "but this is the Temple where the Ark of the Covenant was kept, right?"

"You are correct," Rosen said. "Of course this wall is some distance from where the Ark was. Why do you ask?"

"Oh, nothing really. It's just that I must have seen the movie *Raiders of the Lost Ark*[14] about half a dozen times over the years and I was just wondering if anyone knows what really happened to it."

"Well, there are a number of theories. The Bible doesn't mention the whereabouts of the Ark after the Temple was destroyed in the Babylonian invasion. It's assumed that when the invaders plundered the Temple they took the Ark with them. But the Bible

[12]Josephus, *The Jewish War*, VII, 1. See also *Midrash Rabba*, Lamentations 1:31, where it is reported that Vespasian's General Pangar, when asked why he had not destroyed the Western Wall of the Temple, responded, "I acted so for the honor of your empire . . . When people look at the Western Wall, they will exclaim, 'Behold the might of Vespasian from what he did not destroy!'"

[13]Matthew 24:2.

[14]1981, Paramount.

says that when Ezra returned from Babylon to rebuild the Temple, he brought back everything that had been taken.[15] Some people have speculated that the Ark may have been taken from the Temple when it was destroyed by Titus in 70 A.D. and that it was either melted down or perhaps locked away and later hidden in some secret treasury room in the Vatican. However, there is some evidence to dispute that theory. In Rome there is an arch which was dedicated to Titus in honor of his successful siege of Jerusalem. Carved into the arch are scenes of the Roman destruction and looting of Jerusalem, including a detailed carving showing the treasures taken from the Temple. The Ark is not among the treasures depicted, even though, as the most highly valued item, it surely would have been included had Titus taken it.

"Some people believe the Ark is in Ethiopia, though there are a number of major weaknesses in that theory. Another theory, based on one of the apocryphal books of the Bible, is that to prevent the Babylonians from finding the Ark, the Prophet Jeremiah hid it in a cave on Mount Nebo in Jordan."[16]

"What do you mean, 'apocryphal'?" Tom asked.

"Well, of course you know about the Old Testament and the New Testament, or—as we Messianic Jews prefer to call them— the Old and New Covenants."

Tom nodded.

"Well, not all religious writings were considered worthy of inclusion in the Bible. The other books make up the Apocrypha. Some are simply flights of fantasy, others are obvious fakes written hundreds of years later than their texts would lead you to believe. But there are a few where the question of authenticity is not quite so clear. A number of the apocryphal books appear in the Catholic version of the Old Testament. But these are books that neither the Jews nor the Protestants consider to be inspired by God. The Greek Orthodox Bible also includes the Apocrypha, but the Greek Church does not consider them to be inspired. Today, even the Catholic Church downplays their importance."

[15]Ezra 1:7.

[16]2 Maccabees 2:4-8.

"So, where do you think the Ark is?" asked Tom.

"Actually," Joshua answered, "I have my own theory. I think that whether it was hidden on Mt. Nebo or taken to Babylon, the Ark was probably returned when the new Temple was rebuilt."

"But then where is it now?"

"I think it may be somewhere in southern France."

"France? Why France?"

"Well," Joshua began, "like I said, this is just a theory. I never gave it much thought until a few years ago when they announced the results of the Carbon 14 dating of the Shroud of Turin."

A puzzled look came over Decker's face. "What does all this have to do with the Shroud?" he asked.

"Decker, you remember how impressed we all were with the Shroud," Joshua said. "It really isn't important to my faith whether it's real or not, but from a purely scientific point of view, it's just too good to be a fake. But until recently the Carbon 14 dating seemed conclusive. Then one day I was reading some of the writings of St. Jerome, who lived in the fourth and early fifth century and was the first to translate the Old Testament directly from Hebrew to Latin. In the piece I was reading, Jerome quotes from a book he called the Gospel of the Hebrews, a book which unfortunately either no longer exists or is lost. He doesn't quote from it very extensively, but the small piece he does quote reveals a very interesting piece of information about the Shroud. Of course, there's no way of knowing how authentic this gospel really was. It may have been as spurious as some of the other apocryphal writings, but it says is that after Yeshua rose from the dead, he took his burial shroud and gave it to the servant of the high priest.[17] That's not very much, but it's the only record we have that indicates what happened to the Shroud following the resurrection."

"Who was the servant of the high priest?" Tom asked.

"That was my question as well," Joshua continued. "Who was he and why would Yeshua give him the Shroud? Well, I mulled that over and then I recalled that there is a reference to the ser-

[17]Jerome, on Eph. 5. 4. (Migne PL 26, cols, 552 C-D), cited by J. K. Elliot in *The Apocryphal New Testament* (Clarendon Press, Oxford University Press, 1993).

vant of the high priest in the gospels.[18] In that account, the servant of the high priest, a man named Malchus, was among those who went to arrest Yeshua on the night before his crucifixion. The Apostle Peter attempted to fend them off with a sword and in the scuffle he cut off Malchus' ear. Yeshua told Peter to put his sword away and then picked up the ear and placed it back on Malchus' head and instantly healed it.

"This same Malchus would have been in the Temple on a daily basis and would have seen the curtain, which separated the people from the Holy of Holies, inexplicably torn in two after Yeshua's crucifixion.[19] The Holy of Holies was the most sacred place in the Temple. When Yeshua died, God himself tore the curtain from top to bottom, allowing ordinary men and women—not just the high priests—access to his holy presence. And Malchus, like everyone else in Israel at the time, would have been very much aware of Yeshua's miracles and the evidence of his resurrection. It seems reasonable to me to assume that Malchus, having experienced all this—especially the healing of his ear—may well have become a follower of Yeshua himself. If so, it would explain Yeshua's contact with him after the resurrection; the Bible says that Yeshua appeared to more than five hundred people in and around Jerusalem after the resurrection.[20]

"But it still doesn't explain why he would give Malchus the Shroud. That was the toughest question. Then one day, when I wasn't even thinking about it, something just clicked, and I realized it must have been to preserve the Shroud as evidence of the resurrection! I believe Yeshua told Malchus to put the Shroud in the Ark of the Covenant."

"Why would he do that?" Tom asked.

"It's a little complicated," Rosen continued. "As I said, we're pretty sure that the Ark wasn't in the Temple when it was plundered by the Romans in 70 A.D. So where was it? I believe the Ark

---

[18]Matthew 26:50-52; Mark 14:47; Luke 22:50-51; John 18:10.

[19]Matthew 27:51.

[20]1 Corinthians 15:6.

disappeared a second time, but this time it clearly wasn't stolen. It was hidden by the high priest.

"Between the time of the Babylonians and the Romans there were several other times that bandits tried to rob the Temple. I think the priests probably developed an evacuation plan to hide the Ark whenever the Temple was threatened. Surely when the Romans conquered Israel, the priests realized that the Temple was once again an extremely attractive target for those seeking their fortune.

"My theory is that the Ark was hidden somewhere in the tunnels beneath the Temple to protect it from the Romans. If so, very few people would have known about it, but certainly the high priest would have known. And if the high priest knew, it's likely that his servant—that is, Malchus—would have known as well."

Decker and Tom nodded tentative agreement.

Rosen continued. "Okay, now let's move ahead in time about eleven hundred years, during the time of the First Crusade. Not many people realize that the Crusaders, who were mostly French, were quite successful in their first attempts to take the Holy Land from the Muslims. They even succeeded in capturing and holding the city of Jerusalem and establishing a French-born king over the city. Shortly after that, an order of knights known as the Knights Templar was formed in Jerusalem."

"I've heard of them," Decker offered. "They were pretty powerful, if I remember correctly."

"Yes, but not at first. The stated purpose of the Knights Templar was to protect Jerusalem and to aid European pilgrims coming to the Holy Land. This was a rather unrealistic undertaking, since originally there were only six or seven members in the order. And they were very poor. Ironically, poverty was one of their vows. I say ironically because somehow over the next hundred years this small group of knights not only grew in number, but grew unbelievably wealthy. In fact, these men became the first international bankers, loaning money to kings and nobles throughout Europe. How they acquired their immense wealth has been the subject of great speculation."

"And you think you know the answer?" Decker urged.

"I think so, and if I'm right, it explains a lot more. You see, the headquarters for the Knights Templar was in the Mosque of Omar—that is, the Dome of the Rock—that sits on the site of the old Temple. It has been suggested that the knights excavated the tunnels beneath the Mosque and found the treasures of Solomon's Temple and *that* was the source of their wealth."

"But how does the Shroud of Turin fit into all this?" Tom asked.

"God had Moses build the Ark," Joshua continued, "as a container for certain sacred objects: the stone tablets on which God wrote the ten commandments; the first five books of the Bible written by Moses; a container of manna, which God caused to fall from the sky each morning for the Hebrews to eat while they were in the desert; and Aaron's staff, which God had miraculously caused to sprout, bud, and bear almonds.[21] Those things were placed in the Ark as a witness to later generations of God's power and his covenant with Israel.

"But something always struck me as odd about that list of items. Stone tablets will last forever. Protected in the Ark, the parchment that Moses used to write the first five books of the Bible might last for thousands of years. But the container of manna, under normal conditions, would turn to dust within just a matter of months. And Aaron's staff—though it might survive the centuries as a simple wooden staff—without the budding and the almonds, would not be much of a witness of God's power. That's when it occurred to me that perhaps the power of the Ark is greater and quite different than we may have realized. For instance, think about the staff for a minute. How tall do you imagine Aaron's staff would have been?"

"Oh, gee," Tom said, "I hate to show my ignorance, but all I can think of is another movie, *The Ten Commandments*.[22] In that movie it seemed like Moses' staff was about six or seven feet tall."

"Well, I can't say much for the reliability of your sources, but I think that's a fair guess," said Joshua. "Shepherding hasn't

---

[21]Hebrews 9:4.

[22]1956, Paramount.

changed much over the centuries, and all the shepherd staffs I've ever seen are about that long. So when you think about Aaron's staff, with the limbs and sprouts and almonds growing from it, it would have had quite a large diameter. But," said Joshua, about to make his point, "based on a standard eighteen-inch cubit, the absolute longest that staff could have been and still have fit in the Ark is four feet, nine inches, and that's without any branches."

Tom tried but didn't catch Joshua's point. "So?"

"Well, think about it. The only way that a six- to seven-foot shepherd's staff could have fit into the Ark is if the inside dimensions of the Ark are not limited by the outside dimensions."

Tom's eyes widened. "Oh, I get it! Sort of a *Mary Poppins*[23] effect," he said, referring to another movie. "Where Mary Poppins was able to put all sorts of things in her carpetbag that were much bigger than the bag itself."

Decker and Joshua laughed.

"Exactly," Joshua answered. "If the container of manna and Aaron's staff were to be a witness to future generations of God's power, there must be some miraculous, preservative power to the Ark. I'm sure you know that time is generally referred to as the fourth dimension—with length, width, and height being the first three. What I'm suggesting is that perhaps inside the Ark there is a total absence of dimensions: no length, width or height, which would explain how Aaron's staff could fit; and no *time*, which explains how the manna and the staff could be preserved!"

Suddenly it all became clear to Decker just what Joshua was getting at. "So you think the servant of the high priest put the Shroud into the Ark, where it remained until it was taken out, more than a thousand years later, by the Knights Templar when they discovered the Temple treasures!"

"Exactly!" Joshua said. "Of course, it's mostly just conjecture, but it does offer a unified theory that would provide a consistent explanation for a number of unanswered questions. Besides, it makes sense that the Shroud—the only physical evidence of

[23]1964, Disney.

Yeshua's resurrection and the consummation of God's *new* covenant with his people—would be kept in the Ark of the Covenant together with the evidence of God's *old* covenant."

"Wait a second, wait a second," Tom said, trying to catch up with the thoughts of his companions.

"Don't you see?" said Decker. "That's why the Shroud flunked the Carbon 14 dating. For more than a thousand years it totally escaped all deterioration and aging while it was inside the Ark!"

"Holy—" Tom caught himself, but his excitement showed in his raised voice, and many of the nearby tourists and worshipers turned to stare at him disapprovingly. "That's incredible!" he said in a more controlled voice. "But what about the Knights Templar? Is there any connection between them and the Shroud of Turin?"

"Well," Joshua answered, "as far back as it can be traced, the first person who we can positively prove had the Shroud was a man in France named Geoffrey de Charney. Some years later his family gave the Shroud to the House of Savoy, who later moved it to Turin, Italy."

"So is there a link between de Charney and the Knights Templar?" Decker asked.

"As a matter of fact," Joshua glowed, having been asked the question he was hoping for, "there is."

"So what is it?" Decker asked, when he felt Joshua's pause had gone on long enough.

"Well, as we said, the Knights Templar became very powerful throughout Europe. But then the King of France decided he no longer wanted them around. He accused their members of hideous sins and atrocities. They were arrested and tortured to force them to confess to his trumped-up charges. Those who confessed were locked away in prisons; those who refused were tortured to death or burned at the stake. Two of the last to be executed in this way were Jacques de Molay, the grand master of the Knights Templar, and Geoffrey de Charney, preceptor of Normandy. *That* Geoffrey de Charney apparently was the uncle of the later Geoffrey de Charney, who was the first person we can positively determine had possession of the Shroud."

"Incredible!" said Tom.

"Additionally," Joshua said, "one of the accusations against the knights was that they worshiped the image of a man."

"The Shroud of Turin!" Decker concluded.

"And that's why you think the Ark is in France?" Tom asked.

"Yes," Joshua answered. "It's my belief that the Shroud, the Ark, and the other Temple treasures were taken from Israel and hidden in southern France by the Knights Templar. If so, many of the treasures and the Ark may still be there, hidden away. In fact, there is a secret society in France called the Prieuré de Sion, which traces its origins to the Knights Templar. The head of the society has been quoted as saying that he knows where the Temple treasures are and that they will be returned to Jerusalem 'when the time is right.'"[24]

"Are there really tunnels and hidden passageways under the Temple where the Ark could have been hidden before the Knights Templar found it?" Decker asked.

"Oh, absolutely. In fact, not just tunnels, but large vaulted rooms. Most haven't been excavated, but they have been identified by radar soundings."[25] Rosen pointed to a pair of low arches to the left and perpendicular to the wall. "Over there beyond those arches is the opening of one of the tunnels that has been excavated. It runs south along the inside of the wall and north for more than a hundred yards along what was the western boundary of the Temple. A great deal of fighting broke out when the tunnel was opened to the public in 1996. There's a side tunnel that leads eastward in the direction of what today is the Dome of the Rock, but two thousand years ago would have been the Holy of Holies, where the Ark resided. Some rabbis were excavating that tunnel, but the government stopped them and sealed it off."

"Why?" Tom asked, obviously disappointed with such an uneventful end to the tale.

"When Israel captured Jerusalem in the Six Day War in 1967,

[24]Michael Baigent, Richard Leigh, and Henry Lincoln, *Holy Blood, Holy Grail* (New York: Delacorte Press, 1982), 200.

[25]See, for example, Dan Bahat, "Jerusalem Down Under: Tunneling Along Herod's Temple Mount Wall," *Biblical Archaeology Review*, Vol. 21, No. 6 (November/December 1995), 30-47.

we made a pledge to allow the Muslims to continue to control the area of the Dome of the Rock. When the Muslims found out about the digging, they immediately protested and the tunnel was sealed. Some people believe the Ark may still be buried under the Dome of the Rock and that the Muslims know it's there but don't want the Jews to have it.

"A more likely reason for refusing permission, though, is that the Muslims fear that Jewish zealots might get into the tunnel and blow up the Mosque in order to bring about the rebuilding of the Jewish Temple. It would not be the first time that Israelis have tried to blow up the Dome. A group of zealots, mostly followers of Meir Kahane, tried it back in 1969. Kahane was assassinated while visiting New York in the early nineties, but Moshe Greenberg, one of his followers, is now the Israeli minister of Religious Affairs."

The Tears of Dogs

7

Nablus, Israel

THAT NIGHT DECKER AND TOM stayed at the Rosens' home. They were invited to stay during their entire six-week stint in Israel, but both men felt that would be an imposition. Besides, *NewsWorld* had already made arrangements for them and they said it was best not to let the company get out of the habit of paying the bill.

Decker had trouble sleeping that night. During the day he had catnapped at every opportunity, so sleep now seemed to lose its priority. He thought of home. It was nearly midnight in Israel. He wasn't sure what time it was in Washington, but decided that late or early, Elizabeth would appreciate the call. Walking quietly toward the kitchen to use the phone, he stopped dead in his tracks when he heard hushed voices and saw a light. At first he thought he might be imagining it, and then he became concerned that intruders might be in the house. As he stood motionless it became clear that one of the voices was Joshua Rosen and another was Ilana, but there were others—two or three men. By the time Decker realized that there was no danger, his reporter's instincts had taken over. Later the guilt of spying on his hosts would eat at his conscience, but for right now he let curiosity rule.

"Don't you understand?" said one of the men. "We must not let cost stop us. God will provide what we cannot."

"Of course," responded Joshua Rosen, "but we must not fool-ishly rush into this unprepared. If this is the task God has set before us, we must begin it, but not haphazardly. When God told Noah to build the Ark, he provided adequate time for its com-pletion. If we are faithful, God will not allow the need to arise before the answer is provided."

"Yes!" responded the first man with undiminished zeal. "But Petra must be protected!"

"Yes, yes," said Rosen, "Ilana and I agree, Petra *must* be pro-tected. All we are saying is that cost must be considered—not as an issue in whether to proceed, but rather to allow us to know *how* to proceed, as well as how much we must raise. We are not a large group, you know."

"You don't need to tell me!" the man responded.

"How are things progressing in getting the permits to obtain the equipment from America?" asked Rosen.

This time another man answered. "I'm having a little trouble from some of my fellow Knesset members. Most trust me implic-itly in these matters, but a few of the opposition members are constantly watching over my shoulder and have caused some delays."

"But you will be able to do it?" asked the first man.

"Yes," the other responded. "I think so."

"Good. Then, if there is no other new information," said another man with an unusually rich and measured voice, "let us plan to meet again after the *Shabbat* two weeks hence." Clearly this was the voice of the group's leader. "In the meantime, Joshua, continue your design work; James, continue to arrange for the permits; and Elias, please work with Joshua to determine the costs. I will continue to speak to those of our number from around the world who believe as we do that Petra must be pro-tected, so that we can raise the necessary funding."

"Yes, of course, Rabbi," answered at least two of the partici-pants respectfully.

As the meeting broke up Decker quietly crept back to his room. He would call Elizabeth later.

Jerusalem, Israel

The next morning Decker and Tom went to the Jerusalem Ramada Renaissance Hotel, which was serving as the temporary Middle East headquarters of *NewsWorld* magazine. The office was nothing more than a hotel room with a southern view of the old city of Jerusalem and an adjoining room for the correspondents to sleep in. The room stank of stale cigarettes, which lay in a half dozen overfull ashtrays. It had apparently been some time since the trash had been taken out. A laptop computer and a small printer sat on a table, along with several crumpled sheets of paper and a day-old cup of coffee.

"Nice place you've got here," Decker said dryly as he surveyed the condition of the room. "What's the matter, no room service?"

"Better get used to it," responded lead reporter Hank Asher.

"Why, what's going on?"

"Most of Israel's service workers are Palestinians," answered Bill Dean, the other *NewsWorld* reporter. "When the protests started four months ago, they all refused to go to work. This is the result."

"It's been the same in every recent episode of this never-ending battle," continued Asher, as he took another drag from his cigarette.

At that moment the phone rang. Asher answered it. "When?" he asked the caller after a moment. "Are you sure?" He listened to the caller's reply, hung up and grabbed his camera bag while the other three men moved instinctively toward the door. "I hope you guys ate your Wheaties this morning," Asher said. "This looks like a big one."

The four men crammed into a small car and sped off. "Where are we going?" asked Decker.

"Petah Tiqwa," answered Asher. "There's a major riot in progress. If my source is correct, there may be as many as several thousand Palestinians involved. Israeli security has been using rubber bullets so far, but with that many people throwing rocks and fire bombs, there's no telling what will happen."

"What's going on?" asked Tom. "Why so many?"

"Don't know," answered Asher. "So far the riots have been scattered and limited to a few dozen Palestinians at any one time. This is very unusual."

When they arrived near the site of the riot, the road had been roped off by Israeli security forces. Asher pulled the car to the checkpost and showed the soldier his press credentials. A moment later they parked the car within a hundred yards of the riot and Asher and Dean put large "PRESS" signs in their front, side, and rear windows. "Most of the time they won't bother press vehicles," Dean explained as Tom and Decker looked on.

As they approached the rioting, the size of the crowds became clear. Asher's source had been right about the number. The Israeli security forces had broken the Palestinians into half a dozen smaller groups. From the direction of each of the groups, the sounds of breaking glass and the pop of rubber bullets being fired by Israeli soldiers could be heard above the shouts and chants. Decker and Tom split off from Dean and Asher to cover a larger area. They got as close to one of the crowds as they could and decided to try to circle around behind them. This required the pair to swing wide some five blocks and approach from the side of the conflagration.

Still two blocks from the riot, Decker's pulse suddenly quickened as the pop of rifles firing rubber bullets was replaced by a far more familiar and deadly sound, which Decker recognized from his time in the army as the crack of live ammunition. At first there were just a few shots, but the number grew. Decker assumed he was hearing echoes reflecting back in the distance. Then he realized he was wrong. From the streets around them, in every direction, hundreds of shots were being fired. His first response was to look for cover, but that same reporter's curiosity that sometimes caused him to do things he wasn't proud of now drove him on toward the conflict. Tom readied his camera for the scene that awaited them.

Suddenly the guns went silent and the streets were filled instead with sounds of weeping and cries of pain. On the street before them, more than fifty Palestinians lay wounded or dead.

Above the cries, an order went out and was repeated to unload live ammunition and to reload rubber bullets. Israeli soldiers ran from storefront to storefront, routing any Palestinians they found huddled together. Showing some mercy, they ignored those individuals in the street aiding the fallen.

Near where Decker stood, knelt a young boy, perhaps eleven or twelve years old, holding a dead man in his arms. As Decker watched, an Israeli soldier came near the boy. He was staggering and bleeding heavily from a rock-inflicted wound above his right eye. In anger and grief the boy abandoned caution and reached for the first thing he could find: a brick, broken in half, with corners rounded from being thrown so many times already.

The soldier seemed dazed and unaware of the boy until he was only a few yards away. Through his tears the boy hurled the brick with very poor aim at the soldier, hitting him in the right shin and sending him into a fit of pain. Grasping his leg and then seeing the boy running away, he raised his rifle. With blood dripping from the wound above his eye, he took aim. As he did, the boy approached the corner of the building where Decker was standing. Decker reached out and grabbed the boy, pulling him from harm's way just as a bullet whizzed by. The sound of the shot made it clear to both Decker and to the Israeli soldier that he had fired live ammunition. In his dazed state he had failed to respond to the order to reload rubber bullets.

Decker held tightly to the boy, who struggled for a moment to get away, then stopped fighting. The soldier did not pursue the boy. Soon the riot was over. All that was left was to count the casualties, clean up, and start over.

Decker and Tom asked the boy, who spoke some English, where he lived. The boy responded that he was from Jenin, a town several miles from Petah Tiqwa. Apparently the riot had been an organized effort that brought Palestinians in from towns throughout Israel. Decker told the boy they would take him back to his home in Jenin.

Tom continued taking pictures of the destruction while Decker carried the boy piggyback along the route the riot had followed.

When they arrived at the car, Dean and Asher were waiting for them.

"What do you have there?" asked Asher.

"A witness," answered Decker. "He lives in Jenin. He was recruited to come here today for the riot. That's how they managed to stir up such a large crowd: They recruited extras from outside. If we take the boy home we might be able to get a lead on who the organizers were." It was a long shot, but Decker didn't want to have to depend on Asher's generosity to help get the boy home.

The previously crowded car now felt like the Washington subway at rush hour. The boy did his best to direct the Americans to his home, and after losing about forty minutes to bad directions, they finally stopped in front of his cement slab house. Decker and Tom went to the door with the boy and deposited him with his mother. The boy hugged her around the waist and began speaking to her. Seeing her tears, Decker guessed that the dead man the boy had been holding must have been his older brother. Through her tearful attempts to speak, they ascertained that she spoke almost no English. Nevertheless, it was evident she realized that they had helped the boy.

"If we're going to get any of this in Monday's edition we've got to get back to the office now," Bill Dean called to them from the car. "You can follow up on this later."

❑

Back at the hotel Decker and Hank Asher compared notes while Bill Dean and Tom contacted Israeli officials on the phone for their reaction to the riot and the killing of the Palestinians. When they completed their report, they e-mailed it to the United States.

At six o'clock that evening Decker and Tom took Asher and Dean to Ben Gurion International Airport in Tel Aviv for their flight home to the U.S. After several months covering the Middle East, they were looking forward to a few weeks at home. Before they boarded their plane, Decker pulled Dean off to the side. "Bill, let me ask you a sort of strange question," he began. "You've been over here for a while. If you overheard a conversation in which the people talking said 'Petra must be protected,' what would you think they were talking about?"

"Hmm . . ." Dean began thoughtfully, "You hear so many strange things around here. I guess it depends on who said it. *Petra* is Greek for 'rock,' so they might have been talking about a lot of things. They could have meant the Rock of Gibraltar at the entrance of the Mediterranean Sea. There has been a lot of concern about terrorist activity in that area. Or, if the people talking were Muslims, I'd guess they were talking about the Dome of the Rock. But those are both pretty cryptic references. There's an ancient city called Petra in Jordan, but it's been abandoned for centuries. It's just a tourist attraction now. There's also a reference in the Bible where Jesus refers to the rock on which he would build his church. So, I suppose they could have been Christian zealots referring to protecting the church from some perceived devil or false doctrine or something. That's really all I can think of right off the bat. I don't know if that helps you any. What's this all about, anyway?"

Decker shook his head. "At this point I really don't know. If I come up with anything, I'll tell you when you get back from your vacation."

❑

For the next week things seemed strangely quiet compared to their first day on the job. Israel braced for a Palestinian response to the shootings, but it was slow in coming. There were a few small disturbances, and the strike by Palestinian workers and shopkeepers continued, but there was nothing the Israeli authorities couldn't handle. On the international scene, a United Nations vote to condemn the Israeli action in Petah Tiqwa passed by a large majority, with the United States abstaining. Decker and Tom found plenty of time to engage in such things as taking out the trash and airing out the rooms.

Tom, who seemed to be more interested in sightseeing than Decker, picked up brochures on all the historical and religious places to visit that they had missed on their whirlwind tour with Joshua Rosen. Decker looked over a few of them, making mental notes of where to take Elizabeth and the girls when they arrived the week before Christmas. Since Decker's stay in Israel would last into January, Elizabeth had thought this would be an excellent opportunity to take advantage of an otherwise bad situation and spend Christmas with Decker in the Holy Land.

❏

At about four in the afternoon of their eighth day, Tom returned from visiting one of Jerusalem's many shrines and sat down just as the phone rang. On the other end was a man whose accent gave him away as a Palestinian. "I need to speak to the American, Asher."

"I'm sorry, he's not here," Tom responded. "May I help you?"

"Tell the American, 'Many dogs shall weep tonight, but their tears will find nowhere to fall.'"

"What?" Tom asked. "What are you talking about? What does that mean?" But the man had hung up.

"What was that?" Decker asked, responding to Tom's excited but puzzled expression.

"I don't really know," Tom answered. "I think it must have been one of Hank Asher's informants. Either that or a kook."

Decker waited a second for Tom to continue and when it seemed he might keep the mystery to himself, he finally asked, "Well, what did he say?"

"He said to tell Asher 'Many dogs shall weep tonight, but their tears will find nowhere to fall.'"

"Any idea what it means?" Decker asked.

Tom picked up the phone and began dialing as he answered. "None, but I know who might."

Tom was calling Hank Asher in America. It took four calls to locate him and when they reached him he had no more idea what the message meant than did Tom or Decker.

"The only thing that I can think of," said Asher, "is that sometimes one or more of the Palestinian groups will call after a bombing or a kidnapping to take credit for it. There's quite a bit of rivalry that goes on among the different factions of Palestinians. Maybe the guy that called is trying to establish responsibility before the fact so his group will get credit for it afterward. If so, you can expect a second call from him after the fact. I suggest you call the Israeli police and tell them about the call. In any case, it doesn't seem like you'll have long to wait to find out what he meant. Whatever it is, he said it would happen tonight."

"Okay," said Tom. "Listen, give us a call at the hotel if you think of anything else."

"Sure thing," said Asher. "Oh, one other thing: When you call the police, don't tell them the guy asked for me. I'm trying to take a vacation over here."

Tom called the police, who wasted no time responding to the call. Figuring out what to do about it was another thing. The police inspector, Lt. Freij, said that since the caller was apparently Palestinian, the use of the term *dogs* must refer to Israelis. "We call them dogs and they call us dogs. 'Weep' and 'tears' obviously means that something will happen that will cause grief for Israel. 'Tonight' must mean just that: Whatever is going to happen will occur tonight. Beyond that it's guesswork." Lt. Freij also suggested that it might all be just a hoax and that such things were not uncommon. "Just in case, though," he said, "I'll order all the standard precautions and see that all the appropriate authorities are alerted to the possibility of a terrorist attack."

❏

Tom and Decker discussed the caller's message for a while longer but came to no conclusions. A little after eleven o'clock Tom decided to go to bed and Decker went up on the roof of the building for some fresh air.

As he sat on a large gray fixture on the roof, he thought back to his discussion with Goodman about the boy, Christopher. In truth, the matter was never very far from his mind. *There has to be some way I can write that story without hurting people*, he thought. A dozen scenarios ran through his mind, but all had the same conclusion: too great a risk of exposure. Someone was sure to figure it out.

Decker looked out over the beauty of the old city of Jerusalem. For the most part, the city lay silent in the late evening darkness, with only scattered points of light shining in defiance of the moonless night. The gold-covered Dome of the Rock sparkled in the starlight near the Wailing Wall.

Suddenly he understood. "That's it!"

Decker ran at full speed from the roof to the hotel suite. "Tom!" he shouted as he burst through the door. Tom had not gone to bed, but was watching an old John Wayne and Jimmy Stewart movie. "Quick! Get your shoes!"

Tom grabbed his camera, coat, and shoes while running toward the door. "What's going on?" he asked.

"The phone call!" Decker said, abbreviating his speech to save time. "They're going to blow up the Wailing Wall!"

"Of course!" Tom exclaimed as they ran for the elevator. "'Weeping' but 'no place for their tears to fall!'"

Tom called Lt. Freij from his cell phone while Decker drove the short distance from the hotel to the Joffa Gate and turned down David Street into the old city. They were only about a mile from the Wailing Wall, but at their present speed Tom felt that the car would shake apart on the ancient roads before they reached it. Because it was late, the one way street was fairly clear and Decker had no trouble as he made the sharp right onto Armenian Patriarch Street, past the Zion Gate and then onto Bateimahasse Street. They were almost there.

Decker pulled the car into the parking lot at the Wailing Wall and slammed the door as he and Tom ran toward the Wall. All was quiet and deserted in the cold, late night. Even the tourists had gone to bed. Decker and Tom stopped and looked around for signs of activity but found none. The only sound was the wind and the barely audible late-night sounds of the new city outside the walls. They looked at one another.

Decker was the first one to speak. "You know," he said, "any minute now Lt. Freij is going to be driving up here with his sirens blaring and his lights flashing and we're going to be standing here looking like total idiots."

They sighed together. "I don't suppose we could call him back and tell him to forget it," Tom said in strained jest.

"No use," responded Decker. "He'll be here any minute."

That's when it hit them. They stopped talking and looked around them.

"What's wrong with this picture?" Decker quipped as he scanned the scene more closely.

"No police," Tom answered dryly. The ever-present Israeli security were nowhere to be found.

The next instant they were startled as a young boy emerged from the entrance to the tunnel Joshua Rosen had shown them. Seconds later he was followed by about eight men for whom he apparently had been standing watch. As he ran, the boy passed close enough for Decker and Tom to get a look at him. It was the Palestinian boy from Jenin.

Decker and Tom ran to the tunnel entrance and found the bodies of four Israeli security personnel lying in pools of blood, their throats cut. Decker stooped down over them, vainly looking for any sign of life. Tom turned his head away from the bloody sight. As he did he caught the distinctive smell of a burning fuse.

"Decker! Run!" he shouted as he grabbed Decker's arm.

The two men bolted from the tunnel and ran as fast as they could. Sixty yards away they slowed to a stop, thinking they were probably far enough to be safe. In the distance they heard the sounds of Lt. Freij's sirens. As Decker looked toward the approaching police cars, the ground shook and the blast of a massive explosion thundered through his head. Instantly, he dropped to the ground as dirt and rock flew all around him. Almost at once, a second and third detonation followed, filling the air with a heavy, opaque cloud of dirt and smoke and rock dust, which obscured the lights of the city. For a brief instant there was silence and then the ground shook again and again as hundreds of immense stones tumbled from the Wall with heavy thuds, demolishing the plaza floor and breaking stones that had fallen before them to various states of rubble.

Decker lay on the ground choking for air, his shirt pulled over his mouth and nose to filter out the dust. He could not see what had happened to Tom and for that moment he didn't really care. All he knew was he needed to breathe. His death seemed to him almost certain—only his continued gasping and the pain in his lungs made him sure he was still alive. He could hear nothing but the ringing in his ears.

Then through the dark there appeared flashing lights. Several minutes passed before, nearly unconscious, he felt hands grab him and drag him away. Soon the cloud began to settle and he could see the face of Lt. Freij looking down at him.

"Are you all right?" Freij asked.

Decker tried to answer but immediately began coughing and spitting up dust-filled mucus. From the corner of his eye, he saw Tom lying on the ground nearby. Still coughing, Decker made his way to his friend's side and managed to call his name.

Tom, like Decker, was covered from head to toe with thick gray dust. His breathing was short and labored. Hearing Decker's call, he opened his eyes and began to smile.

"What?" Decker asked, trying to understand Tom's unexpected cheerfulness.

"I got the picture," Tom managed, holding his camera like a trophy before breaking into a fit of coughing.

As Decker scanned the area where the Western Wall had stood, he thought only briefly about how glad he was to be alive. And though he was sickened by the destruction of this awesome historical site, he could not help but envision Tom's picture on the cover of next Monday's *NewsWorld* along with his article as the lead story.

When their lungs had cleared enough to speak, Decker and Tom told Lt. Freij what had happened and pointed out approximately where to find the guards' bodies under the rubble. They did not, however, tell him about the boy. They would talk to him themselves in the morning and maybe come away with a second exclusive.

By the time they left the scene, crowds of Israelis and tourists from the surrounding area had gathered behind the police lines to look in shock and horror at what had been the last remnant of the ancient Temple.

❏

The phone caller had been right: There was much weeping that night. The Palestinians had planted far more than enough explosives to do the job. Bits and pieces of broken stone lay everywhere. The earth of the Temple Mount behind the Wall caved down upon the rubble. And of the Wall itself, not one stone was left standing upon another.

8

When in the Woods and Meeting Wild Beasts

Jerusalem, Israel

THE NEXT MORNING Decker and Tom got up early and drove to Jenin to talk to the Palestinian boy. On the way there it occurred to them that they really didn't have a plan.

"Okay, after we get there, then what?" Tom asked.

"We'll just talk to the kid and tell him to tell the people he was with last night that some American reporters want to talk to them. We're not their enemy. They like the media. That's the only way they can get their story out. Besides, if they didn't want coverage they certainly wouldn't have called us on the phone to tell us it was going to happen. The bigger problem will be Lt. Freij wanting us to reveal our sources once the story comes out."

When they arrived at the boy's house, Tom decided to leave his camera in the car, just to be extra sure nobody got nervous. They walked the short path to the house and Decker knocked on the door.

"Do you think anyone's home?" Tom asked after a moment. But before he had even gotten the words out, the door opened and the boy's mother motioned for them to come in. "Great," Tom said, pleased at the reception. "Maybe I should have brought my camera, after all."

As the door swung shut Decker heard a loud crack and felt a sudden intense pain spread through his head as his skull absorbed the impact of a wooden club.

Somewhere in Israel

The pain in Decker's head crawled down his neck and shoulders and came to rest in the pit of his empty stomach. Ropes bound his feet and hands. They were loose enough to allow circulation but no movement. Lying on his side with his face to the floor, he wondered where he was and how long he had been there. The air was stuffy and from the stench and the slight dampness of his pants it was apparent that while he was unconscious, he had urinated on himself. From this he judged that he had been unconscious for less than a day, because any fluids in his system would have been vacated in the first twenty-four hours. After that his body would retain any remaining fluids as dehydration set in.

He could hear two men talking. For right now it made sense to not let them know he was awake. Slowly he opened the eye closest to the floor. When it became clear no one had noticed, Decker strained to look around as much as he could, wincing in pain with each eye movement. What he saw told him very little. He was in a room with one small, boarded-up window. About five feet away Tom lay on the floor in much the same condition, facing away from him. Two men sat playing some kind of card game on a makeshift table, paying very little attention to their captives. Decker closed his eye and rested from the strain. The men were speaking in an Arabic dialect, so Decker had no idea what they were saying. Still, as he tried to ride out the pain, it seemed somehow reasonable just to lie there without moving, listening to the men in hopes of learning something of his situation.

Some hours later, Decker realized he had fallen asleep. The nausea had subsided and the pain in his head was somewhat less than he remembered. What woke him was the sound of a door closing and men talking, which he took to be a changing of the guard. With his eyes still closed he could feel the men moving about the room, stopping to look down at him and then moving away. Carefully he opened one eye and saw the men gathered around Tom.

"Wake up, Jew," said one of the men in heavily accented English. Decker watched as the man pulled back his right foot to get a good swing and then threw it forward with the full weight of his body, landing the toe of his army boot squarely in the middle of Tom's back. The force of the blow drove Tom several feet across the floor. His back arched in agony as he let out a yelp, muffled by the fact that the blow had also knocked the wind out of him.

"Stop!" Decker shouted. The four men looked over at Decker, who had somehow managed to sit most of the way up. The man who kicked Tom walked over and looked down at Decker. Decker had the feeling that he was being inspected by the man; he was looking for something. When he failed to find whatever it was, he shoved Decker back to the floor with his foot and went back to Tom.

Tom struggled to catch his breath and a deep, anguished moan passed from his lips. The man had hurt Tom badly and he was preparing to do it again.

"Stop!" Decker shouted again.

This time the man returned to Decker and kicked him in his left shoulder. It hurt terribly, but it was obvious to Decker the man had not kicked him with nearly the enthusiasm or force he had used to kick Tom.

"Keep your mouth shut or you'll get the same as the Jew," the man warned and moved back to Tom.

"Wait!" Decker said, sitting up again and failing to heed the warning. The man looked over at Decker, who continued, "He's not a Jew!"

For an instant the man's eyes registered uncertainty. He

paused, and then looked as though he was going to ignore Decker's infraction of his order and concentrate on Tom.

Decker persisted. "He's not a Jew, I tell you. He's an American, just like me. Check his passport. It's in his pocket." Scenes of the bloody death of *Wall Street Journal* reporter Daniel Pearl played through Decker's memory. Pearl, who was Jewish, had been videotaped as he was forced by his Islamic kidnappers to repeat, "I am a Jew. My mother is a Jew." Then, with the tape still running, he was brutally murdered.[26]

"We've already seen your passports," the man responded. Decker had at least bought Tom a little time: he had gotten the man talking. "It makes no difference to me whether he is an Israeli Jew or an American Jew."

"But he's not a Jew at all!" Decker said. Decker remembered also the 1994 abduction of three British tourists by Ahmed Omar Saeed Sheikh, the same man who engineered the Pearl kidnapping and murder. After several weeks in captivity, the Britons were released unharmed. The obvious difference between Daniel Pearl and the British tourists was Pearl's Jewish heritage. Decker knew it was imperative that he convince his captors Tom was not Jewish.

"He looks like a Jew to me," the man said, as though that made it so.

"I'm telling you, he's an American and a Gentile," Decker responded with the same intellectual level of argument.

Decker knew that, right or wrong, if the Palestinian was really sure, he wouldn't be taking the time to argue about it. But there was another force at work in the room, simple but powerful: peer pressure. The other men were watching their comrade to see what he would do. His judgment was being challenged and he felt he had to respond.

Tom had stopped moaning and was lying nearly motionless on the floor, taking short, labored breaths. The Palestinian was unimpressed with Decker's response and decided to refocus his attention on Tom.

---

[26]Daniel Pearl was kidnapped in Karachi, Pakistan, on January 23, 2002, while working on a story.

Decker blurted out the first thing he could think of. It was risky, but neither he nor Tom had anything to lose: Another blow from the man's boot might break Tom's back. "If you don't believe me," Decker said, getting his captors' attention again, "pull down his pants."

The Palestinians looked at each other, not sure that they had understood him, and then started to laugh as they realized what Decker meant. If Tom were a Jew, he'd be circumcised.

The one who had kicked Tom was not so sure about the idea. He didn't want to risk appearing foolish. But the other three laughed and went to work loosening Tom's pants. They were enjoying the contest between their leader and the American. Besides, it seemed an amusing way to settle an argument where a man's life hung in the balance.

There was just one problem, and therein lay the risk: Decker had no idea whether or not Tom was circumcised. But with Tom's life on the line, Decker's only choice had been to set that as the defining criterion. When the three lackeys pulled down Tom's pants, they committed themselves to that criterion. Knowing that many American men, Jew and Gentile alike, are circumcised, Decker was well aware that he still might be condemning his friend to death.

The leader was disappointed with what he saw.

The three Palestinians gave Tom's pants a tug and pulled them most of the way back up. Again they were laughing, but this time, in part at least, they were laughing at their leader. An angry glare abruptly stopped their merriment. The leader quickly changed the subject and, after pushing Decker back to the floor with his foot, signaled for the others to follow him out of the room. As soon as they were gone Decker tried, as best he could, to check on his friend's condition. He helped him get his pants back up, but with their hands tied behind them it was impossible to fasten or zip them.

❏

That night, one of the men brought them food and water. In the morning they were fed again and allowed to clean up, one at a time. Now that there appeared to be less chance they would be killed right away, Decker's mind went to thoughts of Elizabeth, Hope, and Louisa. The fear of torture and death and the physical pain he had already endured seemed somehow entirely different and diminished by comparison to the empathetic pain he felt for the emotional distress he knew his family would suffer.

In the evening two of the guards came in and blindfolded them, shoved rags into their mouths, and gagged them. Decker guessed they were about to be moved to another location. They lay in that condition for about twenty minutes, choking from time to time on the rags, then their feet were untied and they were led outside.

Once outside, their captors did something that seemed very strange to Decker. He was taken by two of the men and laid on his back on top of something he recognized from the way it felt as a mechanic's creeper, used for sliding under a car. His feet were then tied again. All he could imagine was that this might be in preparation for some grisly form of torture by dragging them behind a car or truck. On the other hand, why would they blindfold him? If sadism were the goal, wouldn't they want him to see the torture that awaited him? Certainly, he thought, they wouldn't stuff his mouth full of rags. They'd want to hear him scream.

Decker felt himself being pushed about eight feet, and then rolled off the creeper onto his stomach on the ground. He could sense he was under something large. A moment later eight hands grabbed him and lifted him about eighteen inches until his back pressed firmly against the object above him, and he was strapped tightly into this position. The next thing he heard was the sound of a squeaky metal door sliding shut.

He realized that he was in some sort of coffinlike box. But he thought he could feel air moving around him, so he didn't think he would suffocate. As he hung there face down, strapped in and waiting, he heard the sound of the creeper's wheels again, followed by men straining under a weight and then another metal door closing. Decker assumed his captors had done the same to Tom. The voices of the Palestinians were now muffled beyond distinction, but since no one was speaking English, it really didn't matter.

After about five minutes Decker heard a vehicle's door slam, followed by an engine starting. Now he understood. He and Tom were strapped under the bed of a truck. They had been placed in metal boxes that were built to fit under the truck in order to ship weapons and, on rare occasions, people through check points and past border guards.

Tel Aviv, Israel

Elizabeth Hawthorne and her two daughters walked through the concourse of David Ben Gurion International Airport in Tel Aviv. A few days earlier Elizabeth had been sitting in her office thinking about how slow business was and how much she missed Decker. On the spur of the moment she decided to take some extra vacation time, get the girls out of school, and fly to Israel a week early. Surprises had always been Decker's forte, but this time Elizabeth decided she would do the surprising.

She was totally unprepared for the news that awaited her.

As she and the girls walked toward the exit with their luggage, a somber-looking man and woman in their mid-sixties approached them.

"Mrs. Hawthorne?" the man asked, requesting confirmation.

"Yes," she answered, a bit surprised.

"My name is Joshua Rosen. This is my wife, Ilana. We're friends of your husband."

"Yes, I know," Elizabeth responded. "Decker has mentioned you. Did he send you? How did he find out that I was going to surprise him?" she asked, not discerning the seriousness of the situation.

"Could I speak to you for a moment in private?" Joshua asked.

Suddenly Elizabeth realized that something was wrong. She wanted to know what and she didn't want to wait. "Has something happened to Decker?" she demanded.

Joshua Rosen preferred not to talk in front of Hope and Louisa but Elizabeth insisted. "Mrs. Hawthorne," he began, "according to the clerk at the Ramada Renaissance, Decker and Tom Donafin left their hotel in Jerusalem five days ago. Last night Bill Dean from *NewsWorld* called me on the phone to ask if I had any idea where they were. He said that their editor had been trying to reach them for three days. He tried to call you at your office, but they said you were on vacation. He couldn't reach you at home either."

Elizabeth was growing impatient with Rosen's explanation. She wanted to know the bottom line. "Please, Mr. Rosen, if something has happened to my husband, tell me!"

Joshua understood her anxiety but hated to just blurt it out with no explanation. "I'm afraid that Decker and Tom have been taken hostage in Lebanon."

Elizabeth was struck with disbelief. "What? That's crazy. That can't be," she said, shaking her head. "They weren't even supposed to be in Lebanon. They're in Israel! There must be some mistake!" The denial in her heart hid itself behind the authority in her voice, as if by sufficient insistence she could alter what she could not bear to face.

Joshua and Ilana looked on sadly. "I'm sorry," he said. "This morning the Hizballah, a group of militant followers of Ayatollah Oma Obeji, announced that they were holding Decker and Tom hostage. They sent a note to a Lebanese newspaper claiming responsibility and included pictures of Decker and Tom."

Hope and Louisa were already crying. Elizabeth looked for some place to sit down but, finding none, accepted the offer of support from Ilana Rosen, who held her as she wept.

Somewhere in northern Lebanon

As the truck came to a stop, Decker tried to breathe deeply and relax his muscles from the hours of grueling bouncing over pot-holed roads. With his tongue and teeth, he had managed to force the rag part of the way out of his mouth, so at least he could breathe more freely. He could only pray that Tom had been able to do the same. Decker's head ached from the constant pounding against the inside of his steel coffin and from referred pain from the muscles in his back and neck. He desperately hoped the journey had come to an end, but he was terrified by the thought of what awaited him.

The driver blew the truck's horn and then got out to await his compatriots. Obviously, he was not concerned about anyone seeing him or his human cargo. Whether this was because no one else would be nearby or that no one who was nearby would care briefly played with Decker's curiosity but was soon forgotten. A moment later, Decker heard some other men coming toward the truck. He heard the rusty creak of the door again, this time sliding open, and felt hands loosening the straps that held him in place. The man working the straps at his feet was slower than the others and there was no attempt by the faster men to slow his fall to the street's surface, so he dropped head first, landing on his forehead with his feet still strapped to the underside of the truck. Still not fully recovered from the original blow to the back of his head a few days before, Decker gasped, causing him to suck the rag back into his throat.

Choking for air, Decker was dragged from beneath the truck. After untying the rope that bound his feet, one of the men barked a command that Decker assumed meant to get up. His head was spinning with pain and blood soaked his blindfold and dripped down his face and neck; he felt as though he would vomit. Every muscle in his body was cramped or stiff, but he struggled and managed to stand.

One of the men turned him around and pushed him in the direction he wanted him to go. Decker stumbled repeatedly as his captor shouted commands he couldn't possibly understand. Coming at last to the threshold of a building, Decker stepped inside and somehow felt as though he had entered a stairwell. It would be bad enough if he had to climb stairs blindfolded; it could be deadly if he unexpectedly came to stairs leading down.

Doing everything he could to keep his senses despite the pain, Decker reached slowly forward with his toes for either a step up or a drop off. His captor, impatient at the slow progress, shoved Decker forward. Sprawling ahead and expecting the worst,

Decker's foot hit the base of a step. Adjusting his position, he lifted his foot and began to make his way up the stairs.

Three flights up, Decker was directed down a hallway, through two doors, and finally into a small room. He was placed with his back against the wall and pushed down to a sitting position. The gag was removed and a cup of water shoved into his hands. The man then left and closed the door, locking it behind him. Decker drank the water and rolled over onto his side.

It was a hopeful sign, Decker thought, that the other men had remained behind at the truck. Perhaps they had stayed to get Tom out and would be bringing him into the same room at any moment. Decker lay waiting for the sound of the door and for Tom to be brought in, but it never came. He had no idea how long he had waited, but when he woke up some time later, he found that his blindfold had been removed and his feet retied.

Six and a half months later

As near as he could tell, Decker guessed the date to be June twenty-fourth, his wedding anniversary. Twenty-three years. He tried to remember if he had ever heard what the traditional present was for the twenty-third anniversary. He hadn't. He tried to imagine what Elizabeth might be doing that day. He could almost endure the separation, but the isolation—and not knowing if it would ever end—was more than he could bear. Feelings of total helplessness filled him both with self pity and with rage at his captors. He just wanted to be able to tell Elizabeth that he loved her and that he was alive. The need to reach out and comfort her was the worst pain of all. He knew he might never go home. He might never see his wife's face again—or his children. In his anger and frustration, he pulled at the bonds that held his hands and feet. He could not have broken the ropes even when he was in peak condition, but in his weakened, half-starved state it was doubly futile and only added to his despair.

Decker had gone over and over in his mind the events of the

day he and Tom were captured and all that followed. He couldn't
explain why, but his instincts told him he was in Lebanon. He
searched for any clue to support this hunch. If just once his captors would bring his food wrapped in old newspaper or if he
could catch the sight or sound of a seagull from the Mediterranean . . . But the most he had to go on was the occasional use
of the word *Al-Lubnān*[27] by his captors. He refused to believe Tom
Donafin was dead but he had not seen his friend since that night
in Israel when they were blindfolded and gagged. For that matter,
he had not truly seen anyone. The men who held him captive
wore masks every time they came into the room and they almost
never spoke to him.

He had not seen anything outside the locked door of his room,
but he perceived that he was in an old apartment building. The
ropes on his feet were tied manacle style with about twelve inches
between his ankles so he could take small steps. To prevent him
from untying himself—an act that would have resulted in severe
punishment—the ropes around his wrists provided almost no
slack. He was, however, able to hold his food bowl and take care
of the necessary toilet activities. Personal hygiene was nearly
impossible, and he was provided with a bucket of water with
which to bathe only once a week or so.

Earlier, when Decker had been there about four months, one
of his captors had given him a copy of the Koran in English. He'd
wanted to tear it to shreds but he knew that to do so would probably result in his death. He knew that to Muslims, the Koran is
more than just a book containing what they believe is God's word;
it is in itself a holy object. To deface it is not just to insult Allah,
it is to *assault* him, and thus invite both his wrath and the wrath
of his followers. Besides, with nothing else to do or read, it provided Decker with some distraction. He had heard the claims that
Islam is a peaceful religion—that those who murder and take
hostages and commit acts of terrorism in Allah's name do not represent "true Islam." But as he sat on the floor reading the Koran
with his feet and hands tied, he found it hard to believe.

[27]Arabic for "Lebanon."

He took some consolation in the fact that things could be worse. His captors had not tortured him since early in his captivity. All of the cigarette burns had healed by now. Only the most serious ones left noticeable scars.

At first his captors had seemed to enjoy threatening him with knives and razors. They were not all just threats, however. At one point, one of the men had gone to elaborate lengths for sadistic satisfaction. He began by tying Decker so he could not move and then telling him he was going to cut off his ears for trophies. If Decker moved at all, the man said in broken English, he would slit his throat instead. Starting at the topmost point of Decker's left ear the man made a deep, bloody gash, then pulled the blade away, laughing uncontrollably at the pain in Decker's eyes as he gritted his teeth, trying not to flinch. When the man left the room and closed the door, he was still laughing under his mask. Decker was left tied in that position overnight. With some effort he managed to shift his weight, roll onto his stomach, and turn his head so he could lay it on the floor with the weight resting against his partially severed ear. The pressure was agonizing but necessary to stop the bleeding.

Despite his fear and pain throughout the ordeal, Decker had found it amazingly easy to not cry out. His surprise and curiosity at this fact was an extremely propitious distraction from the pain. Lying there, he remembered a short poem by Nguyen Chi Thien he had read years before that explained his silence under torture. Nguyen, a prisoner of the Communist Vietnamese for twenty-seven years, had written a volume of poetry about his life called *Flowers From Hell*. The particular poem Decker recalled was:

> *I just keep silent when they torture me,*
> *though crazed with pain as they apply the steel.*
> *Tell children tales of heroic fortitude –*
> *I just keep silent thinking to myself:*
> *"When in the woods and meeting with wild beasts,*
> *who ever cries out begging for their grace?"*[28]

[28]Nguyen Chi Thien, "I Just Keep Silent When They Torture Me," in *Flowers From Hell* (Southeast Asia Studies, Yale University, 1984), 105. Used by permission.

Several hours later Decker woke to find that the pool of blood had dried, gluing his ear to the floor. As he tried to pull free he felt the scab begin to tear. He knew he couldn't just lie there. If he didn't move himself, his captors would, and they would not be gentle about it. For the next three hours Decker let spittle run from his mouth down his cheek to the floor to soften the dried blood while he carefully worked his ear loose. Still, some fresh blood was added to the pool.

❏

Now, so many months later, Decker's biggest problems were endless boredom and depression brought on by the feelings of helplessness, hopelessness, and anger. He had long ago read about an American prisoner of war in Vietnam who handled the boredom and kept his sanity by playing a round of golf every day in his mind, but Decker had never had time for sports. For the last twenty-three years it seemed that all he had done was write and read.

For a while, he tried to recall every article he had ever written. Then he hit on the idea of rereading novels from his memory. When he couldn't remember how the story line went, he'd make it up.

Somewhere along the way, like Nguyen Chi Thien, he began to compose poetry. Silently he'd recite each line of the poem over and over in order to be sure to remember it. Mostly he made up poems to Elizabeth.

> *Moments lost, I thought would last;*
> *Promises broken that cannot mend;*
> *Dreams of days from a wasted past;*
> *Days of dreams that never end.*
> *Nights and days form endless blur.*
> *Walls of drab and colors gray,*
> *Pain and loss I scarce endure,*
> *While dirty rags upon me lay.*

I've wasted such time that was not mine to take,
Leaving sweet words unsaid, precious one.
Now walk I on waves of a limitless lake
Of unfallen tears for things left undone.

There are many things a man can think about when left alone for so long, and it seemed to Decker that he had thought about them all. Usually he thought about home and Elizabeth and his two daughters. He had missed so many things because he had always put his job first. And now, because of his job, he might never see them again. So many chances and opportunities lost.

As he lay on his mat in the room, illumined only by the light that came through the cracks in the boarded-up window, it suddenly seemed strange to him—almost funny in some pitiful way—that he had always called his wife Elizabeth and never Liz or Lizzy or Beth. It wasn't that she was somehow too proper to be called by a nickname. It just seemed they had never had enough time together to become that informal.

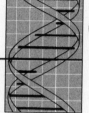

Dream a Little Dream of Me

9

Two years and three months later
Somewhere in northern Lebanon

"Mr. Hawthorne."

"Mr. Hawthorne."

"Wake up, Mr. Hawthorne, it's time to go."

Decker opened his eyes and looked around the room. As he twisted his body and shifted his weight to sit up, the ropes that bound his hands and feet slipped off like oversized gloves and shoes.

"It's time to go, Mr. Hawthorne," the voice of a young boy said again.

Decker rubbed his eyes and looked toward the voice. There in the open doorway of his room stood Christopher Goodman. Now fourteen years old, he had grown remarkably since Decker last saw him.

"Christopher?" Decker asked, puzzled at this obviously unexpected turn of events.

"Yes, Mr. Hawthorne," Christopher answered.

"What are you doing here?" Decker asked in confused disbelief.

"It's time to go, Mr. Hawthorne. I've come to get you," Christopher said, making no attempt to explain.

Christopher walked from the room and signaled for him to follow. Decker lifted the 115 pounds that remained of his body and followed Christopher out of the room and toward the front door. Halfway there, he hesitated. There was something he was trying to remember, something too important to forget, something he could not leave behind.

"Tom!" he said suddenly. "Where's Tom?" he asked of the friend he had not seen since they were brought to Lebanon.

Christopher hesitated and then raised his arm slowly and pointed toward another door. Silently, Decker opened it, looking for any sign of his captors. There was none. Inside, Tom lay on a mat identical to the one Decker had now spent nearly three years sleeping on, sitting on, eating on . . . living on. Tom was lying with his face to the wall. Decker entered and began untying the bonds that held his friend's feet.

"Tom, wake up. We're getting out of here," he whispered.

Tom sat up and looked at his rescuer. For a moment they just stared at each other's faces. Finally, Decker forced his eyes away and began untying Tom's hands. He had not looked in a mirror at any time during his captivity, and though he knew his body was emaciated, he had not seen his face, where the most dramatic effects of his captivity were evident. Seeing Tom's face, he was struck with such grief and sympathy for his friend's similar condition that he had to look away to hold back tears.

Outside the apartment, Decker and Tom walked stealthily down the hall, hoping to avoid detection. Christopher, on the other hand, walked on ahead of them, showing absolutely no sign of concern about the seriousness of the situation. They went down three flights of stairs, cluttered with trash and broken bits of plaster and glass. Still there was no sign of their captors. As they emerged into the open air Decker closed his eyes as the bright sunlight struck him in the face with its warmth and glow.

When he opened his eyes again, he was staring at his empty room. The morning sun shown in on his face through the cracks in the boarded-up window. He realized he had been dreaming.

Usually Decker dreamed of his family. When he awoke from those dreams he would close his eyes again to try to hold on for one more moment to the vestiges of the illusion. It was all he had. This dream, however, was just a curious distraction.

Decker flipped over onto his back. As he twisted his body and shifted his weight to sit up, the ropes that bound his hands and feet slipped off like oversized gloves and shoes.

He shook his head; was he still dreaming? He wasted no more time thinking about it, but quickly got to his feet. The door was unlocked, and he quietly cracked it open to look into the apartment. It looked just as it had in his dream. No one else was there. He crept toward the room that in his dream had held his friend. Until this moment Decker had not known where Tom was, or even if he was still alive, but when he looked into the room, there was Tom.

Moments later Decker and Tom were walking down the hall and then down the same cluttered stairway. When they emerged from the building, Decker used his hand to shield his eyes in anticipation of the sunlight. None of this made any sense, but if he was dreaming, this time he didn't want to wake up.

The two men moved from doorway to doorway, building to building, staying out of sight as much as possible. As they continued down the street they saw no one; it was like a ghost town. They decided to try to put as much distance between themselves and their captors as they could right away and then wait until nightfall to go on. All they knew to do was to move south, which they hoped was toward Israel. They had no idea how far they were from the border, but with their eyes they silently pledged to each other to die rather than be recaptured.

When they were a safe distance away, Decker related the strange dream of their rescue, though he did not tell Tom about Christopher's unusual origin. Later Decker regretted revealing the dream and made Tom promise not to repeat it to anyone.

❑

For the next three nights Decker and Tom worked their way southward. As much as possible they stayed off the roads and away from any sign of population. On this night they had started early, about an hour before sundown. Decker could tell their time was running out. Soon he and Tom would be too weak to travel.

Their diet was limited to what they could catch, which meant mostly insects. On their first day they found a small wild dog that had apparently been killed by another animal, but reluctantly decided it had been dead too long for them to eat. They regretted that decision now.

Just before dark Tom and Decker came to a well-traveled road. Waiting in a field of tall grass, they planned their crossing for after dark, hoping that traffic would be lighter and they could cross unseen. As night fell, the traffic continued nearly unabated, though there were occasional gaps of several minutes between passing vehicles. Slowly, they approached the road, stopping short about fifty yards. The road was straight and flat and they could see several miles in each direction. A series of trucks passed, then there appeared to be a break. The nearest vehicles were coming from the east, about three miles off.

Decker and Tom moved quickly. As they reached the small rise on which the road was built, it seemed they would have no trouble getting across. Then, unexpectedly, halfway up the rise, Decker felt a tug at his leg. Looking down, he saw he had caught his pant leg on some barbed-wire fencing. He tried to pull free but the barbs dug into his leg and he fell, catching his other leg in the same tangled mass.

Tom had already stepped into the road when he heard Decker call out. He hurried back to help, but as the seconds passed they were forced to reassess the situation. The next group of vehicles was getting too close. Their only option seemed to be to lie as flat and still as they could and hope the slight rise of the road would hide them from the direct beams of the passing vehicles.

Tom lay on his stomach next to Decker and they held their breath. The vehicles inched closer, moving much slower than Decker had first thought. As the first truck passed, Tom moved suddenly. Before Decker could stop him, he was running into the road, shouting and waving his arms. *It's over*, Decker thought.

The next truck stopped a few yards from Tom. From the back of the truck came men in uniforms, carrying rifles. They surrounded Tom, their rifles pointing at him. Another group encircled Decker, who was still on the ground. Slowly Decker rolled to his back and looked up at the men. Each man wore a light-blue helmet with an emblem of fig leaves surrounding a globe. The same emblem, which Tom had seen on the first truck, was emblazoned on the flags that flew from the antennas and was painted on the door of each of the vehicles. Decker recognized it. They were from UNIFIL, the United Nations Interim Force in Lebanon.

❏

That night Tom and Decker showered, were given clean clothes, and slept in real beds. Their stomachs could not handle much food, but before they fell asleep in the quarters of the UN compound, they each had two pieces of bread and a half cup of beef stew.

The next morning Tom and Decker were invited to share breakfast with the Swedish UN commander. "I read the report of the team that picked you up last night," the commander said as they walked across the compound to the mess hall. "That convoy you stopped had a very special guest on it. That's why the men responded as they did—they thought you might be Hizballah. That group of crazies would love to get their hands on somebody like Ambassador Hansen."

At breakfast Tom and Decker met the commander's special guest, the British ambassador to the UN, Jon Hansen. He was very interested in the story of their capture and escape, which they gladly told him, although neither mentioned the dream about Christopher. After breakfast they were taken to the compound's communications building. The UN post had one phone link to the United States via satellite, used primarily for contact with the UN headquarters in New York. Tom, who had no close family, insisted that Decker call first.

It was just after one o'clock in the morning in Washington when the phone rang. Decker listened as it rang two more times. Only partially roused from a deep sleep, Elizabeth Hawthorne picked up the phone. "Hello," she mumbled, her eyes still closed.

Decker listened to the sleepy, sweet sound of her voice. "Hello, honey. It's me," he said as tears began to roll down his cheeks.

Elizabeth quickly sat up in her bed. "Decker! Is that you?"

The love he heard in her voice brought new tears to his eyes and he could barely breathe as he answered, "Yes, it's me."

"Where are you?!" she asked anxiously. "Are you all right?"

"I'm in Lebanon at a United Nations post. Tom's with me. We're both okay. We escaped."

"Thank God!" she said. "Thank God!"

"They'll be taking us to Israel to a hospital for a checkup and observation. Can you come to Israel right away?"

"Yes! Of course!" she said as she wiped her own tears.

"How are Hope and Louisa?" he asked.

"They're fine, fine. They won't believe me when I tell them you called. They'll say I was dreaming. I'm not dreaming, am I?"

"No," he answered, reassuringly, "You're not dreaming."

"Do you want to talk to them?" she asked. Her voice was excited and hurried. Her mind raced. She wanted to ask everything, say everything, do everything all at once.

"No, not right now. We're going to leave soon, so I can't stay on very long and Tom wants to call a cousin or uncle or something."

"How is Tom?"

"He's fine. We're both fine. Just tell Hope and Louisa that I love them and that I'm looking forward to seeing them. Okay?"

"Of course," she said. And then it suddenly occurred to her that she didn't know where he was going in Israel. "Where will you be? What hospital?"

"I'm sorry, Elizabeth. I don't have any details, but I didn't want to wait to call you."

"No. No. That's okay," she said and then thought for a moment. "The girls and I will be on the next plane to Israel. When you get to the hospital, call Joshua and Ilana. Tell them where you are, and when I arrive I'll call them for the message."

"Joshua and Ilana?" Decker asked, surprised at the apparent familiarity. "You mean the Rosens?"

"Of course, Decker. They've been a great help and support to me while you've been gone. They're such wonderful people. Here's their number."

Decker took down the number. "I've got to go now," he said and then paused to be sure she would hear him. "I love you," he said softly but clearly.

"I love you!" she answered.

❏

The Swedish commander arranged for two trucks and a squad of armed men to take Decker and Tom the 120 kilometers to the Israeli border. From there Israeli security would take them to a hospital in Tel Aviv. But Ambassador Hansen had other plans. Hansen was a good politician and here was an opportunity for some very positive publicity. It was, after all, *his* convoy that had rescued them.

When they arrived in Israel, Tom and Decker were greeted by reporters from four international news agencies who had been called from Lebanon by Ambassador Hansen's aide. There were more reporters at the Tel-Hashomer hospital in Tel Aviv. Hansen handled questions from the press himself "in order to take the burden off the boys," he said. He agreed to allow the press to take a few pictures of Tom and Decker, but curiously managed to figure prominently in each. Neither Tom nor Decker really minded. They had talked and joked together on the trip through Lebanon and to Tel Aviv. They liked Hansen—he was a "jolly good" sort. He was also a politician; getting publicity was part of his job. They were just happy to be free.

After they checked into the hospital, Decker phoned the Rosens. Feeling more his old self, he decided to be a little playful. "Joshua," he said as though nothing unusual had happened, "this is Decker. So where have you been lately? I haven't seen you around."

"That'll do you no good, Decker Hawthorne," Rosen answered. "I know all about you and Tom. Elizabeth called us as soon as she made her plane reservations to tell us the good news. Besides, you've been on television all afternoon."

Decker laughed warmly. "When will she get in?"

"Just a second. Ilana!" Rosen called to his wife. "Decker's on the phone. What time did Elizabeth say her plane would be arriving?"

There was a pause. Ilana took advantage of her husband's poor memory for such things, and took the phone away from him. "Hello, Decker," she said. "Welcome home!"

"Thanks, Ilana. It's good to be home," he answered, by which he meant anywhere away from Lebanon.

"I saw you on TV," she said. "You're skin and bones."

"Yeah, well, I didn't care for the menu."

"You know, I make some of the best chicken soup."

"Tell him about Elizabeth, already," Decker heard Joshua saying in the background.

"Oh, yes. Elizabeth's plane will be here tomorrow at 11:36 A.M. Don't you worry about a thing. Joshua and I will pick up her and the children at the airport and bring them to the hospital. If you'd like," she added as an aside, "I'll bring you some of my chicken soup. I've heard the hospital food is atrocious."

Decker appreciated their kindness. "Sure, Ilana. Sounds great."

Decker next called the Washington office of *NewsWorld*, where it was nine in the morning, and asked to speak to his editor, Tom Wattenburg. He was all ready to say, "Hi, Tom. This is Decker. Any calls for me?" when the switchboard operator said that Tom Wattenburg had retired and that his replacement was Hank Asher.

"Hank," Decker said when Asher came to the phone, "you mean they promoted you ahead of me?"

"Well, if you'd show up for work once in a while," Asher responded with a faint chuckle. "And by the way, I've got a bone to pick with you. I get up this morning and what do I see? Your ugly mug on the *Today Show*. You guys called NBC but you didn't notify your own magazine! And another thing, you took the key to the hotel room when you left and I ended up havin' to pay for it: cost me four bucks."

"Hey, we didn't have anything to do with calling NBC," Decker said in his defense. "But no kidding? The *Today Show*?"

"Yeah, and seems like everywhere else, too," Asher answered, trying to sound disgusted. "But at least they mentioned you guys work for *NewsWorld*."

Actually the publicity for *NewsWorld* was great and would certainly boost sales for the edition Asher had planned for Tom and Decker's "first-person" article on their lives as hostages.

Tel Aviv, Israel

The next morning as he shaved and brushed his teeth, Decker examined his face in the mirror. He was getting used to his skeletal appearance, but now he was thinking of Elizabeth. How would she react? The important thing was that he was safe; in a few months he'd be back to normal physically. It was best to concentrate on the positive. What would never be "back to normal" was the way he felt about her. The bittersweet truth was that in his isolation he had come to love her in a way he otherwise never could have.

Because of her flight, Elizabeth probably had not seen him on television, so when she walked in the door of the hospital in a few hours she would be seeing him for the first time. As he finished brushing his teeth, Decker noticed a box of sterile cotton balls and was struck by one of those crazy ideas that sometimes hit him. He stuffed several pieces in his cheeks to see if it would make his face look fuller. Looking in the mirror, it appeared he had mumps. Decker laughed so hard he almost swallowed one of the cotton balls. Fortunately, these ideas usually only hit him when he was alone.

One thing was certain, though. Decker did not want to be wearing a hospital gown when Elizabeth arrived. He tried to charm a nurse into doing some shopping for him, to no avail. Then he thought of Hansen. Decker figured Hansen owed him and Tom a favor for all the good publicity, so he called the British Embassy. This time he was in luck. Hansen sent over two aides and a local tailor, who measured Decker and Tom for suits. The aides did some quick shopping at Polgat's on Ramat Alenby, an outlet of fine men's clothes. They brought the suits to the hospital, along with the tailor and a sewing machine, and the tailor hemmed the suits on the spot.

When Elizabeth arrived, Decker and Tom were sitting in the hospital lobby sipping tea and reading the English edition of the *Jerusalem Post*. They looked like transplants from a fancy British gentlemen's club, an appearance they played to the hilt. The act worked fine until Elizabeth's and Decker's eyes met. Then it was all hugs, kisses, and tears. Despite the suit, Elizabeth immediately realized the seriousness of Decker's condition as she put her arms around him. The bones in his back were easily distinguishable through the fabric. Instinctively she understood what Decker was trying to do and attempted not to look too worried.

Ilana Rosen put down her thermos of chicken soup and hugged Tom. Hope and Louisa jointly hugged their dad. Somehow the hugs merged and evolved into a mass hug. Even Scott Rosen, who had come along with his parents, joined in.

After a few moments of this they sat down to talk. Elizabeth sat beside Decker and they held hands as they all talked about what had happened over the last three years. On the other side of Decker, Hope and Louisa took turns sitting next to their father. Decker was amazed at how much his daughters had changed. Hope was now sixteen and Louisa eleven. He had never noticed how much they both looked like their mother. He had missed so much of their lives . . . Decker tried not to focus on his regrets.

Joshua and Ilana introduced Tom and Decker to their son, Scott, a brawny, 260-pound, six-foot-three-inch Orthodox Jew with thick black curly hair and beard. The Rosen family had grown much closer over the past three years.

Everyone wanted to know how Tom and Decker had escaped and what had happened during their captivity. Again, neither mentioned the dream. Sometime later the subject turned to how they had become hostages in Lebanon in the first place. Until that moment no one realized they had actually been abducted in Israel and smuggled over the border. Everyone assumed they had gone into Lebanon to pursue some story and were taken hostage while there.

Upon learning the truth, Scott Rosen asked if they had reported the details to the Israeli authorities. They had not, but agreed to tell the police later that day. Scott didn't want them to wait. He insisted they call the police immediately and when they said it could wait, Scott became indignant. "Well, I'll just go call them for you," he said and walked off to find a phone.

Ilana Rosen, who had been getting more embarrassed by the minute, apologized for her son. "I'm really sorry, Decker and Tom," she said. "He's just so firm in his beliefs that nothing comes before God and Israel."

"Or is it Israel first and then God?" her husband interrupted.

Ilana understood her husband's exasperation. "When the Palestinians destroyed the Western Wall, Scott went crazy with rage," she said. "He wanted to put every Palestinian in Israel on trial."

"He wanted to do much worse than that, and you know it," Joshua interrupted again, this time earning himself a firm pinch on the leg from Ilana. Despite the pinch—or more likely to spite it—he continued. "If he had not been with us at the very time it happened, I might believe he was one of those who attacked the Dome of the Rock after the wall was destroyed."

"What?" asked Decker and Tom in unison. "What happened?" Tom added by himself.

"Did *NewsWorld* have a team here to cover it?" Decker asked.

"Oh, Daddy!" said Hope in recognition of the silly unimportance of his question.

"Exactly one week after the wall was destroyed," Joshua explained, "a group of about forty Israelis attacked the Dome of the Rock. They killed sixteen Muslim guards and drove everyone out of the Mosque before setting explosives. They totally destroyed it. Some have accused the police of being part of the conspiracy because by the time they arrived all of the Israeli terrorists had escaped." Rosen's inflection on "terrorists" made clear his revulsion. He did not like terrorists, no matter which side they were on.

"It was terrible here for many months." Ilana said. "We've been in Israel for some of the worst, but you cannot imagine all the car bombs and suicide bombings. Security was unbelievable. I couldn't even go from our house to the market without going through checkpoints."

Joshua continued, "There were huge protests and the Arab countries threatened war. It didn't come to that, at least not yet, but it probably did more for Arab unity than anything in the past sixty years. Even Syria and Iraq are talking again."

There was something ominous about the way Joshua had said "at least not yet" that Decker couldn't leave unexamined. "Has something happened recently?" he asked.

"Things calmed down some after a while," Joshua began. "The Arabs wanted to rebuild the Mosque; many in Israel wanted to rebuild the Temple. For two and a half years the area remained roped off from both Jews and Arabs. Then three months ago, after Moshe Greenberg became prime minister—"

"Prime minister?" Decker interrupted. "That radical?"

"Don't let Scott hear you say that," Rosen said. "But actually Greenberg doesn't seem quite so radical now as he once did. Nowadays he's considered somewhat of a moderate. That's less because he's changed and more that the mood of the country has swung so much further to the right as a result of the continuing threats from our Arab neighbors. But as I was saying, three months ago after Greenberg was elected prime minister, he announced that Israel would immediately begin rebuilding the Temple."

"Wow. I'm surprised the Arabs haven't already declared war."

"The Arabs never cease their war with us," Rosen replied. "But yes, you are right. They are very upset. But since they have never been able to win an all out war with Israel, the Arab countries prefer terrorist actions. One effect of the years of America's War on Terror is that while the United States monitors and subdues terrorism's backers, politically it has greatly freed Israel to search out and destroy its own terrorist cells. As a result, unless the Arab states are ready to start a full-scale war, there's little else they can do. I don't mean to minimize the danger. Even now the Syrians have troops amassed near our mutual border, and there are always rumors about some huge terrorist attack being planned here or somewhere in the world."

"What about the Temple?" Tom asked.

"Oh, it's really quite a massive undertaking, as you might

expect. They removed all the stones from the remains of the Western Wall and from the old steps that had been excavated. They'll use what they can and the rest will be put in a museum or something. They dug out the tunnels, but found only some minor artifacts," Rosen replied.

"I guess that supports your theory that the Knights Templar took everything and that the Ark of the Covenant is in France," Tom said. "So, how long before the Temple is finished?"

"The completion date is set for four years from now. That is if we don't go to war—"

"Enough news and politics, already," Ilana Rosen interrupted as she gave her husband's leg another pinch. "Maybe Elizabeth would like to talk for a while."

Joshua thought hard for a second. "Uh, oh, yes, of course," Joshua agreed, as though he suddenly recalled his part in some conspiracy with Ilana and Elizabeth. "Maybe Elizabeth has . . . uh . . . something to say."

"Go ahead, dear," said Ilana, urging her on. Decker listened intently as Elizabeth spoke.

"Decker, while you were gone, you know that Hope and Louisa and I spent a lot of time with Joshua and Ilana. They were a great support to us. I don't think we could have made it through all this without them. And, well, I just wanted to tell you that while you were away, I—that is to say, the girls and I—"

At that moment Scott Rosen returned, flanked by two plain-clothes detectives. They wanted the address of the house where Tom and Decker had been taken hostage and they wanted it now. They also wanted descriptions of the men who did it, and any other details that Tom and Decker could remember. Elizabeth's revelation would have to wait.

❑

The police left two hours later. Scott Rosen followed them in a cab to the station to tell them how to do their jobs. Joshua and Ilana took Hope and Louisa to eat, and Tom fell asleep on a couch. Decker and Elizabeth were finally alone.

"I missed you," Decker said softly, as he held his wife close.

"I missed you," she responded.

"I never knew how much you meant to me until I didn't have you. I thought of you every hour. Constantly. When we get back, I'm going to tell Hank Asher that I'm not taking any assignments where I'll have to be away from home for more than three days."

As the night waned, the couple went outside and sat under the stars. Elizabeth listened quietly, holding her husband's emaciated body to her as he recited the poetry he had composed for her over the past three years.

❏

Two days later, Decker was told he would be released from the hospital the following morning. It was nearing Rosh Hashanah, the Jewish New Year, and the hospital wanted to reduce their occupancy as much as possible before the Jewish High Holy Days. Tom, however, had developed serious problems with his back and kidneys while in captivity and was to remain for continued observation and more tests. That night Decker was able to leave the hospital for dinner, so he and Elizabeth shared a romantic candlelit dinner in old Jaffa.

"Elizabeth," Decker said at one point when the mood grew quiet, "I'm sure you must remember all the times I've said that I've never really felt there was any one place I could call home. I guess it's just that I've lived so many places."

Elizabeth remained silent but nodded affirmation. Decker reached across the small table and placed his left hand over hers. With his right hand, he softly ran the back of his fingers along the smooth curve of her face.

"Over the last three years I decided that if I ever got home to you, then that's where home would be. When we get back to Maryland we're going to make that home, whatever that means and whatever that takes."

A single tear came to Elizabeth's eyes. Having Decker back had kept her emotions at a fever pitch since he first called her from the UN outpost. It had been a constant struggle not to cry. Now,

the intensity of Decker's feelings, though she didn't fully understand them, nudged her gently and briefly over the edge, and she
wept.

❏

Decker and Elizabeth finished their meal, then stayed at the table
to talk. They did not speak of their time apart but rather of good
times they had spent together in years past. As Elizabeth spoke,
Decker looked across the table admiringly at his wife, watching
her every move. Elizabeth noticed the attention with no small
amount of enjoyment.

"Decker," she whispered in feigned embarrassment, "you look
like you're undressing me with your eyes."

"Oh," he responded with a smile and a gleam, "I'm way past
that."

Decker was feeling much better.

Derwood, Maryland

The Hawthorne family arrived at Dulles Airport outside Washington early in the morning and were surprised to find a limousine waiting there to pick them up—courtesy of Hank Asher. For
the next three days Decker, Elizabeth, Hope, and Louisa spent
time getting to know each other again. They bought jumbo
steamed blue crabs at Vinnie's Seafood and went to a small park
they knew at one of the C&O canal locks. They stayed around the
house and just talked. They cooked steaks on the grill. They went
shopping. They drove around town so Decker could get reac-
quainted. They did whatever they wanted to do.

At about noon on the third day the phone rang and Decker
answered it. It was Professor Goodman.

"Decker, we need to talk," Goodman said with what seemed to
Decker to be a bit of self-important urgency.

"Sure, Professor. I want to follow up on that story we talked
about, anyway. How about in a month or so?" After three years as

a hostage, even the "biggest story since Columbus discovered America" could wait a few more weeks.

"Not soon enough." Goodman's voice gave no indication he was even aware that Decker had been gone.

"Well, I'm really not in any shape for a long trip," Decker responded. "I've just gotten back from three years in a small room in Lebanon and I thought I'd take it easy for a while."

"Yes, I know all about that," Goodman said. "I *do* read the newspaper, you know. But you don't have to go anywhere. Martha and I are in Washington. In fact, we're here in Derwood, at the German restaurant two blocks from your house."

"What are you doing here?" Decker asked in surprise.

"I came out for a scientific conference. Martha had never seen Washington and insisted on coming along. Christopher is staying with a friend from school. So can we come over or not?"

Decker quickly talked it over with Elizabeth and they agreed to have the Goodmans come over, although Decker insisted that the professor promise it would take no more than an hour. Harry and Martha Goodman arrived in just minutes. Elizabeth had never met Martha Goodman and both women felt a little uncomfortable—Mrs. Goodman for imposing and Elizabeth about being imposed upon. Professor Goodman made it clear that the subject of the conversation was for Decker's ears only, so Elizabeth suggested that Mrs. Goodman go for a walk with her and the girls.

As soon as they left, Goodman began.

"I'm sorry to barge in on you but it isn't really for my welfare that I'm here. There are a thousand other reporters out there who would love to get an exclusive on what I'm about to tell you."

"Of course," Decker said. "It's just that I really need to spend some time with my family."

"I understand that. But what I'm about to tell you will change the world forever. Forgive me, I just thought you might be interested," Goodman added with mild sarcasm.

Decker's once overpowering curiosity had lain dormant for nearly three years. Deep inside he felt it stir again.

"I don't want to impose any more than necessary," Goodman

said, "so I'll leave a copy of my notes for you to study later. Right now, I'll just give you a summary."

Decker retrieved a fresh yellow legal pad and Goodman began.

"First of all, you remember that the last time we talked, we discussed the methodology I used for creating the viral cancer antibodies, and I told you that it would probably also work on AIDS and other viral strains? Well, that work has continued with some outstanding results. But as important as that work is, all I could really ever hope to accomplish with that methodology was to use the C-cells as an agent for producing antibodies. That seemed to me to be little more than running a pill factory. Well, I didn't want to just make pills. Even if they could cure cancer or AIDS, it still seemed to be such a waste of potential. What I really wanted to do was to figure out some way of altering the cells of living people to enhance their own immune system.

"For a long time it just ate at me. How could I ever hope to alter the genetic structure of every cell in the human body? You can make changes on a few cells in a laboratory. With C-cells it's even possible, as we both know, to create a totally immune individual like Christopher. But how do you give that immunity to someone else like you or me? That had me stumped."

Decker listened quietly, nodding when appropriate. Goodman was going to tell his story the way he wanted to tell it, and the best thing to do was just listen.

"Then I had an idea. Decker, do you know how the AIDS virus works?" Decker thought he had a pretty good idea, but before he could answer the question, Goodman continued. "All around the outside of the AIDS virus are tiny spikes that are made of glyco-proteins. These spikes are imbedded in a fatty envelope that forms the outer shell of the virus. Inside this envelope are RNA strands, each with a quantity of reverse-transcriptase enzyme. The spikes bind the AIDS cells to healthy cells of the immune system, called T-cells, by establishing an attractive link with certain receptor molecules that occur naturally on the healthy T-cells. The infection occurs when the virus is absorbed into the interior of the healthy cell. Once inside the T-cell, each individual strand of RNA material in the virus is converted into a complementary strand of DNA by the reverse-transcriptase enzyme. Enzymes that occur naturally in the cell duplicate the DNA strand, which then enters into the nucleus of the cell. That strand then becomes a permanent part of the heredity of that cell!" Goodman paused for Decker's reaction.

"Okay, so then what?" Decker had understood most of Goodman's explanation but failed to comprehend the significance.

"Don't you see? The AIDS virus is able to alter the genetic structure of living cells and it does it inside the body!"

Suddenly Decker realized what Goodman was getting at. "You mean you could remove the harmful genetic material from the nucleus of the AIDS virus . . ."

". . . and replace it with the specific immunity-providing DNA strands from the C-cells," Goodman said, finishing Decker's sentence. "Except, of course, viral cells do not have a nucleus; they have simply a core." Goodman—ever the professor—could not allow such an error, no matter how insignificant to the main topic, to pass uncorrected. "That way it's not necessary to alter each individual cell of the body. We can accomplish nearly the same result by just altering the T-cells!"

"And that result is . . ." Decker urged.

"Total immunity! Maybe even reversing the aging process! Life expectancies of two, three, four hundred years, maybe more!" Goodman's voice had grown as excited as he dared risk without sacrificing the appearance of appropriate scientific aloofness.

"So when can you begin to move beyond theory on this?"

"I already have," Goodman answered. "I began working on it two and a half years ago. For the first six months I focused my efforts on a cold virus. I felt that the dangers involved in using an AIDS virus were too great, and I must concede that the problems I encountered with my previous AIDS research soured me on having any more to do with it."

"Does the cold virus work like the AIDS virus?" Decker asked.

"Similarly, although the AIDS virus is actually a retro- or reverse-virus because of the existence of the reverse-transcriptase enzyme that converts the RNA strand into a DNA strand. There are a number of other differences as well, but for the early studies the differences didn't really matter. All I needed was a carrier—some means of bringing the desired genetic information to the individual T-cells of the immune system. I got as far as the creation of an extremely resilient second-generation test strain. Of course at that time I was still experimenting to isolate the specific DNA strands in the C-cells that were needed for transplant into the carrier virus.

"As my research continued, it became more and more clear to me that the AIDS virus was really the best medium to use as the carrier, and I somewhat reluctantly redirected my studies in that direction. That's when my work really began to progress. Think of it, Decker. Fifteen years ago it looked like AIDS could be on its way to being as bad as the Black Plague. And now, by some time in the next decade, it may—combined with the C-cells—be the source of virtual immortality!"

❏

By the time Decker and Goodman finished their conversation, Elizabeth, Mrs. Goodman, Hope, and Louisa had returned from their walk and retreated to the patio for iced tea. They had talked long enough to find that they liked each other's company. After the Goodmans left, Elizabeth told Decker how much she had enjoyed talking with Martha and that Martha had suggested she come along with Decker next time he went to Los Angeles.

"Well," said Decker, pleased that his wife was pleased, "I'm glad you two hit it off. She really is a nice person. And as far as you coming along, I'd like that too. So what did you two talk about?"

"Well, mostly we talked about you and how wonderful it is to have you back. But, let's see . . . We talked about Professor Goodman. Did you know he's been notified that in December he's going to receive the Nobel Prize for medicine for his cancer research?"

"You're kidding!" Decker said. "He didn't even mention it."

"That's why they were here in Washington. He was invited to address the annual convention of the American Cancer Society."

"I can see I've got a lot of catching up to do," Decker said. "So what else did you talk about?"

"Well, she told me all about her grandnephew, Christopher. She's very proud of him. He's apparently a very precocious child. Oh, and this is kind of interesting: Martha said that two weeks ago she and Professor Goodman were talking about you. He had this important story—I guess what he came over to tell you about today—and apparently he was reluctant to give it to another reporter even though at the time you were still being held hostage. But—and this is the strange part—as they were talking about it, Christopher, came over and just sort of matter-of-factly said that Professor Goodman should wait because you'd be free soon. She said she asked him about it later and he said he wasn't sure how he knew; he just had a feeling."

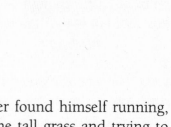

10

Disaster

A LIGHT RAIN BEGAN TO FALL and Decker found himself running, awkwardly making his way through the tall grass and trying to avoid the thistles and wild blackberry bushes. Home and safety from the impending storm were just over the next hill. In his determination he was totally unaware of the strange feeling of being in a small body not yet eight years old.

The storm clouds had gathered quickly and for a while it seemed they might disappear the same way. But as the rain began to fall, the promise of a cloudburst of Noahic proportions seemed to declare itself with the first sudden clap of distant thunder.

As he ran, Decker's nerves twinged with the fear of the somehow inevitable turn of events he knew was about to befall him. It seemed . . . it seemed he had done this all before. There was something in his path—something to fear. But what?

Suddenly the earth disappeared from beneath his feet. Decker's hands flew up above his head as he grabbed at the moist thick air, trying desperately, instinctively, to slow his descent. He felt the earth again as his stomach and chest slammed into a wall of dirt and slipped along a rough incline that threatened to swallow him. The blow had knocked the wind out of him, but before he could catch his breath, a sudden sharp pain surged through him as dozens of odd-shaped protrusions scraped against his body, tearing his shirt and pulling it up over his head as he slid down the incline. His hands, still grasping, caught a tangled mass of small fibers that quickly slipped away but were replaced by one more solid and firm. In shock he hung there, motionless.

Moments passed. Then Decker began to carefully pull himself upward, hoping his hold would not fail under the strain. Raising himself a few inches, he worked his shirt back down over his head and shoulders. Now able to survey his condition, he found he was holding on to a tree root about an inch in diameter. Near tears, he slowly turned his head and looked down. In horror he realized his imagination had not exaggerated the danger. Below him the hole continued for about thirty feet and then narrowed and veered off.

He closed his eyes and thought of the previous summer when he had first heard of such holes. He and his cousin Bobby had been riding two of his uncle's mules in the field north of the milk barn. Bobby brought him to a spot in the field where an old hay wagon had been left sitting long enough for the grass and the purple-flowered thistles to grow up around it. Bobby, who had been riding bareback, lifted his leg and slid off the side of the mule.

"C'mon," he said as he tied the twine of the mule's homemade reins through a rusted iron eye on the wagon. There was a sense of adventure in his voice and Decker was quick to follow.

"Be careful, now," Bobby cautioned as he began to inch his way slowly toward the edge of a hole in the ground on the other side of the wagon. Decker followed Bobby's lead and was soon standing on the edge of the hole looking down.

"Man, that's deep," Decker said. "What is it?"

"A sink hole," Bobby answered.

"A what?"

"A sink hole. It goes on forever," Bobby said authoritatively.

"Aw, that's crazy," Decker responded. "I can see the bottom."

"That's not the bottom, it's just where it turns off in another direction." Bobby gave a slight tug to Decker's shirt and the pair moved to the other side of the hole.

"See down there," Bobby said as he pointed to what had appeared to be the bottom of the shaft. Decker couldn't tell how far it went, but he could see that the shaft continued off in the other direction. He squatted down to get a better look but there simply wasn't enough light to see any farther.

"Where'd it come from?" Decker asked.

"Whadda ya mean, where'd it come from? Ya think we dug it or sumthin'?" Decker gave Bobby a dirty look and Bobby, deciding this was not the place to pick a fight, continued. "They just show up. One day it's flat ground and then the next day there's a sink hole. That's why they call 'em sink holes, I guess."

Decker tried again to get a better look and then an idea struck him. "Let's get a rope and climb down and explore it!"

"Are you nuts?"

"C'mon! We can get a real long rope. Or even better, we can find some flashlights and get that roll of bailing twine in the barn. We can tie the twine to one of the mules and ease ourselves down. I've seen 'em do stuff like that on television a bunch of times."

"Man, you are nuts! My dad told me about three guys who went down in a sink hole over in Moore County. They never came back up, and two months later they found their bodies in the Duck River!"

Decker looked at Bobby, trying to figure whether he was making this up. Bobby continued, "I told ya, these things don't have no bottoms!"

Just then they saw Bobby's dad stomping through the tall grass toward them. He was mad. "Bobby!" he called out, "What in the Sam Hill are you doin' out here? You wanna fall in there and get yourself killed? You get away from that hole right now or I'm gonna beat the livin' tar outta both of ya!" The boys ran as quickly as they could to the mules. All the commotion gave Decker the clear impression that Bobby hadn't been kidding about the danger.

❑

The rain fell harder now and the dirt that Decker's face was resting against had turned to mud. His hands were locked around the root, his clothes were wet, his stomach was scraped and bleeding, and he was getting cold. He tried calling for help but gave up as his voice grew hoarse. He was only a few feet below the surface, but there was no way to pull himself any farther up. He tried to think of this as an adventure; he'd get out somehow and then he could tell the kids at school about it. Maybe he'd get a lot of sympathy and his mom would even let him skip school tomorrow. He thought about taking off his belt and somehow using it as a rope to pull himself out. *Boy! That would make a great story,* he thought. But there was nothing to tie it to. And anyway, he wasn't about to let go with one hand to try to take off his belt.

For an hour or more he lay there on the muddy slope, holding on to the root. The rain had almost stopped, but the sky was growing dark with the night. That's when he heard the voices of his mother and older brother, Nathan. They were calling him and they were getting closer. He called out—not for help, but to warn them.

"Stay back, Mom! There's a sink hole."

But of course she didn't stay back. In a moment he saw her terrified face peering down over the ridge of the hole. She had crawled on her hands and knees to the side and was holding back tears as she looked down at him clinging to the root about three feet below the surface. She struggled to think clearly. She looked at his fingers wrapped around the root. They seemed so tiny. The blood had long since drained from them, and they were white and wrinkled from the rain. Lying flat on her stomach, she reached down, stretching, sliding a little farther, a little farther, knowing full well that the ground under her could give way at any second, sending both of them to a muddy grave. In a last attempt to gain the extra inch she needed, she held her breath, flattened herself against the ground, and dug the toes of her shoes into the soft dirt to keep from sliding in.

"Just hold on, honey. I'll have you out of there in just a minute," she said in her bravest, most reassuring, voice.

Decker watched in hope as her fingers grasped his right wrist. It was already far too numb to be able to feel her grip. When she was sure of her hold she began to pull him upward. She lifted him a few inches while Decker did his best to try to climb with his feet against the muddy slope. "Let go of the root now, honey," she said, "I've got you."

But Decker couldn't let go.

The grip that had held him just out of the reach of death's jaw now refused to release its hold. His hands were numb, locked together, fingers intertwined, and he could not make them move. His mother pulled harder.

"I can't let go! Mommy, I can't make my hands let go," he said, only now beginning to cry.

"It's okay, Mommy's got you and she won't let go." She pulled. With all of her strength and love, she pulled. And then suddenly, she stopped.

❑

Decker sat bolt upright in his bed.

It was a dream.

It had really happened, just that way, but that was years ago.

Still, inexplicably, he felt his mother's tight grip on his right forearm. He tried to move it, but it hurt and it was heavy. In the dim predawn light he looked and realized what was happening.

"Elizabeth, wake up and let go of my arm," he said. "Come on, babe. You've been having some kind of weird dream or something." Decker mused briefly at the irony that *he* would be telling her *she* was having a weird dream. "Elizabeth, come on, you're hurting me. Wake up and let go of my arm!" Decker took her hand and pulled her fingers loose from his arm.

Finally freeing himself and shaking his arm to get the blood flowing again, he lay down to go back to sleep. But something was not right. Elizabeth was a light sleeper.

"Elizabeth!" he called sharply, but there was no response. He rolled over and shook her to try to wake her, but she would not awaken. He shook her again, but still she didn't respond. Suddenly a horrible thought hit him and he grabbed her wrist.

There was no pulse.

He checked for a pulse in her carotid artery. There was none.

He listened for a heartbeat, but there was nothing. His own blood pressure rose as his heart pounded in terror. His jaw clenched and his head began to ache. He tried to understand what was happening.

CPR, he thought suddenly. *Her body's still warm. It must have just happened. I've got to try CPR.* He pulled the covers from her lifeless body. It had been years since he had taken a class in CPR; he prayed that he remembered how.

Let's see, he thought, *put one hand on top of the other on the middle of the chest. Wait! Is it just above the place where the ribs come together or just below? Just above!* he thought. He began to apply pressure, but her body just sank with the mattress. He had to get her onto something solid. He grabbed her arms and pulled her to the floor.

He tried again. "Oh, God!" he said out loud. "I forgot to check her mouth." Decker pulled his wife's mouth open and looked inside for any obstructions to the airflow. It was too dark to see.

He scrambled for the light, but lost more time as his eyes adjusted to the sudden brightness. He checked her mouth again, but could see nothing. He reached into her mouth with his fingers. There was nothing there. "God, help me!" he said, in tears of desperation. *I should have just done that in the first place.* He had lost precious seconds.

He quickly blew two full breaths into her lungs and went back to his position above her, pressing with his palms against the middle of her lower rib cage. "One, two, three, four, five," he counted under his breath, and then blew air into her lungs again. "One, two, three, four, five." He repeated the process. Again. Again. "Don't die . . . Elizabeth, please don't die," he sobbed. Again, and again. Five minutes. "Please, honey. Please wake up! God, please, let her wake up." But there was still nothing.

Got to call an ambulance. Just a few more. "One, two, three, four, five."

Decker grabbed the phone from the nightstand by the bed. His hands were shaking and his fingers struggled to dial 911 as he stretched the phone cord over to where Elizabeth lay. He held the phone between his shoulder and ear and began CPR again. The line was busy. He stopped and dialed again. Busy. *How can it be busy?* "God, help me!" he said again. He pressed the "0" button for the operator. It too was busy. He tried again, but it was still busy.

Decker dropped the phone. He continued CPR for another thirty minutes, stopping every five minutes to try the phone again. Finally it rang. He held the phone between his shoulder and ear, continuing CPR, as over and over it rang. Minutes passed and it just kept ringing. Could he have dialed wrong? Now that it was ringing did he dare hang up? No, no! How could he have dialed 911 wrong? If he hadn't dialed right it wouldn't be ringing. Unless, unless he accidentally dialed 411, the number for information. It was unlikely, but in his state of panic, anything was possible.

He hung up and dialed again. It was busy.

It took only a moment while he dialed, but when he started CPR again he noticed something that had escaped him before. Almost an hour had passed and Elizabeth's body was growing cold. She was dead. There was nothing he could do. She was dead.

Decker sat down on the floor beside her and wept. The thought of losing her now, now that he had finally learned what it meant to truly love her, was more than his heart could bear. His muscles ached from the CPR. Outside their window the sun was rising just as it did on every other morning. Elizabeth always loved the sunrise. The clock-radio came on, and an announcer's voice started in mid-sentence, but Decker didn't hear it. He heard the noise, but that's all it was. Tears streaked his face but he didn't wipe his eyes. If all he had to offer Elizabeth was his tears, he would leave them where they lay.

Soon Hope and Louisa would wake up. How could he tell them what had happened? For their sake, at least, he knew he must be strong. Still weeping, he picked up Elizabeth's body and moved her back to the bed. He pulled the covers up, tucking the blanket in gently around her. Only now did the radio announcer's words begin to pierce through the wreath of grief which encircled him.

"Reports continue to come in from all around the world," the announcer's voice cracked painfully. "Thousands, hundreds of

thousands, maybe more, are reported dead in what is undoubtedly the worst single disaster in human history. The deaths seem
to have occurred almost simultaneously in all parts of the world.
So far, no one has any idea why this has happened."

What! What was he saying?

The thoughts pounded like thunder in Decker's head. Thousands dead? Was this what killed Elizabeth? How could this
happen? Radiation? Poison gas? Terrorist attack? But why would
it kill only some people and not others?

As if in answer, the announcer continued. "There is no
apparent pattern to the deaths: black, white, Indian, Japanese,
Chinese; men, women, children . . ."

"Children?" Decker said out loud. "NO!!!"

Decker ran from the bedroom. A moment passed and then a
scream of anguish ascended the stairs, ripping through the walls
and shaking the tiny particles of dust as they floated through the
morning sunlight. It was like no earthly scream, such a sorrowful
howl. But no one heard it. They were all dead. Decker was alone.

❑

Hovering in the twilight of insanity, Decker stumbled up the half
flight of stairs to the living room and made his way to a chair.
Upstairs in the bedroom, the voice of the radio announcer continued.

"Everywhere there is terror, everywhere there is heartbreak.
Never has the world faced such devastating loss. No war, no
plague, no event in history can compare with the scale of this disaster. And no one can be certain the death is over. Whatever has
claimed the lives of so many, can it truly have struck so quickly
and just as quickly be gone?

"In our studio three of my coworkers have died, one as he
stood speaking with me little more than an hour ago. There was
no warning. As long as I live, the scene of my coworker and
friend simply stopping mid-sentence and collapsing to the floor
will be etched in my memory. And as I recall that moment when
death struck here and around the world, I cannot help but ask

myself, Is it over? Will it strike again? Will this sentence, this word, this breath be my last? Will the same happen again to others, to me, as has happened to so many?

"Is this the end of the world? It's not unreasonable to ask that question.

"Can this be an act of unmatched terror and barbarism? An insidious crowning achievement in the endless parade of man's inhumanity to man? . . . Can it be anything else?

"Tens of millions lay dead around the world for no apparent reason. At least thirty commercial airplanes are reported to have crashed into hillsides or fields or cities. In Brazil and Argentina, where it is mid-morning, carnage covers the roadways. Cars driven by victims of the disaster sped helter-skelter, careening into other vehicles and pedestrians. There are reports of nuclear power plants teetering on the edge of disaster as surviving technicians rush to fill in for those who died at their stations. Some who survived the initial disaster have been forced to leave their dead behind as they evacuate neighborhoods around overturned train cars spilling out streams of chemicals.

"World governments are appealing for calm. People are being asked to stay in their homes. All forms of mass transportation are being shut down; planes have been forced to land at the nearest available airport. Even though the deaths appear to be worldwide, the governments of many countries are responding to the disaster as though it were an attack on their national sovereignty, placing their military on high alert and restricting fly-over rights to their own armed forces. NATO, too, has been placed on high alert.

"No one knows what has happened, but we cannot help but ask: Have all the years of the War on Terror now come back to strike the civilized world? Perhaps this attack has been in the works for decades. Or perhaps it is a radical Islamic response to Israel's construction of a new Temple in Jerusalem on the site where their mosque once stood. Clearly, if this disaster is the result of a terrorist action, they've gone beyond the destruction of a few buildings or the murder of the population of a few cities, and we are now in a world war." The announcer paused, no longer able to hold back tears.

"At this moment all over the east coast of America and Canada, men and women are waking to find their loved ones dead. It is all so hard to comprehend, so difficult to imagine. In time zones to the west, where it is not yet dawn, many are sleeping soundly, unaware of what has befallen our planet. For some it will be hours before they wake to find their loved ones lying dead next to them."

South of Hanoi, Vietnam

Pedaling her heavily laden bicycle steadily along the unnamed road that runs north along the top of a dike on the floodplain of the Red River Delta, Le Thi Dao made good time on her way to the markets of Hanoi, twelve miles to the north. The handmade wicker baskets she carried were stacked tightly, then tied together in two rings and hung on either side of her bike, giving an appearance, to someone from the West, that she was carrying two enormous bagels. Squinting to see better, she stopped pedaling and began to drift. Ahead on the roadside, next to a grazing ox, a small patch of bright blue and red took on a familiar form. Lying there wearing her New York Yankees baseball cap was Vu Le Thanh Hoa, a friend from school. Her stiffening fingers still clutched the ox's lead rope.

North of Akek Rot, Sudan

Ahmed Mufti held his rifle to his chest as he waited quietly but eagerly for the signal. Just fourteen years old, this would be the boy's first time to participate in an actual raiding party.

He had come south from his home in Matarak with his father and uncle and the other men to raid the Dinka and Nuba villages of southern Sudan for booty and slaves. So far, though, his father had made him stay at camp during the actual raids. Officially, the government of Sudan in Khartoum was opposed to the practice of raiding and taking slaves, but in reality, it was encouraged as part of the policy of Islamization.

Driving the booty of cattle, sheep, goats, and slaves northward was painfully slow and with every mile Ahmed had felt the disappointment of not having been in on an actual raid. There was always the possibility of encountering the Sudanese People's Liberation Army (SPLA), guerrilla members of the Dinka tribe, but the Dinka were poorly armed and would not likely attack a raiding party as large as Ahmed's. It had seemed he would have to wait until next year to participate in any fighting.

Then word came from the party's scouts, who had been sent ahead to look for SPLA forces. Following a path that had been heavily traveled recently, the scouts had come upon a large group of perhaps two hundred slaves near a huge mahogany tree. Brought south by slave traders for sale back to their families and tribes or to some humanitarian group intending to free them, the women and children were escorted by no more than ten armed men. It was few enough that Ahmed's father had agreed to allow Ahmed to come along. Now as he waited for the signal to converge on the camp, he stayed low to the ground and considered the number of Sudanese pounds that would be his from the sale of two hundred slaves.

Finally the signal came, but it was not the one he expected. Knowing only to follow the lead of the other men, Ahmed moved slowly forward. In a moment, he came to where his uncle and three others from the party had stopped to look down at the bodies of two dead SPLA soldiers. He had heard no gunshots or sounds of fighting and there was no blood. Before he could ask, another call came from the direction of the slave encampment. With adrenaline rushing through his veins, Ahmed ran to catch up with the others, who were now charging to the encampment. At the clearing they all stopped. There was no sign of battle. Unsure of what he should do, Ahmed stood between his father and uncle. He did not understand what he saw, but he could see in the faces of the others that neither did they. Beneath the shade of the huge mahogany tree were two hundred slaves, just as the scouts had said, but nearly all of them were dead.

Lavaur, France

Albert Faure tugged at the reins, bringing his horse to a halt as he reached for his cell phone. "Faure," he answered crisply. The Andalusian stallion shook its abundant white mane and took advantage of the pause to graze on the clover at its feet.

"Something has happened," the caller said. It was Faure's secretary from his office at the Conseil Régional, the congress of the Midi-Pyrenees region of France. Faure was the region's youngest member of the Conseil and, according to many, one of the most ambitious.

Gerard Poupardin did not know how to explain what had happened. "Do not keep me waiting, Gerard!" Faure demanded. "What is it?"

"Sir, it's difficult to . . . A little more than ninety minutes ago, millions of people all over the world suddenly died without any warning or known cause."

Faure tried to understand, but of course could not. There was the desire to believe he had simply misunderstood. "France?" he asked finally, not knowing where else to begin his questioning.

"There's really very little information available so far. I have heard an estimate of perhaps a quarter million dead, but I do not know how they can estimate such a thing." Faure gasped. "It does seem," Poupardin continued tenuously, "that France and much of Western Europe may have lost far fewer than some parts of the world. Estimates coming from the United Kingdom are more than a million."

"The United States?"

"It's still early there, sir. Based on what we know from their east coast, they seem to have been struck much worse than we."

"Is this some kind of biological warfare? Arab terrorists?" Faure asked. It was an obvious question, but of course Poupardin couldn't answer it.

"Our borders and the borders of many other countries have been ordered sealed and the military reserves are being called to active service," Poupardin reported.

"Is it safe for me to return to the city?" Faure asked.

"I don't know, sir. No one is sure of anything. Nothing makes sense."

Faure thought for a moment.

"There is one other thing, sir." Poupardin paused. "The Conseil president is among those reported dead."

Faure thought on this bit of additional information and quickly considered how it might be used to his advantage. Stroking his horse's neck, he scanned the Pyrenees Mountains, which mark France's southern border with Spain. "I'm coming in to the office," he said finally, and hung up.

Pusan, South Korea

His leg broken in two places, DaiSik Kim finally managed to free himself and struggled to climb from beneath the crushed remains of his tented kiosk at the Chagalchi Fish Market in Pusan. Stunned when half of the men and women in line at his shop had suddenly fallen dead before him, he had not noticed until it was too late that a bus had jumped the curb and was speeding toward him. From beneath the rubble where he was buried for almost two hours, he had called for help, but no one came. Now, as he emerged hoping to find police and ambulance standing by, he instead found a scene of unexplainable destruction. The dead were everywhere. The living sat sobbing or walked confused and dazed among them. The street in front of his stand, which hours before had flowed with vehicles of all sorts, was now frozen in shattered tableau.

Brisbane, Australia

Patrick McClure was working the closing shift at the bookstore in the historic Brisbane Arcade when the disaster hit. Amid screams and cries for help, his boss called the police and hospital, but the lines were already busy. As the sweeping scope of the disaster became apparent, Patrick immediately called his mother at home. After determining his family was alright, he did what he could to help others. The long arcade of shops linking Queen Street Mall and Adelaide Street was littered with dozens of bodies. Some of the victims were attended by friends or family who had been with them. Many other victims were alone. In some cases it appeared that several shopping companions had died together. It was hard to know what to do and there was no help from police or other authorities. Most survivors had fled, and with no other way to help those who had perished, Patrick walked among the corpses, laying them in what seemed a more suitable position than the sprawled knots into which they had fallen. Later he brought food and drink from an Arcade eatery to the few remaining survivors. Two hours had passed, and as he was bringing some clothes from one of the stores for an old woman to sit upon, Patrick noticed a man and woman with shopping bags walking among the dead, collecting wallets, purses, and jewelry.

Kerala, India

Dr. Jossy Sharma sat on the hood of his Mercedes, his laptop computer resting on his propped-up knees, as he typed notes for an article he was writing for the *Indian Journal of Ophthalmology*. He liked to come here to the Thattekkadu Bird Sanctuary to concentrate. Nestled among a forest of evergreens and home to indigenous and migratory birds, including a few rare species, the sanctuary formed a quiet asylum from his busy office at St. Joseph's Hospital in Kothamangalam twelve miles away. After several peaceful hours, Sharma felt satisfied with his progress on the article and decided to head home for supper.

As he got in the car he noticed his pager had an urgent message from the hospital. He was needed immediately. Because the message was now three hours old, he attempted to call but was unable to reach anyone. Driving out of the sanctuary toward

Kothamangalam, he had gone less than a mile before he came upon the first of many auto accidents in his path. Pulling to the side of the road to help the drivers and passengers, he was met by a bizarre scene. In addition to the two adult male drivers, there were three adult women and five children. Though everyone in both cars was wearing a seat belt and the airbags had apparently functioned properly, they were all dead, and they had been dead for at least a few hours. The damage to the vehicles was extensive but the passenger compartments were basically intact. These people, he told himself, should not be dead. And why had no one stopped to help them? Then he noticed something else. Though there were lacerations on the victims, there was very little blood. It was as though when the accident occurred, they were already dead.

Again he tried to call the hospital, but with the same result. He stopped at two more accident scenes before finding anyone alive. A middle-aged woman, who had survived the disaster and the crash that followed, had pulled the body of her dead husband from the car and was sitting beside him on the side of the road. She had no serious injuries.

Continuing on past six more accidents, Dr. Sharma sped to the top of a hill just outside the city. On the road ahead were more wrecked vehicles than he wanted to count. Abandoning his car when the roads became impassible, he walked the rest of the way. Passing people dead in the street, some of whom he knew, he arrived at the hospital only to find that thirty-six of the forty-two doctors were among the dead.

Four days later
Derwood, Maryland

Hank Asher locked his fingers together, forming a step for his young journalist intern to place her foot into. Sheryl Stanford took the task in stride as she climbed through the kitchen window they had just pried open. As she made her way to open the front door, she spotted Decker's pale, motionless form slumped in a chair in the living room. Hank Asher entered the house to the now familiar stench of rotting bodies. At first he assumed that Decker had been among the unlucky ones who had died four days earlier in the "Disaster," as it had come to be known, but Sheryl soon determined he was still alive.

"He seems to be in shock," she told Asher, as she tried to get Decker to drink some water. Decker stared blankly but swallowed eagerly as she put the glass to his mouth.

Asher surveyed the situation and decided she had things well in hand. "You stay here with Mr. Hawthorne. I'll check the house to see if anyone else is alive." Sheryl needed little encouragement to stay among the living. The smell of the house left no doubt what Asher would find. Hank had not known Elizabeth or the Hawthorne children but his heart ached for his friend.

When he returned from the bedrooms a few moments later he directed Sheryl to go around the rest of the house and open up all of the windows. "We need to remove the death from this house. I'll see if I can find a shovel to bury the bodies."

Asher made no effort to try to revive Decker. Even if he *could* rouse him, it seemed to Asher the most humane thing to do was to allow his colleague to "sleep" through the awful tasks that needed to be done.

Sheryl opened as many windows as weren't stuck shut and then went back to the living room. In small part this was to sit with Decker, but mostly it was to allow her to turn on the television news. Without an answer for the cause of the Disaster and a solid assurance it would not be repeated, the anxiety was nearly debilitating. The only people who seemed to be unaffected were looters and opportunists who burglarized the homes and businesses of Disaster victims. The single reason Sheryl was out was that Hank Asher had come by her house to get her. Most businesses were still closed, but as Hank told her in no uncertain terms, that did not include the news business. In a way, she respected his attitude of getting on with life; she just wished he hadn't involved her. Most of the *NewsWorld* staff assigned to the Washington, D.C., office had survived the Disaster, but anyone who had not reported in, Hank called. Decker was the only one he couldn't either reach or confirm dead, and so he had come to see for himself.

Every conceivable explanation for the Disaster and many inconceivable ones as well, had been put forward. With very few exceptions outside the Arab population, the first words out of the mouths of most was "Arab terrorists," and to date no reasonable explanation had been found to dissuade those who held that theory. The common wisdom was that it was some new killer strain of virus developed by the terrorists, or more likely developed by either the U.S., Russia, or China and stolen by or sold to the terrorists.

Gas masks of every kind, respirators, and even disposable surgical masks were bought up or stolen from stores that remained closed. Army surplus stores sold out of masks, and Internet stores took hundreds of thousands of orders they could not fill. In some stores there was fierce fighting among customers for paper masks, even though reason dictated that they could not possibly filter out the agent of death.

Each new explanation brought panic to someone. Just as many were afraid of what might be in the air, others were afraid to drink the water; still others feared genetically enhanced foods. Most weren't sure what to fear and so feared everything equally.

Whatever the cause, if it was in the air or water or elsewhere in the environment, it must have been there for weeks or months or even years, a ticking time bomb waiting to go off. Ships at sea and even submarines submerged for weeks reported deaths. Two astronauts who had been aboard the International Space Station for six months also died.

❑

Outside, Asher found a garden shovel and began digging a single large hole for the burial of Elizabeth, Hope, and Louisa Hawthorne. It was not the grave one would have expected before the Disaster, but it was better than the mass graves at the edges of the city. Here at least Decker might someday place a gravestone.

Asher looked around the yard to be sure he wasn't going to hit any utility lines and went to work. As he was digging, he sensed he was being watched. Turning, he found a boy in his early teens staring at him from the next yard.

"You buryin' sumbody?" the boy asked, as he jumped the fence and came over to where Asher was working. The boy's clothes were new but dirty, as though he hadn't changed or washed in several days.

"Yeah," Asher replied, as he went back to his work.

"I knew 'em, you know. I used to ride bikes with Louisa. I don't guess she'll be needin' the bike no more." The boy paused for a second in thought and then continued. "Too bad it's a girl's bike."

Asher continued digging.

"You want some help?" the boy asked.

Asher had already worked up a sweat and the boy's offer was extremely welcome.

"I'll help you dig for ten dollars," the boy added.

Asher was momentarily disgusted by the boy's profiteering. Instead of offering to help with the burial out of charity or perhaps friendship for Louisa, he looked at the deaths as a way to make some money. But, still, Asher decided it was better to forget about motives and simply get some help. "There's another shovel and some work gloves that might fit you in the shed over there," he said.

The boy found the additional shovel and gloves while Asher went to work with a pick.

"They all dead?" the boy asked, as Asher broke up the ground.

"Everybody but Mr. Hawthorne."

"I didn't know him very good. I remember him some from when I was a kid, but then he was kidnapped by the Arabs. He only got free about a week ago."

Asher continued digging without responding and then stopped and looked up at the boy. "Are you going to dig or just hold up that shovel?"

The boy acted as though he appreciated the reminder and went to work on the hole. "My dad says it was probably Arab terrorists," he said after a few minutes of digging.

"Yeah, well, that seems to be what most people think," Asher answered.

"Yeah, I heard on the news that only a few thousand Arabs died."

"That's old information. The figures I've seen put the number much higher: half a million in Saudi Arabia and Iraq, two hundred thousand in Jordan and Iran, one hundred thousand in Libya, three *million* in Pakistan, and *eight* million in Egypt."

The boy was temporarily caught off guard by Asher's recitation of figures, but he quickly recovered. "That's probably just lies to keep us from knowing it was them."

Asher continued digging while the boy continued talking. Every other sentence or so the boy would throw out a shovel full of dirt, just to keep his hand in.

❑

Inside the house, Sheryl Stanford was watching the Fox News Network.

"In a press conference this morning from Washington," the news anchor said, "Secretary of Health and Human Services Spencer Collins, issued a statement regarding what measures are being taken to deal with this crisis and answered questions from reporters. Here's some of what he had to say."

The picture switched to the secretary of HHS reading a prepared statement. "We want to assure the public that no stone is being left unturned in the search for the cause of this tragedy, determining whether there is further risk, and, if so, what can be done to protect against that risk. Everything, no matter how small or unlikely, is being examined. Emergency funding has been authorized by the president and Congress and we will spend whatever it takes to accomplish this mission. We are working around the clock. Every imaginable kind of environmental test is being conducted: atmospheric, drinking water, soil, chemical, biological, nuclear . . . Because this is a worldwide event we are also looking closely at cosmic data collected from before the Disaster, such as solar activity.

"Simultaneously, the Centers for Disease Control in Atlanta and the U.S. Army Medical Research Institute of Infectious Diseases at Fort Detrick, Maryland, have taken the standard protocols used in the investigation of naturally occurring infectious diseases and biological threat agents and have adapted them to the unique circumstances of this event. In coordination with HHS, they are conducting interviews with tens of thousands of relatives of victims. Together with their counterpart agencies in other countries around the world and with the World Health Organization, they are looking for any similarities in the victims' activities: where they went, what they ate, what they drank, their personal habits, anything they might have received in the mail. As I said, no stone is being left unturned. At the same time, they are looking for similarities in the activities of survivors in a search for anything that may have counteracted the threat agent. This is a huge task and we have enlisted the assistance of thousands of researchers from universities and private institutions around the country.

"We are also asking individuals who lost relatives or close friends to assist in this effort by logging onto our website and answering a comprehensive set of questions for each person lost and also about themselves so we have comparative data from survivors. In this way, we are using the Internet to recruit people from all over America and around the world to help in this effort. Because of the extensive nature of this event, we expect many millions to participate, and we are confident the analysis of all this data will provide us with useful information. In fact, citizen participation in this effort may make the difference between success and failure.

"The National Institutes of Health are conducting DNA studies of large numbers of both victims and survivors, looking for distinguishing genetic markers in the two groups. E-mail requests are going out to local hospitals and health care professionals requesting collection of DNA samples from victims and their close surviving relatives. Again, this is an area where citizen participation is imperative if we are going to succeed.

"The Centers for Disease Control are coordinating the data

gathering from autopsies. To date, we have data from the autopsies of more than a thousand victims and more reports are coming in by the minute. These procedures have been conducted by medical examiners and pathologists from around the world. We have some data from autopsies that were conducted within an hour of the Disaster by astute MEs who recognized the importance of their findings to uncovering the cause of this tragedy."

Secretary Collins finished his statement and then took questions from reporters. The first two questions sought some assurance from the secretary on behalf of viewers that the Disaster would not be repeated. Though he attempted to be upbeat, he could offer no assurances. The third reporter asked a more direct question, but the secretary's answer was neither more helpful nor reassuring: "Based on the autopsies, what can you tell us about the actual cause of death of the victims?"

Secretary Collins adjusted his glasses. He knew his answer would only raise more questions that he could not answer. "Normally," he began, considering his words carefully, "whatever the cause of death, we would expect that during the autopsy, we'd find indications of how the agent of death had acted. It may, for example, have caused the failure of normal functions of the heart, lungs, liver, kidney, brain, blood . . . something. Whatever we are dealing with here," Collins said, "appears to be entirely asymptomatic. Or, rather, having only the one symptom: death. Nearly all of the common markers we would expect to find in an autopsy of someone who went through the normal death process are missing in these victims. The evidence strongly indicates that death occurred extremely quickly and with an almost instantaneous shutdown of all the body's organs. This has made it impossible, so far, to say exactly how the agent worked or even why the victims died."

This statement brought the expected flurry of questions, but in the end, Collins was able to provide no more information than he had already offered.

Finally a reporter pursued a different matter. "In the U.S. the number of deaths in rural areas appears to be higher, on a percentage basis, than it is in the cities. This seems counterintuitive. Is there some explanation for this?" she asked.

"We are aware of this anomaly," the secretary answered, "and it is being factored into our investigation. There are a number of bacteriological agents that can remain dormant for years in soil, and perhaps the higher percentage of rural deaths would indicate that contact with the soil is involved. We are investigating that possibility. On the other hand, this hypothesis certainly cannot account for the deaths of the two astronauts aboard the space station.

"But let me point out that there are a number of other anomalous patterns that are beginning to emerge as well, some of which are conflicting from country to country or from region to region. We must stress that this analysis is based on very preliminary figures of the number of victims, but clearly there is evidence that the death toll was not evenly distributed worldwide. We hope that together this information will provide some clues, but right now we are still gathering data."

"What other anomalous patterns have been identified?" the reporter asked in follow up.

"Well, for example, losses in the U.S. are currently estimated at between 15 and 20 percent. Some European countries, on the other hand, lost as few as one or two people for every one thousand of their population. As a result, the logistical impact of the Disaster in these countries is almost negligible and their governments have been able to finish what they believe are nearly complete counts. Largest among these is Greece, which lost approximately ten thousand out of a population of more than ten million. Also in this group are Albania, Monaco, Andorra, Luxembourg, Macedonia, and Malta. Other European countries with losses of one percent or less include France, Austria, and Belgium.

"Another example," continued the secretary, "is India, which estimates say lost as many as twenty-five million, or about two percent of their population. This is not a high percentage, but what makes India unusual is that as many as 90 percent of the victims lived on India's southwest coast, on the Arabian Sea."

"What information do you have on the death toll in Arab countries?" another reporter asked.

"As you may know, it is not always easy to get accurate information from some Islamic countries. Additionally, in most cases, their ability to gather data is not as advanced or accurate as it is in the Western world. Based on what we have been able to gather on these countries, however, this may be the most surprising information so far."

The secretary paused for a moment and then corrected the possible misperception of his statement. "I don't mean that it is particularly surprising from a medical standpoint, but rather because it poses some serious challenges to theories that the Disaster was caused by Arab terrorists. It seems that several Islamic countries have lost a larger percentage of their population than did the European countries I just listed. These include Saudi Arabia, Oman, Iraq, Jordan, and most notably Egypt, which may have lost as much as 10 percent of its population. Indonesia, which is not Arab but is predominantly Islamic, also suffered significant losses. With the exception of Egypt, those percentage numbers are still low as compared to many other countries, but it raises doubts in my mind that Islamic terrorists would develop a weapon and then kill a greater percentage of their own population than that in many of the countries of the European Union. It also begs the question of why the death toll in Israel was not greater."

The tape of the press conference ended and the camera returned to the news anchor.

"As you just heard HHS Secretary Collins say, there is evidence that some Arab countries may have been hit worse by the Disaster than some countries in Western Europe. Nevertheless, vigilante attacks against Muslims continue. For more on that we go to a special Fox report with Greg Culp."

The picture changed to show a reporter standing outside the smoldering remains of a building, in front of which stood a partially destroyed marquee that read "Gilbert Arizona Islamic Academy." The reporter began, "Throughout the non-Islamic world, Muslims fear for their lives, and with good reason. Islamic homes have been burned, businesses have been looted, their inhabitants beaten and even murdered in mob actions. Islamic schools like this one behind me have been destroyed by local citizens. Fortunately, the school was empty and no one was injured. Throughout America, Islamic schools have been closed since the day after the Disaster, when three men entered an Islamic school in Cincinnati and shot sixteen students and four teachers.

"Despite the president's plea for calm and his promise that FBI and law enforcement will hunt down anyone who participates in such acts, thus far police and other authorities have been unable to stop or even contain the violence. Contributing to the problem, authorities tell Fox News, has been the trend since the terrorist attacks of 9-11, of Americans to arm themselves, frequently with unregistered, illegally purchased firearms." The news report then shifted focus to a sidebar story on the sale of illegal firearms.

❏

When they had dug about four feet, Hank Asher decided the hole was deep enough; the standard six feet under was simply more than he could manage. He was about to pay the boy his ten dollars but paused with the bill in his hand as he looked at the boy and then down at himself. The distribution of dirt and sweat left no doubt that the boy had done less than his share. Hank checked his wallet again and, as a matter of principle, decided to pay the boy eight dollars instead of ten.

"Hey, what about my other two bucks?"

"Eight dollars is more than you deserve for the little bit of work you did."

"Man, what a rip-off! I'm gonna go get my dad. He'll make you pay me." With that the boy threw down the shovel and stomped off.

Asher rested for a moment. It suddenly occurred to him that he still had to carry the bodies out and fill the hole back in. "That was really stupid!" he said, realizing he had gotten rid of the boy too soon.

❏

Inside the house, Sheryl Stanford tried talking to Decker from time to time, but there was no indication he could hear her. He just stared blankly into space. She found some food in the kitchen and when she put it in his mouth he chewed and swallowed, but still he just stared. As she fed him, she continued to listen to the news in the background. There was an urgent and growing concern about disease from decaying bodies. Reports from around the world said that thousands of suicides were adding to the world-wide death toll. Most of these suicides took place in the victims' homes, but others were more public: jumping from buildings and bridges, driving off cliffs, and the like. A few chose to murder others before turning their weapons on themselves.

There was a great deal of rallying around the flag. People flocked to houses of worship to find answers, but the Disaster had struck everywhere and large numbers of clergy had died as well, leaving a vacuum. Stock markets and exchanges in the U.S. remained closed and analysts predicted worldwide financial chaos and a serious economic depression. Insurance companies were seeking legal relief in the form of exemption from payment on deaths from the Disaster. Insurers said that without such legal relief, every life insurance company in America would have to declare bankruptcy, and analysts agreed that if the markets reopened before Congress and the president acted, insurance company stocks would not survive the first hour of trading. Opponents of these measures and other critics argued that insurance companies were certainly not the only industry at risk. Everyone had suffered, and no one could predict what would happen when the markets reopened. The government couldn't bail out everyone.

❏

After Asher finished the burial he came in and collapsed on the couch across the living room from Decker. "Has he said anything?" he asked.

"Not a word. He just stares," Sheryl answered as she muted the television. "What are we going to do with him?"

"He needs to be cared for, but the hospitals are packed. I don't suppose you'd take him home with you?"

Sheryl looked at Decker and then back at Asher. The desperate look on her face made it clear that she did not like the idea at all but was not comfortable saying no to her boss. As she struggled to respond, Asher let her sweat it out. He knew it was an unusual request, but these were unusual times.

Just then there was a knock at the door.

"I'll get it," Sheryl said, jumping up from her seat, hoping to evade her boss's question. Asher was too tired to argue.

A moment later, she came back. "It's a kid," she said. "He says he wants to see Mr. Hawthorne."

"Tell that lousy kid to go away, that he's not going to get one penny more than I've already paid him! No, wait! I'll tell him myself."

Energized by his anger, Asher picked himself up off the couch and headed for the front door. "Look, you, I'm not—" Asher stopped himself in mid-sentence as he realized this was not the boy from the backyard. "Oh. I'm sorry, kid. I thought you were someone else. Look, Mr. Hawthorne isn't feeling well right now. Can you come back later?" he asked, trying to get rid of the boy.

"I'm sorry, but I need to talk to Mr. Hawthorne," the boy persisted.

"Like I said, kid, Mr. Hawthorne isn't feeling well. Come back tomorrow."

The boy held his ground.

"Okay," Asher said, "look, maybe I can help you. What is it that you need to talk to Mr. Hawthorne about?"

From the living room, Sheryl Stanford called to Asher, "Hey, he moved his eyes a little!"

Asher went to his friend's side and looked, but saw no sign of awareness.

"Mr. Hawthorne, it's me, Christopher Goodman." Asher turned around and saw that the boy had followed him into the living room.

"Mr. Hawthorne, please tell these people you know me. I've come a long way and I don't have anywhere else to go. Uncle Harry and Aunt Martha both died in a plane crash. I don't have any other family. Uncle Harry told me if anything ever happened to them I should call you. But you didn't answer your phone."

Asher, who knew of Harry Goodman from Decker's articles, put the pieces together. "Your uncle is Professor Goodman from Los Angeles?"

"Yes," Christopher responded. "Did you know him?"

"I know his work. What are you doing in Washington?"

"Uncle Harry told me that if anything ever happened to him and Aunt Martha, I should find Mr. Hawthorne," he repeated. "I don't have any other relatives and Mr. Hawthorne was my uncle's friend."

"How'd you get all the way out here from Los Angeles?"

Christopher paused, apparently hoping to avoid an answer that might get him in trouble. "I drove my uncle's car," he admitted finally.

"You drove from Los Angeles?" Asher said, surprised. "How old are you, kid?"

"Fourteen," Christopher answered. "I didn't have any other way to get here."

Asher shook his head in disbelief. "How'd you get all this way without getting stopped by the cops?"

"I guess they're pretty busy with looters."

"I guess so. Well, look, kid. I'm sorry you drove all the way out here for nothing, but Mr. Hawthorne won't be able to help anybody for quite a while."

Christopher looked at Decker.

"In fact," Asher continued. "I'm going to have to find someone to take care of *him*."

"But, I don't have anywhere else to go. Most of Aunt Martha's friends are dead and Mr. Hawthorne is . . . well," Christopher paused to think. "Can I just stay here for a while? Maybe I could help you take care of him."

"I think that's a great idea!" Sheryl chimed in, still fearing she'd be stuck with taking care of Decker. "Let him stay."

"Let him stay," another voice repeated hoarsely.

Asher, Sheryl, and Christopher all turned toward the only other person in the room.

"Let him stay," Decker said again.

11

The Master's Promise

THE COOL MOISTURE of morning soaked slowly through the seat of Decker's jeans as he sat on the grass beside the grave of his family. Mindlessly he stared at the upturned soil, still numb from his loss. It would be spring before the surrounding grass would begin to encroach upon the settling mound of bare dirt.

Decker had put in an order for three gravestones but was told that it could take as long as a year and a half to get stones with names on them. Generic stones with "Beloved Wife," "Beloved Father," "Beloved Daughter," etc. and no date of birth could be had in half the time and at about one fourth the price of a personalized stone, delivery included. Someone else was offering four-week delivery on personalized grave markers made of reinforced plastic with a "marble look." Decker had decided to wait for the real thing.

His wife and children were not all Decker had lost. Shortly after Christopher arrived, Decker had learned that his mother and older brother were also dead. His uncle had buried them, together with others, on his farm in Tennessee.

Still, some had it much worse. The dead who had no one to bury them had been laid by the thousands in mass graves. In the city of Washington the poor had tried to bury their dead on the Mall—the strip of park that runs from the Capital to the Lincoln

Memorial—and in other city parks, but were turned away by U.S. Park Police and National Guard. Some expressed their frustration and protest by leaving the dead on curbs with the garbage.

Among those who died were many celebrities of one sort or another: politicians, religious leaders, heads of state, a few actors and actresses. The U.S. lost twelve senators, sixty-odd congressmen, three Cabinet members, and the vice president. It seemed that everyone had lost someone: wives, husbands, children, parents.

❑

As the sun rose above the fence slats on Decker's right, the individual blades of grass released their moist coats of dew into the morning air. Decker heard the sliding glass door open but did not raise his eyes from the ground to look.

Christopher Goodman approached Decker, stopping a few feet short. After a moment he seemed to realize he would have to speak first. "Breakfast is ready," he said softly but brightly, adding that he had fixed Decker's favorite—waffles with plenty of bacon and scalding hot syrup.

Decker looked up after a second, smiled appreciatively, and extended his hand toward Christopher. "Give me a hand up," he said. Christopher never asked Decker about the hours he spent sitting by the grave in the backyard. He just seemed to understand and allowed Decker the privacy of his thoughts.

"What about your family?" Decker asked, opening the subject as if in mid-conversation.

Christopher didn't miss a beat, but answered as though he knew and understood exactly what Decker had been thinking. "When they didn't come home and they didn't call, I decided to call the airline. They told me that Uncle Harry and Aunt Martha were listed on one of the planes that crashed when the Disaster struck. They said they didn't have enough people to handle all of the calls, much less to clean up all of the crash sites and evacuate all the bodies and notify their next of kin." Christopher paused. "They did tell me where the plane went down," Christopher said, pausing again. "I tried to find it on my way here but it was a long way from any roads." Christopher seemed distraught by the memory of the agonizing decision he had made to leave his aunt's and uncle's bodies in the wilderness where their plane crashed.

Decker was touched by Christopher's obvious pain. For three weeks now Christopher had provided Decker with supportive companionship, never once saying a word about his own loss. Perhaps, Decker thought, it was time to start thinking of someone besides himself. Without thinking it through, he asked, "Would you like for me to go with you to find them? We could take them home to Los Angeles and bury them there, or we could bring them here and bury them in the backyard near Elizabeth, Hope, and Louisa."

Christopher seemed to appreciate the offer but responded that he didn't think it was a good idea. "No, it's, uh . . . too far," he answered.

"That's all right. I can help you drive," Decker told the precocious fourteen-year-old, trying to make a joke and not catching the hint in Christopher's voice that he preferred not to talk about it.

"Mr. Hawthorne," Christopher said directly, "their bodies have been up on that mountain, exposed to the elements and animals for nearly a month. I don't think . . ."

Decker was shocked at his own stupidity. How could he have missed that? "I'm sorry, Christopher. I didn't think."

"It's okay, Mr. Hawthorne," Christopher said, and from the understanding look on his face, Decker could tell it really was. Christopher had apparently accepted the harsh truth with determined resolve to go on. "Come on," Christopher urged. "The breakfast is getting cold."

Decker was beginning to understand Harry Goodman's fear of disclosing Christopher's origin. Over the past few weeks, without knowing it, Decker had come to think of Christopher almost as his own son. Perhaps it was because of the loss of Elizabeth, Hope, and Louisa. Much of the feeling, though, was due to Christopher's totally unselfish attitude, always giving of himself and never asking for anything more in return than room and board. Decker finally and firmly resolved that the story of Christopher's origin was one the world could do without.

❑

Three days later Decker was spending the afternoon reading through recent copies of *NewsWorld* that Hank Asher had brought over to help bring him up to date on the world, restore his interest in life, and assist in his recovery. He was scanning an article on possible theories for the cause of the Disaster when he read something that tied his stomach in knots.

"The search for a cause," the article read, "has been so elusive that the CDC has even considered a great many concepts out of science fiction. One such theory, called Andromeda for its resemblance to *The Andromeda Strain*[29] by author Michael Crichton, was that some widespread, commonly occurring—and therefore overlooked by researchers because it was assumed innocuous—virus or bacteria simultaneously underwent an evolutionary change that made it extremely virulent." Decker felt his stomach tighten as he considered the possible implication of what he was reading. "If so," went the hypothesis, "then the reason that additional similar deaths have not occurred is due either to some natural immunity of the remaining population, or else the killer bug just as quickly went through a second evolutionary change that rendered it harmless."

Decker scanned the words again: "widespread, commonly occurring—and therefore overlooked . . ." His mind went back to the night before the Disaster. He struggled to remember what Professor Goodman had told him about the research he had done on the cold virus. Was it possible the Disaster had been caused by the genetically engineered cold virus Goodman had been working on two years earlier?

"Such a simultaneous evolution of geographically dispersed cultures," continued the article, "would require genetic engineering beyond anything currently known to exist, and would virtually rule out a natural cause."

[29]Knopf, 1969.

Decker could not breathe. He would have to tell someone what he knew.

"Like many others, however, the Andromeda theory has been ruled out based on the evidence of the autopsies. Such a viral or bacterial agent would have left clear and definite indicators that have not been found in any of the victims' autopsies."

Decker caught his breath. In just those few seconds, he had been torn by so much stress and anxiety that he had the beginnings of a major tension headache. He breathed deeply and tried to relax his mind and muscles, taking the time to think through what he had read and consider whether he should still call someone at the CDC. No, he decided, the article was right. The autopsies would have revealed some kind of evidence. The theory had been investigated and found lacking. Besides, this was more than he had strength to think about.

Decker got an ice pack for his headache and lay down for a short nap. When he awoke, he again began going through the pages of *NewsWorld*. If it did not entirely focus on the Disaster, every article had at least some mention of it. In the most recent edition he came to an editorial written by Hank Asher:

> There comes a time following every great tragedy when someone very authoritatively states that those who have lived through it will never be the same. Perhaps it is a cathartic statement. Perhaps it marks or at least helps to mark the point at which we all agree it's time to begin to move on, time to get back to the business of life. It is never easy, but it is necessary.
>
> I am not suggesting that we try to forget what happened, or that we forget those who meant so much to us. Most certainly I am not suggesting that we stop looking for an explanation for what happened or a way to prevent its recurrence.
>
> In an age in which we've come to expect quick answers, it only adds to the horror that no one can provide an explanation for this tragedy. They say funerals are for the living, that they give a stamp of finality to the loss

of loved ones. But that finality can never really come so long as the mystery of cause remains. Scientists are doing everything in their power to determine the cause and prevent it from happening again, but for most of us there is nothing we can do but wait and hope.

The world has no choice but to go on with life. A psychologist friend told me that in one way, recovering from this disaster will actually be easier than recovering from the individual tragedies that plague our mortal lives. In this disaster, everyone lost someone: a relative, a friend or a neighbor. At the very least they know someone who knew someone who died. In that way this bears some resemblance to soldiers marching into fearsome battle, each drawing strength from the others and from the fact that they are not alone.

As I write this I cannot help but think of each of the relatives, friends, and coworkers I've lost. As I picture their faces and remember events where our lives intersected, I notice that many of them are smiling. It seems that is how I usually saw them in life, but maybe that is just how I choose to remember them. For many, I am gnawed by regret that I did not treat them more kindly, that I did not get to know them better, that I did not give them more of myself while I had the chance.

I know my regrets are shared by many who are reading these words. What wouldn't any of us give for the chance to spend just one more day with those we lost? If we could just go back to one day before the Disaster, how different we would seem, how differently we would behave, how much kinder we would be. But there is nothing we can do to bring back that day. There is nothing we can do to bring back into our lives those who died.

I wonder about the children. How will their lives be affected? Many of the children of the Great Depression, remembering their parents' reaction to sudden poverty, went through their entire lives in imagined financial insecurity, holding so tightly to every penny that they denied themselves much of what they wanted or needed. What will children of this generation remember when they look back at how we handled this tragedy? What will they carry with them for having experienced this event?

Regret is natural, but if we allow it to rule our lives, how many more regrets will we pile up? How many more missed opportunities will there be with others whom one day we will wish we had treated with more kindness or gotten to know better or given more of ourselves to? Let us then not flounder in our regrets, but rather let us carry them as reminders to cherish every day we have, to value everyone we meet.

As we lick our wounds in the wake of any new tragedy, we all believe it when we hear the words, "None of us will ever be the same," but inside we know better. Our experience tells us we forget all too quickly. Each time we vow "This time will be different," but we are a resilient lot. We may carve words like "We will never forget" into limestone or granite to remind us, but carving them into the human soul is not so easy. It is made of much more pliable stuff, easily impressed but quick to rebound. And while we may curse that stuff for its conspiracy with time to steal from us the only thing we have left of those who died—our pain—without that resiliency our species would have died out millennia ago.

In a few years our lives may give every appearance of being unchanged by the event we now call the Disaster. But having lived through it, can any of us ever greet another day without the thought that this may be our last? Will any of us ever pass children playing or a flower growing or friends chatting and not look back and thank our lucky stars that we're still alive to witness it?

Perhaps this time it will be different. Perhaps this blow has come with sufficient force to make an impression that will endure. Only time will tell. All we can say for now is none of us will ever be the same.

This was not the typical biting editorial by Hank Asher that Decker was used to reading. He sat quietly for a few minutes, considering Asher's words. Then the phone rang.

"Mr. Hawthorne's residence," Christopher answered, sounding more like a domestic servant than a fourteen-year-old boy. "Yes, just a moment. I'll get him for you." Decker got up and headed for the phone as Christopher reported that it was Mr. Asher calling from *NewsWorld*.

"Hank, how are you?" Decker asked warmly.

"I'm fine. How are you?" Asher's voice made it clear he was willing to listen to a detailed response.

"Much better, actually. Really, I'm doing all right," Decker said resolutely.

Asher understood the determination in his voice. Decker was probably a long way from being all right, but he was determined to be all right and that in itself was a major step in the right direction. "Good," Asher said. "How's the boy?"

"Oh, he's great. He's been a big help around here."

"Look, I know we haven't really talked about your plans on getting back to work, but I need a favor. I need you in New York on Monday for a story."

"Monday!" Decker blurted. "If you've got a story in New York why not just have someone from the New York office cover it?"

"The New York office is understaffed since the Disaster. And really, it's just a small assignment. It'll be good for you. You'll be in and out in one day. I'd send someone else, but it's an interview with Jon Hansen and you're the only one I could get him to talk to."

"The British ambassador to the UN?" Decker asked, more out of surprise than for confirmation.

"I've already set up the interview for Monday afternoon and bought your plane ticket."

"I don't know, Hank," Decker said reluctantly, although yielding a little ground to the man to whom he owed so much. "What's this all about? What's the story?"

"It's about Hansen's report on the situation in the Middle East. The UN lost nearly two thousand men assigned to that area in the

Disaster. They've tried to replace them with reinforcements but many of the countries that provide the UN with soldiers were hit just as badly. The U.S., Britain, Germany, Switzerland—all have major losses. With the threat of war in the Middle East because of the Jews building a temple on the site of the Dome of the Rock, there's serious doubt that the UN forces can maintain the peace.

"We have a tip that Hansen is going to recommend that unless Israel agrees to halt construction of the Temple, the UN should immediately withdraw its remaining thirteen-thousand-man force from around Israel's borders. If the UN removes its troops, war is almost certain."

"How many people know about this?" Decker asked, as he felt his resistance slipping away.

"There are a lot of rumors and suspicions, but no one knows the facts. Hansen has refused to talk to the press, but I was able to get him to agree to talk to you. Come on, Decker. This is the quintessential 'right place at the right time' scenario if I've ever seen one."

Decker laughed to himself, but his pause made Asher think he needed to push for the answer he wanted. "So . . . will you do it or not?" he asked finally.

"Yeah, I'll do it." Decker looked over at Christopher, who had been listening quietly to Decker's end of the conversation. "But, I'll need two tickets instead of one." Christopher understood and nodded with great enthusiasm. "And can you set up a tour of the UN for Christopher?"

"That's a great idea," Asher said. "The kid must be going crazy with cabin fever by now. I'll even make reservations for you in the Delegates Dining Room for lunch. Your appointment with Hansen is set for two o'clock Monday afternoon."

New York, New York

"Where to?" the cabby asked.

"The UN building," Decker answered. Christopher got in first. When Decker joined him he noticed a very strange look on the boy's face. Something was not quite right. It took only an instant for Decker to understand. Sealed in the cab, a strange but familiar smell made its way into their lungs. It was not overpowering, but it was definitely there and it wasn't pleasant. Decker thought about getting out and hailing another cab, but it was too late. The driver punched the gas pedal, pulled his cab across two lanes of traffic and was off.

Decker and Christopher looked at each other. Christopher silently mouthed, "May I roll down the window?"

Decker held up his hand with his thumb and forefinger spread apart, indicating that about three inches would be acceptable. It was pretty cold outside but that seemed a good compromise with the smell.

After a few minutes, Decker cracked his window as well. It was then that he noticed the driver looking at them in his rearview mirror. He seemed to be studying them. *If he asks me to roll up my window,* Decker thought, *I'll make him stop and let us out.* Their eyes met in the mirror and the cabby realized Decker had been watching him looking at them. He quickly reached up, as if he had been checking the adjustment on the mirror.

"So what ya goin' to the UN for?" he asked a moment later.

"Just a visit," Decker answered.

"Oh, yeah?" he said. "Ain't been too many tourists around here lately."

Decker chose not to respond.

A moment later the driver added, "Well, ya wanna be careful over there."

"Why do you say that?" Decker asked.

"Call me paranoid, but I wouldn't go in there widdout a gas mask on."

Decker found it almost impossible not to respond with a crack about needing one to ride in the cabby's car. "I don't follow you," he answered instead.

"Well, I don't care what anyone says. The way I see it, it was definitely Arab terrorists that caused the Disaster. Or if not, then it was the Russians, 'cause no way you're gonna tell me all those people just dropped dead for no reason. And, well, I don't know if you ever been to the UN before, but they got foreigners crawlin' all over the place over there. 'Course, that's true everywhere in New York, only especially at the UN."

"If the Arabs or Russians are responsible for the Disaster," Decker responded, "why would they release it on their own people?"

"Yeah, that's what they say, but how can we really know how many of them died? They could be lyin' through their teeth. And besides, accidents happen."

Decker realized there was no sense in trying to reason with the driver, so he settled back in his seat for the ride and kept silent. The cabby, however, didn't need an active partner to carry on a conversation.

"'Course, I wanna get the creeps that did it as much as the next guy—and I don't mean to be cruel or nuthin'—but if ya ask me, I'd tell ya we wuz better off widdout so many people in the world. 'Course, there ain't near as many fares on the streets nowadays. Not live ones, anyway. But an entrepreneur like me, well, I figure there's a *green* linin' to every cloud. So I asked myself, how can a guy like me make some money when the fares're down. An' it didn't take no time till it comes to me. If there ain't as many live ones around, haul the dead ones! So I called up this guy I know who works at a land-fill in Jersey. And next thing ya know, I'm in business."

If Decker needed any confirmation of what the smell was, he now had it.

"Yeah, I figured it was a great idea," the cabby said, continuing his discourse. "The wife says it makes the car stink. So, I just stopped at the 7-11 and bought this air freshener." The cabby pointed to a cardboard pine tree dangling from the rearview mirror. "And I ain't had no more problem with it. 'Course it was a little creepy at first, but I can make upta two hundred dollars a head for haulin' off bodies, dependin' on how bad a shape they're in. 'Course, most of the stiffs from the Disaster have been hauled off by now. Still, I get a call maybe two or three times a day, mostly to haul off suicides—folks that lost everybody in the Dis-aster and decided ta join 'em. But for a while there, I was rakin' it in. One time I got twelve stiffs in here all at the same time."

The cabby paused just long enough for Decker to get his hopes up that he would remain silent. "And then there's another thing," he said, after catching his breath. "It sure is easier to get apartments around here now. 'Course, most of the apartments that ya find still smell like dead folks, but, hey, ya just let it air out a few hours an' it's jus' like home."

The cabby looked over and nodded toward a pawn shop as they passed. "I tell ya another guy that's makin' a buck on the dead besides the grave digger and me: the pawn broker. Ya see this ring," he said, holding his right hand up for them to see. "Pretty nice, huh? I picked this up dirt cheap from a pawn shop last week. But I bet I paid four times what the pawn broker had ta give for it. An' the guy he got it from probably got it for free off some stiff. Some people don't like wearin' dead folk's stuff, but I figure, hey, they don't need it no more."

"Was there a lot of looting?" Christopher asked the driver, apparently unaware that Decker was hoping the driver would just be quiet and drive.

"Oh, yeah, plenty. Let me tell ya, the looters wuz breakin' windows an' rippin' off stores left and right. A bunch of 'em got shot by shop owners, but then pretty soon the looters started shootin' back. But that only lasted a few days. Then Hizzoner, the mayor, declared open season on anyone on the streets after curfew. So far, I hear the cops have shot more than thirty of 'em."

"Well, here we are," the cabby concluded as he pulled up to the UN General Assembly building.

Decker paid quickly, not wanting to spend an extra moment in that car. The driver thanked him and warned them again to be careful.

"I hope you know that that cabby didn't know his head from a hole in the ground," Decker told Christopher as the two walked toward the entrance of the UN.

"You mean about the Russians and Arabs?" Christopher asked.

"Well, yes, that too. But not just that."

"Sure, Mr. Hawthorne, I know that. But, still, it was an interesting experience."

Decker laughed to himself. "You'd make a good reporter," he said.

Decker and Christopher walked across the North Courtyard to the entrance to the UN General Assembly building. After going through the security check, they went to the information and security desk to get visitor's badges for the Delegates Dining Room. Both enjoyed the lunch buffet immensely. There was more variety than either had seen before at one meal and they liked almost everything they tried.

After their meal, as they were in the lobby returning their badges, someone called to Decker. They turned toward the voice and, through a group of colorfully clothed people, saw a tall blond man who smiled at them and gave a nod of recognition. It was Jon Hansen.

Decker smiled back and made his way across the lobby toward him.

"Mr. Ambassador," Decker said as he approached and extended his hand. "It's good to see you again. But I certainly didn't expect you to come to greet me."

"No problem," Hansen answered with a friendly smile. "But to be honest, I had some business in the building. How have you been? You look much improved over our first meeting."

"Yeah, well, that's not necessarily saying very much," Decker joked. "But I have been eating a lot better. Christopher here is a pretty good cook."

Hansen looked curiously at Christopher, who was listening intently to their conversation.

"Ambassador Hansen, this is Christopher Goodman," Decker responded in answer to Hansen's glance. "He's been staying with me since the Disaster. His granduncle was Professor Harry Goodman of UCLA, who before his death was scheduled to be awarded the Nobel Prize in medicine."

"Well, it's very nice to meet you, Christopher," Hansen said as he shook Christopher's hand. "I've read about your uncle's work in cancer research. He was a brilliant scientist. The world will miss him. Maybe someday you'll continue his work."

"Professor Goodman and I were friends from my college days," Decker continued. "I lost—" Decker bit his lower lip to get a grip on his emotions. For a brief moment he thought he would be able to just say it, but as the words approached his lips, they began to quiver and his cheeks began to ache. Releasing his bite, he tried again. "I lost my wife and two daughters." He paused briefly and took a breath. "So when Christopher showed up on my doorstep, I invited him to stay. The professor and Mrs. Goodman were his only family."

"I'm terribly sorry about your families," Hansen offered. Decker nodded appreciation.

"Mr. Ambassador," Christopher said politely, waiting for permission before continuing.

"Yes, Christopher," Hansen replied.

"I'm very interested in what the World Health Organization is doing to help find the cause of the Disaster. Are they any closer to finding an answer?"

"Well, Christopher," Hansen began, pleased at the boy's interest, "they tell me they've been able to determine several hundred things that it was not. So I guess that's progress. But they still don't know what it was. I have faith in them, though. They'll figure it out soon, I'm sure."

Christopher seemed satisfied with the answer.

"So," Hansen asked Christopher, "is this your first trip to the United Nations?"

"Yes, sir," Christopher answered. "Is your office in this building?"

"Oh, no. I think most people assume that the delegates' offices are here at the UN, but actually each country has its own mission elsewhere in the city. The British Mission is about four blocks from here on Dag Hammarskjöld Plaza, which is really the same as Second Street."

"Christopher is quite a big fan of the UN, so I brought him along," Decker interjected. "He's scheduled for the one-thirty tour."

"Well, why don't we walk Christopher over to where the tour starts, and then we can go over to my office."

❑

When Decker and Hansen reached the British Mission on the twenty-eighth floor of One Dag Hammarskjöld Plaza, they were met at the door by an attractive blond woman in her late twenties who stood at least six feet two inches tall, just two inches shorter than Hansen. Decker was struck not only by her height, but also by her remarkable resemblance to the ambassador. The features were softer, the skin smoother and younger, but there was no mistaking the kinship.

"Mr. Ambassador," she said hurriedly as Hansen and Decker entered through the lobby past the security desk, "Ambassador Fahd called. He said it was urgent that he speak with you. He left a number but said if you didn't call soon you may not be able to reach him. I'll place the call," she said as she went quickly to her desk and Hansen went to his office.

"Decker, come on in and have a seat," Hansen said, not pausing to look back.

Hansen's office was large with sturdy antique furnishings and solid wood paneling. Decker sat in a comfortable leather chair facing Hansen's desk while Hansen sat down and drummed his fingers on the desk in front of the phone.

"It's ringing," came the young woman's heavily accented voice from the outer office.

Hansen picked up the receiver and waited as the phone rang for nearly a minute. "There's no answer, Jackie," he said to his assistant. "Try it again."

Hansen waited anxiously as, this time, Jackie listened while the phone rang. Still there was no answer.

"Okay," Hansen said. "Well, there's nothing we can do then except wait until he calls back and hope nothing happens in the meantime." Hansen turned his attention back to Decker.

"Ambassador Fahd?" Decker quizzed before Hansen could speak. "Isn't he the ambassador from Saudi Arabia?"

"Yes, we're old friends. School chums, actually. Oxford, class of '72. We've worked together on a number of projects for the UN."

"Like the Middle East project your committee is preparing a report on?"

"Well, yes. But tell me, how can I help you?"

"Well," Decker began, unsure of why Hansen would interrupt the conversation on the Middle East project and in the next breath ask how he could help. *That*, after all, was what Decker understood this meeting to be about. Could Hansen have forgotten the purpose of the interview? "I'd like to ask you some questions about the committee's report," Decker finally responded.

"But, Decker, surely you know that that information is strictly confidential," Hansen answered in surprise.

"Wait a second," Decker said slowly, the confusion showing in his voice. "Didn't you agree to talk with me about the report?"

"Of course not!" Hansen was taken aback at the whole idea, but there was no anger in his voice. He was simply surprised. "What exactly did my editor tell you I wanted to talk with you about?"

"Well, Mr. Asher . . . your editor?" Hansen asked, seeking verification. Decker nodded painfully, embarrassed by the course this meeting was taking. "He said that you wanted to do some sort of profile piece on me for your magazine."

Decker dropped his forehead into his open hand and expelled a deep breath in frustration and embarrassment. "Mr. Ambassador," he said, "I'm afraid you and I have both been misled. Hank Asher told me that I was to interview you about your report—that you had refused to talk to other reporters about it but that you *were* willing to talk with me."

"Well, now that wouldn't be quite fair, would it?"

"I'm sorry, Mr. Ambassador," Decker said as he felt his face redden. "I should have thought to question him when he told me you had agreed to talk with me. I guess I let him appeal to my vanity. I—stupidly, I realize now—thought you would . . . Oh, never mind."

Ambassador Hansen's response to this revelation was completely unexpected: He laughed. It was a friendly laugh.

"I don't understand," Decker said. "What's so funny?"

"I'd like to meet this Mr. Asher of yours. He must be quite a good judge of a man's character. I could use a few people like him on my staff."

Decker's expression showed he still didn't understand.

"Oh, but don't you see, Decker? He pulled the same trick on the both of us. I didn't even think to question his motives when he said you wanted to write a profile story on me. I too was a victim of my own vanity."

Decker forced a smile. He didn't think it was very funny, but he didn't want to deny the Ambassador his fun. And besides, it was much better to have him laughing than angry. "Well," Decker said after a moment, "I don't see any reason we shouldn't go ahead and do that profile. Maybe we can still get the last laugh on Hank Asher. You'll get the coverage. And he won't be able to say I didn't bring back the story."

"I like the way you think, Mr. Hawthorne. You'd make a fine politician," Hansen said in all sincerity.

Decker assumed it was a compliment.

❏

Christopher Goodman stayed close to the guide as she took the UN tour group through two of the three council chambers—first the Economic and Social Council (ECOSOC), and then the Security Council Chamber. From there, they went to the Hall of the General Assembly. As they were leaving the General Assembly, Christopher went to look over the balcony at the visitor's lobby four floors below them. Midway between floors hung a replica of the Russian *Sputnik,* the first artificial satellite.

At that moment a group of men and women approached the rear entrance to the Hall of the General Assembly, led by a man in his early seventies. Each member of the group was politely but intently jockeying for position, staying far enough back to be respectful but close enough to hear what the man was saying and hoping to be the next to ask him a question. From their clothing it was obvious they represented many different cultures and nationalities.

"I consider," the man was saying, "Secretary-General U Thant to have been not only my political mentor but my spiritual mentor as well. It was while I was serving him as assistant secretary-general that I first learned—" The man stopped suddenly and turned sharply to examine the profile of the boy he had noticed out of the corner of his eye.

"What is it, Mr. Assistant Secretary?" someone asked, but for the moment he seemed unable to respond as he stared at the boy.

Christopher turned and saw that his tour group had moved on and was preparing to board an elevator. In his rush to rejoin the group he didn't even seem to notice the attention of the old man or the others in the entourage as he scrambled directly through their midst, coming within scant inches of the old man and then dashing away to reach his tour group before the elevator's doors closed.

"That boy!" the man said finally, as Christopher began to weave his way through a group of Japanese businessmen that stood between him and the elevator. "It's him. I know it is." Trying to recover from the apparent shock while there was still a chance to act, he yelled, "Stop him! Someone stop that boy!" But no one moved except to look around to see what was happening. The former UN assistant secretary-general had no time to explain or to wait for the others to get their bearings. He pushed his attendants aside and ran after the boy himself. He made a remarkable effort for a man his age, but there was no real contest; his momentary hesitation had cost him his chance. Christopher was on the elevator and the doors closed behind him.

There had only been an instant of indecision, a moment's hesitation, but it was enough to make all the difference. Christopher was gone. "No! It's not fair," the man said, without explanation. He took no notice as the others rejoined him. They stared at him and at each other in confusion, hoping to find some hint of meaning to the strange episode.

"No!" he said again. "It wasn't supposed to be like this. It's not fair! I didn't even get to talk to him." His voice was now barely audible. No one had any idea of the significance of what had just taken place or what the old man was saying, and he seemed to have no interest in letting them in on it. Then a thought occurred to him. "Alice," he said. "I must find Alice."

❑

After the tour, Christopher looked for Decker but was met instead by a young aide sent by Ambassador Hansen to retrieve him. When they arrived at Hansen's office, Decker was just preparing to leave. "Well, Christopher," Jon Hansen asked, "how was your tour?"

Christopher was about to answer when a thin bald man with an auburn-red mustache and a deadly serious expression rushed through the open door into Hansen's office. Every eye in the outer office was on the man; every face took on a uniform look of dread. It seemed they all recognized him, and though no one tried to stop him, it was clear there was something to be feared about this man's arrival.

"Jon, they've done it," the man said in a thick German accent. "I just talked to Fahd, and he confirmed that Syria, Jordan, Iraq, and Libya have launched a united attack against Israel."

"Blast!" said Hansen. "When did it happen?"

"Only moments before Fahd called. The Syrians have attacked from the north, along their mutual border with Israel and through Lebanon. Jordanian and Iraqi forces have launched a joint attack from the east. Syria, Libya, and Iraq have launched coordinated air strikes against Israeli airfields. There's no word yet on damage or whether the Israelis were able to get their planes off the ground."

"Blast!" Hansen said again.

Decker and Christopher had backed away to keep from interfering with what was going on, but both listened intently to the conversation, and apparently no one cared. It would all be on the news soon anyway.

As Hansen and the other man talked, they were interrupted by the tall blond woman. "Father," she said, "Ambassador Rogers is on the phone and says he must speak with you immediately." Her manner was calm and typical of her high upbringing, but Decker could sense the concern in her voice—that, plus the fact that she had called him Father rather than Mr. Ambassador.

Decker had no idea who Ambassador Rogers was, but it seemed both Hansen and the German were very anxious to talk with him. "Hello, Frank," Hansen said. "This is Jon. Ambassador Reichman is here with me. I understand it's hit the fan over there. What can you tell us about the situation?" Hansen paused to listen but the look on his face said that he wasn't prepared for Rogers' answer.

"Tel Aviv! In the city?" Hansen said into the receiver in dismay. "Are you sure it's not just the military bases around there?"

Decker's ears perked up and he listened with new interest.

Hansen paused again and then put his hand over the phone and spoke to Reichman. "They're shelling civilian areas of Tel Aviv. Rogers says scores of bombs have already fallen."

Up until now, Decker had been satisfied just to listen to the ambassadors' conversation, but now he had a personal stake in what was happening. He too broke with formality and came right up to the two men. Hansen didn't seem to even notice the breach of protocol, but continued to listen to Ambassador Rogers on the phone.

"Frank, are you all right?" Hansen asked with some concern. "Is the embassy in any danger?" Rogers' answer seemed to reassure Hansen about the immediate safety of the embassy staff.

"Okay, Frank," he said after another pause. "Hold on, I'll do it right now. Jackie!" Hansen said, directing his eyes to his daughter. "Get the Syrian ambassador, the Russian ambassador, and the Iraqi ambassador on the phone right away, and in that order!"

The momentary break in the phone conversation allowed Hansen's glance to pass to Decker, who took advantage of the opportunity. "Tom Donafin is still in the hospital over there!"

Hansen paused for a brief fraction of a second, his eyes intently fixed on Decker's. The look on his face was of sincere concern but he did not answer. He had greater, more immediate, concerns and responsibilities. He spoke back into the phone. "Frank, I'll apply every ounce of pressure I can on this end to get them to stop bombing civilian targets, but I don't know what good it will do.

It would help if you can give me a few specifics on what parts of the city are being hit and how much damage has been done." He grabbed a pen and paper from his desk and began taking notes, every few seconds letting out an "Uh-huh."

Decker realized the comparative triviality of his plea and stepped into the background.

"I have the Syrian ambassador's office on the phone, Mr. Ambassador," Hansen's daughter said, this time remembering to use the proper title. "He'll pick up as soon as you're on the phone."

Hansen was still writing and listening, while looking up at his daughter. "Frank, I've got Ambassador Murabi on the other phone. I'll talk to him first and then make the other calls. If I don't call you back within fifteen minutes, then you call me."

Hansen was just about to hang up when he remembered something and put the phone back to his ear. "Frank," he said loudly into the mouthpiece, hoping to catch Ambassador Rogers before he hung up. There was a brief anxious silence and then he continued. "Frank, one other thing. It's a personal favor. You recall those two Yanks I brought back from Lebanon? Well, one of them is here with me in the office and he says that the other is still in the hospital there in Tel Aviv." Hansen listened. Decker listened. "Yes, that's right." Ambassador Hansen looked at Decker, obviously needing details.

"The Tel-Hashomer Hospital in Tel Aviv," Decker responded.

"Tel Hashomer," Hansen repeated. "His name is Tom Donafin. How much longer is he supposed to be there?" he asked, looking over at Decker.

"He's supposed to get out any day. They were just keeping him for observation after his final surgery last week," Decker answered.

"Frank," Hansen said back into the phone, "apparently he can leave anytime. If you could have someone check up on him, and if he's fit to travel, get him on a plane out of there."

Hansen hung up the phone and acknowledged Decker's look of appreciation. "Rogers is a good man. He'll do what he can." Decker didn't have a chance to reply before Hansen continued.

"Right now though," he said as he poised his finger above the blinking light on the phone, "I'm afraid I have to ask you to leave." Decker began to move toward the door. "Leave your number with Jackie and we'll call you if we hear anything about Tom."

❑

Robert Milner, former assistant secretary-general of the United Nations, came through the door of the Lucius Trust with the energy of a man half his age. "I must speak to Alice," he hurriedly told the receptionist. "Where is she?" He didn't wait for an answer, but moved quickly around the young woman's desk toward Alice Bernley's office.

"I'm sorry, Mr. Secretary, Ms. Bernley isn't in," the receptionist said, but Milner's momentum carried him the rest of the way to Bernley's office door.

"Where is she? I must speak with her immediately!" he said, as he moved crisply through a 180-degree turn back toward the receptionist.

"She didn't say. But I expect her back any minute."

Milner's energy seemed to lose direction as he began aimlessly, anxiously to pace the floor of the Trust's front office. The receptionist offered Milner a cup of herbal tea, which he accepted but didn't drink.

Twenty minutes passed before Milner saw the red-haired Alice Bernley returning to her office from across the UN Plaza. She was walking quickly, excitedly, but not fast enough to satisfy Milner, who ran to meet her. As she saw him coming toward her, she quickened her pace. Almost in unison they called out the other's first name.

"Alice!"

"Bob!"

Then in unison: "I've seen him!"

"Where? When?" she asked, hurriedly. She had been running and was trying to catch her breath.

"In the UN, not more than half an hour ago! He passed within inches of me. I could have reached out and touched him! But, quickly, where did *you* see him?"

"Only moments ago, on Second Street, in front of One Dag Hammarskjöld. He was with a man, getting into a cab. I tried to . . ." Alice Bernley dropped the rest of her sentence as she watched the smile on Milner's face grow broad with the excitement of a promise fulfilled. Only then did she come to fully appreciate the significance of this moment. For a minute they just looked at each other.

"We've seen him," she said, finally.

"We have seen him," he confirmed. "Just as Master Djwlij Kajm promised!"

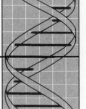

Why Hast Thou Forsaken Me?

12

Tel Aviv, Israel

TOM DONAFIN SAT ON THE EDGE of his bed in Tel Aviv's Tel-Hashomer Hospital, adjusting the strap on the new camera Hank Asher had sent him as a get-well present. Outside Tom's window, a performance of major proportion in the night sky was made surreal by the glow of fires from the ground. The sparkle of anti-aircraft artillery painted narrow stripes across the sky as now and then the bright flash of an explosion added terrifying color to the canvas. Tom had captured it all, beginning only moments after the first shots were fired. He had even photographed a dog-fight between a squadron of Libyan MiG-25s and Israeli F-15 Eagles.

Tom walked back to the open window and scanned the horizon for action. Like most of the other lights in the city, those in the hospital had been extinguished to avoid drawing the attention of enemy pilots—a condition that, coincidentally, also allowed for better night photography. Behind him Tom heard a knock on his hospital room door and turned quickly, a little startled.

As Tom turned in the darkened room, the person at the open door suddenly found himself with a barrel pointed directly at him. Instinctively he ducked, but even as he did, he realized that the sinister barrel that seemed at first to be some type of small bazooka or shoulder-held anti-tank weapon was in fact, only the telephoto lens of the American's camera.

"I'm terribly sorry!" Tom said, lowering the camera as he hurried to offer his hand to help his unexpected visitor up from the floor. "Are you all right?"

"I'm fine," the man muttered in a British accent through his embarrassment while brushing himself off. "Are you Donafin?"

"Yeah, I'm Tom Donafin," Tom responded, offering his hand again, this time in greeting. "Who are you?"

"I'm Polucki from the British Embassy," he said formally. "On behalf of Ambassadors Rogers and Hansen I'm here to offer you the assistance of His Majesty's government in expediting your evacuation from the State of Israel. Please accept my apologies for not notifying you earlier. We attempted to alert you to the situation but the telephone lines are down. At the direction of Ambassador Rogers, I've taken the liberty of inquiring of your doctor regarding your fitness for travel. He entirely agrees that, under the present circumstances, your full recovery would be facilitated by your immediate departure from the area of present hostilities. Besides," he added less formally, "they'll be needing the bed for the wounded."

"Where exactly do you plan to take me?" Tom asked.

"My instructions are to drive you to the British Embassy where you will be provided for until suitable arrangements can be made for your departure on the next U.K., U.S., or UN flight or vessel. If you prefer, I am to deliver you to the U.S. Embassy, where similar arrangements will be made."

Tom had been anxious to get out of the hospital, so he eagerly accepted Ambassador Roger's offer. In ten minutes they were on their way out the front door. There were no lights in Tel Aviv that night except the fires of burning buildings, which reflected against the smoke-filled sky and shrouded the city with an eerie glow.

"Polucki," Tom said, as his young British escort slowly drove the Mercedes through the abandoned streets, turning his lights on only when absolutely necessary and only for a few seconds at a time. "What's your first name?"

"Nigel, sir," Połucki replied.

"Połucki is a Polish name, isn't it?" Tom asked.

"Yes, sir. My grandparents escaped to Britain when Germany invaded at the beginning of the Second World War. They were part of the Polish government-in-exile, which the British officially recognized as the true government of Poland."

At that moment the air around them began to rumble and convulse, finally culminating in the sound of an explosion, followed almost immediately by the screaming whine of a disabled Israeli jet as it careened in a tight spiral toward the ground. From inside the car it was impossible to determine what the sound was, but from the unearthly noise that shook the ground around them, it sounded like the gates of hell were opening.

The pilot was already dead as the jet slammed headlong into the side of a six-story office building just two blocks away from where Połucki had brought the car to a screeching halt. His foot was planted firmly on the brake, and his fingers were locked around the steering wheel, but it did little to steady his shaking hands.

Tom was shaking too, but he grabbed his camera and jumped out of the car to get a shot of the destruction. "Wait here," he told his young escort. Nigel didn't argue—he needed a few minutes to steady his nerves before he would feel ready to drive again. Tom had gone only about thirty yards when again he heard the roar of jet engines. To his left, the horizon was filled with the wingspan of an oncoming Israeli F-35.

Flying just above the rooftops, the plane's engine swallowed up huge gulps of air as it passed directly over Tom's head, followed a moment later by a second jet, a Libyan MiG-31, in hot pursuit. The far more maneuverable F-35 banked sharply to the right but, amazingly, the Libyan followed. The Israeli went left, but the Libyan was right behind him. Then, as Tom recorded the images of the duel on his digital camera, the Israeli made what Tom thought was a fatal mistake: he started to climb. Tom knew the F-35 could never match the MiG-31 in climbing speed. The Libyan closed on his target. As the two planes streaked skyward, the MiG released an AA-6 Acrid air-to-air missile.

The Acrid closed in for the kill and Tom readied his camera to capture the impact. At what seemed the last possible second, the F-35 rolled into a dive. It was a good maneuver, but it had come an instant too late. The heat-seeking missile had caught his scent and turned with him. Downward the Israeli sped, racing for his life against the single-minded Acrid. Soon the pilot would have to pull up, and when he did the missile would easily overtake him.

Closer and closer he came to the ground, maintaining his course as long as possible in order to build speed. A few seconds more and it would be too late to pull up; the F-35 would crash into the earth, followed by the unrelenting Acrid.

The flyer made a valiant attempt, but as he passed the point at which Tom thought he must pull up, it seemed all had been in vain. Tom prepared to record the crash as, finally, the pilot raised the plane's nose. *It's too late*, Tom thought, but to his amazement the pilot raised the machine in a tight arch that missed the tops of buildings by less than fifty yards. The plane shook violently at the demanding effort but the pilot held its course, streaking directly overhead. The missile began to follow but was unable to fully make the radical course adjustment.

As Tom searched the sky for the trailing missile it suddenly came into full view. It was headed directly toward them. The missile pierced the metal roof of Nigel's Mercedes and exploded in a sun-bright flash, killing Nigel instantly as his body disintegrated into minute particles and joined the wash of other charred projectiles flying in all directions at cyclone speed. Before Tom could even blink, small shards of steel and glass cut painful, bloody paths deep into his body and face, followed an instant later by the car's hood, which knocked him violently to the street.

Derwood, Maryland

Decker sat at the computer in his study, typing up the profile piece on Ambassador Hansen. It was early morning, a few minutes before six. He would e-mail the article to *NewsWorld* later in the day, but there was no rush. The real news was the war in the Middle East. Hansen's profile would probably make for an interesting sidebar story to the war. Decker's angle was to look at Hansen as the man who had almost stopped the war. It was an exaggeration, but he would tone it down in the body of the story.

In Louisa's old room, Decker could hear Christopher's alarm clock ringing. He was starting school in a few days and he wanted to readjust to early mornings. By the time Christopher was dressed, Decker had breakfast on the table.

"Good morning, sleepyhead," Decker said when Christopher came into the kitchen. "I fixed your favorite: waffles with plenty of bacon and scalding hot syrup!"

Christopher gave Decker a knowing smile and responded, "Uh, Mr. Hawthorne, as I recall, that's *your* favorite breakfast. Remember?"

Decker put his hand over his mouth and gasped in mock surprise. "Why, so it is!" he said, continuing the act. "Well, now isn't that a wonderful coincidence!"

He laughed at his own joke and reached for the remote control to turn on the kitchen TV set. It was six-thirty and the news was just starting. "Our top story," the news anchor said, "is the war in the Middle East. For two reports we go to Peter Fantham in Tel Aviv and James Worschal at the State Department. Peter?"

"Thanks, John. Today is the Sabbath in Israel, a day of rest, but few are resting. Last night, just after dusk, as the Sabbath began, Syrian, Libyan, and Iraqi jets penetrated Israeli air space, headed for dozens of strategic targets. At the same time, Syrian ground forces crossed into Israel from Syria and Lebanon, supported by additional ground forces from Jordan. Throughout the night and into the late morning, widespread fighting has continued on several fronts, with heavy casualties on both sides.

"Behind me are the still smoldering remains of a Russian-made Libyan MiG-25, one of the most modern planes in the Arab arsenal, shot down last night in a dogfight over Tel Aviv by an Israeli F-15 Eagle. But sources tell CNN that while there may have been far more Libyan and Iraqi MiGs than Israeli aircraft shot down in last night's fighting, the real story of the first day of this war was not in the air, but on the ground.

"CNN has learned that most of the Israeli Air Force never even got in the air. According to one source, dozens of Israeli fighters and bombers were destroyed and had to be bulldozed off runways to allow undamaged planes to take off. The Israeli military has refused comment and has ignored requests to allow our camera crew onto any of their bases, but unofficial estimates of losses range as high as 60 percent of the entire Israeli Air Force. If these figures are correct, Israel may be in a struggle for its very existence."

The scene switched to another reporter standing in a large hall with flags of various nations behind him. The caption identified the man as James Worschal and the place as the U.S. State Department. "This is the fourth time Israel has been in an actual war with her Arab neighbors," the reporter began. "Each time before, she has emerged the victor against far superior numbers. But this time the odds seem to have changed dramatically in favor of her Arab neighbors.

"In the past, Israel has depended on four basic strategic advantages: superior intelligence capabilities, more highly trained and motivated soldiers and officers, a world-class air force, and distrust and disorganization among Arab allies at the command level. But this morning three of those four strategic advantages seem to have been severely damaged or lost altogether.

"The successful attack not only decimated the machinery of the Israeli Air Force, as Peter Fantham just reported from Tel Aviv, it has also shown that the perennial problem of cooperation between Arab states may have come to an end. Military experts tell CNN that last night's unified attack was nearly flawless. The level of coordination between the Syrians, Libyans, Iraqis, and Jordanians was a classic display of synchronized modern warfare. In part, at least, the Arab participants can thank the United States for that. U.S. military sources all seem to agree that the experience gained by Syria while working with the U.S. during Operation Desert Storm and subsequent operations played a large role in the success of this attack.

"Finally, John, the key to the success of last night's attack was surprise. The Arabs successfully launched a massive three-pronged attack in total secrecy. Israel's intelligence agency, the

Mossad, has a reputation second to none in the world, but last night they appear to have been asleep on the job. John."

The scene switched to a split screen of the news desk in Atlanta and the reporter at the State Department. "Jim, what about Israel's strategic defense that we've heard so much about? Isn't that a factor?"

"No, John. Although, as you say, Israel is believed to have a highly developed strategic defense—which unofficial estimates say may be more advanced than the U.S. program—this highly touted system is not considered to be a factor in the present conflict. The reason for this is that the Arab attack used entirely conventional forces, while Israel's strategic defense—as its name implies—is designed to defend against a *strategic* attack by incoming missiles ranging from SCUDS to ICBMs. Against small, low-flying aircraft and ground forces their strategic defense was useless."

"What's the prognosis there at the State Department?" the anchor asked. "Has the possibility of direct U.S. intervention been discussed? And even if the U.S. does become involved, is there much hope that Israel can recover from this?"

The reporter at the State Department adjusted his earphone. "John, no one is talking openly about direct intervention, although it is very likely that both the U.S. and Britain will respond with assistance in the form of military equipment. To answer the second question, no one is making any bets on the outcome one way or another, but there is some quiet optimism being expressed. Despite the successful first strike, it's important to remember that this is not the first time Israel has suffered a surprise attack. The first time was in the Yom Kippur War—a war the Israelis came back to win and win big. The other point of optimism is still Israel's air force. Despite the heavy losses, it's possible that the Israelis may be able to make up in quality what they are lacking in quantity. Two examples have been repeatedly brought up: the first, as I mentioned, is the Yom Kippur War, in which the Israeli Air Force shot down more than two hundred Syrian MiGs without the loss of a single Israeli aircraft. The other example, which in its own way is no less impressive, is that in

July of 1970, in their only head-to-head meeting with the Soviet Union, the Israelis shot down six Russian MiG-21s while the Soviets failed to damage even one Israeli aircraft. If the air force can duplicate that kind of record in this war, they may still have a chance of surviving."

"Thanks, Jim. Now, for more on this story we go to Tom Slade in Jerusalem." The scene switched to the Temple Mount.

"John, Arabs and Israelis have never really needed a reason to fight, but on this occasion the reason is clear. This is a holy war, a *jihad*, bringing together Arab countries that only a few years ago were bitter rivals. Surprisingly, their cause is a piece of land only about the size of two football fields.

"Behind me, construction of the Jewish Temple goes on despite the war, on land claimed by both the Jews and Muslims. For nearly twelve hundred years, until it was destroyed by Jewish extremists three years ago, this spot was occupied by the Mosque of Omar, the third most holy shrine in Islam. Before that, on this same spot, stood the ancient Jewish Temple, which was itself destroyed in 70 A.D. by the Roman army.

"Orthodox Jews, who have tried to muster support for rebuilding the Temple since before Israel became a state in 1948, attempted to portray the destruction of the Mosque as a sign from God, but for most Israelis, the Temple was a nonissue.

"For nearly three years, since the destruction of the Wailing Wall by Palestinians and the subsequent destruction of the Mosque by Israelis, the land sat cordoned off, guarded and undisturbed behind Israeli police lines. During those years, Israeli politics has moved sharply to the right in response to continuing Palestinian riots and suicide bombings. Last year Moshe Greenberg's Ichud party, campaigning on hard-line promises including expulsion of Palestinians suspected of rioting and the symbolic promise of rebuilding the Temple, won a small but solid plurality in the Knesset. Minority religious parties made the reconstruction of the Temple a key issue when they agreed to support the Ichud party in forming a coalition government.

"Today, after years of increasing tensions and violence between Palestinians and Israelis, even many nonreligious Israelis defiantly support the rebuilding of the Temple as a cultural and historic landmark. So, ironically, while fighting goes on all around it, here on the Temple Mount the construction crews continue their work."

"Tom, aren't the workmen at great risk of being caught in an Arab air strike to destroy what has already been built?" the anchorman asked.

"Actually, no, John. Remember that even without the Mosque of Omar, this mount is the third holiest location in Islam. For the present, it's considered highly unlikely that the Arabs will do anything that might damage this site. They will not bomb the construction site, but many have vowed that if they are successful in taking Jerusalem, they will tear down the Temple with their bare hands."

"Thanks, Tom," said the anchor as the scene switched back to the studio. "In New York, the United Nations Security Council will meet this afternoon in emergency session to consider what action to take in response to this outbreak of hostilities. British ambassador to the UN, Jon Hansen, has been outspoken in his response to the attack. Hansen, who recently led a UN delegation to the Middle East, called on the United Nations to respond with strict economic sanctions, and suggested that if the fighting continues, he may seek deployment of the UN's recently commissioned naval forces to blockade the combatants' ports.

"But with the world still grieving for those who died in the Disaster and awaiting the official report on its cause, there is a sense that while the words and posturing may be the same as in any other war, realities are actually very much changed. Most of the world has seen all the death it can stomach for a while."

Decker turned down the volume with the remote, "Well, Christopher, it seems our trip to New York allowed you to get a bird's-eye view of history in the making."

Christopher looked upset. "'Holy war,'" he said quoting one of the reporters. "Once again, man uses religious differences to justify his personal desires. Religion should lift men up, not be used as an excuse to kill and destroy."

Decker was unprepared for such a thoughtful response from

his young ward. It took him a moment to shift gears and meet the boy on level ground—ground much higher than his comparatively petty statement about a bird's-eye view of history. He waited to hear what else Christopher might say, but Christopher seemed satisfied to keep his thoughts to himself and go back to his breakfast. Decker decided to probe. He didn't know what he expected, but here, sitting at his breakfast table was the clone of Jesus of Nazareth—a fact that seemed strangely easy to forget—and he was talking about religion. Decker wanted to keep him on the subject a while longer.

Decker had already determined never to reveal to Christopher the secret of his origin. But like most people, Decker thought about things like the meaning of life, whether or not there is life after death, and if so, what it's like. He really wanted to hear what Christopher had to say on such subjects. As he was about to speak, though, he hesitated. Christopher was, after all, only fourteen years old. How much insight could he really have into such things? It wasn't as though Decker would actually be talking to Jesus; Professor Goodman had made it clear that Christopher had no memory of his past life. Still, Decker had to ask.

"Christopher," he began, "I don't want to pry into your private thoughts or anything, so if you don't care to talk about it, just say so. But I'm interested in what you were saying about religion." *Yeah, that was pretty good*, he thought. *Not too pushy; not too probing.* He didn't want to say anything he'd have to explain.

What Decker was about to hear would go far beyond anything he possibly could have expected. Christopher didn't answer right away. It seemed as though he was deeply considering something. At first Decker thought it was just an answer to the question, but the look on Christopher's face said it was something altogether different. Could he have understood the real reason for Decker's question?

"Mr. Hawthorne," Christopher began, looking as serious as Decker had ever seen him, "I've been meaning to talk with you about something, but the time just never seemed right."

Christopher took a long breath while Decker looked at him in anxious surprise. "I know who I am," he said. "I know that I was cloned from cells Uncle Harry found on the Shroud of Turin."

"What? How do you know?" Decker managed to sputter despite his shock.

"Well, I always had a feeling I was different from other kids. But whenever I mentioned it to Aunt Martha she would just tell me that every kid feels that way from time to time and that I shouldn't let it bother me. Aunt Martha was a wonderful lady; she could always make me feel better.

"But when I got a little older, just before my twelfth birthday, I had a terrifying nightmare of being crucified—literally! It was so real. I didn't tell Aunt Martha or Uncle Harry about it because I thought it was just a nightmare. But over the next few months I had the same dream several more times. Of course, I had heard of crucifixion, but it didn't particularly frighten me, certainly not enough to cause a recurring nightmare. The dreams were always terrifying while they were happening, but when I'd wake up, it all just seemed kind of crazy, and pretty soon I'd go back to sleep.

"Then about a year ago, I was in Uncle Harry's study. He was doing some work at his desk and I was doing my homework in his big over-stuffed chair and I fell asleep. When I did, I had the dream again and apparently I started talking in my sleep. When I woke up Uncle Harry was sitting in front of me with the strangest look on his face. He had recorded most of what I said in my sleep on his old tape recorder. He asked me what I had been dreaming and I told him. When he played the tape back for me I didn't understand a single word. It was my voice, but the words weren't English.

"Uncle Harry called someone he knew in the language department at the university, played the tape for him over the phone, and asked him if he could identify the language. The man said I had been talking in ancient Aramaic with some Hebrew thrown in.

"That's when Uncle Harry told me the whole story about the Shroud and everything. According to the man on the phone, a couple of things I said in my sleep were similar to things Jesus was supposed to have said when he was crucified.

"It was scary, but to tell you the truth, it was kinda neat too, especially when Uncle Harry told me his theory that Jesus might have been from another planet. I guess every kid likes to think he's special. He made me promise not to tell Aunt Martha or anyone else because he was afraid of what people might think or do. He was especially worried about the fundamentalist Christians who would think it was a sin to clone Jesus. He said that the only other person who knew about me was you. And, of course, you were in Lebanon."

"But how can you remember these things?"

"Uncle Harry wondered about that, too, and he had a theory that he thought might explain it. He said that each cell in the body has the blueprints for the whole body—not just things like race and sex and hair color and eye color and whether you'll be tall or short, but everything that every other cell in the body needs to know to function. That's how the single cell of a fertilized egg can reproduce to form something as complex as a human being. The information even tells the cells in a finger which finger they're in and how they're supposed to grow so that finger fits with the other fingers on the hand and is the same size as the matching finger on the other hand. He said that information is also what makes cloning possible.

"Uncle Harry's theory was that the cells may include even more information than all of that. He said that about 95 percent of human DNA is called 'junk DNA' by scientists because it's repetitive and they're still not entirely sure what it's all for. He thought maybe the junk DNA is used by cells to record any changes in other cells, so that every cell stores the information from every other cell, including the cells of the brain. He said that might also answer some questions about evolution and something he called the collective unconscious of the species, but he didn't really explain that."

Decker recognized the reference to the theories of Sigmund Freud's protégé, Carl Jung.

"Before he and Aunt Martha died, Uncle Harry was experimenting with some white mice to see if a cloned mouse would remember its way through a maze that the original mouse had been trained to go through. I don't think he ever completed his work on that.

"He thought that maybe the reason my memory is only partial is because of the cellular trauma of crucifixion, resurrection, and cloning."

"Do you remember anything after Jesus' resurrection?" Decker asked.

"No. Uncle Harry said I wouldn't remember anything about that because I was cloned from a cell left on the Shroud only seconds after the resurrection."

"Is there anything else besides the crucifixion that you remember about your life as Jesus?"

"Uncle Harry tried to spur my memory by having me read parts of Aunt Martha's Bible. It was interesting, but it didn't help me remember anything. There was one thing in the Bible that seemed really confused, though."

Decker was intrigued. "What was that, Christopher? What was confused?"

"Well, the Bible makes it seem like Jesus knew he was going to be killed, like it was all planned out, but that's not the way it was. I know this all sounds kinda strange, but in my dream, before the crucifixion, I remember being in front of Pilate and he was asking me questions. The whole time I just kept thinking that any minute I'd be rescued by angels. But something went wrong. Mr. Hawthorne, I don't think the crucifixion was supposed to happen! For hours I hung on that cross with spikes driven through my wrists and feet, trying to understand what went wrong. That's why I said, 'My God, my God, why have you forsaken me?'[30] I don't think I was supposed to die. I think God was supposed to rescue me!"[31]

Remembering this was obviously a painful experience for Christopher.

"I'm sorry," Decker said, as he put his hand on the boy's shoulder and tried to comfort him.

At that moment the phone rang.

[30]Matthew 27:46.

[31]Readers are reminded of the *Important Note from the Author* at the beginning of this book.

Decker gave Christopher's back a comforting rub and went to answer the phone. It was Ambassador Hansen. "Decker, I don't know any way to say this to make it any easier on you," Hansen said, "so I'm just going to read you the dispatch I received from Ambassador Rogers in Tel Aviv.

> As per your request, at about 5:00 Eastern time, midnight Israel time, a driver was dispatched to Tel Hashomer Hospital to bring Mr. Tom Donafin back to the British Embassy with the intention of expediting his departure from Israel. The driver and Mr. Donafin were expected back within two hours. Three hours later, that is about 3:00 A.M. Israel time, the driver had still not returned to the embassy and could not be reached by mobile phone.
>
> In keeping with standard operating procedures, a search team was dispatched to cover the route that the driver had indicated on his itinerary. The search team was unsuccessful in finding either the driver or the car, but they did verify that Mr. Donafin had checked out of the hospital and left with the driver from the embassy.
>
> The search team expanded their search to include some likely alternate routes and at about 7:30 A.M. Israel time, they located what was left of the car, which was positively identified by the license plate.

"Decker, I'm sorry," Hansen concluded. "It appears that the car took a direct hit from a stray missile or artillery shell and was completely destroyed. There were no survivors."

New York, New York

The wealth of the Bragford family was clearly evident in the solid cherry wood paneling, rich carpeting, and highly polished brass that presented former UN Assistant Secretary-General Robert Milner and Alice Bernley with perfect mirrored images of themselves and the operator who was piloting the private elevator to the penthouse office of the family's guiding force, David Bragford.

Most of Robert Milner's adult life had been spent in the presence of the wealthy and powerful. Raising large amounts of money from rich patrons for special projects at the UN came with the job of assistant secretary-general, and Milner was quite good at it. The experience had its benefits. He knew what it took to separate the rich from their money—at least small portions of it. He had become adept at getting what he wanted by alternately stroking an ego and stoking a sense of guilt for having so much while others starved.

Still, Milner held a deeply seated distrust of those with great wealth, and certainly there were few on earth who possessed such wealth as did the Bragfords. Men like David Bragford were altogether different from the garden-variety rich. While it was true the Bragford family had been very extravagant in their support of the UN—indeed, the Bragfords had been instrumental in financing the original organization of the UN—Milner had found that such extravagance is never born purely of generosity. When they gave, there was usually something they expected in return, and in Milner's experience, at the very least that meant intrusion.

It was, therefore, with some discomfort that he agreed to accompany Alice Bernley to Bragford's office. Bernley was positive, she said, that this was the right thing to do and that Bragford would help them. She had consulted her spirit guide, Tibetan Master Djwlij Kajm, and he had left no doubt that Bragford was to be consulted.

At the conclusion of their ascent to the penthouse, they were met by David Bragford's administrative assistant, who escorted them past two security posts to a mammoth office where David Bragford sat comfortably on the edge of his desk, talking on the telephone. Beside the desk, on the white carpeting, lay a full-grown black Labrador retriever who, unlike their host, seemed to take no notice of their arrival. Bragford quickly finished his conversation and joined his guests in a sitting area of the office.

"Alice, Mr. Assistant Secretary-General, welcome," Bragford said, affording Milner the honor of his previous post. "Can I get you anything? Would you like some coffee?" Bragford had his secretary bring coffee for his guests while he shared niceties with Bernley and Milner about their recent projects. The arrival of the coffee marked the end of small talk and the beginning of discussion of the business at hand.

"So," Bragford said, directing his opening to Milner, "Alice tells me you would like my help with something."

"Yes," Bernley said, taking the lead. "As you know, Master Djwlij Kajm many years ago prophesied that both Bob and I would live to see the true *Krishnamurti*, the Ruler of the New Age. Yesterday we saw him."

One would never have guessed it from the look on his face, but with each word Alice spoke, Robert Milner was dying inside of embarrassment. Why, he asked himself, had he allowed Alice to do the talking? He should have known this would happen; Alice was not one to control her emotions. This was not the correct approach for the uninitiated. Sure, it was all true. They *had* seen him, but Milner knew very well that David Bragford did not believe one word of this about Bernley's spirit guide. Bragford, after all, had never been present at a demonstration of Master Djwlij Kajm's power.

"That's great," Bragford replied to Bernley's introduction. "When can I meet him?"

Though there was absolutely no evidence of it, Milner was sure Bragford was patronizing them, but he was suffering too greatly from embarrassment to respond.

"Oh, well, that's the problem," Bernley said. "We don't know where he is. He was at the UN, but then he left with a man, possibly his father."

"His father?" Bragford asked. "Just how old is this . . . uh . . ." Bragford was trying hard not to say anything that would make his skepticism too obvious, but he could not for the life of him remember what Bernley had called this person.

Alice spared him the difficulty of finishing his sentence. "He's just a boy," she said. "I'd guess he was about, oh, what would you say, Bob?" But 'Bob' wasn't saying. It didn't matter, though. Alice was already starting to answer her own question. "Fourteen or fifteen, I'd say."

"Fourteen or fifteen?" Bragford echoed.

"Yes," Bernley said, ignoring Bragford's raised eyebrows and the skepticism in his voice. "What we need is your help finding out who he is."

To Milner's surprise, Bragford was ready with an answer. "I think I have just the right person to help you. Just a moment," he said as he reached for the phone on the coffee table. "Betty, would you ask Mr. Tarkington to join us in my office?"

Almost immediately, the door opened and a tall, muscular man entered the office. "Come in, Sam," Bragford said as he sat his cup down. Bernley and Milner rose to meet him. After the introductions Bragford got right to the point of explaining what was required, although leaving out the stranger aspects of Bernley's and Milner's interest in finding the individuals.

"Do you think you can do it?" Bragford asked.

"I believe so, sir. The security cameras at the UN record everyone entering and exiting the guest lobby. I can get the tapes. If Ms. Bernley and the assistant secretary-general can identify the man and boy from the tape, then I'll put our people to work finding out who they are. If they went anywhere in the building that required signing a registry, such as the Secretariat Building or the Delegates Dining Room, it'll make our job a lot easier."

"Great," Bragford said, satisfied with the prospects and confident of Tarkington's abilities.

"Great," echoed Bernley. "Now, once we find out who they are, there's one other thing we may need your help with."

Tel Aviv, Israel

The darkened streets were nearly silent as the tall, bearded man walked through the rubble scattered across the pockmarked asphalt. His long, purposeful strides and the soft, muffled sounds of the leather soles of his shoes gave no hint of the great weight the man bore over his shoulder. The long, brown, curled hair of his traditional Hasidic earlock was flattened against his cheek, sandwiched tightly between his face and the load he carried. For more than six miles the darkly dressed man had carried his burden, from the business district of the city down long straight streets to a cluster of apartment buildings near the shore of the Mediterranean.

Finally, the man stopped in front of a ten-story apartment building on Ramat Aviz and went to the front entrance. The glass doors, which had been destroyed in a blast the night before, had been replaced with sheets of plywood. The man knocked, and a moment later the door was cracked open and two eyes peered out at him. As recognition registered in the eyes, the door was quickly shut again and a table moved so the door could be fully opened. A rather plain woman in her mid-thirties, dressed in a blood-stained surgical gown, greeted her unexpected guest.

"Welcome, Rabbi," she said, as she led him to an area of the lobby that had been converted to a makeshift clinic. Here and there family members of some of the patients were camped out near their relatives to assist with their care.

"Not here with the others," he said, his words revealing a voice unusually rich and measured. "You must take him to your apartment."

Only now did the woman see the face of the man the rabbi carried over his shoulder. The blood that covered his face and soaked his clothes was foreboding enough to his prognosis, but his misshapen skull led her to believe that the patient was as good as dead, and perhaps would be better off if he were.

"Rabbi, I think we're wasting our time with this one," she said.

"You must see to it that we are not," he answered firmly as he turned and walked toward the stairwell. "You are a good doctor. I have full confidence in your abilities."

"But Rabbi, he's nearly dead if he's not dead already."

"He is not dead," the rabbi said as he opened the door and began to ascend the first flight of stairs, the woman following closely behind. The woman moved quickly, dipping and swerving to get around the rabbi, then placed herself in the middle of the stairs, stopping his advance. The rabbi stared insistently, his eyes telling her to let him pass.

"At least let me check his pulse!" she pleaded.

The rabbi paused as she took the man's wrist and checked his pulse. He watched her eyes, entirely certain of what she would find. To her amazement the pulse was reasonably strong. The rabbi moved past her and continued up the steps.

"Okay," she said, "so he's alive, but you can see the condition of his head. He's probably hopelessly brain damaged."

"There's nothing wrong with his brain. It's an old injury he received when he was a child." The rabbi reached the third floor and opened the stairwell door.

"Okay, okay, so maybe he'll survive." She was becoming frantic to stop him as he made his way ever closer to her apartment with his unwelcome patient. She knew her only hope was to talk him out of his plan. If he insisted, however, she knew she would have to submit; he was, after all, the rabbi. The problem was that as far as she knew, no one had ever talked the rabbi out of anything.

"But why does he have to stay in my apartment?! Why can't he stay downstairs with the others?"

The rabbi, who had now reached her apartment, turned to answer as he waited for her to unlock the door. "He is unclean," he answered in a whisper, though no one else was within earshot. "He is uncircumcised," he added in clarification. "Also, he will need your personal care."

Convinced it was futile to resist, the woman relented and opened the door. "Put him in the extra bedroom," she said as she grabbed some old sheets from the linen closet. "Is he a Gentile?" she asked, as she began spreading the sheets on the bed.

"He believes he is," he answered. "In a week or so, when he is better, I will see to his circumcision."

"Who is he?" she asked, now reluctantly reconciled to her situation.

"His name is Tom Donafin." The rabbi waited while the woman ran water into a basin and began to clean Tom's wounds. "He is the one of whom the prophecy spoke, 'He must bring death and die that the end and the beginning may come.'"

The woman stopped her work and looked back at the rabbi, stunned at what she had just been told.

"He is the last in the lineage of James, the brother of the Lord," he continued. "He is the Avenger of Blood."

13

The Color of the Horse

Derwood, Maryland

IT WAS AN EXTREMELY PLEASANT late fall day in Washington, D.C., with temperatures in the upper sixties and the sky clear and sunny. It seemed to Decker a great day to play hooky from work. On the other hand, he had not been into the office for more than three years and he figured he was about due.

Decker boarded the Metro at the Shady Grove station and noticed that the train was less crowded than usual. Several stations later, when the cars continued to be less than fully occupied, he realized the reason: the Disaster. He was aware the D.C. area had lost about 14 percent of its population—nearly 1.5 million people—but seeing the impact in microcosm on the Metro brought the figure home. The thought continued to occupy him as he exited at the DuPont Circle station and made his way to the offices of *NewsWorld* magazine.

When Decker walked into the lobby of *NewsWorld,* the receptionist insisted that he sign in and wait for an escort before going back to the working offices. Decker was not a rude person, but he was somewhat territorial, and despite having been gone for so long, to him this was his territory. He had no intention of either signing in *or* waiting for an escort. Fortunately for the receptionist, Sheryl Stanford arrived on the next elevator. "It's all right," Sheryl told the receptionist, "he works here."

Very few familiar faces greeted Decker that morning. Over the last three years, most of the people he knew had been transferred to other offices or had retired or taken other jobs; a few were victims of the Disaster.

When Sheryl caught up to Decker he was staring unhappily at the person who now occupied what had been his desk and his office. Far worse, though, was the fact that some young jerk was in what had been Tom Donafin's office. "Mr. Hawthorne," Sheryl called, preventing Decker from saying something to the new occupant that he might regret later. "Mr. Hawthorne," she repeated as she got closer, "Mr. Asher would like to see you."

Decker gave the young reporter in his old office one last dirty look and proceeded on toward Hank Asher's office. "I want my office back," he barked at Sheryl.

"This is not going to be a good day," Sheryl muttered, trying to maintain a smile.

"I want my office back," Decker repeated as soon as he walked through Asher's door.

"That's what I wanted to see you about," said Asher. "We're giving you a new office, a corner office with windows and a view."

Decker's mood changed quickly as he looked around covetously at Asher's office. He knew that Hank's description could only fit one office at *NewsWorld*, and they were sitting in it.

"Wait a second," Asher said, reading Decker's thoughts. "Not this office!"

"So where, then?" Decker asked.

"Decker, word just came down today. You're being promoted. They're putting you in charge of the New York office."

Decker thought for a second. "What if I don't want the New York office?"

"Why wouldn't you want it?"

Decker thought about his house in Derwood—the house he had told Elizabeth they would make their home. He thought about the grave in the backyard in which his family lay. "I'm just not interested," he answered.

Asher thought he understood what the problem was. After all, he'd dug the grave. "Decker if it's about your . . . uh . . . house, there's no problem. I've been authorized to offer you a very generous raise. You should be able to afford an apartment in New York and still keep your house here."

"Are you crazy?" Decker asked. "Do you have any idea how much an apartment in New York goes for?"

"It's less now than you may remember. There are a lot fewer people in New York since the Disaster. It's a buyer's market."

Decker cringed a little as he recalled what the cabby in New York had said about dead people's apartments. "Yeah, that may be so," Decker answered, "but I hate apartments."

Asher closed the door and lowered his voice. "Look, Decker, just between you and me, I've been told to offer you whatever it takes."

Decker looked at Hank to be sure he wasn't kidding. "What do you mean, 'Whatever it takes'?" he asked.

"Don't get crazy on me now, Decker."

Decker thought for a moment. "Why?" he probed.

"Why what?" Asher responded.

"Why are they being so generous?"

"They need a new head for the New York office, and I guess they think you're the man for the job."

"Look, Hank, I'm flattered but there must be more to it. *News-World* is not the type of organization to throw money around. How can they possibly offer to pay me enough to maintain two homes?"

"I don't know, Decker. It sounds a little out of character to me too, but I think you'd be crazy to look a gift horse in the mouth."

"So what else did they tell you?"

"Look, Ima Jackson just called me this morning and told me the decision had been made to give you the New York office. I asked her how much I was supposed to offer and she said 'Whatever it takes.' When I asked her to be a little more specific, she just repeated herself. She told me not to ask questions, that the decision had come down from way above her head, and that I was to see to it you accepted the position. I guess somebody on the board of directors must want you there. To tell you the truth, I was hoping you might be able to fill me in on what's going on."

"I have no idea at all," Decker shrugged.

Asher took a deep breath and shook his head. It made no sense that the board of directors should care about the promotion of a particular reporter. They almost never got involved at this level.

"When do they want a decision?" Decker asked.

"ASAP."

"I don't know. I'll get back to you."

❏

That evening Decker took Christopher out for dinner. He wanted to talk with him about his first days in his new school and to see how he'd feel about moving to New York. Christopher had been given a battery of tests at his new school because his records from California had not yet arrived.

"How do you think you did?" Decker asked him.

"Okay, I guess. The tests were pretty easy."

Decker had always thought of Christopher as bright; he decided to pursue it a little. "Christopher, what sort of grades do you usually get in school?"

"I've always had a 4.0," Christopher answered.

"That's good," Decker said, not really surprised. "Have any of your teachers ever suggested that you should skip a grade?"

"Yes, sir. Almost every year the subject was brought up, but Aunt Martha said I should be with kids my own age. She said it would be bad for my social growth to be put with a bunch of older kids."

"What do you think?"

"I guess she was probably right," Christopher answered. "She said that once I got to college I could go as fast as I wanted because I'd be old enough to make my own decisions."

"Your Aunt Martha must have been a remarkable woman. I wish I had gotten to know her better," Decker said. Christopher smiled. They took a few more bites of their food and Decker changed the subject. "How would you feel about us moving to New York?" he asked without explanation.

"New York?" Christopher said with unexpected enthusiasm. "Would we be near the UN?"

"Well, I don't know. I've been offered the job as head of the New York office for *NewsWorld*. The office is just a couple of miles from the UN but I don't know where we'd actually live. We'd have to shop around for an apartment."

Christopher's excitement was obvious. "You really *are* a big fan of the UN, aren't you?" Decker asked.

"Yes, sir! I bet if we moved there I could get a job as a page to one of the delegates. And did you know they have their own university?"

"I had no idea you would be so favorable to the idea."

"Oh, yeah! It'd be great!"

"Well, don't get too excited. I haven't taken the job yet."

Decker still wasn't comfortable with the circumstances of the promotion, but he did check the Internet for prices of apartments near the UN.

After Christopher went to bed Decker got out the financial records Elizabeth had kept while he was in Lebanon to determine how much he needed to ask for to be able to keep the house *and* get an apartment in New York. He had only studied the figures for a few moments when he dropped his head and began to cry. In Lebanon he had wondered so often what Elizabeth was doing. The figures provided a partial answer. Not only were they debt-free except for the mortgage, but Elizabeth had made frequent extra payments on the house, and she had put a tidy sum in their savings account. The tears he cried were not of joy but of pain as he came to realize that Elizabeth must have pinched pennies the whole time he was in Lebanon, saving for when he got home. How many things, he wondered, had she denied herself? How many times had she and the girls eaten leftovers of leftovers? How many times had they made do with less when everyone around them had all they needed? Now he was home and here was all the money, but they wouldn't be able to share it with him.

Between Elizabeth's frugality and the apartment prices he found on the Internet, Decker determined he wouldn't need to ask for as much from *NewsWorld* as he thought he might. Still, as he neared the bottom line he wondered just how much they were willing to pay him. This brought back the question of what was behind this sudden and uncharacteristic generosity. He was torn between keeping his mouth shut and taking the job, and wanting to know what was behind the offer. Was this really a gift horse, as Hank Asher had suggested, or was it a Trojan horse? As he continued to think about it, he became more and more resolved to know the answers and to know them *before* he took the job.

❑

Decker went directly to Hank Asher's office, closed the door behind him, and gave Asher a slip of paper with a figure written on it.

"What's this," Asher asked, after he looked at it.

"That's how much I want to take the job in New York," Decker answered without flinching.

"Are you crazy?! That's twice what I make! There's no way they're going to pay you that much!"

"You're probably right," Decker answered, "But let's see."

Asher thought it was a dumb idea, but he placed the call anyway. No sooner had he told his boss, Ima Jackson, how much Decker wanted than she authorized it. Asher put his hand over the phone and looked at Decker dumbfounded. "She says yes," he mouthed silently.

This wasn't the way Decker planned it at all. He had assumed that Jackson would refuse and then he'd offer to negotiate. Then, once he was talking with her face-to-face, he could get some answers. "Ask her why," Decker directed in a whisper.

Now Hank's pride was on the line. He didn't particularly appreciate that *NewsWorld* was willing to pay Decker so much more than he was making. He asked, but Jackson directed him to simply comply with her instructions. Asher gritted his teeth and took his orders like a good executive, but this would not be the end of it. Whatever happened with Decker, Asher planned to demand a substantial increase in his own pay in the very near future.

"So, what are you going to do?" Asher demanded, after he hung up the phone. He was angry about the whole situation and didn't want to be pushed any further.

"Call her back and tell her I'm not interested. Tell her that if they want me that badly they're going to have to tell me why. Tell her I'm in no mood for games and either I get some straight answers or else leave me where I am and give me my office back! Tell her she can reach me at home. I'm taking the day off."

❏

When Decker arrived at his house the phone was ringing. He recognized the caller's voice immediately as Ambassador Hansen's daughter, Jackie.

"Mr. Hawthorne," she said, "Ambassador Hansen asked me to call you. He was very impressed with your article about him in this week's issue of *NewsWorld* and he wishes to thank you for all the nice things you said about him."

"Well, please relay my regards back to the ambassador. Tell him I appreciate his graciousness, especially considering the circumstances of the interview."

"Thank you, I will," she answered. "Ambassador Hansen would also like to know if you would be at all interested in discussing the possibility of accepting a position as his press secretary and chief speech writer. The position has just come open and the ambassador feels that you would be an excellent choice to fill it."

Decker was surprised by the offer. Was this opportunity knocking? Perhaps another case of being in the right place at the right time? He was uncomfortable with what was going on at *NewsWorld*. If he took the job as head of the New York office, he would have to live with Asher's ire about his higher salary. But should he really turn down that much money? On the other hand, it made sense to look at another offer. Then he remembered the expression on Christopher's face when he talked about the UN. Decker hadn't quite realized it yet, but since the deaths of Elizabeth and the girls, Christopher was quickly becoming his family.

"Sure," he said. "I'd be interested. I'd be glad to consider it."

"Good," she responded. "When could you come to New York to discuss it further?"

"I can be there tomorrow afternoon, if that's okay with Ambassador Hansen."

"That would be fine. We'll arrange for your airline ticket and I'll have someone call you back within the hour to confirm the time."

Decker hung up the phone and immediately went to work updating his résumé.

❑

In New York Jackie Hansen sat at her father's desk with the door closed. In a moment she would instruct her secretary to make the arrangements for Decker's flight. Right now she needed privacy to make another call. "This is Jackie Hansen," she said into the receiver. "I need to speak to the director."

"Yes?" she heard after a moment.

"He said yes," Jackie Hansen said without explanation. "He'll be here tomorrow for the interview."

"Excellent! You've done very well," Alice Bernley said.

❑

Alice Bernley hung up the phone and smiled at Robert Milner. The look on her face left no doubt that the plan had been successful.

"I guess we can tell Bragford to call off the people at *NewsWorld*," Milner said. "I think this is a better arrangement anyway. We'll be in a much better position to direct the boy's future with Mr. Hawthorne working for Ambassador Hansen than if he had accepted the job at the magazine."

"Assuming Jackie is able to ensure that her father offers him the job," Bernley said, "how can we be sure Mr. Hawthorne will accept the offer?"

"When *NewsWorld* abruptly withdraws its offer of a promotion and a raise, Hawthorne will have to consider it a professional insult. He'll be looking for some way to preserve his honor. Ambassador Hansen's offer will provide him that opportunity," Milner answered.

Dark Awakening

14

A SMALL ELECTRIC SPACE HEATER blew a warm breeze across Tom Donafin's face as sounds began to fill his ears with the reality that surrounded him. Still more asleep than awake, his mind wandered aimlessly between dream and consciousness. Finally he committed himself to wakefulness and opened his eyes, but was suddenly struck with intense pain as tiny bits of glass scraped across the inside of his eyelids. Instantly his eyes closed again as he winced and moaned and rolled in pain.

He lay still, trying to relax his eyes as he sorted through his memories. The last thing he recalled was the missile that killed Nigel and destroyed the car. He did not recall being knocked unconscious, nor did he have any idea where he was now. He listened for voices or some distinguishable sound but heard none.

"Hello," he said finally to anyone who might be nearby.

No one answered.

"Hello," he called out louder.

"So, you're awake," a man's voice answered in a not altogether friendly tone.

"Where am I?" Tom asked.

"You're in the apartment of Dr. Rhoda Felsberg on Ramat Aviz in occupied Tel Aviv." The man spoke quickly and his voice gave the clear impression that Tom was an unwelcome guest.

"How did I get here?"

"You were brought here nearly a month ago by my sister's rabbi, who found you on the street."

"A month ago?" Tom gasped. "Have I been unconscious the whole time?"

"Pretty much."

"What do you mean, 'occupied' Tel Aviv?"

"Just that," the man responded, not offering any more information.

"Occupied by whom?" Tom probed, becoming a little exasperated at the man's apparent unwillingness to provide substantive answers.

"The Russians," the man answered.

Tom didn't know whether to take the man seriously. He began to wonder if he had awakened in a psychiatric ward and the man he was talking to was a patient.

"You said I was brought here by your sister's rabbi. Is your sister the Dr. Felsberg you mentioned?"

"You got it," he answered.

"And she has been taking care of me?"

"Yep."

Tom desperately wanted to know what was going on and what had happened to him, but he wanted to talk to someone who would give him reliable, complete answers. "Well, can I talk to her?" he urged.

For a moment there was silence. "Yeah, I guess so."

Tom heard the man dial the telephone.

"Hey, Rhoda," the man said. "He's awake and he wants to talk to you."

"I'll be right there!" Tom heard the woman answer.

A moment later Dr. Rhoda Felsberg arrived, went directly to Tom's side, and began to check his vital signs. "Is he cognizant?" she asked, a little out of breath from running up the three flights of stairs from her office on the first floor. Like her brother, she had a New Jersey accent.

"Hi, there," Tom said with a half grin in answer to her question.

"Oh," she said, a little surprised. "How do you feel?"

"Well, I have a terrible headache and when I opened my eyes it felt like somebody was dragging razor blades over them."

"I thought I got all the glass out," Rhoda Felsberg said, followed by an indiscriminate sound that Tom interpreted as a negative assessment of his condition. "When you opened your eyes, did you see anything?"

The full meaning of her question was apparent at once. "I don't think so," he said haltingly. "Am I . . . blind?"

"We can't say yet," she answered. Her voice had no emotion but seemed somehow reassuring. "I need you to open them again slowly and let me look inside. Then we'll go from there."

Tom felt her sit down on the bed beside him. Wincing, he opened his eyes, hoping desperately to see something. He didn't. He felt Dr. Felsberg's hands on his face as she examined him. They were strong but soft, and despite all else that was going on, he noticed the faint sweet fragrance of her perfume as she leaned down close to him and peered into his eyes with her ophthalmoscope.

"Can you see the light in my hand?"

"I can see a light spot."

"Good, at least that's a start," she said. "Your pupils both seem to be working properly. But I'm afraid there must still be a few tiny particles of glass." Tom felt her put some eyedrops in his eyes, which brought quick relief from the pain. "I'm going to bandage your eyes to keep them closed until we can get you to an ophthalmologist."

"Will I be able to see again?"

"It's too soon to say for sure," she answered as she helped him to a sitting position and began to bandage his eyes. "You should be glad just to be alive. I removed several pieces of glass from each eye when you were first brought here. You're actually very fortunate. If the glass had gone much deeper, the vitreous fluid would have escaped and your eyeballs would have simply collapsed."

Tom had no idea what vitreous fluid was, but the thought of his eyeballs collapsing was quite alarming and at least in this regard he did indeed consider himself fortunate.

"The scarring to your corneas is quite extensive," she continued. "In addition, both of your retinas have been burned. Was there a bright flash when you were injured?"

"Yeah, I think so," he said, thinking back to the last thing he remembered.

"The burns on your retinas are our biggest worry. The corneas can be replaced with transplants but there's no way to repair a damaged retina. I may be able to remove the remaining glass myself, but I'd feel better if we had a qualified ophthalmologist do it."

"How soon can that be done?"

"Well, it could take a while." The tone of her voice said a while might be a very long time indeed.

"Why? What's going on here, anyway? Will you please tell me why I'm here instead of in a hospital?" Tom was trying not to panic, but it wasn't easy. He had just been told in gruesome detail that he may never see again.

"Please, Mr. Donafin. We're friends. We want to help you, but you've got to realize a lot has changed since your accident. Israel is an occupied country. If you'll be patient I'll explain everything. But first you need to try to eat something."

Only then did Tom notice he was starving, so he didn't object.

❏

In the kitchen, Rhoda Felsberg and her brother Joel spoke in hushed tones.

"So, now that he's awake, are you finally going to move him in with your other patients?" Joel Felsberg asked.

"No," Rhoda answered. "I'm not."

"Why not?"

"Because Rabbi Cohen said he should stay here."

"There's no reason for him to insist that you keep this man in your personal care."

"He's the rabbi," Rhoda answered, as though no further justification were necessary.

"Yeah, well he may look like Hasidim, with his earlocks and all dressed in black, but I've heard that the other Hasidic rabbis won't have anything to do with him." Right now Rhoda was glad Joel wasn't more aware of religious matters; if he had been he would have known that Cohen's standing with the other rabbis was actually far worse than he imagined. It had not always been this way. At one time Cohen had been thought by many to be the heir apparent to the Lubavitcher Rebbe: Rabbi Menachem Mendel Schneerson, considered the most politically powerful rabbi in the world. Now, however, it was not only the Hasidic rabbis who wouldn't have anything to do with him; *none* of the other rabbis, not even the most liberal ones, would even mention his name without spitting to show their disgust.

"Oh, and since when did you start to care what the rabbis think?" Rhoda asked her brother, not letting on.

"The point is, he's a kook," Joel answered.

"Come eat," she said, not wanting to argue the matter.

"Rhoda!" Joel said, trying to get her back on the subject as she took the pot of soup and some bowls and headed back to Tom.

"Come eat," she said again more sternly, then added, "We'll talk about it later," though she had no intention of allowing the subject to reemerge.

❏

Rhoda put a spoon into Tom's hand and set his soup on a tray in front of him. Tom found it difficult to eat without being able to see, and his first few bites were a bit messy. Rhoda gave him a napkin but as he began to wipe his mouth, he felt the scars that covered his face from the explosion. Silently, he traced the scars with his fingers.

"How bad am I?" he asked.

"You had lacerations over most of the front of your body. Most of the scars will disappear eventually," Rhoda answered. "Some minor plastic surgery may be needed later for some of the scars on your face. We'll just have to wait and see."

Tom reached down and felt his arms, shoulders, and chest. "Well, I guess I was never really that much to look at anyway," he said, trying to hide his pain in humor. He paused. "So, how about that explanation? What am I doing here and when can I see an ophthalmologist?"

"The night after the war began," Rhoda explained, "you were brought here by Rabbi Saul Cohen, who found you buried under rubble about five or six miles from here. Since then you have been either unconscious or disoriented and delirious."

Tom shook his head. "I don't remember anything since the explosion," he said.

"Well, unfortunately, the war didn't go so well," she continued. "Israel fought hard but it soon became apparent that the Arabs were getting the upper hand. The United States and Britain tried to help by providing emergency supplies and food. I think they could have done more, but a lot of their politicians kept saying they couldn't afford a war, especially after both countries had lost so many people just two months earlier in the Disaster. Then it was discovered that the Russians were supplying arms to the Arabs. Of course the Russians denied it, but the UN Security Council voted to set up a blockade of the Arab ports."

"You're kidding! How on earth did they ever get the vote past the Russian delegate on the Security Council?" Tom asked.

"That's the really strange thing. The Russian delegate didn't show up for the vote," Rhoda answered.

"That's crazy," Tom blurted. "The Russians made that mistake in 1950 when they boycotted the UN because of its exclusion of Red China. That's what allowed the Security Council action against their allies in Korea. The Russians would never let that happen a second time."

"Well, I don't understand it, but they did," Rhoda said.

"I don't know what the big mystery is," Joel said sarcastically. "I think they had the whole thing planned ahead of time."

"What do you mean?" asked Tom.

"Joel, just let me tell the story," Rhoda said. "You can give us your theories later."

"Sure, go ahead. But he'll figure it out pretty quickly for himself if he's got half a brain."

"Where was I? You made me forget," Rhoda chided her brother.

"The UN voted for a blockade," Joel reminded her.

"Okay, so there were a lot of charges back and forth but finally the Russians agreed not to provide any more arms to the Arabs, and the UN agreed not to impose the blockade. A few days later things seemed to be changing in Israel's favor. We had taken back a lot of land that we lost earlier and what was left of our air force was clobbering the Arab air and ground forces.

"Then the Israeli Intelligence—the Mossad—found out that because the Libyans couldn't get additional conventional weapons from the Russians, they were planning to launch a chemical attack. To prevent that, the Israeli Air Force launched a preemptive strike against the Libyan chemical weapons storage facilities. Unfortunately, most of the air strike didn't get through because the Libyans anticipated the attack.

"When it became apparent there was no other way for Israel to stop the chemical attack, Prime Minister Greenberg sent a message to the Libyans saying that if Israel was attacked with chemical weapons, we would immediately respond with a massive nuclear attack on Libya."

"So Israel finally admitted it has nukes?" Tom asked.

"The exact wording of the message wasn't released to the press, but he apparently made it very clear that's what he meant," Joel answered.

"Anyway," Rhoda continued, "despite their agreement with the UN, the Russians agreed to sell the Arabs additional conventional weapons, claiming it was the only way to prevent a chemical/nuclear exchange."

"Yeah," Joel interjected. "It was a perfect excuse for the Russians to do exactly what they wanted in the first place."

Tom still didn't understand what Joel was driving at, but for now he let it pass. Rhoda continued. "So the Mossad tracked the Russian ships they thought were going to deliver the arms to Libya, and just before they entered Libyan waters, our air force attacked. They sank four cargo ships and a bunch of escort vessels, but it turned out the whole thing was a decoy. While most of the Israeli Air Force was busy in the Mediterranean and the army was busy with the Arabs on our borders, advance teams of

Russian commandos landed north of Tel Aviv and took over an airstrip. The whole thing must have been planned perfectly because no sooner had they taken the airstrip than Russian troops and equipment began landing."

"Wait a second," Tom said. "You mean Joel was telling the truth about Tel Aviv being occupied by the Russians?"

"Not just Tel Aviv," Joel answered. "It's the whole country."

"Man, what a world to wake up to!"

"Yeah, seems that some of the Russians weren't happy with the way things have worked out since the collapse of the Soviet Union," Joel said. "Some of them still want to rule the world. Of course, they told the UN they were simply responding to our 'unprovoked' attack on their naval vessels and that they were really just a peace-keeping force. They said their only intention in occupying Israel was to prevent a chemical/nuclear war. And just to make it seem more legitimate they brought a few troops from Ethiopia, Somalia, and a few other countries so they could say it was an 'international' peacekeeping force. Only now they refuse to leave."

❑

The next morning Tom awoke to the smell of breakfast cooking and the sound of Rhoda Felsberg's voice calling his name.

"Mr. Donafin, are you awake?" It was hard for her to be sure with his eyes bandaged.

"Yes," Tom answered.

"Do you feel like having some breakfast?"

"That sounds great, thank you. But actually the first thing on my mind is finding the bathroom."

"I can bring you a bedpan, or if you feel like you're ready to walk a few steps, I'll guide you there."

Tom was already standing, though his legs felt incredibly unsure beneath him. "I think I'm ready for the real thing," he said.

"Come on then," she said and put his hand on her arm to lead him through the apartment.

"I'll take it from here," Tom said when he felt tile instead of carpet beneath his bare feet.

"Can you find your way back to your room? I need to go check the breakfast."

"Sure," Tom said. "I'll bet I can even find the kitchen."

After Tom finished, he slowly made his way to the kitchen, where Rhoda had set the table for two and finished cooking the meal.

"A little to the left," she said as he started to walk into a door-jamb.

Tom found the table and sat down. He had a very strange look on his face. "I . . . um . . ."

"Is something the matter?" Rhoda asked.

"I'm not sure," he said. "When I was in the bathroom I noticed something that didn't seem . . . uh . . . quite right. I, uh, well . . . I . . ." Tom stammered for another moment. Had he been able to see, he would have seen the look of embarrassment on Rhoda's face as she realized what he was talking about. "Never mind," he said finally.

Rhoda was glad to let the subject drop. "I have some good news," she said, quickly changing the subject. "I called an oph-thalmologist friend and he said he can see you first thing tomorrow."

"That's great!" Tom said.

"Don't get too excited yet. He only said he could examine you and try to get the rest of the glass out, not that he can get you admitted for surgery."

"Oh. Well, maybe he can at least tell me what my chances are of getting my sight back."

"Yeah, that's what I'm hoping for."

"You know," Tom added, "there's no reason I have to have the surgery done here, is there? I could go back to the States."

"Well, yes, you could," Rhoda said hesitantly. "Ben Gurion Air-port is in pretty bad shape, but I understand that the Russians are still letting a few flights out."

Tom noticed an unexpected hint of disappointment in her voice.

"Speaking of the States," Rhoda continued. "Isn't there anyone you need to call to let them know you're alive?"

Her voice said she was fishing for something she didn't want to ask outright. Tom let it pass and replied to her direct question. "I don't have any family," he said. "My parents, two brothers, and a sister all died in a car wreck when I was six. That's how I got this mangled-looking skull. I was the only one to survive."

"Sounds like you've had your share of close calls," Rhoda offered.

"Yeah. I guess so."

"Did they do surgery on you?" she asked out of professional curiosity.

Tom let out an odd chuckle. "Yeah. They waited awhile though. They figured I'd die within a few days anyway, and even if I did make it, I'd be a vegetable. I guess I'm lucky it happened so long ago, back in the days before they'd pull your feeding tube to hurry you on your way. Anyway, four days after the accident I woke up and started talking to the nurse. That convinced them I might make it," he said dryly, "so they went in and dug around and pulled out a bunch of broken pieces of skull and a few extra brains I guess I didn't need. They left me with a steel plate that has a habit of setting off metal detectors at airports."

Rhoda smiled awkwardly.

"I do have a friend I should call," he continued, getting back to her original question. "He probably thinks I'm dead."

"Is that Decker?" Rhoda asked.

Tom gave her a funny look. "How did you know that?"

"You mentioned him several times while you were delirious."

"Oh."

"Anyone else?" she asked.

"Well, I had some friends named Rosen here in Israel, but they died in the Disaster." Tom was going down a very short list of the people he counted as his friends. Until the Disaster, Joshua and Ilana Rosen had visited him every day at the hospital in Tel Aviv. Their son, Scott, had survived the Disaster, but Tom hardly considered him a close friend. "I really ought to call *NewsWorld*," he said. "That's where I work. But to tell the truth, I'd rather wait until after we've been to the ophthalmologist before I call them.

I'm a photojournalist, or at least I was. I'm not sure there's much call for blind photographers."

"No. I guess not."

"How about you?"

"Pardon?"

"Your family."

"Oh, well, of course, there's my brother, Joel, whom you met yesterday. His wife and son died in the Disaster. I really liked her, and he was a real sweet kid. The three of us used to go to worship services together. That's how I know Rabbi Cohen. Joel's a computer systems analyst for the Israeli government, doing something with strategic defense, but he's not allowed to say what. That was before the Russians relieved him of his responsibilities, of course. I feel bad for him; he's lost nearly everything in the past couple of months. My parents and younger sister live in the States."

Tom nodded and after an appropriate pause asked Rhoda if she knew what time it was in Washington.

"About midnight," she answered after doing a quick mental calculation.

"Good, Decker ought to be home. Can I use your phone?"

"Sure," she said. "I should warn you that getting an overseas call out is not an easy task. There's really no logic to it. After the occupation began, I called repeatedly to let my folks know I was all right. I must have dialed a hundred times before I got a call through. When I did, it went straight through and sounded as if they were right next door. Of course, it's not just from the occupation. There was a lot of damage from the war."

Rhoda dialed the number Tom gave her, and handed him the phone. "The middle button at the very bottom redials," she said. "If you don't get through, feel free to try as many times as you like."

"It's ringing," Tom said, surprised.

"That won't happen again in a million years," Rhoda said, astonished by Tom's stroke of luck.

Tom waited as the phone continued to ring.

"What's the matter?" Rhoda asked after a minute.

"No one's answering."

"Well, don't give up too quickly. You may not get another call through for a long time."

New York, New York

Decker was already in his chair at the conference table when Ambassador Hansen and the other members of his senior staff arrived for a special meeting. The excitement of Decker's new job was still fresh.

"Decker," Hansen said before he even sat down, "I need one of your best speeches for this."

"I'll have the draft ready by one o'clock, sir," Decker responded. "I've done a search in the computer archives for any speeches you've given in the past on the makeup of the Security Council and I ran across one where you talked about reorganizing the Council on a regional basis. Of course we don't want to detract from the main issue, but if you like, I think I can work that in as a minor theme."

"Yes, that will do nicely. That's been a hot topic for years with the countries not on the Council. Peter," Hansen said, turning his attention to his chief legal council, "what's your final prognosis for this effort?"

"Well, for the benefit of the others in the meeting, let me just restate that there's no way on earth that this measure will ever pass, if for no other reason than simply on the grounds that it violates the United Nations Charter. There is no provision for removing a permanent member from the Security Council. You might, however, expand on Decker's suggestion and go for a complete reorganization. Another option you might consider would be to attempt something along the lines of what was done in 1971 when the Republic of China was removed from its seat in the UN because the General Assembly recognized the People's Republic of China as the true representative of the Chinese people."

"Let's not get carried away, Peter," Hansen said. "Remember, this is entirely for effect. We don't actually want to get the bloody thing passed."

"Jack, what about the poll of support from the other members?" Hansen asked his legislative assistant. "Are we sure that we can at least get this thing to the floor?" Jack Redmond was a native of Louisiana and the only other American besides Decker on Hansen's staff. When Hansen came to the UN he had wanted someone who understood American politics and this outspoken Cajun seemed just the man for the job.

"There should be no problem getting it to the floor, but I can't guarantee seconding support," Jack answered.

"That's fine. As long as we can get the proper coverage of my speech, I think we'll be all right."

"Ambassador," Decker interrupted, "from a media point of view, I think that may be a mistake. Unless we can get someone to second the motion, there's a good chance that the press may focus more on the hopelessness of the motion than on its symbolic nature."

"Good thought," Hansen said after mulling it over for a second. "I think you're probably right. If nothing else, perhaps we can get one of the Arab countries to second the motion. After all, they're not very happy with the Russians right now either. Jack, find me that second."

"Okay, any other thoughts or objections before we pull this thing together?"

There were none.

"Jackie, do you have anything to add?" Hansen asked his daughter.

"Your meeting with Russian Ambassador Kruszkegin is set for noon tomorrow in the Delegates Dining Room."

"Okay," Hansen said, "then we're set. Tomorrow at three o'clock, in plenty of time for the evening news in America and the morning news in Asia and Europe, I will make the motion that in response to their invasion and occupation of Israel, the United Nations General Assembly should permanently remove Russia from its position on the Security Council.

"All I have to do now is have lunch with Ambassador Kruszkegin and convince him it's nothing personal."

Tel Aviv, Israel

"Are there a lot of Russians on the streets?" Tom asked as Rhoda drove him to the ophthalmologist's office.

"Too many," she answered, but then added, "Actually there are not as many as you might expect. They patrol the streets, but the main forces are camped in the hills in the wilderness areas. Apparently they're trying to limit the resentment of the people. I think they realize that filling the streets with soldiers would just result in more violence, both by the soldiers against the people and vice versa. Besides, if they had a bunch of tanks rolling through the cities it wouldn't do much for their claims that they're just a peacekeeping force. It's really the best possible arrangement for the Russians, I suppose. They keep their soldiers on a short leash in the unpopulated areas and maintain a minimum show of force in the cities."

"Sort of the 'iron fist and silk glove' approach," Tom interjected. "Is it the same in the other cities?"

"Yeah, as far as we can tell. In Jerusalem the Russians shut down work on the Temple to pacify the Arabs. But they want it both ways, so to keep from further angering the Jews, they haven't destroyed any of the work that's already been done."

"Is there any kind of organized resistance?" Tom asked.

"There are reports of small groups sniping at the Russians in the hills, but I don't think they're very well organized. In the cities the people are less violent, but they're just as resistant."

"What about the Russians' ultimate goal? Your brother seemed to think the whole thing had been planned out from the very early stages. Does anybody know what the Russians want with Israel? Have there been any public statements of their long-range plans?"

"They say they'll leave when the threat of a nuclear/chemical war is removed from the region. But Joel says they already control all of Israel's nuclear weapons. If they planned to dismantle them they would have started by now. Of course if they *do* leave we'll be sitting ducks for the Arabs. The Russians have confiscated and impounded all military equipment as well as most of the small arms from the people. It's a lousy situation, but right now if the Russians left we'd have no way to protect ourselves except with picks and shovels.

"I suppose I'm not looking at this very optimistically, but at best this is going to be a long-term arrangement. At worst the Russians will declare the occupation a success and leave us to be slaughtered by the Arabs. It's actually quite clever—it's a perfect excuse for them to stay indefinitely."

"I wonder when the next plane leaves for the U.S.," Tom mused, but Rhoda didn't laugh.

❑

When they arrived at the ophthalmologist's office, Tom took Rhoda's arm and she led him to the door. Inside, the receptionist greeted her like an old friend.

"So this is the special patient you called about. How's he doing?"

"Well, that's what we're here to find out. How long before Dr. Weinstat can see us?" Rhoda asked as she surveyed the nearly full waiting room.

"Dr. Weinstat said to handle this as an emergency since the patient may still have some particles in his eyes. He's finishing up with a patient now, so it should be only a few minutes."

Tom continued to hold Rhoda's arm as they sat down to wait. The chairs were closely placed and it seemed natural to continue the contact. It was a moment before Tom realized he was still holding on. His first thought was to let go, but at the same instant it occurred to him that Rhoda did not seem to object. Even through the soft fabric of her blouse, the warmth of her skin seemed to penetrate the cold darkness that surrounded him.

The two sat silently. The receptionist's comment about him being the "special" patient had not escaped his attention. He didn't want to assign it too much meaning, but he thought briefly about asking Rhoda to explain the reference. *No*, he thought. If he spoke he would disturb the moment and she might feel compelled by propriety to lightly pull away her arm, and then he would be compelled by the same propriety to release it. Better to leave things as they were.

Unexpectedly, she spoke. "Dr. Weinstat is a good doctor."

"Good," Tom answered, inanely.

It was only small talk. Apparently she was as aware of the silence as Tom was. What was important was that they were carrying on a conversation, however unimaginative, and she gave no hint she wanted him to let go of her.

❏

In the examination room, it took the ophthalmologist only one quick look in each eye to make his diagnosis. "I'm sorry, Mr. Donafin. The damage to your corneas is very severe. The scarring from the shards of glass and the corneal burns have formed a nearly opaque cover over about 90 percent of your crystalline lens, and the rest isn't much better. As bad as it is, I'm surprised you still have any light perception at all. Ordinarily we might consider corneal transplants, but in this case, with the ancillary burn damage to the retinas, I think we'd only be causing additional suffering with no real hope of improvement in your sight."

It was all so quick. So quick and so final. In those few short words, stated with such stark clinical coldness, the doctor had pronounced him permanently blind.

"If you'll lean back, I'll put some fluorescein in your eyes so we can locate the glass that's still bothering you," the doctor said. When he finished, the doctor put an antibiotic ointment in Tom's eyes and reapplied pressure bandages to keep the lids from moving. "Now, leave that on and come back tomorrow so we can see how you're doing. Dr. Felsberg," he continued, now addressing Rhoda, "will you be bringing Mr. Donafin back in tomorrow?"

Rhoda nodded, and then stated her intention verbally for Tom's benefit.

"If you'll let Betty know on your way out, she'll try to set up a time convenient with your schedule."

"Thank you."

"Oh, and ask her to give you some pamphlets about learning to live with blindness."

Tom knew that it was entirely normal for doctors to carry on conversations as if their patients were nowhere within earshot, but right now what he knew made little difference. What he felt, there in the blackness that he had just learned would be his permanent home, was that he was being talked *about* and not *to*. It was as if he weren't a real person anymore because he was blind. He knew it was just the beginning. He had known blind people over the years. He knew how they were obliged by their blindness to always wait for the conversation of others. Even in a crowded room he had seen blind people forced to stand silently until someone spoke to them. The day before, Tom had joked about it, but now the reality of the end of his career as a photographer hit him full force.

In the car he was silent as Rhoda got in the other side. "How are you doing?" she asked sympathetically, as she put her hand on his.

"Not very well," he answered. "And what's worse, I don't think the whole thing has really hit me yet. I keep thinking that I'll just get these bandages off and I'll be able to see again."

"Well," she began as she caressed his hand to comfort him, but she obviously couldn't think of anything else to say.

Tom turned his hand to hold hers; he needed all the support he could get right now. "I have no idea what to do from here," he said. "I can't work. I have some savings and three years of pay from *NewsWorld* in the bank. That'll last me for a while, but then what?" He felt like saying something cliché like, "I'd be better off dead," but the warmth of Rhoda's hand told him that wasn't true.

"Tom, I know you're feeling angry right now, and cheated, but there are things in life we must simply accept, because even if we don't they remain the same." She sounded as though she was speaking from experience.

They sat for another few minutes in silence holding each

other's hand. "Tom," Rhoda said finally, "there's someone I want you to meet."

Tom thought he knew who she was talking about. "Your rabbi?" he asked.

"You'll really like him," she said, confirming Tom's question. "He asked me to bring you by when you were back on your feet."

"Yeah, I guess it's about time I thanked him for digging me out and bringing me to you." Reluctantly, Tom let Rhoda's hand slip free so she could drive.

15

Plowshares into Swords

SCOTT ROSEN SAT IN A SMALL CAFÉ eating a bowl of soup, waiting for his friend Joel Felsberg. Soon Joel entered, removed his coat, and sat down without speaking.

"You look upset," Scott offered, in what seemed to Joel to be a rather irritating tone.

"I hate these arrogant Russians—always stopping you on the street and wanting to see your papers." Joel was exaggerating; most people went days without being stopped. "They're never going to leave, you know."

"Yeah, I know," Scott answered with uncharacteristic resignation as he sipped his soup. "But everything is not so gloomy," he added with equally uncharacteristic good cheer. "I heard the resistance hijacked a supply truck, stole all the supplies, and then loaded it with dynamite and sent it into a Russian camp by remote control. They say it killed nearly a thousand Russians."

Joel ordered his lunch before responding. "I've heard that story twenty times in the last three weeks and it gets more ridiculous with every telling," Joel responded.

"You don't believe it?"

"Yeah, I believe it. But I believe it the way I heard it the first time: The resistance hijacked a truck and drove it into a Russian camp, where it ran into a water tower, accomplishing next to nothing."

"Well, at least there *is* a resistance."

"Yeah, and they're outgunned and completely disorganized. If Ben Gurion had used their tactics we'd still be a British protectorate! No matter how you paint it, Scott," Joel continued after stirring his coffee, "we're still occupied! I don't care how many water towers we run into or supply trucks we hijack! We were a free, independent state and now we are not!"

"What do you think the resistance should do differently?" Scott asked, as if Joel's opinion made a difference.

"I don't know." Joel shook his head in resignation. "Nothing I guess. That's the whole problem—there's nothing we can do. Even if we got rid of the Russians, as soon as they were gone we'd be attacked by the Arabs, and we'd have nothing to fight them with."

"Yes, but—"

"Stop it, Scott! Is that why you brought me here? So I could wallow in my anger and frustration?!"

Joel and Scott were zealous in their love for their country; either could easily be brought to a fever pitch when it came to Israel. But strangely, on this occasion, only Joel's blood pressure had risen. An unusual calm accompanied Scott's speech, but Joel didn't notice it. Neither had he noticed that since his arrival no one had entered or left the café, nor that the café owner had turned the sign to read "Closed." Likewise, the two men standing watch outside the café had escaped Joel's notice entirely.

Suddenly Scott became animated. "We must drive the Russians from Israel and bloody their noses so badly they'll never come back!" he said.

"Big talk. Big talk," Joel responded. "I suppose you think the resistance will accomplish that with their puny disruptions to the Russian supply lines. And just how do you propose we deal with the Arabs when and if the Russians leave?"

Scott studied his soup. "If only we had used our nukes on the Russians instead of just waving them around as a threat to the Libyans."

"You're a fool, Rosen! By the time we knew we were being invaded, the Russians were all over the place. The only way we could have nuked them was to launch on our own soil," Joel said, growing even more angry.

Scott Rosen did not allow his friend's anger to distract him. He had a mission to accomplish and all was working exactly according to plan. "Yeah, I guess that's true." Scott's voice seemed resigned to the hopelessness of the situation, but he continued. "Too bad we can't get control of the nukes now. With the Russians all concentrated in the hills, we could wipe out 90 percent of them with just a few well-placed missiles and the resistance could take out the other 10 percent in the cities."

"You really are a fool," Joel said. "What about Moscow? You think they're just gonna sit back and let that happen without responding? What's to stop them from striking back against our cities?"

This was the question that Scott had been waiting for. Suddenly his mood grew much more serious. The gravity of what he was about to say was clear even to Joel. "Our strategic defense," he whispered finally.

Joel stared coldly at Scott, studying his expression. Twice he opened his mouth to speak, ready to accuse Scott again of being a fool, but he held back. It appeared that Scott was serious and when it came to strategic defense, Scott Rosen deserved to be heard. Next to his late father, Joshua Rosen, Scott knew more about Israeli strategic defense than anyone. Finally Joel responded, "You're talking impossibilities. Even if a plan like that *could* work, there's no way in the world our puny, disorganized resistance could get control of the Strategic Defense Control Facility."

"We don't need to go anywhere near the control facility," Scott said confidently.

Suddenly Joel became aware of his surroundings. When he'd thought he and Scott were just griping, he hadn't cared who heard them. There was nothing unusual about two Israeli men complaining about the Russians. Everyone in Israel was complaining. Indeed, it might have been considered unusual for them to be talking about anything else. But now they had crossed the line; they were no longer just complaining. The wrong person listening to their conversation might easily have mistaken this for a conspiracy. He looked around quickly to make sure no one had overheard them.

Scott didn't interrupt him to mention he had nothing to worry about; each of the seven people in the café had been handpicked for the occasion.

"You mean a remote?" Joel asked finally, under his breath.

Scott signaled an affirmative with his eyes.

Joel had heard talk about a remote, an off-site test facility for the Strategic Defense Control Facility (SDCF), but he had written it off as speculation by people who didn't know any better. If the Off-Site Test Facility (OSTF) was real, it would have been evident in the communications configuration needed for such an operation. True, the communications links could have been intentionally mislabeled to conceal its existence, but Joel had worked at the SDCF for more than five years and had run numerous configuration scenarios on the facility's computers. If the OSTF existed, it would have turned up in the simulations.

Joel was intimately familiar with the concept of an OSTF. Early in his career, before leaving the U.S., he had been a low-level software analyst for Ford Aerospace, assigned to North American Aerospace Defense Command (NORAD). He remembered those long walks down the cold tunnels in Cheyenne Mountain to test software upgrades. He had been there in the mountain on November 9, 1979, when for several terrifying minutes it had appeared as though the Soviet Union had launched a full-scale nuclear attack on the United States. American Strategic Air Command (SAC) bombers were launched and nuclear missiles were put on alert, awaiting the president's order. As it turned out, the alert had been caused by a test scenario inadvertently being fed into the on-line NORAD computer network. As a result of that false alarm the U.S. Congress immediately authorized the construction of the NORAD Off-Site Test Facility in downtown Colorado Springs.

Prior to the establishment of the Colorado Springs OSTF, the standard operating procedure for testing software upgrades had involved taking NORAD's backup systems for the critical missile warning computers off line while the tests were run. It was risky business at best. What if there had been a failure in the primary system? In the fifteen minutes it would take to get the backup system out of test mode and back on line, it could be all over. The OSTF was definitely the way to go. Besides, as far as Joel was concerned, downtown Colorado Springs was a much easier commute than Cheyenne Mountain in the middle of the night. The OSTF included a complete duplicate of all the systems at Cheyenne Mountain. All testing of new software was performed there. Only after the software passed testing were the cryptographically check-summed object modules—used to authenticate and ensure system security—electronically downloaded to the operational center at NORAD. And there was one other benefit to the OSTF: In the unlikely event of a total failure of the NORAD systems, the OSTF could take over the actual operation. Computers, communications, and cryptographic equipment were all in place. All that was needed was loading of the proper cryptographic key material into the cryptos.

When Joel went to work at the Israeli Strategic Defense Control Facility, he tried for two years to convince his superiors of the need to develop the same type of system for Israel, to no avail. At one point he considered resigning to protest their refusal to even talk about it, but his wife convinced him to be patient and wait until those in charge were more sympathetic to the idea. Actually, that was one of the most irritating parts: The head of the Israeli SDCF was Dr. Arnold Brown, one of the men who had played a crucial role in developing the OSTF concept for NORAD. It never made any sense to Joel that Brown would refuse to consider providing the same capabilities for Israel.

Joel's initial response to Scott Rosen's suggestion that the Strategic Defense Control Facility had an OSTF was that Scott was simply believing more rumors like the one about the hijacked supply truck. Still, there were some things to which Scott, with his compartmentalized clearances, might have had access that Joel could have been totally unaware of. And the look on Scott's face said he was serious.

"Scott," Joel said as he leaned across the table, "is this a game? Are you putting me on?" Scott's eyes answered the question. "But, Scott, I worked at SDCF for more than five years. I ran configuration scenarios on the facility's computers a thousand times. If there was an OSTF, why didn't it turn up in the simulations?"

"It was there. Its functions were masked to hide its true purpose, but it was there."

Joel's eyes asked, "Where?"

"SF-14," Scott answered.

There was no way of knowing whether Scott was telling the truth. Sensor Facility 14, as far as Joel had known, was a non-operational and entirely redundant infrared tracking station for terminal-phase acquisition and discrimination of ballistic reentry vehicles. Perhaps by coincidence—and then again, perhaps not—SF-14 was one of only two remote facilities Joel had never actually visited. Now that he thought about it, he couldn't remember ever seeing anyone's name on the duty roster for a site check of SF-14. This would certainly explain Dr. Brown's lack of interest in considering an OSTF. After all, why talk about building something that was already fully operational?

If Scott Rosen knew what he was talking about, then Joel wanted to know. But if this was just more wishful thinking, then he wanted to be done with it, and the sooner the better. "Okay," he said, abruptly, "take me there." To Joel's surprise Scott didn't come back with some flimsy excuse but instead got to his feet, put on his coat, and started to leave the café with Joel in tow. "What about the check?" Joel asked Scott.

"It's on the house," answered the café owner.

❑

Scott drove straight into the eastern business section of Tel Aviv and parked in the basement parking lot of a tall but otherwise nondescript office building that appeared to have only minor damage from the recent war. Joel followed as Scott walked toward the elevators, pausing to look up at a security camera near the ceiling. In a moment a red light on the camera blinked and Scott pushed the call button for the elevator. As the elevator door closed behind them, Scott flipped the emergency "Stop" switch, and, on the numbered buttons of the elevator, punched in a seven-digit code. Despite already being in the basement, the elevator lurched downward, taking them, Joel guessed, several floors farther beneath the building. The elevator door opened to a small room about twelve feet square, where two armed guards waited. Badges were out of the question under the circumstances, so they were operating strictly on a recognition basis. Joel would soon learn this was not that difficult a task; very few people were involved in this operation. As Scott introduced him to the guards who were obviously studying every aspect of his appearance, Joel noticed his photograph lying on the desk beside an array of security monitors, one of which was focused on the elevator in the garage where they had entered.

Scott opened the cipher lock of an armored door that was the only other exit from the room. Before them lay a small sea of computers and defense tracking equipment on a raised floor, filling a room about 8,500 square feet. An array of symmetric multiprocessors made up the heart of the operation, with integrated routers/ATM switches feeding real-time input via broadband fiber links. Joel had seen this hardware configuration before, at the Strategic Defense Control Facility in the mountains near Mizpe Ramon in southern Israel. There was much less room here than in the mountain, but at first glance this seemed to be an exact duplicate of the core of the SDCF.

Scattered around the facility were a handful of men and women busy at Sun workstations. A few slowed their pace just long enough to look up and acknowledge Scott's and Joel's presence with friendly smiles before going back to their work. While Joel looked around in disbelief, a short well-built man entered from another room and approached them. Scott abruptly ended the brief tour to greet the man.

"Good afternoon, Colonel," Scott said, formally. "Allow me to introduce Mr. Joel Felsberg. Joel, this is Colonel White."

"Welcome to the team," White said. "Glad you could join us."

"Uh . . . thank you, sir," Joel said, unaware that he had.

"You're coming in at a crucial time. Scott has told me all about you and I've seen your record. I'm sure we can count on you to help us make this thing happen.

"Scott," he continued, "introduce Joel to the rest of the team and get him briefed on what his role is. We'll talk later." With that the colonel left.

"Uh, yeah, that's a good idea, Scott. Get me briefed on what my role is," Joel repeated. And then, more to the point, "What on earth is going on down here?!"

Scott smiled. "Welcome to SF-14."

❑

In the facility's briefing room, Scott poured coffee and proceeded to present an overview of the project and a discussion of the highly classified maximum capabilities of each of the four phases of the Israeli strategic defense. After nearly an hour, he finally got around to explaining where Joel fit into all of this.

"The reason you're here," Scott explained, "is that two nights ago Dr. Claude Remey, our software guru, very stupidly got in the way of his neighbors' domestic quarrel. As a result, he's now lying unconscious in a hospital with a stab wound three quarters of an inch from his heart. You've been brought on to finish the project he was working on."

Joel knew Remey. They had worked together on a couple of projects but had never gotten along well. Still, Joel was sorry to hear of his injury.

"What you see here is a fully operations-capable backup facility to the Strategic Defense Control Facility. It is not simply a test facility. Dr. Arnold Brown, who was in charge of its development, determined from the outset that knowledge of its existence should be limited to as few individuals as possible. It was felt that, should Israel ever be invaded, this facility should be maintained at all costs.

"Colonel White—actually Lieutenant Colonel White—whom you just met, was part of a chain of officers, decreasing in rank from general to captain, charged with operation of the facility in case of an invasion. The purpose of the chain was to prevent any invading force from disrupting the operation of this facility by systematically arresting all high-ranking officers. As it turns out, each of Colonel White's superiors were arrested in the first days after the invasion and the responsibility fell to him.

"The initial plan for this facility, in an invasion where the SDCF was lost, included three scenarios. First, should the opportunity present itself, this facility could be used to launch on the invader's flank, thus cutting off its supply lines and weakening the forward forces. Second, should there be an attempt by an invading force to use our own nuclear capabilities against us, this facility could frustrate that attempt by overriding the controls at the SDCF. And third, should there be any attempt to remove a warhead from a silo, this facility has the capability to neutralize the nuclear device. Had either the second or the third scenario occurred, the established procedure would have been to initiate the destruction of each threatening, or threatened, missile by remotely setting off small explosives in the silos that would disable both the silo and the warhead—without, of course, detonating the nuclear device.

"What actually happened with the Russian invasion was something that had not even been considered. As I alluded in the café—oh, by the way, the café is one of several safe houses around the city—the Russians have presented us with a totally unexpected opportunity. By concentrating their forces away from populated areas"—Scott paused to point out the Russian troop locations marked on a large wall map—"they have literally made themselves sitting ducks to the capabilities of this facility.

"The first phase of our plan, then, is to neutralize the SDCF and launch six neutron-tipped, short-range Gideon missiles, one against each of the Russians' positions. There are three very important reasons we've chosen the neutron-tipped Gideons. The most obvious is that since we will be launching on targets within our own borders, it is absolutely imperative that we limit the area of destruction. We'll come back to that in a minute.

"The second reason is that the Gideon-class warhead produces the most rapidly dissipating radiation pattern of any of our warheads. Our forces will be able to reenter the initial kill radius within six to eight hours after impact. Ground Zero will be entirely habitable in three weeks.

"Third, if the launch is successful and our strategic defense successfully defends Israel against a Russian retaliatory nuclear strike—that's phase two of the plan—we will very quickly face a second threat from both Arab and Russian conventional forces. We hope to limit the immediate response of the Arabs by, one, creating a communications blackout, thus maintaining the highest possible level of confusion for our enemies; and two, by planning the strike during the Hajj." Scott was referring to the annual pilgrimage of Muslims to Mecca in Saudi Arabia. The rites of the Hajj include circling the Ka'bah in Mecca and going seven times between the mountains of Safa and Marwa as Abraham's concubine, Hagar, is believed to have done during her search for water. This can take several days and is followed by group prayer on the plain of Arafa. During the Hajj, Muslims are forbidden by the Koran to harm any living being, including their enemies.

Scott spread out a handful of photographs on the table. "As you can see, our satellite reconnaissance of the Russian encampments reveals extraordinarily large caches of weaponry, both Russian-made and captured Israeli weapons."

Joel was surprised by what the photos showed. Dozens of huge temporary warehouses had been constructed, with tanks, helicopters, and armored personnel carriers parked nearby in neat rows. It looked like a massive car lot. "What are they doing out there?" he asked.

"We suspect the Russians are storing up military equipment for a conventional attack on Saudi Arabia and Egypt. After that, we have to assume they will go after each of the other oil-rich countries in the area. We have only limited intelligence reports to support that assumption, but it's obvious they don't need that kind of armament simply to keep Israel under thumb."

"They're planning on using Israel as home base to go after the Arab oil fields and the Suez Canal!" Joel concluded in disbelief.

"That's what it looks like," Scott said without emotion.

"But if we have these satellite photos, then surely so does the U.S. Why haven't they done anything to stop it?"

"They are pursuing the matter through diplomatic channels. If they have plans for a military response, we have not been informed of it. Apparently their assumptions of the Russians' immediate intent do not match our own. As you know," Scott continued, getting back to the subject at hand, "the neutron bomb was developed to destroy personnel, not materiel. It kills primarily by an immediate burst of radiation, not by heat or the sheer power of the blast, as in the case of other nuclear weapons. The third reason, then, for selecting the Gideons is to eliminate the Russian personnel while preserving the weaponry. As you said earlier, even if we get rid of the Russians, we don't have any weapons to defend ourselves from the Arabs. The Russian stockpiles will provide us with the weapons we need. To further reduce the damage to materiel, we are actually targeting a point four hundred meters outside of the perimeter of the Russian camps. Targeting is being coordinated by Ron Samuel, who will be briefing you on that part of the project when we're finished. With a little luck, he'll be able to finish his work in the next few days and then he can help you with your project.

"Now let's get back to the first reason I mentioned for selecting the Gideon. The initial kill radius for the Gideon-class warhead is only one kilometer, with a secondary radius extending another three kilometers. In most cases those limits will allow us to hit the Russians and entirely avoid initial or secondary kill of our own population. However, there are two places where because of adjacent villages and *kibbutzim*, that will not be possible. In those cases, and in the case of nearby farmers at the other sites, an evacuation team will be given approximately eight hours to effect evacuation of all civilian residents before the launch. The plan is for this to occur under cover of darkness, and to avoid tipping our hand the evacuation team will not be given the word to begin evacuation until after we have secured control of operations from the SDCF.

"Neutralizing the SDCF and transferring operations to this facility is the easy part, relatively speaking; that's what this facility was set up to do. The hard part is to make the Russians believe they are still fully in control long enough for us to evacuate our people and launch the six Gideons. That's where you come in. We need you to give us those eight hours. Your job is to create the illusion, through a software dump to the SDCF computers, that their systems are operational.

"After we transfer control to this facility, it will take approximately twenty minutes for us to download the retargeting data into the missiles. If the Russians realize what's happened, they will first attempt to regain control and then very quickly disperse their troops in the mountains. Should that happen, we will have no choice but to launch immediately, killing more than a thousand Israeli civilians and evacuation team members."

Joel mulled over what he had been told. It was a lot to digest so quickly. "What about the Russians in the cities?" he asked.

"Immediately after the launch, teams of Israeli commandos will take over all radio and television stations from the Russians. Where they are unsuccessful, other teams will destroy those stations' antennas. It is critical to our success that the Israeli people be rallied to attack the Russians in the cities, but it is equally important that we keep the rest of the world, especially the Arabs, confused about exactly what is going on. If we make things too clear for our own citizens, it will be equally clear to the Arabs, who—Hajj or not—may seize the opportunity to strike while we're still disorganized and before we can take control of the Russian weapons caches. Rather than broadcasting reports that would be picked up by the Arabs, the radio and television will play a continuous loop of a single message, the words of the prophet Joel, from Joel 3:10."

Scott paused. He may have been a scientist but, like his father, he was a zealot first, though for a different religious cause. He was hoping his friend at least might have studied enough Scripture to be familiar with the writings of the prophet whose name he bore. But, if Joel was familiar with the verse he gave no indication of it to Scott. Scott gave a sigh of noticeable disappointment and then continued, "'Beat your plowshares into swords and your pruning hooks into spears.'"

"That's kind of obscure, don't you think?" asked Joel, unaware the idea had been Scott's.

Scott started to argue but held back. "I suppose so," he admitted. "But that's the signal that has been passed to the resistance forces. Hopefully, others will join in when they see the fighting start in the streets."

Over the next two hours Joel was given concise briefings by each of the eight people in the operations room concerning their individual parts of the project.

Three weeks later
New York, New York

The phone rang three times before Ambassador Hansen could rouse himself from his sleep to answer it. "Hello," he said, as he checked his alarm clock. It was just after eleven.

"Mr. Ambassador," said Decker, "I'm sorry to disturb you, but I've just heard that about thirty minutes ago, at 5:30 A.M. Israeli time, there were an undisclosed number of nuclear explosions in Israel."

The sleep suddenly rushed from Hansen's brain as his eyes opened wide. "The Russians?" he asked.

"Reports are very sketchy so far. It's not clear who's responsible, and there have been no official statements from the Russians."

"Decker, is there any chance there's been a mistake?"

"No, sir. I don't think so. The detonations were detected by U.S., U.K., and Chinese satellites. To make things worse, the explosions were followed by a major earthquake along the Dead Sea Rift."

"Okay, hold on a second while I switch on the telly." A moment later Decker heard the sound of Hansen's television through the phone. "Okay, I'm back," Hansen said, but he and Decker stayed silent as each listened to the report just being read.

"Fox News has just learned that the United States has scrambled Strategic Command bombers. The State Department has emphasized that this is only a precautionary measure and that STRATCOM has been ordered to remain in U.S. air space pending further orders."

"What the devil is going on?" Hansen asked.

"I don't know, sir," Decker answered, stating the obvious.

"Do you have the Russian ambassador's phone number?"

"I have Ambassador Kruszkegin's number right here, sir," Decker said. He relayed it to Hansen.

"Okay," Hansen said. "I'll call Kruszkegin. You call Jackie, Peter, and Jack and have everyone get to the office ASAP."

❏

The phone rang only once at Ambassador Kruszkegin's residence before it was answered by an official-sounding "Hello."

"This is Ambassador Jon Hansen," Hansen said. "I would like to speak with Ambassador Kruszkegin immediately on a matter of utmost importance."

"I'm sorry, Ambassador Hansen," the voice answered. "Ambassador Kruszkegin is in a meeting right now and cannot be disturbed."

"I'll take it," Hansen heard Kruszkegin say in the background. Obviously the person who answered the phone had lied.

Ambassador Kruszkegin stood by the phone wearing a finely woven black and gold silk dressing gown, his warm Italian slippers protecting his feet from the cold marble floor. "Good evening, Jon," he began. Jon Hansen liked Kruszkegin as a person and respected him as an adversary. For his part, Kruszkegin was fond of referring to Hansen as "a man who has failed to notice that Britain no longer rules the world." Kruszkegin had found that, when possible, it was more productive to cooperate with Hansen than not to.

"Jon," he continued, anticipating Hansen's question, "I honestly do not know what is happening in Israel. I've just spoken with the foreign minister in Moscow and he swears we have not launched an attack. I believe they are just as confused as we are."

Hansen was surprised that Kruszkegin had even taken his call; the straight answer was even more unexpected. Hansen knew the Russian well enough to have a pretty good idea when he was lying and when he was telling the truth. Right now he seemed to be telling the truth—at least as far as he knew it.

"Thank you, Yuri," Hansen said. Kruszkegin's straightforward answer left little else to be said.

❑

Ambassador Hansen's senior staff members watched the news reports on television at the British Mission as they awaited the ambassador's arrival.

"Can anyone tell me what's going on?" Hansen asked as he walked in the door and handed Jackie his coat, just before 2:00 A.M. New York time.

"The Russians claim they had nothing to do with it," began Jack Redmond, Hansen's legislative assistant. "They say the attack was against the Russian troops in Israel's mountains."

This was a new twist on the story. "How the devil could that happen?" Hansen asked, incredulously.

Redmond shook his head.

In the brief silence, Hansen's attention turned to the reporter on television. "There is speculation at the State Department," the reporter was saying, "that the attack on Israel could be the result of some internal power struggle inside the Russian government. The battle for power and control of policy has been heated, to say the least. Hard-liners like Foreign Minister Cherov and Defense Minister Khromchenkov want to lead Russia back to communism and world power, while others like President Perelyakin favor a more moderate approach. The Russian invasion of Israel still has many analysts unsure of who's in charge."

Redmond shrugged his broad shoulders as Hansen looked at him for his comment. "It's possible," he said. "But it doesn't really answer the big questions. We know that no cities were hit; apparently the missiles fell in the wilderness areas of the country. That would seem to support Russia's assertion that it was their troops that were hit, but I can't imagine any kind of political situation so bad that one group of Russians would bomb another."

"Okay, let's assume for a moment that the Russians are telling the truth: They're not responsible for the bombing," Hansen said. "Which country with the capability to launch a nuclear attack would actually do it?"

No one had an answer. "All we can do is wait for release of the satellite data to identify the origin of the launch," Redmond concluded.

"Mr. Ambassador," Decker interjected, "whoever launched the attack, the Israelis have apparently taken advantage of the combined confusion of the explosions and the earthquake. There are reports of fighting between Russians and Israelis in every major city, and Israeli resistance fighters apparently have taken over all of the television and radio stations not destroyed by the quake."

Hansen ran his hand through his hair, thought for a second, and then shook his head. "Except for the quake, I'd wonder if this whole thing was the work of the Israelis!"

Tel Aviv, Israel

Deep beneath the streets of Tel Aviv the mood was bright and hopeful. It was now five hours since the launch, and the quake had left the OSTF shaken but undamaged. Phase one of the plan had been a complete success: The Russians had been completely unaware of the transfer of control from the SDCF to the OSTF; the evacuation of civilians had taken place with only a few delays; the Gideons had been launched (much to the surprise of Russian security teams guarding the missile silos); and all of the designated targets had been hit.

Russian troops who had been outside the initial kill radius of the bombs vainly sought relief in the surrounding mountains, but the seed of death planted within them by the neutron radiation would not yield until it had consumed them. Their dead bodies, leached of the quickly decaying neutron radiation, would provide carrion for wild animals and birds, and for the next seven months their scattered bones would be collected by the survivors and laid to rest with their comrades in a massive cemetery in the Valley of Hamon Gog.

Far from hindering the Israelis' efforts, the earthquake along the Dead Sea Rift, where the African and Arabian tectonic plates meet, had actually aided their cause by adding to their enemies' confusion. In the streets of Israel, citizens were attacking the occupying Russians troops. In the mountains near Mizpe Ramon, an Israeli squadron had surprised the security force outside the SDCF and was now preparing to wait out the surrender of those inside. It would be useless to try to force them out; the facility, with its three-foot-thick steel walls and doors, was impervious to anything, with the possible exception of a direct hit by a multi-megaton nuclear warhead. When the Russians invaded four months earlier, those in control of the facility had surrendered it only after they were ordered to do so by the Israeli defense minister. Though the facility had been completely overridden by the OSTF and was therefore useless to the Russians, it would likely be a long wait before the occupants surrendered.

Any celebration would have to wait, however. Phase two required the full attention of Colonel White and his team at the OSTF. While the Israelis would soon be able to secure the weaponry warehoused at the Russian camps, those in Colonel White's team had the immediate responsibility of directing Israel's strategic defense against a possible retaliatory nuclear strike from the Russians.

Scott Rosen estimated that Israel's strategic defense could eliminate 97 percent or more of anything the Russians might send at them in a full-scale attack. The throw-weight of the Russian nuclear arsenal had been substantially reduced since the collapse of the Soviet Union, and Israel's strategic defense was made practicable by the fact that it has a very limited land mass to defend. But a full-scale attack would still mean that several soft targets— that is, cities—could be hit. If the attack were of a lesser scale— a "limited" response—the strategic defense could probably destroy all incoming warheads. The most likely scenario was that the Russians would choose a strong but limited response in order to reduce the possibility of a response from the West. What everyone hoped for, however, was that the Russians, realizing Israel was once again in control of its own strategic defense, would see that a nuclear attack would ultimately prove futile and therefore would not launch at all.

There was no way to be certain how the Russians would respond and each person in Colonel White's team understood that every warhead that got through meant the deaths of tens of thousands of their countrymen. This was not a game of sighting targets and pulling triggers, however; the strategic defense was fully automated. It had to be. Destroying the maximum number of approaching missiles required a nearly instantaneous response to launch. There was no room for "man in the loop." Once the order was given to place the Battle Management/Command, Control and Communications (BM/C³) computers on threat status, the role of humans was reduced to support and repair. Some argued that it was dangerous to turn the control of the system over to the system itself, but as Joshua Rosen and his colleagues had successfully countered, it was the best way to ensure survival.

The strategic defense was now initiated for immediate response to any sign of launch from Russia, her allies, or from the sea.

16

The Hand of God

Moscow, Russia

ELEVEN HUNDRED MILES and nearly due north of Tel Aviv, the Russian Security Council was meeting to discuss the events in Israel. It was now 12:05 P.M. in Moscow, 4:05 A.M. in New York, and 11:05 A.M. in Israel.

At eighty-six years old, Defense Minister Vladimir Leon Josef Khromchenkov was the oldest of the thirteen men assembled in the Kremlin's war-room. Khromchenkov had been born in the early days of the Russian Revolution. His father had missed the birth, choosing instead to take part in the fighting in Petrograd. Throughout the revolution and the years that followed, Khromchenkov's father somehow managed to walk the fine line of being close to Lenin, Stalin, and Trotsky and yet was never so close to any one of them that he was considered a threat by the other two. His ability to maneuver through politically treacherous waters had been passed on to his son. After serving for nearly forty years in the Soviet Army, Vladimir Khromchenkov had come to the Kremlin during the early days of Gorbachev as a candidate of the hard-liners who opposed Gorbachev's reforms and were afraid he might "give away the store."

Boris Yeltzin and Vladimir Putin had both attempted to weaken Khromchenkov's political power and even to remove him from the Security Council, without success. Khromchenkov knew the inner workings of everything and used it to his advantage. Had he wanted it, he might well have become president, but Khromchenkov preferred manipulating to being manipulated. It was said of Khromchenkov that he believed it was his destiny not to die until the Soviet Union had been restored as a world power. And though he gave the credit to others, it was Khromchenkov who had engineered the invasion of Israel as a key step toward bringing about that destiny.

"Comrades," Defense Minister Khromchenkov began in old Soviet style, which always irritated some of those around him but warmed the hearts of others, "our intelligence reports have just confirmed that this morning's strike against our international peacekeeping forces in Israel was conceived and initiated by Israeli insurgents. We have very recently regained communications with General Serov, who is in charge of the Strategic Defense Control Facility at Mizpe Ramon. He reports that the Israelis apparently took control of the nuclear forces from a remote facility, from which they launched this morning's attack. At present the insurgents are fighting our troops stationed in the cities, and a small force of Israelis has set up camp outside the control facility. General Serov has sealed the blast doors so his forces are in no danger from the insurgents outside. Presently, he reports, he is working to isolate the breach in operations in order to attempt to regain control. One other point," Khromchenkov said, as if it were only an afterthought, though in reality it was the most significant thing he would say, "in addition to having control of their launch facilities, the Israelis have also taken control of their strategic defense."

Foreign Minister Cherov recognized the importance of Khromchenkov's final point. If the Israeli resistance had control of the strategic defense, then it greatly limited Russia's options for response.

"Our damage estimates indicate that the warheads used were Gideon-class five-megaton neutron devices targeted for just outside the perimeter of each of our six temporary installations. We believe the loss of personnel in the camps was total."

"What about the materiel?" asked the minister of finance, concerned more about the stockpiles of weaponry than the thousands of lost lives.

"At this moment we have no assessment of damage to our weaponry, but it is likely the equipment has survived the attack."

"What do you suggest?" President Perelyakin asked the defense minister.

"We must assume," Khromchenkov began, "that the use of low megatonnage neutron bombs was intended to kill our soldiers while allowing the Israelis to seize our weapons for their defense against the Arabs. While we can hope that General Serov will regain control of the nuclear capabilities and strategic defense, we must plan a response in the event those attempts are unsuccessful. Therefore, in addition to immediately replacing our peacekeeping forces, I recommend we prepare both a nuclear and a conventional response. First, if we regain control of the strategic defense, then our response to the Israeli nuclear attack should be in kind. I recommend a launch of six low-yield neutron bombs on Israeli targets to match the unprovoked Israeli attack on our troops. Second, if we are not able to regain control of the strategic defense, then within twenty-four hours, before Israel can avail itself of our equipment, we must launch an air strike against those same six targets, followed by additional strikes against any Israeli troops who attempt to take our equipment. The second option is not as colorful, but it will make the point."

"Defense Minister Khromchenkov," said Interior Minister Stefan Ulinov, "if we can regain control of the Israeli's nuclear forces, then I recommend that the launch come from their own silos."

"Excellent," approved President Perelyakin, and everyone agreed.

"As for a nuclear response," Ulinov continued, "if Israel's strategic defense is anywhere near as effective as our intelligence reports indicate, then Defense Minister Khromchenkov is absolutely correct. We must not launch a nuclear response unless we are sure the warheads will reach their targets. We cannot afford to provide the world with a demonstration of what a well-developed missile defense can do. It would be," Ulinov said, measuring his words for effect, "a catastrophic mistake if the net result of this entire event was to encourage the West to finally deploy their own full-scale strategic defense." Ulinov paused to allow the members of the Security Council a moment to consider what he felt was the great wisdom of his words and then looked over at Defense Minister Khromchenkov to surrender the floor to him.

"Ultimately," said Khromchenkov, "if we are unable to retake the nuclear capabilities or the strategic defense, we will have to expend much greater forces to disable the missile silos with conventional air strikes. Once they have again been stripped of their nuclear forces I believe we can count on Israel to surrender its strategic defenses."

"Excellent," the president said again. "I commend you, Mr. Defense Minister, for your clear thought and planning of a sensible response to this incident."

❑

When the meeting was over, Defense Minister Khromchenkov hung back to catch Foreign Minister Cherov alone. Khromchenkov felt sure he knew Cherov's feelings on what he was about to ask, but one could never be too careful. "Tell me, Comrade Cherov," he said when he was sure no one could overhear their conversation, "what did you think of my recommendations for a limited response?"

"I think they were well planned . . . if your intent was to satisfy the wishes of President Perelyakin." Cherov's voice hid nothing; it was obvious he was not satisfied with Khromchenkov's plan.

"Perhaps you would prefer a response that was a bit . . . stronger? One that took greater advantage of the opportunity?"

"I had hopes, yes."

"I did prepare an alternate recommendation. Perhaps you would like to have a look?" Khromchenkov handed a large unmarked envelope to his fellow minister and left the room.

New York, New York

By 8:00 A.M. New York time, the world had begun to learn what had actually happened in Israel. Early reports had suggested that the bombing was an accident on the part of the Russians. Many of the Russians had even thought this was the case. Now that it was clear the attack had been somehow engineered by the Israelis, concern at the UN quickly turned to calls for restraint by the Russians.

Jon Hansen had learned early in his political career that the most effective diplomacy is usually carried out in private; the speaker's dais in the hall of the General Assembly was for show business. Still, there were times, such as when he had called for the reorganization of the Security Council—a move that was entirely for spectacle—when the dais was indispensable. The present occasion would require both.

It was ingenious that the Israelis could engineer such a maneuver, Hansen thought; it was insane that they'd actually do it. And it was impossible for anyone to tell how the Russians were planning to respond to the attack. Hansen knew enough about Russian politics to recognize there would probably be serious discussion of launching some sort of limited nuclear attack in response, but he hoped the moderates would win out. Unfortunately, he could learn nothing more from Russian Ambassador Yuri Kruszkegin, who was playing it very close to the vest.

Unknown to Hansen were the cards in the hand of the small group of men and women deep beneath the streets of Tel Aviv. They were the ones who held history in their hands, along with the control of Israel's nuclear forces and strategic defense.

Moscow, Russia

Defense Minister Vladimir Khromchenkov had just walked into the rest room and gone over to one of the urinals when he realized that someone had followed him in. Out of the corner of his eye he recognized Foreign Minister Cherov. Khromchenkov knew at once this was no chance meeting; he could count on the fingers of his free hand the number of times he had seen Cherov in this wing of the building. Still, it was not wise to make assumptions. "Good afternoon," Khromchenkov said.

Cherov only nodded.

"Have you had a chance to examine my alternate proposal?"

"I have," answered Cherov. "It offers some intriguing possibilities for both the short- and long-term goals of our country." Cherov's voice said he was interested and Khromchenkov knew it.

"Of course," Khromchenkov said, "such a plan would depend greatly on the response from the Americans. I have made some assumptions, and of course it is all conjecture; I am not an expert in these things." There was no doubt in Cherov's mind that this was said both to fulfill Khromchenkov's obligation to defer to Cherov's position as Foreign Minister and to position himself to avoid the blame later if his assumptions on the matter proved incorrect. "Perhaps you would have a different assessment," Khromchenkov suggested as he left the urinal to wash his hands.

"No. Your assessment seems correct," Cherov said as he joined him at the sink. "Of course, we shall never know for sure. It would be impossible to overrule the wishes of President Perelyakin on this matter." Cherov's voice made it clear he was eager to hear more, if indeed there was more to hear.

"I suppose you are correct," Khromchenkov said with an insincere sigh, and then added, "On the other hand, were it to be proposed by the right member of the Security Council, there are doubtless others who would follow."

"The right member?" Cherov asked, wanting Khromchenkov to confirm what he seemed to be suggesting.

"Yes, someone who could offer the strong leadership required to lead the Russian Federation, should the president find it, er . . . impossible to support the view of the majority."

There was now no doubt about what he was suggesting. Khromchenkov's plan was obvious: Cherov was "the right member." President Perelyakin would obviously oppose the plan. That was the easy part. The difficult part—impossible, unless it could be prearranged—was to have the majority side with

Cherov. Perelyakin was not a forgiving man. If the plan failed it would cost Cherov dearly.

"Can one be sure of the numbers?" Cherov asked cautiously.

"As sure as one may be of anything," Khromchenkov answered, drying his hands. "There are three members who supported Perelyakin in the past who have confided to me that they do not wish to see an opportunity such as this pass unanswered."

Cherov did a quick tally of the numbers. It suddenly occurred to him that, despite the accuracy of Khromchenkov's math, everything did not add up. Why had not these three members simply gone to Perelyakin to press for a stronger response to the problem?

"And have these members gone to President Perelyakin with their plea?" Cherov asked.

"Yes, of course."

"And he refuses to listen?"

"He listens. He just does not hear. His world is built on caution."

"A sound foundation," Cherov answered.

"Yes, but one that may let destiny slip past unanswered and ignore an opportunity that would restore Russia to its rightful place as a world power."

"You speak of opportunity. But there is no such opportunity unless your General Serov is successful in regaining control of the Israeli strategic defense."

"True enough," Khromchenkov admitted. "If he does not, then the alternate recommendation will not be made and there is nothing lost. And yet, if he does succeed . . . we must be ready to act."

Cherov considered Khromchenkov's comment. "I will think on it," he said finally.

Tel Aviv, Israel

In the Off-Site Test Facility the members of Colonel White's team took turns sleeping. It had been thirty hours since the successful launch of the Gideon missiles; it might be days or even weeks before they saw the outside again. Joel was munching on a bag of Tapu potato chips in front of a computer console and Scott had just stretched out on a cot to rest when something unexpected happened.

"What's this?" Joel said under his breath. "Colonel White," he called, requesting the team leader's presence.

Colonel White downed the rest of a cup of coffee and walked over to where Joel was sitting. "What's up?" he asked.

Joel moved closer to the console, studying the computer monitor. "A bad reading, I hope. The master icon for the defense grid just went red."

Colonel White took one look and didn't like what he saw. "Danny, get over here quick," he yelled to one of the two female members of the team.

Danielle Metzger was the one person, other than White, with the most experience in the OSTF, but unlike the Colonel her work had all been hands on. She knew the facility inside and out.

"Oh, no!" she yelled. The noise woke the three team members who were sleeping.

"Quick," Metzger shouted, taking command of the situation. "Everybody, we've got a problem!!"

"Tell me what's going on," White ordered.

"We've lost control," Danielle responded as she ran a series of diagnostics to be sure the readings were correct.

"What happened?" several voices said at once.

Danielle continued working, madly trying to reestablish control. Finally she confirmed that this was not simply a faulty reading. "Colonel, it appears that somehow the Russians have taken control of all defensive capabilities."

"Can we get them back?" he asked, terrified of what her answer might be.

"I don't know, sir. I—"

"Wait a second," Joel interrupted. "We still have control of our offensive forces. How could we lose one but not the other? Could this just be an aberration in the system?"

Like the others, Scott Rosen was studying the situation, trying to get some idea of what went wrong and what could be done to correct it. It was he who answered Joel's question. "It's not an aberration," he replied. "I can't explain *how* they did it but I can explain *what* they've done. The fiber optics used for communication between the various sites in the offensive and defensive systems go through both the SDCF and the OSTF. For reasons of logistics, control communications of missile silos go first through this facility and then to the SDCF; defensive control communications go first through the SDCF and then to this facility."

"What idiot decided to do that?!" Joel exclaimed.

"Dr. Brown," answered Danielle Metzger. "But he couldn't have predicted we'd ever be in a situation like this," she continued, becoming a little defensive on behalf of the late doctor who had been her mentor.

Scott continued his explanation. "Somehow they must have discovered that Sensor Facility 14 was a counterfeit facility and traced its input/output cables."

"So can we get control back or not?" Colonel White asked, reasserting his authority. There was a long pause.

"I don't think so," Scott answered finally. "I think they may have cut the cables."

In all the confusion and disarray, no one noticed the faint sound of the radio in the background as it monitored the continuous loop of the words of the prophet Joel. Nor did they notice at first when the loop abruptly stopped and was replaced by another voice. It was the low, rich, and measured voice of Rabbi Saul Cohen. As the room fell silent for a moment, the familiar voice registered in Joel Felsberg's ears. At first he ignored it, but then suddenly he recognized it. "That's my sister's rabbi," he announced, surprising the others, who were trying to figure a way out of the present predicament. "What's going on up there? Why have they shut off the loop?" he asked as he turned the sound up enough to be heard more clearly.

"Cohen? That traitor!" Scott Rosen said, temporarily distracted from the more pressing subject at hand by his intense hatred for the rabbi. Scott was only too familiar with Cohen's powerful voice. Once, when he'd stayed overnight at his parents' house,

Scott had been awakened in the morning by that same voice as it joined with his parents and a few others in singing songs proclaiming Yeshua as the Jewish Messiah. It took all the forbearance he could muster to refrain from going into the kitchen and slugging the rabbi, and still he would have, had it not been for his mother. It was one thing for individual citizens of Israel like his parents to believe in Yeshua, but it was something else altogether for a rabbi—an Hasidic rabbi at that—to believe it. More recently, before their deaths in the Disaster, Scott's parents had spent every spare moment with Cohen on some mysterious project. Several times the three had disappeared for weeks, leaving only a note to indicate their expected date of return.

"All the earth has seen what has been done here today," Cohen said over the radio. "But you, oh Israel, have not glorified God. Instead you have congratulated yourselves for destroying your enemy. You have glorified yourself and now you have falsely used the words of the prophet Joel to suit your own needs. 'These words must not be used as a rallying cry for my people,' says the Lord. These are the words of the son of Satan, who will rally his evil forces to destroy you in the day of the Lord that is coming. Nevertheless, the Lord your God is a patient and merciful God. Hear now the words of the prophet Ezekiel for the enemy of my people Israel:

> I will execute judgment upon him with plague and bloodshed; I will pour down torrents of rain, hailstones and burning sulfur on him and his troops and on the many nations with him . . . On the mountains of Israel you will fall, you and all your troops and the nations with you. I will give you as food to all kinds of carrion birds and wild animals. You will fall in the open field, for I have spoken, declares the Sovereign Lord . . . and they will know that I am the Lord![32]

[32]Ezekiel 38:22; 39:4-6.

"Today, oh Israel, today you shall behold the power and wrath of God! Here, oh Israel, is your true battle cry. 'Behold the hand of God! Behold the hand of God!'"

New York, New York

Decker was suddenly awakened as a scream of pure terror erupted from Christopher's room. Decker found the boy covered in sweat and trembling in fear. "What's wrong?" Decker shouted, his own heart racing to match Christopher's.

Christopher sat up straight in bed, seemingly unsure of his surroundings. As he looked around, the disorientation was slow to leave him. Finally, Decker saw a look of recognition in his eyes.

"I'm sorry," Christopher said. "I'm okay now. It was . . . just a dream."

Decker had been a father long enough to recognize when a child was attempting to be brave. Christopher was visibly shaken and Decker wasn't about to leave him alone.

"Was it the crucifixion dream again?" Decker asked.

"No, no," Christopher answered. "Nothing like that."

"Well, why don't you tell me about it."

Christopher seemed a little reluctant but Decker insisted. "It was really just a dumb dream," Christopher said apologetically. "I've had the same dream before." Decker didn't budge. "Okay," Christopher said, giving in to Decker's insistence. "The dream has a weird feeling about it. It seems almost ancient, but at the same time it's clear and fresh. When the dream starts, I'm in a room with huge curtains hanging all around me. The curtains are beautiful, decorated with gold and silver threads. The floor of the room is made of stone and in the middle of the room is an old wooden box, like a crate, sitting on a table. I can't explain why, but in the dream I feel like I need to look in the box."

"What's in the box?" Decker asked.

"I don't know. In the dream it seems like there's something inside that I need to see, but at the same time, somehow I know that whatever it is, it's terrifying."

Decker read the terror in the boy's eyes and was glad he had insisted Christopher tell him about the dream. This was not the sort of thing a fifteen-year-old should have to face on his own.

"In the dream, when I approach the box and I'm just a few feet away, I look down and somehow the floor has disappeared. I start to fall, but I grab onto the table that the box is sitting on." Christopher stopped.

"Go on," Decker urged.

"That's as far as the dream ever went until tonight."

"So, what happened tonight?" Decker prodded.

"Well, usually I wake up at that point, but this time there was something else: a voice. It was a very deep, rich voice and it was saying, 'Behold the hand of God! Behold the hand of God!'"

Decker had no idea what the dream might mean, but it certainly had his attention.

"And then there was another voice," Christopher continued. "Well, it wasn't exactly a voice. It was a laugh."

"A laugh?"

"Yes, sir. But it wasn't a friendly laugh. I can't really explain it except to say it was cold and cruel and terribly inhuman."

Moscow, Russia

Lieutenant Yuri Dolginov hurried down the long hall of the Kremlin toward the office of the Defense Minister. Despite the importance of his message he knew well that he had better take the time to knock before entering. "Sir," he said, when he was permitted to enter, "we have regained control of the Israeli strategic defense."

This was good news, indeed. "Excellent," Khromchenkov said to himself. "Then the time has come to strike." He made a quick call to Foreign Minister Cherov before notifying President Perelyakin of the change in status in Israel. The president called for an immediate meeting of the Russian Security Council.

When the meeting convened a few minutes later, President

Perelyakin immediately turned the floor over to Khromchenkov. He had no idea of the intrigue that was brewing and simply felt it was good politics to allow the defense minister to have the pleasure of informing the Security Council of the good news from Israel.

Khromchenkov read the words of the communiqué from General Serov in the Israeli Strategic Defense Control Facility:

> Have regained control of Israeli strategic defense. Unable to achieve same for offensive missile forces. Recommend immediate action as condition could change without warning.

The members of the Security Council applauded General Serov's accomplishment. Several of the men in the meeting had already been notified of the situation and were obliged to act as though this was the first time they had heard it.

"Thank you," President Perelyakin told Khromchenkov. "Now, I suggest we comply with the general's recommendation and respond immediately."

"One moment," Foreign Minister Cherov interrupted.

"Yes," responded Perelyakin, who had already risen from his seat. Perelyakin's face showed only the slightest hint of concern as Cherov began. Inside, however, his stomach muscles tightened as if in preparation for a physical blow.

"It has occurred to me that we face a remarkable opportunity to restore Russia to its rightful position as a great world power. At this moment the American forces are struggling to rebuild. Now, certainly I will acknowledge that similar conditions exist for the Russian Federation. The Disaster, as the Americans call it, has struck both sides with severe losses. But the measure of superiority is not what is, but how one uses what is, to his final advantage."

Perelyakin listened to Cherov's words with his ears but his eyes studied the faces of those around him. He didn't like what he saw anymore than he liked what he heard.

New York, New York

"I appreciate you meeting me for breakfast, Yuri," Jon Hansen said as he greeted the Soviet ambassador.

"Good morning, Jon," Kruszkegin responded. "That's all right. I'm on a diet," he added in jest, anticipating the distasteful nature of the conversation that was about to follow.

Kruszkegin's eyes were red from having to operate in two different time zones. He had been awakened early that morning to be apprised of the situation in Israel. His nephew, Yuri Dolginov, who worked for the defense minister, had sent him an encrypted e-mail from Moscow that Russia had regained control of the Israeli strategic defense, and Kruszkegin had stayed up expecting official notification from the foreign minister of what action was intended. None came. This was not the first time he'd had to depend on his nephew for word of what was going on. The foreign minister, under whose direction all Russian ambassadors functioned, was not comfortable with men like Kruszkegin, whom he considered far too internationally-minded to be very useful to the Russian Federation.

Hansen and Kruszkegin continued to exchange small talk for a while as their breakfast was served, and then Hansen attempted to elicit some information. "You seem worried," Hansen said. He was lying. Kruszkegin's face showed no emotion at all except possibly enjoyment of his breakfast. Hansen had said it solely to observe Kruszkegin's response.

"Not at all," Kruszkegin answered.

Hansen tried a different tack. "You don't have any more idea what's going on than I do, do you?" But Kruszkegin only smiled and continued chewing. Hansen tried a few more times, to no avail. Kruszkegin just continued eating his breakfast.

"I thought you were on a diet," Hansen said in frustration. "Why did you even accept my invitation to breakfast if you weren't going to talk?"

Kruszkegin put down his fork. "Because," he began, "one day I will want you to come to breakfast as my guest and *I* will be the one asking all the questions."

"When that happens," Hansen responded, "I shall endeavor to be as tight-lipped as you."

"I'm sure you will be," Kruszkegin said. "And then I will notify my government that we met but that I was unable to learn anything new, just as you shall do today."

Hansen gave a brief chuckle and went back to his nearly untouched breakfast. A few moments later, however, the gravity of the current situation resurfaced and Hansen began to push the food around on his plate rather than eat it.

"You look worried," Kruszkegin said, echoing Hansen's earlier statement.

"I am," Hansen answered. "Yuri, things have changed. I can't tell what's going on in Russia anymore. The men in power are unpredictable. Men like Yeltzin and Gorbachev, even men like Putin, would never have taken chances like these men have. I just don't know what we can expect from them."

Kruszkegin stopped eating, and unlike before, it was obvious he was not thinking about his food. Hansen had struck a nerve. In truth, Kruszkegin was as concerned as Hansen, probably more so. Still, he offered no comment.

❑

After breakfast Hansen and Kruszkegin left for their separate missions. When Kruszkegin arrived at the Mission of the Russian Federation on East 67th Street, his personal secretary handed him a message.

"It came while you were at breakfast," she reported.

Kruszkegin looked at the note. It was from his nephew at the Ministry of Defense. The message was simple but unusual. "Uncle Yuri," it began, which was unusual in itself; in the past his nephew had always addressed his correspondence, "Dear Mr. Ambassador." Kruszkegin did not pause long over the informality, though; his mind was on the message that followed. "Say your prayers," it said.

Kruszkegin went to his office and locked the door. Sitting at his desk he took out a Cuban cigar and lit it. He thought about the brief message from his nephew and looked at it again. "Say your prayers."

It was a joke. That is, it had been a joke four years earlier when he had helped young Yuri, his namesake, get the position on Khromchenkov's staff. "What shall I say," his nephew had asked him at that time, "to warn you, should we ever decide to launch a major nuclear attack?"

Kruszkegin remembered his response: "Just tell me to say my prayers."

Russia

The heavy, German-made cover slid quickly back from the underground silo, clearing the way for the missile inside. At eighty-seven locations scattered around the Russian Federation, the same foreboding sound of metal against metal was followed by the release of mooring clamps and then by the roar of rocket engines firing. Slowly the missiles rose from their tranquil catacombs, hidden at first by the white clouds of exhaust that rose around them. Emerging above the banks of smoke, the missiles crept heavenward, picking up speed as they continued in their course. Their targets were not limited to Israel alone. In truth, Israel had now become insignificant. Khromchenkov's plan for restoring Russia to world prominence was to control the world's oil supply. With this launch it would no longer be necessary to use Israel for a staging ground to take control of Egypt's and Saudi Arabia's oil fields. Now that would be accomplished with one stroke. Israel needed to be taught a lesson and so six warheads had been targeted at its cities. But the hundreds of other warheads, as many as sixteen MIRVed[33] warheads in each missile, were targeted at every major city in every oil-rich country in the Middle East. Throughout Russia the military was put in readiness for the invasion to follow.

West of St. Petersburg a farmer ceased milking his cows as the

---

[33]Multiple Independently targetable Re-entry Vehicle.

frozen ground shook and the roar of engines reached his ears. Running from his barn in confused wonder, he saw the sun briefly eclipsed by a rising missile, which cast a shadow over him and his efforts.

Outside the Cathedral of St. Basil in Moscow a wedding party looked skyward toward six rising plumes of exhaust.

On a bridge in Irkutsk, children watching a puppet show were startled as the puppeteer suddenly ceased his craft to stare at the foreboding display in the sky.

In Yekaterinburg, at a ten-kilometer race, ice skaters and spectators alike stopped in silent terror as the sun reflected off the hulls of four missiles speeding skyward.

Throughout Russia similar scenes played out.

Eighteen and a half seconds into their course, at a point approximately two miles into the air, as people in cities, towns, and farms around the country watched . . . the unexplainable happened.

At the core of each of the multiple warheads carried by the missiles, in an area so infinitesimally small, an incomprehensibly immense burst of energy was released. In less than a hundredth of a millionth of a second the temperature of the warheads rose to more than a hundred million degrees Kelvin—five times hotter than the core of the sun—creating a fireball that expanded outward at several million miles per hour. Instantly everything within two to four miles of the blasts was vaporized: not just the farmer, but the tools with which he had worked; not just the wedding party, but the cathedral from which they had come; not just the children and the puppeteer, but the bridge on which they stood; not just the skaters and spectators, but the frozen river on which they had raced. Even the air itself was incinerated. For eight to fifteen miles around each of the exploding warheads, what was not vaporized burst instantly into flame.

As the fireballs expanded they drove before them superheated shockwaves of expanding air. Reflecting off of the ground they had not vaporized, the secondary shockwaves of the blasts fused with the initial shockwaves and propagated along the ground to create Mach fronts of unbelievable pressure. Buildings, homes, trees, and everything that had not already been destroyed were sheared from the surface of the earth and carried along at thousands of miles per hour.

The death toll in the first fifteen seconds alone was more than thirty million.

The huge fireballs, having expanded to as much as six miles in diameter, now rose skyward, pulling everything around them inward and upward like huge chimneys. Hundreds of billions of cubic meters of smoke and toxic gases created by the fires, together with all that had been blown outward by the blasts, was now drawn back to the center and carried aloft at five hundred miles per hour into scores of mammoth irradiated mushroom clouds of debris that would rain deadly fallout for thousands of miles around.

Tel Aviv, Israel

The unsecured black phone rang and Lieutenant Colonel Michael White answered according to standard operating procedure, simply stating the last four digits of the phone number. The voice on the phone was that of the Israeli prime minister calling from his recently liberated office in the Knesset. "Congratulations," he said. "Not one missile left Russian airspace. All Israel owes you their life and their freedom."

"Thank you, Mr. Prime Minister," Colonel White said. "But it wasn't us. Our line of control was cut hours ago. Our strategic defense is still entirely inoperable."

17

Master of the World

FORMER ASSISTANT SECRETARY-GENERAL Robert Milner and Namibian Ambassador Thomas Sabudu paused briefly to be sure everything was in order before stepping onto the elevator. When they reached the British Mission on the twenty-eighth floor they were warmly greeted by Jackie Hansen and shown into Hansen's inner office.

"Good afternoon, Bob, Ambassador Sabudu," Hansen said as he left his desk to show his guests to the sitting area in his office. "How have you been, Bob?" Hansen asked.

"Not bad for an old man," answered Milner.

"For an old man, you certainly haven't slowed down at all. I think I see you around the UN more now than when you actually worked there."

Milner laughed. "Well, now that I don't have to be there, it's a lot more fun."

"So, are you just operating out of your briefcase now?" Hansen asked.

"Oh, no," Milner answered. "Alice Bernley let me set up shop in a spare room down at the Lucius Trust." Jackie brought in tea and scones and the three men sat down to business.

"So, what can I do for you?" Hansen asked, looking alternately at Sabudu and Milner.

"Jon we're here—Ambassador Sabudu officially and me unofficially—on behalf of certain members of the Group of 77," Milner began, referring to the caucus of Third World countries that had originally consisted of seventy-seven countries but that had since grown to include more than one hundred and fifty nations.

"We have come," said Ambassador Sabudu, "because on two previous occasions you have addressed the General Assembly on the subject of reorganizing the UN Security Council."

"Yes," Hansen recalled. "But I'm sure you understand that on both of those occasions my intent was to dramatize the seriousness of another point. Most recently—just after the Russian invasion of Israel—it was to make the point that Russia could not just start invading other countries and assume the United Nations would do nothing about it. It was never my intent that the motion would pass. If Russia *had* been removed from the Security Council, I think it's a pretty safe bet they'd have dropped out of the UN altogether and we'd have lost the opportunities the UN provides to settle disputes diplomatically. So, as I said, my motion was simply to make the point, not to actually change the Security Council."

"Yes, of course," Sabudu responded.

"Jon," interjected Milner, "we'd like for you to bring it up again, this time in earnest."

Hansen sat back in his chair.

"Ambassador Hansen," Sabudu began.

"Please, call me Jon."

"All right then, Jon. As you know, many things have changed since the Disaster and in the two months since the nuclear devastation of Russia. Many of us in the Group of 77 believe it is now time for the UN to change as well." In truth, the Third World countries had been wanting to change the Security Council since they began to make up the majority of members in the UN. "It is totally unreasonable," Sabudu continued, "that five nations should exercise such dominance over the United Nations as do the five permanent members of the Security Council." Sabudu's voice was spiced with the conviction of his message.

"Let me assure you, Thomas," Hansen said, taking the liberty to call Sabudu by his first name, "even though my country is one of those five you refer to, I personally share that view."

"Jon," said Milner, "Thomas and I have polled most of the members of the Group of 77 and a great many of them—one hundred and seven at this point—have committed their support to such a motion. Another thirty-two are leaning strongly in our direction."

Hansen raised his eyebrows, a bit surprised at the level of support for the proposition. "But why have you decided that I should be the one to make the proposal?"

"Three reasons," answered Milner. "First, as Thomas said, you've made the motion before. Second, you're very well respected by all the members, especially the Third World countries. And third, because we feel it's absolutely imperative that the motion be made by the delegate of one of the permanent members of the Security Council. Some members I've talked to have told me that because of the devastation of the Russian Federation, they think that some sort of restructuring will probably occur anyway in the next four or five years. They're just not sure they want to be involved in rocking the boat to make it happen now. That's why it's so important that one of the permanent members of the Security Council make the motion. Quite frankly, they want someone bigger than them to pin it on if the motion fails. If Britain makes the motion, I believe we can pull all or most of the votes from the Third World countries that are leaning our way. With that, we'll be within a dozen votes of the two-thirds majority needed for passage."

"I don't know, Bob," Hansen interrupted, "I have no idea how my government will feel about such a motion. It was one thing for me to suggest it when it had no chance of passing, but it's quite another if it might actually come about. I don't even know how I'd be instructed to vote on such a measure."

"How do you feel about it, personally?" Milner asked.

"As I said, I agree it's unreasonable that five countries should exercise dominance over the UN, but on the other hand, I'm not sure I know of a better way to run things and still accomplish as much as we do." Hansen thought for a moment. "Off the record, if we could come up with a more equitable approach and it wouldn't bog down the system for lack of direction and leadership, I guess I'd be for it."

"Would you be willing to work with us to develop such an approach, perhaps based on some regional plan?" asked Sabudu. "And if we *are* able to come up with something you're comfortable with, would you present it to your government for consideration?"

Hansen nodded. "I'll do what I can. But it's possible that even if we can come up with a workable plan and I can persuade my government to support it, I may not be allowed to actually make the motion if it is felt that by doing so we would anger the other permanent members. Is there any possibility one of the other permanent members would make the motion?"

"We don't think so," said Milner.

"I see."

Milner opened his briefcase to retrieve a document. "To get the ball rolling on this," he said, "I've brought along a proposal on restructuring the Security Council based on regional entities. We may want to use it as a point of departure, at least, in developing a final plan."

Hansen glanced at the document and put it on the table beside him.

"What Secretary Milner has said about your personal sway with the Third World members was not just flattery, Mr. Ambassador," said Sabudu, becoming more formal to make his point.

"Thank you, Mr. Ambassador," Hansen responded in kind.

"Jon," Milner said, "there is one other item we need to talk about, and I think it may just soften the blow to your government of losing its permanent place on the Council. As you know, in order to ensure impartiality, the secretary-general has always been selected from among the members of the UN who have no ties to any of the permanent members of the Security Council. For years that has served as a major counterweight to the power of the five permanent members on the Security Council. But if the Security Council were reorganized on some other basis, there would be no reason for continuing that requirement. There would be no defensible reason that the secretary-general shouldn't be from, say, Britain or the U.S. or any of the other former permanent members of the Council.

"Jon, the secretary-general has already indicated his intention to retire at the end of this session. If you are the one to make the motion and we can get the votes we need for passage, we believe that you would be the obvious candidate to take his place."

Jon Hansen took a deep breath and leaned back in his chair.

❏

In the outside office Jackie Hansen was working at her computer when she looked up to see Christopher Goodman coming in the door. "Hi, Christopher," she said. "How was school?"

"Okay," he answered. "Is Mr. Hawthorne here?"

"He's out right now, but I expect him back shortly. If you want, you can wait in his office."

"No, that's okay," he said. "I just wanted to let him know that I'd be a little late this evening. I'm going to the seminar and exhibit the Saudi government is sponsoring. Would you tell him for me?"

"Sure, Christopher," Jackie answered. "You seem to stay pretty busy going to all those exhibits."

"Yeah, it's great. There's a different seminar or exhibit or program to go to every couple of weeks. And some of the exhibits can take days to go through."

"I envy you," she said. "I wish I had the time to take advantage of all the educational programs the UN has to offer."

Jackie saw the ambassador's door start to open and put her finger to her lips to indicate that they'd have to continue the conversation after Ambassador Hansen's guests left.

Christopher picked up a magazine to keep busy until he and Jackie could continue, but before he could start reading, he heard someone call his name. He looked up to see Assistant Secretary-General Milner standing next to Ambassador Hansen, looking straight at him.

"Oh, hello, Secretary Milner," Christopher answered.

"You two know each other?" Hansen asked Milner.

"Yes. We've bumped into each other on several occasions at some of the exhibits, but we weren't formally introduced until a few days ago when I spoke at Christopher's high school about my World Curriculum project and the goals of the United Nations. He's quite a good student, his teacher tells me. It wouldn't surprise me at all if Christopher went to work for the UN himself someday," concluded Milner, who then turned his full attention back to Hansen and Sabudu.

"As soon as you've had a chance to review the draft document I gave you and to come up with recommendations on how to improve it, please call me and we'll get back together," he told Hansen.

"I'll do that," answered Hansen.

With that the men shook hands and Milner and Sabudu left. Afterward Hansen told Jackie to inform the senior staff that there would be a 4:30 meeting and they'd all be working a little late.

"Well," Jackie told Christopher, as soon as Ambassador Hansen closed the door to his office, "it looks like you'll have plenty of time at the Saudi exhibit. I'll give Decker the message for you."

"Thanks," said Christopher, as he headed for the door. Before he reached it, though, it opened again. It was Milner.

"Christopher, will you be at the Saudi exhibit this evening?" he asked.

"Yes, sir. I'm going there now."

"Good, I'll see you there. They have a really wonderful presentation on Islam, including some exquisite models of the mosques in Mecca and Medina."

Six weeks later
Tel Aviv, Israel

Tom Donafin dabbed his finger across the bristles of his toothbrush to see if he had applied enough toothpaste. Satisfied that he had, he replaced the tube in its assigned spot on the counter by the sink. He had now been blind for about six months and was learning to live with it. Fortunately, he had always preferred wearing a beard so he didn't have to worry about shaving. And when he'd taken an apartment on the same floor in her building, Rhoda had helped him set up his closet and drawers so that he could pick out matching clothes to wear.

He thought it might still be a little early, but as soon as he was dressed he locked up and walked down the hall toward Rhoda's apartment. Feeling his way with his long white cane, he reached the end of the hall, turned, and counted his steps to her front door. He had done this many times by himself, and there was really no possibility he would go to the wrong door. Still, he had suggested to Rhoda that they carve a heart and their initials into her door so he could always be sure he had the right apartment. Rhoda had thought better of the idea.

Tom knocked at the door and was greeted a moment later with a very warm kiss, which he gladly returned. "You're early," Rhoda said. "Come on in. I was just about to change."

"Should I cover my eyes?" Tom joked.

"It's not your eyes I'm concerned about; it's the pictures in your mind. You just wait here. I'll be back in a minute." In the past Tom had always avoided any real involvement with a woman because he feared rejection because of his disfigurement. Strangely, now that he couldn't see, it was no longer a problem.

Tom made his way to the couch and sat down. On the coffee table Rhoda kept a book for beginning Braille students. He picked it up, intending to get in a little practice, but noticed a single sheet of paper sitting on top. Running his fingers over the formations of bumps one at a time, he determined the characters on the page. "I love you," it said.

Tom didn't mention the note to Rhoda when she came from her bedroom.

"All ready," she said.

Tom got up and walked toward the door. Rhoda met him halfway and placed his hand in the now familiar spot on her arm. "Rabbi won't know what to think when we get to Havdalah early," she said.

"That won't be his only surprise tonight," Tom added, and though he couldn't see it, he was confident that there was a smile on Rhoda's face.

❑

After dinner at Rabbi Cohen's house, everyone moved to the living room. Benjamin Cohen, who alone with his father was the only member of the rabbi's family to survive the Disaster, turned off the lights as his father prayed and lit the three wicks of the tall blue-and-white braided Havdalah candle. The Havdalah, or "separation," marked the end of the Sabbath and the beginning of the work week, the distinction of the holy from the secular. Along with the Cohens and Tom and Rhoda there were nine others present. Originally there had been many more in Cohen's congregation, but the Disaster had reduced their number by more than a hundred and fifty. Now they could fit easily into Cohen's living room. Of those present, some, like Rhoda, had started attending Cohen's services only a few weeks or months before the Disaster. Others had joined the group afterward.

As the flame grew, Saul Cohen took the candle and held it up. In accordance with tradition, those in the circle responded by standing and holding their hands up toward the light with their fingers cupped. Though he could not see the flame, Tom could feel the heat of the large candle and he did as Rhoda had taught him. It meant nothing to him beyond simply being a tradition, but it was important to Rhoda and so he did it.

❑

As they had planned, after the Havdalah, Tom and Rhoda waited for everyone to leave so they could talk with Rabbi Cohen alone.

"Tell me, Tom," Cohen asked, "how did my favorite skeptic like tonight's message?"

"Well," Tom said, "I understood what you were saying, but don't you think it's kind of narrow-minded to say that there's only *one* way for a person to get into the kingdom of God?"

"It would be, Tom," Cohen answered, "were it not for the fact that the one way God offers is entirely unrestricted, completely free, and totally accessible to each and every person on the planet. God is no farther from any of us than our willingness to call upon him. Would it be narrow-minded to say there is only one thing everyone must breathe in order to live?"

"But air is available to everyone," Tom countered.

"Tom, so is God. The Bible says in the book of Romans that God has made himself known to *everyone*. It doesn't matter who you are or where you live or what your religious background is. It's up to each person as an individual whether he will answer God's call. And Tom, one of the great things about it is that once you've answered that call you'll find it's absolutely the most natural thing in the world. Even," Cohen laughed at his own unexpected turn of phrase, "more natural than breathing."

The subject was worthy of further discussion but right now Tom had something else on his mind. As a transitional step to what he really wanted to talk about, Tom decided to ask the rabbi something he had wondered about for a while. "Rabbi," he said, "there's something I don't understand: if you no longer believe as the other Hasidim believe, why do you still wear the attire and earlocks of Hasidim?"

Rhoda looked away in embarrassment; she would never have asked the question herself, but it was something she had often wondered about. She felt sure the rabbi would know she had mentioned it to Tom. After all, how else could Tom know *what* the rabbi wore?

"It is my heritage," Cohen answered. "Even the Apostle Paul, whom Messiah charged with bringing the word to the Gentiles, did not change his ways, except as it was necessary to accomplish his mission. Besides," added Cohen, "there are many years of wear left in these clothes. Why should I buy new?"

Cohen smiled, but Tom, who could only assume that Cohen was serious, had to bite his lip to hold back laughter.

"So, what is it I can do for you?" asked Cohen, assuming correctly that Tom and Rhoda had not stayed late just to ask him about his wardrobe.

"Well," said Tom, glad for the opportunity to get to the subject he wanted to talk about, "Rhoda and I would like for you to officiate at our wedding."

Cohen didn't respond.

"Is something the matter, Rabbi?" Rhoda asked.

Cohen hesitated. "I'm sorry. Rhoda, could I speak with you alone for just a moment?"

Cohen began to move away and Rhoda automatically followed before Tom could even think to object. In a moment so brief he couldn't speak, they were gone and Tom heard one of the interior doors of the house close behind them.

❏

"Rhoda," Cohen said, as soon as he was alone with her, "do you remember what I told you when I brought Tom to you?"

"You mean the prophecy?" she asked.

"Yes."

"How could I forget it? I've thought about it every day."

"Then you know that this will not be an easy marriage. You may have several years of peace—I don't know exactly how many—but then you will lose him. The prophecy is clear: 'He must bring death and die that the end and the beginning may come.'"

"I know and I understand," Rhoda answered.

"And you still want to go ahead with the marriage?" Cohen's voice showed concern but gave no hint of disapproval.

"Yes, Rabbi. More than anything."

Cohen gave her a look of caution concerning her last statement.

Rhoda saw the look and quickly corrected herself. "I mean, more than anything, as long as it is within God's will."

Cohen let it pass. "All right, then. Just as long as you're going into this with your eyes wide open."

"I am, Rabbi," Rhoda assured him.

"There is, of course, the issue of being yoked to an unbeliever, but with Tom, I have always known it was just a matter of time.

We shall have to see to that immediately, and by all means before the wedding takes place."

Rhoda willingly agreed.

"Oh, by the way," Cohen asked as an afterthought, "have you told Tom about the prophecy?"

"No, Rabbi. I didn't think I should."

Cohen nodded thoughtfully. "Yes, it's probably best that you don't. Better to let God act in his own time and not put any ideas in Tom's head."

Cohen and Rhoda went back to where Tom was waiting for them. "Well, Tom," Cohen began, by way of explanation, "your Rhoda assures me that she's going into this with her eyes open."

Tom knew how much stock Rhoda put in Cohen's opinions, but he didn't much care for being talked about when he wasn't around to defend himself, and he wasn't at all sure he liked the scrutiny Cohen had apparently placed on their plans. Nonetheless, he decided to hold his tongue. He would soon be glad he did.

"Speaking of going into things with your eyes open," Cohen said, "Tom, I have a wedding gift for you. Actually, it's not from me. I was told to give you this when I first found you under the rubble. The exact timing was left up to me, and, I guess this seems like as good a time as any." Cohen came close to Tom, reached out his hand, and placed it over Tom's eyes. "Not through any power of my own," Cohen said, before Tom could even figure out what was going on, "but in the name and through the power of Messiah Yeshua: Open your eyes and see."

Two weeks later
New York, New York

British Ambassador Jon Hansen was widely applauded as he approached the speaker's dais at the United Nations General Assembly. His speech would be translated simultaneously into Arabic, Chinese, French, Russian, and Spanish, which together with English are the six official languages of the United Nations.

Twice before Hansen had spoken on the subject of reorganizing the UN Security Council, but this time there was no doubt the plea would be made in earnest.

Over the preceding three weeks Decker had spent countless hours working on this speech: writing drafts, condensing, expanding, adding, deleting, polishing, and working with linguists to ensure that the words spoken in English would have the proper impact when translated. What Hansen was about to propose would involve a major restructuring of the United Nations and his words would have to be both clearly understood and thoroughly compelling.

The message of Hansen's address was not unexpected. The press was out in force to cover the address and the seconding speeches. There was still no guarantee of getting the two-thirds vote necessary to carry the motion; too many nations would not make a commitment before the actual vote.

What made it possible now that Hansen's motion might actually pass, when before it had not been taken seriously, were the recent events in Russia. The nuclear holocaust had reduced the Russian Federation to a mere specter. Even the name was threatened as survivors in one federated region after another emerged from the rubble and declared themselves independent republics—much as had happened when the Russian Federation's predecessor, the USSR, fell apart decades before. Those were the lucky ones; in some parts of Russia there were not enough survivors to even worry about things political.

The world had been a much different place on October 24, 1945, when the United Nations officially came into being. The Second World War had just ended, and the victors who had made up the major powers of the world—the United States, Great Britain, France, the Soviet Union, and China—had established themselves as the "Big Five," giving themselves permanent member status and veto power in the United Nations Security Council. Since that time Britain had divested herself of her colonies and, though influential, remained great only in name. She would trade her power on the Security Council for temporary control of the Secretariat under Hansen and the opportunity to direct the UN's reorganization. "It is better to trade away now what might well be taken tomorrow," Hansen had told the British Parliament. Britain knew that the evolution of the UN was unstoppable. Guiding that evolution was a responsibility for which Britain felt itself uniquely qualified.

France, never truly an economic world power after World War II and ever the libertine, had turned to neo-isolationism and so had voluntarily surrendered her position as a world leader. She would not, however, so willingly surrender her power. Even as Hansen spoke, France was lobbying other members to vote against the measure.

China was an anomaly. Despite being one of the poorest countries, it remained a world power, if only because of its military strength and its enormous population. Because of its size, China alone of the five original Security Council members would be guaranteed a seat on the reorganized Council. Nonetheless, China would oppose the measure because its power would be diluted by half in the proposed ten-member council. Her great size would make little difference in the General Assembly. Concessions made two years earlier had removed veto power of the Big Five over amending the UN Charter. China, like the tiniest of countries, would have only one vote.

The Russian Federation, though it would protest loudly, certainly no longer had legitimate claim to permanent status on the Security Council or to veto power over its actions.

Only the United States could truly claim a right to permanent status based on its position as a world power. Yet in a very real sense, this proposal might be seen as a logical next step toward the "New World Order" first proposed by former U.S. president George H. W. Bush, and it appeared to have the support of, if not a majority, then at least a large and vocal minority of American citizens as well as a majority of those in Congress. The U.S. would not stand in the way of reorganization if it was what the members of the United Nations wanted.

Hansen's proposal would eliminate the permanent positions of the Big Five and instead structure a newly defined Security Council around representatives of each of ten major regions of the world. The details would have to be worked out by all member nations, but it was expected that these regions would include North America; South America; Europe and Iceland; Eastern Africa; Western Africa; the Middle East; the Indian subcontinent; Northern Asia; China; and the nations of Asia's Pacific basin from Japan and Korea through Southeast Asia, down to Indonesia and New Guinea, along with Australia, and New Zealand. Each region would have one voting member and one alternate member on the Security Council.

As he stood before the great assembly of nations, about to give the most important speech of his life, Hansen was running on adrenaline. He had spent night and day for the past several weeks lobbying for approval. Now was the moment for show business, but immediately afterward the lobbying and arm twisting would continue anew. Hansen stepped up to the speaker's lectern and began.

"My fellow delegates and citizens of the world: I come to you today as the ambassador of an empire now divested of all her colonies. I say that not with regret, but with pride. Pride that over time we have grown to recognize the rights of sovereign peoples to set their own course in the history of the earth. Pride that my beloved Britain, though she will bear a great cost at its passage, has placed justice ahead of power and has authorized the introduction and the support of this motion.

"Since the foundation of this august body, five countries, Great Britain among them, have held sway over the other nations of the world. Today the history of nations has come to a new path.

"A new path—not a destination, for there is no stopping.

"A new path—not to a crossroads, for in truth there *is* no other way that just and reasonable men and women may choose.

"A new path—not a detour, for the path we were on has taken us as far as it will go.

"A new path—not a dead-end, for there can be no going back.

"It is the most tragic of situations that has brought us so abruptly to this point in history. And yet, were it not so we would have reached it still. From the first days of the United Nations, it has always been the visionaries' dream that one day all nations would stand as equals in this body. We have come too far toward that dream to refuse now to continue the advance toward its fulfillment.

"The time has come for all peoples of the world to put off the shackles of the past. The day of the empire is gone, and just as certainly the day of subservience to those born of power must also come to an end. Justice is not found in the rule of those who consider themselves our betters, but from the common will of peers. The greatness of nations comes not from the superiority of their armaments, but from their willingness to allow and aid the greatness of others."

Decker listened closely, anticipating the pauses and hoping for the applause he expected each line would draw. Although at the UN the timing of applause can sometimes be embarrassingly delayed by the translation to another language, Decker was not disappointed. Clearly the motion would do well.

❏

In the end, the vote turned, as history so often does, on an ironic twist of fate. At the UN's founding, the Soviet Union had insisted that two of her states, the Byelorussian S.S.R. and the Ukrainian S.S.R., be granted admission to the General Assembly with the full rights of sovereign nations. At the time it had been a way for the USSR to gain two extra votes in the General Assembly. Today the independent Ukraine cast the deciding vote to expropriate Russia's seat on the Security Council. The motion passed.

One week later

The vote to reorganize the Security Council did not mark the completion of the effort, but only the beginning of a new phase. Now that the motion had carried, press representatives from around the world were calling, wanting information about this man who likely would become the new secretary-general. Decker brought in extra personnel to support the more routine functions of the effort, but he was wary of delegating too much. As he went over a press release for the third time, he realized he had no idea what he was reading. He was just too tired. Closing his eyes, he slumped down in the chair and thought back to his days at the *Knoxville Enterprise*. It had been a long time since he had worked this hard.

Unnoticed, Jackie Hansen had entered the room and was now standing directly behind his chair. As he sat with his eyes closed, she reached down and placed her long, slender fingers on his shoulders. Decker jumped, but seeing Jackie's smiling face, relaxed as she began to massage his tired, knotted muscles. "Oh, that feels good," he said gratefully. "I'll give you just twenty minutes to stop it." It was an old joke, but Jackie laughed anyway.

"Your back is one solid knot," Jackie said sympathetically. "I'll bet you're tired."

Decker started to nod his head but decided it might interrupt the massage and instead answered, "Uh-huh."

"My father really appreciates all the work you're doing. He told me you were working so hard that sometimes he wasn't sure which of you was trying to get elected."

Decker appreciated the compliment. It was nice to know his work was appropriately acknowledged. He smiled up at Jackie, then closed his eyes again to concentrate on the relaxing feel of her hands. Suddenly she stopped. "You know what you need to really relax?" she asked.

"What's that?" Decker responded.

"Well, whenever I get real tense, I meditate." Jackie started to rub his shoulders again. "I may seem pretty relaxed to you most of the time, but I used to be a jumble of nerves. When I first started to work here I was so concerned about doing a good job. I didn't want people thinking the only reason I had the job was because my father was the ambassador." Jackie found a knot and began rubbing in circles to work it out. "That's when I met Lorraine from the French Mission. She invited me to go to a meditation class at the Lucius Trust." Jackie stopped again and looked at her watch. "Oh, my gosh," she said in surprise, "speaking of the Lucius Trust: it's 7:55. If I don't hurry I'm going to be late. I've

missed the last three weeks because of work; I really don't want
to miss tonight."

"Miss what?" asked Decker.

"My meditation class," Jackie answered. "It meets at the Lucius
Trust every Wednesday. Tonight Alice Bernley, the director of the
Trust, is going to show new members how to reach their inner
consciousness, the source of creativity. It's like an inner guide."

"Oh," Decker said, making no attempt to hide the fact that he
had no idea what Jackie was talking about.

"Come with me."

"Uh . . . I don't know, Jackie. I'm not really into this New Age
stuff. I'm pretty square, I guess."

"Oh, come on," she insisted, as she took his hand and gave it
a tug. "Really, I think you'll enjoy it. When you leave there tonight
you'll be more relaxed than you've been in weeks. I find it helps
me reach a higher plane of thinking. It frees my creative mental
processes."

Decker sighed. "Well, I guess I could use some of that, but
we'll just have to be a little late. I refuse to run."

❏

The class had already started when they arrived. Quietly Jackie
moved through the crowd of about a hundred and fifty people,
pulling Decker along, until they reached two empty chairs.
Around them people sat silently with eyes closed, some with their
legs crossed, all listening intently to the speaker. They seemed
totally unaware that others were around them. Even in the subdued light, Decker recognized nearly two dozen of the attendees
as UN delegates. The speaker was Alice Bernley, an attractive
woman in her late forties with long flowing red hair. "Just sit
down, close your eyes, and listen," Jackie whispered.

It was easy enough to relax in the deep, comfortable chairs.
Decker listened to the speaker and tried to figure out what he
was supposed to be doing. "In the blackness ahead of you,"
Bernley was saying, "is a small point of light just coming into
view. As you walk closer to the light, you are beginning to

narrow the distance, and the light is growing brighter and warmer." Decker became aware of a soft, barely audible hum, almost like a cat's purr, coming from those around him. As he closed his eyes, to his amazement, he too saw a light. It was very distant, but it was clearly visible. He wondered at the sight, and in his mind it *did* seem as if the light was getting closer, or possibly he was getting closer to it. He was certain it was all just a mental picture painted by the woman, but he was surprised at how open he was to her suggestion. *It must be from lack of sleep*, he thought briefly. The woman's delicate voice seemed to softly caress his ears. "Approach the light," the woman continued, and Decker did. "Soon you will find that it has led you to a beautiful place: a garden." In his mind Decker followed her words and soon he saw it.

Bernley went on at some length describing every detail of the garden. It was so clear, so real and precisely described that later, as Decker looked back to this event and thought of all the others in the room, his greatest wonder—though logically he knew better—was that so many could be sharing the same vision so clearly and yet each be totally alone in his or her own garden. Even in his memory the place seemed so real that he expected to see others from the room there with him.

"Just beyond the shining pool of water you see someone approaching." Decker looked but saw no one. "It may be a person," Bernley continued, "but for many people it will be an animal, perhaps a bird or a rabbit or perhaps a horse or even a unicorn. What form it takes is unimportant. Do not be afraid, even if it is a lion. It will not hurt you. It is there to help you, to guide you when you have questions."

Still Decker saw no one. "When it has come close enough, talk to it, ask it anything you would like to know, and it will answer. You might start by asking its name. As some of you know, my spirit guide is a Tibetan master who goes by the name Djwlij Kajm. For some, your spirit guide may be a bit more shy. You may have to coax it out, not by speaking to it, but by listening. So listen. Listen very closely." Decker listened. He moved closer to the pool, trying to hear. Bernley's voice had fallen silent, apparently to allow those with "shy" spirit guides to listen more closely. Still he saw and heard nothing.

It was not that there was nothing there. If they had spoken any louder, he surely would have heard.

"Why does no one approach him?" one of the voices whispered.

"The Master forbids it," another voice answered. "He has special plans for this one."

❑

Bernley remained silent for another eight or ten minutes. For a while, Decker continued to try to hear or see the guide Bernley said he would find, but when she spoke again he opened his eyes and realized that he had fallen asleep. "Now say farewell to your new friend but thank him and let him know you'll return soon."

Decker watched the others in the group as Bernley brought them back from this expedition of the mind. In a moment they opened their eyes and looked around. Everyone was smiling. Some hugged those around them. A few wept openly. Decker looked over at Jackie Hansen, who seemed to be nearly floating. From a corner of the room someone began to applaud and soon the whole room was filled with applause.

"Thank you, thank you," Bernley said graciously, "but you really should be applauding yourselves for having the courage to open your minds to the unknown. Now, whenever you need guidance on something that you just don't know how to handle, all you have to do is go to a quiet place for a few moments, close your eyes, and open your mind. Seek out your guide at every opportunity and ask it the questions you can't answer. What you are doing is allowing the creative nature that is within all of us to do what it most wants to do: provide visionary solutions to the problems in your life."

Some of Bernley's assistants brought in refreshments and everyone began to talk together in small groups about what they had experienced. Decker politely thanked Jackie for the invitation and told her he had found the experience interesting, but said he really needed to get back to work. She seemed surprised that he was leaving but did not try to stop him.

❏

As soon as Decker left, Alice Bernley called to Jackie, who quickly made her way across the room. Without speaking, Bernley took Jackie's arm and led her to a quiet corner where they would not be overheard. "Was that Decker Hawthorne with you?" Bernley asked, sounding a little concerned.

"Yes," Jackie answered. "I asked him if he'd like to sit in on the class. Did I do the wrong thing?"

"No. It's okay. Actually, it was my fault. I should have told you: The Tibetan has made it very clear that Decker Hawthorne is not to be a part of the Trust. The Master has special plans for Mr. Hawthorne."

Two days later

At the Israeli Mission in New York, Jon Hansen was shown into the office of Ambassador Aviel Hartzog who was at his desk, talking on the phone. He neither looked up nor acknowledged Hansen's arrival. It was an obvious snub. As Hansen waited he couldn't help but overhear Hartzog's conversation, which didn't sound like very important business. This made the snub all the greater. To be talking petty business with some bureaucrat while a guest ambassador waited was inexcusable. What made it even worse was that Hartzog undoubtedly realized Hansen was not only a fellow delegate but most likely the next secretary-general.

Nearly three minutes later the Israeli ambassador finally hung up the phone and joined Hansen. He made no apology for the delay and immediately began by calling Hansen by his first name, even though the two had never been formally introduced, the Israeli ambassador having just been assigned to the UN. *What a cheeky monkey*, thought Hansen.

"So, Jon, what have you come to offer us?"

Hansen held his temper like a true Englishman. "Reason, Mr. Ambassador. Reason."

"You have brought me a reason that Israel should cut her own throat?" Hartzog asked mockingly.

"No. I have—"

Ambassador Hartzog cut Hansen off before he could even begin. "Ambassador Hansen," he said, now becoming formal, "my government considers the decision by the General Assembly to reorganize the Security Council along regional lines a noble gesture. It is, unfortunately, one with which we cannot abide. Did it not cross your mind that by restructuring the Security Council on a regional basis and then grouping Israel with the other nations of the Middle East, you would force us into a position where we would constantly be at the mercy of our Arab neighbors? In case you were not aware, Israel has a Jewish population of five million. We are surrounded by twenty-three Arab nations with a total population of 250 million. Now, tell me, just what do you think Israel's chances are of having a representative on the Security Council who is favorable to our country?" Hartzog paused and then added, "Most of the Arab world still hasn't acknowledged that Israel even exists!"

"But leaving the UN is not the answer, Mr. Ambassador," Hansen said, finally getting a word in.

"Unless you can make some guarantees . . . perhaps by increasing the number of seats on the Security Council to eleven and guaranteeing that seat to Israel . . ." Hartzog paused for Hansen's reaction. He was certain Hansen would never agree to such a proposal, but as Hartzog saw it, he had nothing to lose.

"You know we can't do that," Hansen responded. "It would destroy the whole restructuring. There's no way we can make that kind of exception for Israel without setting the precedent for others wanting the same." Hansen didn't mention it, but there was another precedent he didn't want to set—that of having a nation leave the UN. It had never been done before.

"Then there seems little choice," Hartzog concluded.

"Mr. Ambassador, if Israel leaves the UN, it will be giving in to the very countries you fear. They'd like nothing more than to see Israel out of the United Nations."

"Unfortunately you are correct. But neither can we stay."

❏

The conversation did not improve and Hansen left without having gained an inch of ground. When he returned to his office he was met by Decker Hawthorne. "How'd it go?" Decker asked.

"Not well," Hansen answered in understatement. "Israel is just too blasted cheeky about what happened with the Russian Federation."

"But they've acknowledged that their strategic defense had nothing to do with the premature detonation of the Soviet missiles, so what do they have to be so arrogant about?" Decker really wanted to say "cheeky" too, but he didn't think he could say it without sounding as though he was poking fun.

"The official position of the Knesset is that the destruction of the Russian missiles was a miracle of God."

"You don't think the Israeli ambassador actually believes that, do you?" asked Decker.

"The point is a great many of the Israeli people are convinced that what happened *was* a literal act of God, foretold by their prophet Ezekiel thousands of years ago."[34] Hansen shook his head and sighed. "I can't really blame them for their response to restructuring, though. It doesn't offer them much to look forward to."

[34]Ezekiel 38-39.

Revelation

```
Seven years later
New York, New York
```

DECKER SHOOK THE RAIN from his umbrella, unbuttoned his raincoat, and walked past the UN guard toward the main elevators.

"Good morning, Mr. Hawthorne," the guard said. "And happy birthday!"

Decker paused long enough to smile and nod. "Thank you, Charlie," he responded.

How did he remember that? Decker wondered, as he stepped into the elevator and pushed the button for the thirty-eighth floor. Once he reached the top floor of the United Nations Secretariat building, he proceeded to his office, three doors down from the office of Secretary-General Jon Hansen. The view of the East River and Queens from Decker's office was almost obscured by the rain beating hard against the window.

Decker looked through the notes on his desk to decide what he wanted to do first this morning. Among the neatly disorganized clutter were two photographs: one of Decker with Elizabeth, Hope, and Louisa taken in that brief period between his escape from Lebanon and the Disaster and a two-year-old picture of Christopher at his graduation from the Masters program at the United Nations University for Peace in Costa Rica.

Other than being Decker's fifty-eighth birthday it was an ordinary day at the UN, a fact for which Decker was grateful. As director of public affairs for Secretary-General Jon Hansen,

Decker had been personally involved in much of the planning and implementation of the worldwide United Nations Day celebration three days earlier, so the return to normalcy was welcome. The observance of the UN's founding had been a big success, with celebrations in nearly 200 of the 235 member nations. Secretary-General Hansen placed great importance on the event. He wanted it to be bigger and better each year in order to build public acceptance and support for the UN and its programs. In some countries the UN Day celebration had actually grown more important than the individual nations' own birthday celebrations. There were a few countries where they might have even dispensed with their own national celebrations altogether were it not for the fact that it was an extra day off for the bureaucrats.

Relatively speaking, the world was at peace, and Decker was, for the moment, at rest, recovering from the massive effort of coordinating celebrations in more than a dozen time zones.

Twenty minutes later Decker finally let Mary Polk, his secretary, know that he was officially in.

"Mr. Hawthorne," Mary said in surprise, "I didn't see you come in. Have you forgotten about your meeting this morning with the secretary-general?"

"What meeting?" Decker asked.

"You're scheduled for a meeting with the secretary-general this morning. It was supposed to start about fifteen minutes ago. Jackie has already called twice to find out where you were."

"Oh, no! Why didn't you check to see if I was here?" He didn't wait for an answer. "Call Jackie and tell her I'll be right there." It was only about thirty yards to Secretary-General Hansen's office, so Decker was at the door only seconds after Mary reached Jackie Hansen on the phone.

"They're waiting for you in the conference room," Jackie said as Decker altered his course toward the adjoining room and opened the door.

"Surprise!" about three dozen voices suddenly yelled in unison.

In the center of the crowd stood Secretary-General and Mrs. Hansen. Both seemed to be enjoying the surprised look on

Decker's face. It was incumbent on Decker to laugh, but all he could manage at first was a pained moan and a disbelieving shake of the head. Finally an appreciative smile broke through. Behind Decker, Mary Polk entered the room to join the party. "You're in big trouble," Decker told his secretary as he caught sight of her.

"Don't blame her," interrupted Hansen. "She was just following my orders."

"Don't you people know surprise birthday parties are supposed to be in the afternoon?" Decker asked.

"If we had done it that way we might not have surprised you," Jackie said with a laugh.

On the table were several dozen doughnuts stacked tightly together to look like a cake, with about half the candles Decker was actually due waiting to be lit. "You guys are nuts," Decker said.

"What's that?" Hansen asked in mock offense.

"You guys are nuts, *sir.*"

"Much better," Hansen joked.

But there was still one more surprise for Decker. In a corner of the room was a guest who at first had been concealed behind the others. "Christopher!" Decker said. "What on earth are you doing here?"

"You didn't think I'd miss your birthday, did you?" Christopher, now twenty-two, answered.

"You're supposed to be on a cruise around the world."

"I decided to take half now and half later," Christopher said. "So I flew back."

"Hey, are you going to blow out the candles or not?" Mary Polk asked.

Decker blew out the candles and everyone dug into the doughnuts and coffee. As with most office parties, a few people stayed only long enough to make an appearance, others just long enough to get seconds of the goodies and take a couple of doughnuts back to their desks. Others stayed on and told jokes or gathered in small groups to talk business. Decker positioned himself close to the door and made sure to thank each person for coming. Christopher circulated among the attendees, adding his jokes to the till and, where they were welcome, offering his opinions on the topics of conversation in each of the clusters he visited. Decker watched, pleased at how well accepted Christopher was by Decker's colleagues, and at how well he handled himself with these people.

Among the well-wishers were three Security Council members: Ambassador Lee Yun-mai of China; Ambassador Friedreich Heineman of Germany, representing Europe; and Ambassador Yuri Kruszkegin, formerly of the Russian Federation and now of the independent Republic of Khakassia, representing Northern Asia. They had grouped on one side of the room and were discussing a recent vote on trade barriers. Christopher seemed just as comfortable with them as he had been with the administrative staff.

Finally the crowd began to thin and Secretary-General Hansen came over to talk with Decker. "I want to thank you again, Decker, for the spectacular job you did with this year's United Nations Day celebration," Hansen said as he gave him a pat on the back.

"Thank you for saying so, sir."

"I think you're due for a little time off, so I told Jackie to put you down as being on vacation for the next four or five days. I think your staff can hold the world together in your absence."

The offer was a surprise but, like the party, it was a welcome one. "I believe I'll take you up on that, sir," Decker said willingly. "It would be nice to spend some time with Christopher."

"That's quite a boy you've got there," Hansen said, motioning with his coffee cup in Christopher's direction.

"Yes, sir," Decker said with fatherly pride.

"Someone else who thinks so is Bob Milner. He sent me a letter—a very favorable letter—recommending Christopher for a position with ECOSOC," Hansen said, referring to the United Nations Economic and Social Council.

"Yes, sir. The former assistant secretary-general has been quite supportive of Christopher's endeavors. He even flew down to Costa Rica last month for Christopher's graduation from the UN University's Doctoral program." Decker said this more to brag on Christopher than anything else. He was always willing to tell anyone who asked that Christopher had graduated first in his

class, simultaneously earning both a Ph.D. in Political Science
and a second masters degree in World Agricultural Management.
At this moment he was supposed to be on a cruise around the
world, taking a well-earned vacation before starting to work at
ECOSOC in the position for which Milner had recommended
him.

"Well, with friends like Bob Milner, he'll go a long way,"
Hansen said.

"Have you heard anything recently about Secretary Milner,
sir?" Decker asked. "Someone said he wasn't feeling well."

"Jackie tells me he checked into the hospital three nights ago
for observation because of his heart, and he's still there."

"I've been so busy I didn't know that," Decker said, obviously
both surprised and concerned.

"He's eighty-two now, you know," Hansen said.

"That's not so old," Decker responded, thinking about the
recent addition of a year to his own age.

Hansen laughed. "Christopher can probably tell you better
than I can about how Secretary Milner is doing. I understand he
went to see him this morning before coming to the party."

"Oh," said Decker, a little surprised, but now understanding
more fully why Christopher had cut his trip short.

❑

When the party broke up, Decker went back to his office to tie up
some loose ends and clear his calendar. It was nearly noon before
he was ready to leave. "Where do you want to go for lunch?"
Christopher asked. "I'm buying."

"In that case, there's a hot dog stand downstairs," Decker joked
as he gathered up a few papers and stuffed them into his briefcase.

"I think we can do a little better than that," Christopher
answered.

They finally settled on the Palm Too, a nice but reasonably
priced restaurant on Second Avenue near the UN. "So," Decker
began after they had ordered, "are you ready to start putting that
education of yours to work at ECOSOC?"

"Ready, and anxious to get started," Christopher answered. "I'm not supposed to start work for another two weeks, but maybe I could spend some time reading through their archived literature."

If it had been anyone else, Decker might have complimented his enthusiasm, but from Christopher he had come to expect it. "I spoke with Louis Colleta last week," he said, referring to the head of ECOSOC. "He asked me about you and said he was looking forward to having you on his staff. He told me two or three times how pleased he was to be able to hire someone of your caliber. I'm sure that if you called him and let him know you're available, he'd want you to start right away."

"I'm glad to hear that. I'm just as pleased to have gotten the job."

"I think you made a wise decision in pursuing it. The expansion of ECOSOC's role is a major part of Secretary-General Hansen's plan for greater centralization of authority during his current term." Decker tapped his finger on the table to make his point. "As the role of the UN expands, ECOSOC is going to be more and more on the leading edge of world policy."

"When you look at the growth Secretary-General Hansen has brought about over the last seven years and the spirit of cooperation he inspires among the members of the Security Council, as well as the other member nations, it's hard to imagine how we could get along without him if he were ever to retire," Christopher said.

"Well, I don't think you have to worry about that. He's not the kind to ever willingly walk away from an opportunity to work for world betterment. Besides—off the record—I think he's having too much fun to ever retire." Christopher smiled. "But, you're right: I don't know how we could ever get along without him. So much of his success is based on his own popularity. Peter Fantham in the *Times* called him the 'George Washington of the United Nations' and I have to agree."

Decker paused briefly to take a bite of his sandwich. "We run regular public opinion polls on current and possible future policies, and we also check approval ratings for the various agencies and officials. Secretary Hansen continues to build a higher and higher overall approval rating in all of the ten regions. Last month his worldwide approval rating reached 78 percent. Sure, there are those who oppose everything Hansen or the UN does—a few religious kooks mostly. They think he's the Antichrist or something and that world government is somehow inherently evil."

"Yeah, well, I suppose you're always going to have a few of those," Christopher responded. "But a 78 percent approval rating, that's incredible!"

"You bet it is," Decker continued. "Unfortunately, if there's a weakness in Hansen's government, it's that it's based too heavily on Hansen himself." Decker looked around to be sure no one was listening and then, for good measure, leaned over the table closer to Christopher and whispered, "Left to themselves, some of the Security Council members would fight like cats and dogs." This fact was no big secret; it was just that because of Decker's position with the UN it would be embarrassing if he were overheard making such a statement. "But Hansen has been able to use his personal charm and skills to bind the Council together, helping them overlook their differences and getting them to work as a single unit for the common good. The more I watch him, the more I believe he was born for this moment in world history. I shudder to think what the Security Council meetings would be like without him.

"You know," he continued, "I've frequently been amazed at the human ability to adapt to the situation at hand. I suppose that's why we've survived as long as we have as a species. But at the same time, we seem to have this crazy notion that the way things are at the moment is the way they will remain. Maybe it's just that humans are naturally optimistic. We've gotten pretty used to living in a world at peace, but there's no guarantee that condition will last. Rome fell and so might the United Nations one day. My fear is that we won't last nearly so long as Rome. I'm convinced that as long as Jon Hansen holds the reins the world will stay at peace, but unfortunately there's no structure for succession. The UN Charter lays out the means for electing a new Secretary-General, but how do you find a leader of Hansen's stature and quality?"

Decker and Christopher sat quietly for a moment, both recognizing there was no more to say on the subject and neither was there a proper way, other than silence and taking a few bites of their lunch, of making the transition to another topic.

"Well," Decker said finally, "the last time we talked on the phone you said you had some news for me. Something to do with your dreams."

"Oh, yes. It's about some classes I took during my final two semesters. Secretary Milner suggested them."

Decker, who had been doing most of the talking and little of the eating to this point, took advantage of the opportunity while Christopher talked.

"The first class dealt with New Age thought and eastern religions like Buddhism, Taoism, and Shintoism. Secretary Milner was involved in the development of the curriculum for the class."

"I thought Milner was a Catholic," Decker said.

"He is. That's one of the most interesting things about the eastern religions: They don't make any claims to exclusivity. You can be a Catholic, a Protestant, a Jew, a Muslim, a Hindu or any other religion; it doesn't matter. They believe there are many routes to God and that it's wrong to suggest there's one single way to reach him. Secretary Milner said he was first introduced to the eastern religions by Secretary-General U Thant. Anyway, the other class got into things like altered states of consciousness, channeling, and astral projection."

"I know that stuff has gotten real popular. There's a large contingent of New Agers at the UN. I don't mean to be judgmental, but it all sounds pretty weird to me."

"Yeah," Christopher answered, "I thought so too, at first. The classes I took really only scratched the surface, but I learned a great deal. Some of it still seems a little crazy, but I think they may be on the right track about some things. I read a little about New Age thought eight or nine years ago when I first found out about my origin. You remember that when I told Uncle Harry about the crucifixion dream he had me read some things in the Bible to see if it would spur any memories?"

"Sure," Decker responded.

"Well, I didn't stop with the parts Uncle Harry wanted me to read. I read the whole thing, from Genesis to Revelation. Afterward I became very interested in reading what other religions had to say. So I read the Koran, the *Book of Mormon*, *Dianetics*, *Science with Key to the Scriptures*, and about a dozen other religious books. After growing up around Uncle Harry, I guess I was a little surprised to find that a lot of what they said made a great deal of sense. Some of the books talked about things like karma and reincarnation, meditation, and astral projection."

"Astral projection?" Decker asked. "You mentioned that a minute ago. What exactly is that?"

"Well, like most things in the Eastern religions, it's really pretty simple when you stop and think about it. Nearly all religions teach that man is made up of both body and spirit. Astral projection is a process used during meditation that is supposed to allow you to travel in the form of spirit energy to other places while your body remains in one place."

"Yeah, okay. I've heard of that; Jackie said something about it, oh, I guess a few months ago. But that's just a bunch of silliness," Decker said, ready to drop the subject.

"Maybe not." Christopher said. His expression said there was more.

"You've tried this?" Decker asked, recognizing that Christopher was not the type to believe something as bizarre as this without close scrutiny.

"Yes," answered Christopher. "The first time was eight years ago."

The revelation took Decker entirely by surprise. "You never told me about this before."

"Well, as you said, it sounded pretty crazy—especially before I took these classes."

"So where did you go in your astral projection?" Decker asked, still far from convinced.

"Lebanon," Christopher answered.

Decker put down his fork and knife and stared at Christopher, unsure whether he was serious. He apparently was. Finally, Decker broke the silence. "Christopher, the night before the Disaster, your Aunt Martha and Uncle Harry came to visit Elizabeth and me. Martha told Elizabeth that you knew before the escape that I would be coming home soon. Do you remember telling her that?"

"Yes, sir."

"How did you know?"

"I was there with you in Lebanon. I untied you."

Decker swallowed hard.

After a moment, Christopher continued. "As I said, besides the Bible, I read about a dozen other religious books, including some that dealt with astral projection. It sounded interesting, so I read as much as I could find about it. And then I tried it. I was surprised at how easy it was. At first I just went to places I knew, but then I started going farther. I tried to reach you several times, but even after I found you, you couldn't see me. That's when I decided to try to appear to you in a dream. Do you remember the dream?"

Decker finally found his tongue to answer. "Yes. But until this moment I thought that was all it was. I never even told anyone about it except Tom Donafin, right after we escaped, and Elizabeth. From what your Aunt Martha said I thought you might have had some premonition or something about the escape, but I never imagined this. Why didn't you ever tell me?"

A look of relief swept over Christopher's face. "To tell you the truth, I wasn't entirely sure about it myself until this moment. It was so dreamlike that I thought the whole thing might have been my imagination. Why didn't *you* ever mention it?"

Decker shrugged his shoulders. "It seemed so crazy."

Decker and Christopher just looked at each other for a moment. "I guess I owe you an awful lot," Decker said.

"Not nearly as much as I owe you for taking me in when I had nowhere else to go."

"I probably would have died in Lebanon if it weren't for you."

"I guess we owe each other a lot. You've been like a father to me."

"And you've been like a son." Decker was starting to get a little choked up, so after a deep breath he took a drink and brought the subject back to its previous course. "So, have you done any more of this astral projection?"

"No. Perhaps I made more out of it than I should have, but there was something strangely frightening about it. Every time I did it, it was as if there was something more going on than I realized."

"What do you mean?"

"Well it was like . . ." Christopher seemed to be struggling for words. "The only way I can describe it is by analogy. Imagine you're walking through a peaceful field. All around you, as far as you can see, everything is totally tranquil. And yet, even though you can't see or hear it, you seem to know that somewhere just beyond your view, perhaps over the next rise, there's a tremendous battle taking place. That's about the best way I can explain it, except that somehow I knew *I* was the subject of that battle, and every time I traveled by astral projection, even though I still couldn't see or hear it, it felt as if the battle had gotten closer and fiercer. It was as though someone or something was trying to get to me—at me—and someone or something else was trying to prevent it. After the last trip to Lebanon I never did it again.

"Without being specific," Christopher continued, "I asked my professor at the university if she had ever heard any report of fear or other negative feelings by people during astral projection. She said all the literature indicated only positive reports." Christopher shrugged and Decker shook his head, having no idea what to make of it all.

"But let me tell you about some other things I've discovered from taking these courses," Christopher said. "I think I've been able to piece together some more parts of my past. One of the classes taught us to do a type of meditation in which you go into a dreamlike state while you're still fully conscious, so it's possible to have full control and nearly full recollection of everything you dream. Since most of the things I've remembered about my life as Jesus have occurred in dreams, I tried using this type of meditation to draw out other information."

"So what have you discovered?"

"I remember, as a child, working in my father's carpentry shop and how hard the work was, and I remember playing with the other children. One thing that's a little odd is that I've had several dreams involving Indians."

Decker did a double take. "Indians?!" he said. "You mean like Sitting Bull, Cochise, Geronimo?!"

"No! No! I mean real Indians—East Indians, from India."

"Oh!" Decker laughed at his understandable error. "But, that's not much better. There's nothing in the Bible about Jesus ever going to India, is there?"

"No, not in the Bible, but there's considerable evidence in other literature that suggests he did. There's a church in Montana called the Church Universal and Triumphant that teaches that Jesus studied under an Indian maharishi. To tell you the truth, sometimes it's hard to be sure which memories are based on something that actually happened and which are the product of imagination. What I remember, or at least seem to remember, are scenes of life in an Indian village and of one particular Indian who must have been my teacher or spiritual leader. In my dream I'm very young, sitting on a mat listening to him, though I've not been able to make any sense out of what he was saying."

"Is there anything else you remember—in particular, any events that happened differently than what the Bible describes?"

"No, mostly just personal experiences," Christopher answered regretfully.

"How far back have you been able to remember?" Decker asked. "Do you remember anything about . . . God?" Decker's tone bore a strong hint of reverent caution.

"I'm sorry," Christopher answered, "I wish I did. I can usually remember my dreams while I'm meditating, and I *have* had a number of dreams that I think involved someone who seemed like a god, but each time when I wake up and try to remember, it just won't come back to me. I *do* remember that the dreams were very unusual and I remember a feeling of awe mixed with a heavy dose of fear."

"In your dream," Decker probed, "did it seem like you were in heaven?" The word *heaven* coming from his mouth reminded Decker of the bizarre circumstances of this whole conversation and he looked around again to be sure no one was listening.

"I don't know," Christopher answered. "It didn't seem at all like the heaven Aunt Martha described. I suppose it could have been the planet Uncle Harry thought I came from. I've searched my memory time and again, but all I can see of that world is shadows. It's like trying to hold water in your hand. I'll start to remember something, and for a moment it seems so real and solid, but the instant I start to grasp it, it's gone. I *do* remember seeing lights— glowing bodies, sometimes in human form, sometimes with no form at all." Decker's expression said that he wanted to hear more. "Angels, maybe," Christopher added with an uncomfortable chuckle. "And there was one other thing: a voice. I don't remember what it said; I just remember the voice, the sound of the voice. Something about it was strangely familiar, but I can't say exactly why or how. What's even more puzzling is that I think I've heard that voice somewhere else, just recently, within the past several years."

Decker's eyes grew wide. "Can you re—" He stopped abruptly as a sudden look of recognition registered on Christopher's face. "What is it?"

"I just remembered where I heard the voice!" Christopher fell silent, apparently analyzing the new data in his mind.

"Where?" Decker asked, trying to urge him on.

"Remember the dream I had about the wooden box on the night the missiles blew up over Russia?" Decker nodded. "In the dream there was a voice saying 'Behold the hand of God,' followed by laughter—cold, inhuman laughter. That was the really frightening part of the dream."

"Yeah, I remember you telling me that."

"That's what made the voice I heard in my meditations seem both familiar and yet at the same time so strange. The voice and the laughter are the same. They are the same person or being or whatever. I'm sure of it."

Decker waited while Christopher silently continued his analysis. "I'm sorry," he said, finally. "That's all I can remember."

"Do you have any idea what it all means?" Decker asked.

Christopher frowned and shook his head.

Decker waited a moment just in case Christopher had any afterthoughts. He didn't. "Well," Decker concluded with a smile, "having you around sure makes life interesting." He started to take a bite of his meal but was struck by another thought. "Uh, Christopher," he began, unsure of exactly how to word his question, "these classes and meditation—I don't suppose they've given you any insight into why you're here? Whether you're here for a purpose or anything? If you have a mission?"

Decker was entirely in earnest, but for the first time in the conversation Christopher began to laugh. "What's so funny?" Decker asked, quite surprised by Christopher's reaction.

"I guess that somewhere in the back of my mind I had always hoped *you* might someday answer that question for *me*," Christopher responded. Decker gave him a puzzled look. "After all, the cloning wasn't my idea."

Nor had it been Decker's idea, but in the absence of Professor Goodman, Decker suddenly felt the weight of a responsibility he had never considered his own.

Christopher broke the brief but uncomfortable pause. "I'm just trying to make the best of a very strange situation," he said. "I might just as well ask you why *you* were born. I guess none of us actually chose to be here. We just are." Christopher paused again. "I guess that's one big difference between me and the original. Apparently *he* had some choice in coming to this planet. I had none. I suppose in some ways my lack of choice actually makes me all the more human." Christopher's voice seemed to carry a real note of longing—a longing to be like everyone else.

"No, I'm not entirely human," Christopher continued. "I don't get sick and if I hurt myself I heal quickly. But I feel what other people feel. I hurt like other people hurt. I bleed like other people bleed. And I can die, too." Here Christopher paused. "At least I guess I can." And paused again. Decker didn't interrupt. "If I were to die, I'm not sure what would happen. Would I be resurrected like Jesus was? I don't know. What was it that resurrected Jesus? Was it in his nature? My nature? Or was it some special act of God? I don't know."

Decker had seen Christopher's humanity time and again: in the pain he carried with him over the loss of his adoptive aunt and uncle; in the compassion he showed toward Decker for the loss of Elizabeth, Hope, and Louisa; in his desire that his life and profession be directed toward helping those less fortunate than himself; and in the concern he had for the well-being of his friend and mentor Secretary Milner. And here again was another sign of Christopher's humanity, one that Decker had never seen before: his feeling of being lost and alone in a life and a world he had not chosen.

"I don't think I'm here for any reason in particular," Christopher concluded, "except maybe, like everyone else, to be the best me I can be."

Abruptly, Christopher's thoughts shifted to Milner, almost as if they had been pushed in that direction by Decker's own fleeting thought of the former assistant secretary-general a moment earlier. "I'm really worried about him," he said.

Decker knew immediately who Christopher was referring to. He would have preferred to stay on the subject of Christopher's dreams and recollections, but they could return to that later. Right now Christopher was displaying the very humanity that Decker had just been pondering. He was obviously more concerned with Milner's well-being than with his own circumstances.

"He put up a good show at the hospital," Christopher continued, "but I think he's in much worse condition than he let on. I asked the doctors, but they said they were prohibited from talking about the case, except to say his surgery went well."

"That's pretty much standard policy," Decker said. "I wouldn't let that worry you. I insist on the same policy with Secretary-General Hansen's doctors. They don't say a word to the press or anyone else without my approval."

"Sure, I know that," Christopher said, a little reluctant to be reassured. "I guess mainly it's just a feeling. I've never seen him like this. I know that he's getting on in years, but he's always been so strong. I just wasn't prepared to see him so pale and short of breath. I wish you could have been with me."

"Well, look, if it'll make you feel any better we can drop by the hospital on the way home." Decker immediately realized he was making an assumption. "You are planning to stay at the apartment?"

"Sure, if that's okay with you."

"Of course it's okay. Your room's just the way you left it."

❑

At the hospital Decker and Christopher headed for Milner's room. They were in the elevator when a sudden look of concern swept over Christopher's face. "What is it?" Decker asked.

Christopher shook his head as if he were trying to shake off a dizzy spell. "It's that feeling—the one I told you about where a battle is raging somewhere nearby. Maybe it's because I was just telling you about it, but suddenly I had it again." The conversation ended abruptly as the elevator reached their floor and the door opened, revealing something unusual. There was a steady stream of people—mostly elderly, but a few younger ones as well—moving as quickly as their feet or wheelchairs would carry them, which in the case of some was not very fast at all. There was no apparent panic. They were not running from something. Rather they seemed to be going toward something.

"Have you seen him?" one nurse asked another at the nurse's station as people walked, rolled, or shuffled past. "Only a peek," the other answered. "There are too many people around the door to get a look at him."

As they walked down the hall with the flow of people, Decker and Christopher couldn't help but notice the excitement. "I wonder what's up," Christopher said.

"Looks like somebody's giving away free money and these people want to get there before it's all gone," Decker suggested.

When they rounded the corner, it became clear that the excitement was centered around a room at the end of the hall. Outside the door stood about forty people, most in hospital clothes and slippers, some dressed in the garb of orderlies or nurses, each trying to get closer to the door.

"That's Secretary Milner's room," Christopher said. They immediately picked up their pace, intending to press headlong through the crowd, but were quickly engulfed in the melee. Just as they arrived, a very stoutly built nurse led four orderlies toward the same crowd. Soon Decker and Christopher were pushed away along with the rest of the throng. They might have stood their ground; the others probably would have made their way around anyone who seemed unwilling to move. Instead, they made for an empty alcove as the mass moved by them, driven on like a herd of cattle. "What is going on?" asked Decker in disbelief. But the only one who heard him was Christopher, who seemed as bewildered as Decker.

"Do you think something has happened to Secretary Milner?" Christopher asked.

"Nah," responded Decker reassuringly. "Didn't you see those people? They weren't acting like they were headed for a funeral. In fact, from the looks on some of their faces, I'd think it was more likely that Milner had a baby."

Christopher smiled. Soon the final stragglers passed, followed closely by the stout nurse and her armor-bearers. From there it was only a matter of getting past the guard at the door, an easy task for someone of Decker's experience and credentials. As the door to Milner's room swung open they saw two doctors huddled around the bed, leaning way over as if working on their patient. On closer examination it became clear that the bed was unoccupied except for some medical charts the doctors were examining.

"Where is Secretary Milner?" Christopher asked anxiously.

For a moment the doctors ignored them, and then one turned and called for the guard to escort the intruders out of the room. "It's okay," the second doctor said as he recognized Christopher from his visit earlier in the day.

"Where is Secretary Milner?" Christopher repeated insistently.

"He's in the lavatory," the second doctor answered.

"What was all the commotion about? Is he all right?" Christopher asked, a little less urgently.

"See for yourself," said a voice from their left. There, standing in the open bathroom door was former Assistant Secretary-General Milner in his hospital gown. His appearance gave no hint as to why he was even in the hospital. His eyes were clear and bright, his complexion restored to its ruddy glow, his stance tall and erect, with shoulders and chest broad and firm.

Decker gave his head a quick shake to check his orientation. Christopher simply stared.

"How do I look?" Milner asked proudly.

"You, uh . . . look great," Christopher answered. "What happened?"

Milner cast his eyes toward the doctors, though it seemed he did so less for an answer and more to gloat over their lack of an explanation.

"We're not sure," one of the doctors admitted. "He seems to be in perfect health. He's no spring chicken, but if I didn't know better I'd swear he was twenty years younger than when he checked in."

"They're not sure," Milner said, repeating the doctor's first remark with glee. "Actually, they haven't the foggiest idea."

"He's right," one of them confessed.

"Why don't you fellas just go on back to your offices and study those charts while I talk to my visitors," Milner urged as he motioned his physicians toward the door.

The doctors didn't resist but warned Milner not to overexert himself.

"Of course not," Milner responded, unconvincingly.

When they were gone, Milner checked the ties on his hospital gown, dropped to the floor and began doing push-ups. "Count 'em for me, Christopher," he said as he began. Christopher resisted but counted them anyway as Milner, refusing to let the feat go unmeasured, started to count for himself. As he reached twenty-three Christopher insisted he cease, which he promptly did after two more.

Decker was too busy chuckling at this strange scene to speak, but Christopher asked again, "What's going on? What happened?"

"What do you mean, 'What happened?'" Milner responded. "It's obvious: I'm well and I feel ready to take on the world."

"But how did this happen?" Christopher pressed.

"It's obvious," Milner repeated, unharried by Christopher's

insistence. "It all started after I got the transfusion of the blood you donated."

Decker was momentarily stunned, not only by the fact that Christopher's blood had this effect, but by Milner's matter-of-fact response. Did Milner know about Christopher? How could he? He wondered whether he should pursue this any further and risk giving away Christopher's secret. "What are you saying?" he asked, unable to control his own curiosity.

"Mr. Hawthorne," Milner said, formally, "I have known of Christopher's history since the first moment I saw him. And to some small extent I also know his destiny—though I am forbidden to reveal it, even to him. I cannot claim I knew *this* would happen," he said, referring to his improved condition, "but neither does it surprise me in the least!"

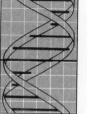

19

The Prince of Rome

Eight years later
South of Frankfurt, Germany

THE TRAIN FROM HEIDELBERG to Frankfurt sped quietly along the track through the German summer evening. A few hundred meters to the left, the foothills of the Odenwald Mountains burst forth from the flat plains of the Rhine Valley to form the western wall of what in millennia past had been a massive sea. Every eight or ten kilometers along the crest of the mountains, castles sat in various states of repair, some in ruins, others still inhabited. Along the mountain's base, the beautiful towns and villages of the Bergstrasse were punctuated by the seemingly requisite steeples and onion domes of the state-supported Catholic and Lutheran churches. Farther away in the west, but within clear sight of the train, the steeples of the small village of Biblis Lorsch were overshadowed by the seven massive cooling towers of Germany's largest nuclear power plant.

Behind the powerful electric engine that pulled the dingy yellow and blue train were three private cars that had been commissioned for the secretary-general of the United Nations, his party, and the ever-present members of the press. Two hours earlier, at the castle of Heidelberg, Secretary-General Jon Hansen had given a speech to a group of international business leaders on the benefits of the recent United Nations decision to remove the remaining barriers to trade among nations. To the casual listener the speech would not have been particularly stirring, but Hansen was preaching to the choir—an audience of men and women from all over the world who had been at the forefront of the effort to eliminate trade barriers. World peace under Hansen had been good for capitalism and for capitalists.

Most notable among the rich and powerful in attendance was billionaire David Bragford, who had introduced the secretary-general to the assembly. It was commonly believed that five years earlier Bragford had been the driving force behind the elimination of most of the trade barriers established by the European Union. It was only a question of time before he sought the total elimination of all trade barriers.

Jon Hansen was now in the fourth year of his third consecutive term as secretary-general, a position that had grown continually in importance since his first oath of office. Now, as more and more power was consolidated both under Hansen and the restructured Security Council, the pace of that consolidation was increasing. The time had passed some years earlier when politicians and news commentators addressed themselves to the subject of *whether* there would be a unified world government. Now they pondered such topics as how that government might best be administered. There were still significant hurdles to be cleared before its final realization. No one of major consequence was calling for the complete dissolution of independent nations—not publicly, anyway—yet the direction was undeniable.

It was not as though one day mankind awoke to find a world where national interests were of no importance and all power resided in a global dictatorship headquartered in New York. Rather, the centralized management of international matters by the UN—under the guidance of Hansen and the Security Council—had facilitated remarkable advances by allowing compromise and cooperation among nations that would have been unimaginable a few decades earlier. The regionalized structure of the Security Council and the even-handed leadership of Jon Hansen had brought balance to the treatment of all nations and had succeeded in bringing about a general peace that was accompanied by prosperity throughout most of the world. As Hansen pointed out quite regularly, now that international matters were handled internationally, the governments of the individual countries were free to focus on their provincial interests.

There were of course exceptions to the general prosperity, for no amount of good government could alleviate natural disasters. One such exception was the Indian subcontinent and especially northern India and Pakistan, which were in a rapidly worsening state of famine due to a combination of drought and wheat rust.

In the secretary-general's private train compartment, Jon Hansen and Decker Hawthorne were conferring on the upcoming annual State of the World Address. "I've received drafts of the annual reports from all of the members of the Security Council and from each of the agencies of the Secretariat with the exception of the Food and Agriculture Organization," Decker told Hansen. "This is the fifth draft of your address, containing everything except for the information from FAO." Decker handed Hansen an eighty-four page document, which Hansen proceeded to page through, scanning the contents.

"As you can see," Decker continued, "we've already prepared most of the text dealing with world hunger and agricultural production and we just need to fill in the figures once we have the FAO report. Then we'll liven it up a bit with some personal insights from your upcoming trip to Pakistan."

"Have you addressed each of my eight points on distribution of agricultural resources?" Hansen asked.

"Yes, sir. That begins on page sixteen."

Hansen flipped to the page and began reading. While it was not possible to legislate away things such as famine, Hansen felt it was imperative that the United Nations do everything in its power to reduce the suffering by providing massive food shipments to the affected countries. The problem with this was that someone had to pay for the food and it was *this* problem that Hansen's eight points on the distribution of agricultural resources was intended to address.

"Yes, this looks good," Hansen said after a brief review. "You're flying to Rome from Frankfurt?" he asked Decker.

"Yes, Jack Redmond and I are meeting with Christopher at

FAO headquarters in Rome to iron out the final projections and recommendations for the agricultural quotas from each region for distribution to the poorer nations. We'll meet you on Wednesday in Pakistan."

"Good. I think it's important we get Jack's input," Hansen agreed, referring to his chief political adviser. "We need to have a solidly defensible position for the distribution quotas when I introduce the measure to the General Assembly next month." Decker nodded acknowledgment. "This program won't be easy to implement," Hansen said. "Those who have an abundance are not exactly standing in line to give it away. The problem with the New World Order is that it's still populated by the same 'old' people," Hansen said, repeating one of his favorite phrases, "Anything you, Jack, and Christopher can come up with to make it politically more palatable will be helpful."

"I think Jack and Christopher have a few ideas that might help," Decker said. Decker was always careful to make any comment about Christopher an understatement. His pride in Christopher was obvious even to a casual observer, but no one could doubt that Christopher's rapid rise as a member of the UN Secretariat was entirely deserved. His success over the past three years as director-general of the UN's Food and Agriculture Organization (FAO), headquartered in Rome, made him the heir apparent to Louis Colleta, the executive director of the Economic and Social Council (ECOSOC) in New York, who had announced he would retire the following spring. Indeed, most of Hansen's eight-point plan had been developed by Christopher in his role as director-general of FAO.

Until the reorganization of the Security Council, ECOSOC had been the umbrella agency for more than half of the UN's dozens of organizations, including FAO. After the reorganization, all the UN organizations were divided into more or less logical groupings and placed under ten agencies chaired by each of the Security Council Alternates.

What remained under the name ECOSOC was far less than it had been when it was one of the five principal organs of the United Nations, but it was still a major agency. And although each alternate member of the Security Council served as the chairman and titular head of one of the ten agencies, actual operations were the responsibility of the agency's executive director, who was usually a career professional trained in the respective field.

In addition to the greatly expanded area of responsibility, the promotion to executive director of ECOSOC offered Christopher one other benefit over his current job as director-general of FAO: The new position would put him geographically and politically much closer to the reins of power.

"We should be ready to brief you on our recommendations on the flight back from Pakistan," Decker said.

"No, I need you to remain in Pakistan with Christopher when I return to New York. Jack will have to brief me on the plane," Hansen said.

This was not what Decker had in mind; Jack Redmond was a good man, but Decker had planned to direct the briefing himself. "Yes, sir," he answered without argument.

"Good, good," Hansen responded, as he went back to his review of the draft document. "What are your readings from Ambassador Faure?" he asked without looking up.

"I don't think we can count on his support for your agricultural distribution plan, if that's what you mean."

"That man is going to drive me to drink," Hansen commented dryly as he took a swallow from a glass of German beer. "It seems no matter what I try to do, he's always there ready to oppose me."

Decker was well aware of Hansen's feelings about the French ambassador. Albert Faure had always been a thorn in the flesh for Hansen and it was getting worse. About a year before, Faure had managed to get himself elected as the alternate member of the Security Council from Europe. The position carried little actual power on the Council.[35] Perhaps the single greatest power held by the alternates, though it was seldom used, was the right to address the Security Council at any time on behalf of the agency they chaired, if they felt the circumstances warranted—even if it

---

[35]Under the new structure, alternates could not introduce, second, or even vote on Security Council motions. Those privileges were limited to the ten primary members (one from each of the world's ten regional divisions).

meant interrupting other proceedings. Faure's agency was the World Peace Organization.[36] In the past, the position had been one of considerable prestige and power, but since there had been no major wars for nearly five years, it proved to be of little consequence to a man as ambitious as Faure. Unfortunately for Hansen, this left Faure with plenty of time to pursue other goals, including lobbying other members against Hansen's positions. So far, Faure had been unable to mount any sizable opposition to Hansen in either the Security Council or the General Assembly, but if he succeeded in putting together a coalition of the farming nations to oppose the agricultural distribution measures, he could make real trouble.

"It seems there should be some way to handle this fellow other than just ignoring him while he goes on sniping at me," Hansen said.

"Perhaps you could convince the French president to replace him with someone more agreeable. That worked a few years back with the ambassador from Mexico," Decker offered.

"Yeah, and with the ambassador from Mali," Hansen added.

"Oh? I didn't know that we were involved in that."

"Well, actually I had Jack Redmond handle that one for me."

Decker made a mental note of this fact for what it might be worth in the future.

"The problem," Hansen continued, "is that Faure is far too popular among the French people to be so easily deposed."

"What about Ambassador Heineman?" Decker asked, referring to the German ambassador who represented Europe as primary on the Security Council and who was loyal to Hansen. As the primary from Europe, Heineman carried considerable clout with the nations in his region, including France.

"I think Ambassador Heineman is well aware of my feelings about Faure, but I suppose I could take advantage of our trip to Pakistan this weekend to approach him directly on the matter."

[36]The World Peace Organization was organized under the new UN structure to consolidate the United Nations Disengagement Observer Force, the United Nations Interim Force in Lebanon, the United Nations Military Observer Group in India and Pakistan, and the UN's other ground, air, and naval peacekeeping forces.

As the representative from one of the major food-producing regions, Heineman was one of the three Security Council members accompanying Hansen on his visit to Pakistan.

"Maybe Jack could come up with something Ambassador Heineman could use to convince Faure to see things your way," Decker suggested.

"Find a weak spot and then apply a little pressure, you mean?"

"Yes, sir. And Jack is the best person I know to find out what and where those weak spots are."

Secretary-General Hansen liked the idea. "Take that up with Jack when you see him in Rome."

Rome, Italy

Decker's plane from Frankfurt arrived the next morning at the Leonardo da Vinci Airport in Fiumicino, just southwest of Rome. Having been warned about pickpockets and luggage thieves in and around Rome, Decker held tightly to his briefcase and carry-on luggage as he scanned the crowd for any sign of Christopher, who was to meet him there. As director of public affairs for the United Nations, Decker had access to the UN's small fleet of private jets, but whenever possible he chose to fly on commercial aircraft. "Much safer," he told anyone who asked.

From behind a group of Italian businessmen Decker saw a hand waving and then Christopher emerged and hurried toward him. "Welcome to Rome," Christopher said as he gave Decker a hug. "How was your trip?"

"Fine. Fine."

"Do you have luggage?"

"Just this," Decker answered, lifting his briefcase and a large piece of carry-on luggage from his side.

"Great. We can get started on your tour of Rome right away. You've never been to Rome before, have you?"

"No. The closest I came was when I was in Turin and Milan on the Shroud research team."

"Well, I think you're really going to like it."

"I have no doubt of that."

As they moved through the crowds to the exit, Decker noticed that several people seemed to be pointing at them, and as they waited on the curb for the limo, several cars nearly collided when a very attractive young woman suddenly stopped her car to stare at them. Christopher ignored the woman's curious gape, but Decker couldn't help but remark. "I think she thought she knew you," he told Christopher as they got in the limo.

"Shall we start with the Colosseum?" Christopher asked, taking no notice of Decker's comment. "I'm afraid all the museums are closed on Monday except the Vatican, but there's still more than enough to see to fill the rest of the day."

"Roma, non basta una vita!" Decker answered in Italian, meaning "For Rome, one life is not enough."

"I didn't know you knew Italian," Christopher remarked.

"You just heard every word I know," Decker confessed. "The flight attendant taught it to me." Christopher smiled. Answering his earlier question, Decker added, "Whatever you say. You're the tour guide. There is one thing I want to see that may not be on the usual list of must-see places."

"What's that?" asked Christopher.

"The Arch of Titus."

"Oh, sure. It's at the Forum, near the Colosseum. We can start there if you like."

"Great," Decker said. "Actually, I think you'll find it more interesting than you realize."

❏

The Triumphal Arch of Titus rose imposingly against the backdrop of the Colosseum, barely scarred by the twenty centuries that had passed since it was constructed to commemorate the successful campaign against Jerusalem by Titus. Decker scanned the carved images in the arch and quickly found what he was looking for. "Here it is," he said. Christopher looked at the carving over Decker's shoulder. The scene depicted the spoils of war being taken from the conquered city of Jerusalem.

"Okay. Now will you tell me what this is all about?"

"Sure," answered Decker. "I don't know if I ever mentioned Joshua Rosen to you." Christopher's face gave no indication that he recognized the name. "Well, he was a man, a scientist actually, whom I knew years ago. We met on the Turin expedition." Christopher's ears perked up. "Later he moved to Israel and I did a story on him. Anyway, when Tom Donafin and I were in Israel, just before we were taken hostage, Joshua Rosen gave us a tour of some of the sites in Jerusalem, one of which was the Wailing Wall. That's what they used to call the western wall of the old Jewish temple before the Palestinians blew it up and the Jews built the new Temple." Christopher nodded, indicating his familiarity with the recent history of the Jewish Temple. "Well, while we were there, Joshua told us about the Ark of the Covenant and gave his theory on what had happened to it. I'll have to tell you all about it sometime. But anyway, the point of the story is that he told us about the Arch of Titus and this carving. Titus was the commander of the Roman forces that pillaged and destroyed Jerusalem in 70 A.D."

"Yes, I know. I prophesied that before the crucifixion," interjected Christopher.

"You never told me you remembered that!"

"Don't get too excited," Christopher answered. "I don't remember it. I read about it in the Bible."

"Oh," said Decker. "Well, anyway, as you can see, the carving is intricately detailed. Despite its age, you can clearly make out the items being taken from Jerusalem." Christopher looked more closely.

"Yeah, I see that. It's really well preserved."

Christopher didn't seem to be getting the point. "Don't you see?" Decker asked. "The Ark of the Covenant is not among the treasures shown in the carving."

"I'm sorry, Decker. I don't get it. So what?"

Decker suddenly realized there was a lot he had not explained. "I'm sorry. I guess I need to give you some more details, but the reason for the interest has to do with the Shroud of Turin. Joshua

Rosen had a fascinating theory involving the Ark of the Covenant that would explain why the original Carbon 14 dating of the Shroud showed it to be only about a thousand years old." Decker proceeded to tell Christopher the whole story of the Ark as it had been told to him and Tom Donafin by Joshua Rosen.

"So you think the Shroud was in the Ark all those years?" Christopher asked after listening to Decker's story.

"I don't know, but it would answer some questions about the Shroud. And about you," Decker added.

As they talked and looked at the carvings on the Arch, they were unaware that two young boys had approached them from behind. *"Scusi, Signor Goodman, potremo avere la sua firma?"* the older of the two boys asked.

Decker had no idea what the boys wanted, and was quite surprised when Christopher took a pen out of his jacket pocket and began to sign his name on some scraps of paper the boys handed him. "Autographs?" he asked, making no attempt to hide his amusement.

Christopher nodded in answer to Decker's question. He spoke for a moment with the boys in perfect Italian, smiling broadly and shaking their hands as if they were important dignitaries, before dismissing them. The boys walked a few steps, each showing the other the autograph he had received. Then, waving their scraps of paper in the air like trophies, they broke into a run toward a lady whom Decker took to be their mother, shouting, *"Il Principe di Roma!"*

For a moment Decker just looked at Christopher, who seemed a little embarrassed by the whole thing. "So that's what all the attention was about at the airport. You're a local celebrity."

Christopher shrugged.

"Don't be embarrassed. I think that's great. You must be doing quite a job here."

"It's not really anything I've done: I've just gotten a lot of credit for some of the United Nations programs we've implemented. Popular programs make for a popular administration."

❑

The next morning Decker and Christopher arrived early at Christopher's office at the UN Food and Agriculture Organization. Jack Redmond's arrival time would be dependent on Rome's morning traffic. FAO headquarters occupied an immense building complex covering more than four square blocks and towering well above the surrounding architecture. Located on Viale delle Terme di Caracalla, the FAO employed more than twenty-five hundred professional administrative personnel with a biannual budget of $2.5 billion.

At Christopher's office they were greeted by a young, attractive Italian woman. *"Buon giorno, Signor* Goodman," the woman said.

"Good morning, Maria," Christopher answered in English. "This is my very good friend Mr. Decker Hawthorne, Director of Public Affairs of the United Nations. Decker, this is Maria Sabetini."

"Mr. Hawthorne, it's a pleasure to meet you. Mr. Goodman mentions you frequently."

"The pleasure is all mine," Decker answered. "Are you any relation to President Sabetini?" he asked, recognizing that she bore the same last name as Italy's president.

"Maria is the president's youngest daughter," Christopher answered.

"Oh . . . uh, well, then it's even more of a pleasure." Decker tried to not seem too surprised, but the question about her name had just been small talk; he never expected the answer he got.

"Mr. Redmond will be arriving a little later," Christopher told Maria. "When he gets here, please show him in."

After Christopher closed the door behind them Decker blurted out, "Your secretary is the Italian president's daughter?"

Christopher shook his head, trying not to make too much of it. "She's not a secretary. She's an administrative assistant," he said. "She wanted a job, and I needed an administrative assistant."

"Yeah, but the president's daughter?"

"It was Secretary Milner's idea." Decker's expression requested an explanation. "Secretary Milner was here on some business shortly after I became director-general of FAO. He and the president are old friends. I just happened to mention to him in passing that I needed to find an administrative assistant."

"I don't suppose it's hurt your relationship with the Italian government any," Decker said.

"No, things have been very cordial."

Christopher's office was spacious and luxuriously decorated and furnished. On the walls were pictures of Christopher with several members of the United Nations Security Council; numerous Italian government officials including the Italian prime minister, the Italian ambassador to the UN, and the Italian president; and with leaders of the Roman Catholic Church, including three cardinals. Most prominent in the room were two pictures displayed side by side, one of Christopher with Secretary-General Jon Hansen, and the other of Christopher with Robert Milner and the Pope. "You've been a very busy boy," Decker commented as he scanned the photos.

"To tell you the truth, most of this has been Secretary Milner's doing. He's been here four or five times a year since I've been director-general," Christopher said. Milner, now ninety, seemingly had not aged a day since the transfusion of Christopher's blood eight years before. If anything, he seemed far younger. "I had no idea Secretary Milner had so much business in Italy."

"Hmm, neither did I," Decker responded. Decker was certain that Milner's frequent trips were not a coincidence. He was obviously doing everything he could to advance Christopher's position with those in power in Italy. It was not that Decker objected in any way. Still, there was a mystery here. He didn't have long to think about it, though. His eye was caught by a familiar face in another picture of Christopher with a very distinguished man in front of the Coliseum. "When was David Bragford here?" Decker asked.

"Oh, that was last summer. He was here with Secretary Milner for a meeting of world bankers." At that moment Maria announced Jack Redmond's arrival.

"All hail the Prince of Rome," Redmond said, addressing Christopher and bowing in mock obeisance as he came in.

Decker had no idea what had prompted Jack's greeting but

assumed it to be a joke; the look of mild annoyance on Christopher's face indicated there was more to it than that. "Okay, I'll bite," Decker said. "What's going on? What's this 'Prince of Rome' stuff?"

"Haven't you seen last week's issue of *Epoca?*" Jack asked Decker, referring to the Italian magazine that is the equivalent of *Time* or *Newsweek*.

"No," Decker answered, looking back and forth from Jack to Christopher and hoping for an explanation.

"Here," Jack said, as he opened his briefcase and handed the Italian magazine to Decker. On the cover was a very complimentary picture of Christopher with the words "*Christopher Goodman, Il Trentenne, Principe di Roma*" boldly displayed underneath.

Decker examined the photo for a moment and then asked for a translation of the caption. Christopher just sat silently, looking a little embarrassed, as Jack answered. "It says, 'Christopher Goodman, the Thirty-Year-Old Prince of Rome.'"

Decker was proud enough to burst. He couldn't read a word of Italian, but he quickly flipped through the magazine trying to find the accompanying article. "Will somebody please tell me what this is all about?" he asked impatiently.

"It seems our boy Christopher has made quite a name for himself around these parts." Jack's voice was laden with an exaggerated Cajun accent—something he did whenever he wanted to do a little friendly ribbing.

"It's nothing," Christopher protested. "The editor of the magazine came up with that to insult the *priministro della republica*. The prime minister," he added in translation. "They've had a running battle for months. Apparently the people at *Epoca* thought it would serve their purposes to build me up while tearing down the priministro. The article right after the one about me calls the priministro a useless, ineffective bore."

Decker flipped to the article about the prime minister and found a most unflattering picture of the man. He wondered if the photo had been altered to make him look so bad.

"Methinks the prince doth protest too much," Jack said with a grin, intentionally misquoting Hamlet.[37]

[37] Act 3, Scene 2.

"I just think the whole thing is a little silly. I called the prime minister as soon as I saw the article and let him know I had no idea they were going to use the story as they did. Fortunately, we've had the opportunity to establish a very affable relationship over the past several years. He took the whole thing very well. Now, could we please get some work done?"

"Okay, okay," Jack said, still joking, "I'll behave."

"Wait a second," interrupted Decker. "I want a copy of this *and* an English translation."

"You guys make it awfully hard to be modest," Christopher protested.

"Listen," said Jack Redmond, donning his political advisor's hat, "you can be very proud of that article. It's not often a UN official other than Hansen gets that type of recognition in the press. I mean, after all—and not to belittle your job—you *are* just a bureaucrat. Normally that means you do your job behind the scenes and no one ever notices, except possibly other bureaucrats. From what I saw in that magazine you've done an outstanding job, not only as a bureaucrat but as a representative of the United Nations to the people of Italy. You keep playing your cards right and there'll be no stopping you."

Christopher accepted the compliment graciously. Decker was too busy smiling to add anything.

"Oh, and speaking of the people of Italy," Jack continued, "the article says you're an Italian citizen. Whose idea was that?"

Decker was sure he knew the answer. "Secretary Milner's," Christopher answered. "He recommended it back when I first took over FAO. He thought it would be popular with the Italian people. With the liberalization of citizenship requirements over the past ten years, it only required a ninety-day residency before I could apply. I've been an Italian citizen for nearly five years now. It's really just a symbolic thing."

Jack Redmond nodded approvingly. "Like I said, there'll be no stopping you."

"Now, can we please get started on this?" Christopher pleaded.

"Not quite so fast. There's one other thing in the article Decker might find interesting." Christopher sat down, folded his hands, and looked up at the ceiling. It was useless to try to stop Jack when he was on a roll. "According to the article, you and the Italian President's daughter are quite an item. Rumors are that marriage may be in your future."

"What?" Decker said in surprise. "You and Maria?"

"No!" Christopher answered quickly. "They're talking about his oldest daughter, Tina."

"Wait a second," Jack interrupted, "who's Maria?"

"Nobody!" Christopher blurted before Decker could answer and thereby give Jack even more to speculate about. "Look, there's nothing to that business. Tina and I are just friends. I needed a date for a few political functions, and so we went together. That's all there is to it."

❑

It took a while longer, but the subject finally got around to agricultural quotas. The meeting went on well into the evening and had to be continued on the flight to Pakistan, where they were to meet with Secretary-General Hansen and his party.

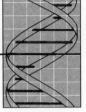

20

Through a Glass Darkly

Sāhiwāi, Pakistan

A DARK FIGURE MOVED QUICKLY along the dry river bed, checking each low-lying area for any sign of water. If he did not find it soon, death would surely overtake him as it had all the others. Up ahead, a tree, still green despite the brown that surrounded it, gave shade to the end of his search: a small pool of water. It was there; he knew it was. He could smell it. Running to it, he put his face down to the water and drank until he was satisfied. He would stay here until the water was gone or hunger drove him on. It was possible that the water might draw some small animal he could eat, but he couldn't wait for food to come to him. He would have to scout out the area and hope for the best.

It was shortly after dawn, but the sun already beat down on the dry plain as he emerged from the river bed and peered cautiously through the dry thicket. A motionless form lay about thirty yards away. The week without food and the days without water had dulled his senses or he surely would have noticed it earlier, so close to him. He paused only a moment to examine the area for danger; he was too hungry to expend much caution. As he approached the figure, it became apparent it was dead. There were two more smaller ones lying nearby.

In the distance, he heard a roar that sounded like a large herd of hoofed animals. It was a long way away but it seemed to be coming toward him. Fear grew as the sound drew near more swiftly than he could imagine possible. Quickly he took hold of a leg and tried to drag his meal to the river bed, but his strength was not up to the task. With insane determination born of unbearable hunger he decided to make his stand. Soon the sound was almost upon him and it became clear that it was coming, not from a herd of any sort, but from a single huge bird like none he had ever seen before.

❑

Overhead, the secretary-general's helicopter slowly approached the famine relief camp, as those on board got a close look at the surrounding conditions. The drought had been devastating. For twenty miles the helicopter had followed a dry river bed, but they saw no more than a few pools of water. Just below, about two miles from the relief camp near one of the pools, they spotted a lone emaciated wild dog looking up at them. It stood over the carcass of a young woman who had died of starvation or thirst before reaching the camp. Nearby lay the bodies of her two small children.

The stark evidence of famine and drought that the secretary-general's party now saw firsthand in Pakistan was mirrored by similar devastation in northern India, where wheat rust had severely reduced the annual harvest. In southern India, tropical storms during the monsoon season had driven seawater into many of the already flooded areas to form brackish water, making the land salty and unarable. The latter was a fairly common occurrence in India, and all that could be done was to try to grow whatever they could and wait for subsequent monsoons to leach the salt from the land over the next few years.

The helicopter landed in an open area outside the camp, creating a huge dust cloud that blew into the faces of those waiting. Along with the twenty or so cameramen and reporters, the relief camp's director, Dr. Fred Bloomer, waited for the blades to stop before approaching to welcome the secretary-general and his party. Christopher, the only one on board who knew Dr. Bloomer, made the introductions.

"I'm anxious to get started," Hansen said as he shook Bloomer's hand.

"I fear you'll find conditions worse than you imagined, Mr. Secretary-General," Dr. Bloomer said. "We've had nearly a thousand new arrivals in the last four days. We're just not set up to handle this many people. We've had to severely reduce rations."

To feed the people in the camp, he explained, the kitchen operated with a full contingent on a fourteen-hour shift throughout the daylight hours. During the night, a skeleton crew was on hand for any who had just reached the camp—a single hour in some cases could make the difference between life and death. Dr. Bloomer's goal was to provide two meals a day for everyone in the camp.

The official purpose of this visit was fact finding, but what Hansen really hoped to accomplish was to build support for the distribution of agricultural resources. He had specific reasons for inviting each of those who accompanied him on this trip. Ambassador Khalid Haider from Pakistan was there because it was his country. The Indian ambassador had been invited because of similar problems in his country and because of the concern that the refugees from Pakistan might begin to spill over into India.

The members from North America and Europe had been asked to come along because it was their regions that Hansen's plan would ask to give the most for the food distribution effort. Ambassador Howell of Canada, who represented North America on the Security Council, had been ill for several months and was expected to resign soon. In his place was Ambassador Walter Bishop from the United States, the alternate from North America, who hoped to replace the Canadian ambassador as primary. Aware of this likelihood, Hansen wanted to take the opportunity to get to know the American better and win his support for the plan. Ambassador Heineman from Germany, who represented Europe on the Security Council, really didn't need to be convinced about the need for food redistribution, but the people of his region did. At Decker's recommendation Hansen had invited Heineman to ensure coverage of the trip by the European press. It was an effective way of making sure the people of Europe learned of the urgency and magnitude of the need.

The team started with a tour of the camp and what was left of the surrounding villages. In the afternoon Christopher briefed the ambassadors on the findings from a study by the Food and Agriculture Organization on projections for future years. Later in the afternoon, in what was mainly a photo opportunity, the team members worked in the serving line for the evening meal. They spent the night at the camp under nearly the same conditions as the camp's inhabitants.

The next morning the secretary-general and the ambassadors planned to fly by helicopter back to Lahore, Pakistan, near the Indian border, while Decker and Christopher remained at the camp to represent Hansen to a second team from the UN who would be arriving in the late afternoon.

Tel Aviv, Israel

Rabbi Saul Cohen finished his morning prayers and rose to his feet to answer the knock at the door of his study. Benjamin Cohen, the rabbi's seventeen-year-old son and only living relative since the Disaster took his four older children and wife, stood outside, nervously shifting from side to side. He knew not to disturb his father's prayer time without good cause, and he did not relish comparing his own evaluation of what constituted a 'good cause' with that of his father. Nevertheless, he relished even less the possibility of angering the man who waited in the sitting room.

The man—*guest* hardly seemed like the right word—had arrived without appointment. Benjamin had opened the front door to let him in but then backed away, sensing instinctively that there was something very unusual about this visit, if not about the man himself. As the man closed the door behind him, it seemed to Benjamin that the sitting room grew strangely crowded. He was only too glad to leave the room to retrieve his father and was halfway to his father's office before he realized he had not asked the man his name. Like it or not, he would have to go back and ask.

Peering around the corner of the doorway, Benjamin's eyes met those of the visitor. He wanted to look away, but he saw something there that held him. He could see clearly now what so unsettled him about this man. Benjamin had been trained to discern wisdom in a man's face. He had been taught that wisdom came with age, but the wisdom in this man's eyes was unnatural for a man no older than this. It would be unnatural for a man of any age.

He asked the man his name. The answer only added to Benjamin's disquiet, but he felt it unadvisable to probe further.

Ordinarily Saul Cohen's morning prayers lasted at least an hour, but for some reason this morning he stopped after only thirty minutes. When he heard the knock on his study door at that very moment, it seemed to him a confirmation. He did not know what news Benjamin brought, but he was sure it was important or the boy would not have interrupted him. Cohen opened the door.

"What is it?" he asked, with no sign of the consternation Benjamin had expected.

"There's a man here to see you, Father."

Cohen waited for more information, but Benjamin was not forthcoming. "So what is this man's name?" Cohen asked finally.

"He didn't say," Benjamin responded in a muffled voice.

"Well, did you ask him?"

"Yes, Father."

"And, what did he say?"

Benjamin wasn't sure how this was going to sound. It seemed very authoritative when the man in the sitting room said it, but coming from his own lips, Benjamin thought it might sound a little dumb. Still, he had to say something: his father was waiting. "He said to tell you that he is 'he who has heard the voices of the seven thunders.'"

Cohen did not respond but the look on his face registered

recognition. Finally he managed a nod and Benjamin went back to the sitting room to retrieve the man.

Saul Cohen closed the door and mechanically began to straighten his desk. A few seconds later, he heard footsteps coming down the hall and watched as the doorknob began to rotate. Suddenly it seemed as though he had forgotten how to breathe. Benjamin pushed the door open, and Cohen, remembering his manners, managed to move around from behind his desk to meet the man. If this man was, indeed, who he claimed to be, then Cohen had no desire to insult him with bad etiquette. For a moment, the man stood in the doorway just looking at Cohen as if savoring the moment, and then finally he entered.

Cohen didn't know how it could be possible for this man to be who he claimed, but in Cohen's vocation he had learned that nothing was impossible. He had known since the Disaster that someday a prophet would come. But could this man really be who he claimed to be? It was almost more than Cohen could accept.

"Hello, Rabbi," the man said cordially as he extended his hand. He was not at all what Cohen expected. He didn't appear to be a day over sixty. Most disconcerting of all was the way he was dressed—in a modern, dark-gray business suit with a red tie. Somehow, as silly as it seemed, Cohen had expected the man to be wearing sandals and a long robe, tied at the waist with a rope. Yet, despite his appearance and the impossibility of his claim, there was something about the man that made Cohen believe he was exactly who he said he was.

"I'm the one you've been waiting for," the man said, still extending his hand. "But believe me, I've been waiting for you for a lot longer than you've been waiting for me." Cohen was silent, still unsure of what to say. "And you are Saul Cohen," the man continued, "of the lineage of Jonadab, son of Recab, about whom Jeremiah prophesied."[38]

Cohen's mouth dropped open. "That secret has not passed outside of my family for nearly twelve hundred years," he said.

[38]Jeremiah 35:18-19.

"It is the only explanation for why you were not taken in the
. . . um, 'Disaster'," the man explained. "And when you have
completed your work, your son will take your place in the Lord's
service, as was promised through Jeremiah."

Cohen grew pensive.

"Why don't we just sit down," the man suggested. "We have a
lot to talk about." Cohen complied silently. "As our meeting indicates, the time is at hand for the end of this age." Without pausing
to allow Cohen to consider the full impact of this statement, the
man continued. "I've observed you for a number of years and I
am now certain that you are the other witness. The fact that you
recognize me confirms that belief."

"You were not sure before?" Cohen asked.

"I was not told who the other would be. I now see I was led to
you, but confirmation was left to the discernment and wisdom
God has granted me. I had no special revelation on the matter."

This discovery caught Cohen off guard. "But . . . I don't understand. How could you not know?"

"Well, as the Apostle Paul wrote, 'For now we see through a
glass, darkly; but then face to face: now I know in part; but then
shall I know even as also I am known.'[39] I can assure you that as
long as you and I remain on this side of life, that will never
change—not even if you were to live to be two thousand years
old."

"Rabbi," Cohen said, not knowing how else to address this man
whom he considered to be hundreds of times his spiritual senior.

"Please," the man interrupted, "call me John."

This had gone on long enough. Cohen had to be sure he
understood what was happening. "You are John?"

The man nodded.

"Yochanan bar Zebadee?" Cohen said, using the Hebrew form
of the man's name.

"I am," he answered.

"The apostle of the Lord? You were there, at the foot of the
cross?"[40]

---

[39] 1 Corinthians 13:12 (KJV).

[40] John 19:26.

"I was there," John answered with an expression that showed he still felt the pain of that event nearly two thousand years earlier.

"But how? Have you returned from the dead?"

The man smiled. "In many ways I would have preferred that. But, no, I've been here, alive on this decaying world, waiting for this moment for two thousand years."

Cohen didn't repeat his question, but his eyes still asked "How?"

"Do you not recall what our Lord told Peter about me on the shore of the Sea of Tiberias?"

Cohen knew the words but he had never thought their meaning to be literal. After his resurrection, Jesus told the Apostle Peter how he, Peter, would die. Peter then asked what would happen to John. "If I want him to remain alive until I return, what is that to you?" Jesus replied.[41]

"But you also wrote that what Jesus said didn't mean you'd *never* die, just that you might not die until after his return."[42] As soon as the words left his mouth, Cohen realized he did not need an answer; both he and John were fully aware of the fate that soon awaited them—and *that* fate matched Jesus' words perfectly.

"The Lord told my brother James and me that, like him, we would both die a martyr's death.[43] James was the first of the Lord's apostles to die[44] . . . and I shall be the last. I suppose in *this* way at least, my mother's request to Jesus will be granted: James and I *will* sit at the Lord's right and left hands in his kingdom."[45]

Cohen still struggled.

"In the Book of Revelation," the man continued, "I said that an angel gave me a scroll and I was told to eat it. I wrote:

> I took the little scroll from the angel's hand and ate it. It
> tasted sweet as honey in my mouth, but when I had eaten

[41]John 21:22.

[42]John 21:23.

[43]Matthew 20:20-23.

[44]Acts 12:1-2.

[45]Matthew 20:20-23.

it, my stomach turned sour. Then I was told, "You must prophesy again about many peoples, nations, languages, and kings."[46]

Cohen nodded recognition. "The words of the scroll were sweet," John explained, "because in that moment I came to know I would live longer than even Methuselah.[47] But the scroll became sour in my stomach as I understood I would have to wait longer than any other man to see the Lord again. Then I was told the reason my life must continue: I have remained on this earth to prophesy *again*, this time with you, about many peoples, nations, languages, and kings."

Knitting his brow, Cohen lapsed into an introspective state. He believed but, then again, it was almost too much to believe. "I suppose it should have been expected," he said finally, "after you survived being immersed in boiling oil.[48] And it explains the prophesies of Yeshua concerning the end of the age, when he told the disciples, 'Some who are standing here will not taste death before they see the kingdom of God come with power.'[49] If you are John, then indeed that generation has not passed away. Still, what of Polycarp?" Cohen asked, referring to the late first- and early second-century bishop of Smyrna who, according to his student Irenaeus, had said John died during the reign of the Roman emperor Trajan.[50]

"Have you not read Harnack?" the man responded, referring to the German theologian who had propounded that Polycarp was referring not to John the apostle but to another man, a church elder, also named John.[51]

It occurred to Cohen that this might also explain one of the mysteries of the Bible that had always puzzled him. "And is this

[46]Revelation 10:10-11.

[47]According to Genesis 5:25-26, Methuselah lived to be 969.

[48]As Tertullian reported, *De praescriptione hereticorum* 36.

[49]Mark 9:1; also Matthew 16:28, 24:34.

[50]*Adversus haereses,* 2.22.5.

[51]*Lehbuchder Dogmengeschichte,* 1885-1889.

the reason for the apparent later additions to the original text of your gospel?"[52] he asked for confirmation.

The man nodded. "I regret the confusion that has caused. From time to time I'd tell someone about something Jesus did or said that I had left out of my Gospel and they'd urge me to include it. It never even occurred to me that, by adding a few things I had left out of the earlier versions, I would cause so much confusion later on.

"Saul, I understand your reason for questioning, and yet I know that at the same time, the Spirit gives witness to you that I am who I claim to be."

"But where have you been?" Cohen asked. "How could you have kept your identity concealed?"

"It's easier than you might imagine," John answered. "I must admit, however, I've not always been as successful as I would like. There was a period of a few hundred years that no matter where I went—from China, to India, to Ethiopia—the stories would follow me."

A thought occurred to Cohen. "Prester John?" he asked, refer- ring to the mysterious figure mentioned in dozens of legends and by a few more reliable sources such as Marco Polo, over a span of several hundred years and in widespread locations.[53]

John nodded. "Though how I ever got tied in with the legends of King Arthur, I can only guess. Perhaps it was the result of spec- ulation that I had the Holy Grail. Since then, I've been a lot more careful about concealing my identity. To avoid questions I've had to move frequently—never more than ten or fifteen years in one place. And I have always tried to find work in the Lord's service that would not draw attention. I've pastored a hundred small churches in every corner of the world. But is it so surprising that

[52]John 7:53 through 8:11 does not appear in the earliest manuscripts of John's gospel, and the original inclusion of John 21 is questioned based on contextual issues.

[53]For information on Prester John, see for instance: E. D. Ross, "Prester John and the Empire of Ethiopia," Arthur P. Newton (ed.), *Travel and Travellers of the Middle Ages* (New York: Barnes & Noble, 1968; first published in 1926), 174-194; C. F. Beck- ingham, "The Quest for Prester John," *Bulletin of The John Rylands University Library*, LXII (1980), 290-310.

I could have gone unnoticed in a world of hundreds of millions? After all, God himself became a man and lived on the earth and went unnoticed by the world for thirty years until the time was right for him to begin his ministry. Now the time is right for me, and for you as well, my friend."

Sāhiwāi, Pakistan

Decker tried to maintain an encouraging smile as he walked among several small groups of people who were sitting on logs or squatting on the ground eating their rations. It was just after six o'clock and the day's second meal—one could hardly call it dinner—was being served. It had been nearly two hours since Secretary-General Hansen's helicopter had left, four hours late, with the rest of the UN contingent. Decker and Christopher remained to await the second team of ambassadors who were coming to the camp to survey the conditions. Christopher had gone to his tent to take a nap shortly after Hansen left.

"Christopher, wake up; it's time for supper," Decker called as he approached the team's small stand of greenish-gray tents. "Come on, Christopher, rise and shine," he said a little louder, but there was no answer. "Christopher, are you in there?"

Decker stuck his head between the two tent flaps and past the mosquito netting. Inside, Christopher sat unmoving on the floor of the tent. Sweat dripped from his face and body and a pained stare filled every feature of his face.

"Are you all right?" Decker asked, though it was obvious he was not.

"Something is wrong," Christopher said finally.

"Are you sick?" Decker asked, but as soon as he said it, he realized Christopher had never been sick; he probably wasn't capable of it.

"Something is terribly wrong." Christopher answered.

Decker ducked inside the tent and closed the flaps behind him. "What is it?" he asked.

"Death and life," Christopher replied slowly. Each word seemed as if it tore an agonizing track from his lungs to his lips.

"Whose life and death?" Decker asked in the more traditional order in which those words are used.

"The death of one who sought to avoid death's grip; the life of another who sought to accept death's release."

"Who has died?" Decker asked, wanting to cover one item at a time and seeing the second reference as both less pressing and more obscure.

"Jon Hansen," Christopher replied.

Decker never got around to asking about the second reference.

21

When Leaders Fall

New York, New York

IT WAS THREE DAYS LATER before search parties spotted the secretary-general's helicopter, forty-five miles off course and crumpled like tissue paper among a stand of trees southwest of Gujränwalä, Pakistan. There were no survivors. It was the second time a secretary-general of the United Nations had been lost in an aircraft crash, the first being Secretary-General Dag Hammarskjöld in 1961, whose plane crashed in Northern Rhodesia (Zambia), killing all on board. The earlier crash, though tragic, had hardly carried the impact on the world and its peoples as did the deaths of Jon Hansen and three members of the Security Council. In 1961 the position of secretary-general, like the United Nations itself, had had little if any influence on the lives of most people in the world. Now, it seemed, the world revolved around the United Nations, and its secretary-general was at the center of it all.

Not since the assassination of the American president John Kennedy or the death of Princess Diana of England had there been such an international outpouring of emotion. At the United Nations, the General Assembly adjourned for two weeks to honor the man who had led them for nearly fifteen years through some of the most remarkable times in recorded history.

The members of Jon Hansen's staff struggled to get through each moment while attempting to carry out their duties. Few attempted to hide their tears as they spoke of him. It was not unusual to see small groups huddled closely together, weeping openly as they reminisced.

As much as anyone else, Decker Hawthorne grieved the loss of his boss and friend, but for Decker there was no time to commiserate with his colleagues. At this moment the world waited for him. As director of public affairs, he had to put aside his own mourning in order to coordinate the funeral and numerous memorial events. His staff was inundated with calls from the press and from mourners wanting to share their grief. Thousands called requesting photographs of Hansen, and hundreds of dignitaries wanted to be included in the many memorial ceremonies. Of the latter group, each believed that Decker should take their call personally; in many cases he did. Staying busy was probably the best thing for Decker at the time and he knew it.

But the lust for power never ceases, and it was during this period of mourning that Decker saw the first indications of the odious dealings that were afoot to replace Hansen. The once-united members of the Security Council each called upon Decker, requesting special favors with regard to the funeral or the ceremonies surrounding it. Ambassador Howell of Canada wanted to be the final speaker to eulogize Hansen at the funeral, the ambassador from Chad wanted to be seated near the center of the dais from which the speeches would be made, and the ambassador from Venezuela wanted to escort Hansen's widow. The request that angered Decker most was made by French Ambassador Albert Faure, who, though he had never said a kind word about Hansen while he was alive, now wanted to be a pallbearer for the secretary-general. Worse, he also insisted he be given the right lead position among the bearers. Though he wouldn't say why, Decker understood the reason: In that position, Faure hoped to be able to be most frequently seen by the television cameras.

As one of his more pleasant duties, Decker sent a limo to pick up Christopher at Kennedy Airport, but could not spare anyone to greet him. Christopher, like hundreds of other diplomats and hundreds of thousands of mourners, had come to New York for the funeral, filling the already crowded streets to capacity. In the sixteen years since the Disaster and the devastation of the Russian Federation, the population of the world had grown very quickly. Overall, world population was still more than a billion fewer than before the Disaster and the war, but one would not have guessed it to look at New York on this occasion.

As Decker emerged from his office after a long meeting, he called one of the senior secretaries to be sure the limo had left to get Christopher.

"No, sir," the secretary answered, quickly adding, "Alice Bernley called during your meeting and said she and former Assistant Secretary-General Milner would meet Director-General Goodman."

❑

At Kennedy airport, Robert Milner and Alice Bernley waited patiently for Christopher's flight. When Christopher arrived, he seemed genuinely pleased to see his mentor waiting for him at the gate, and the two embraced in a warm, extended hug. "How are you, Mr. Secretary?" he asked.

"Just great, Christopher," Milner answered.

"And Ms. Bernley. It's so nice to see you again."

"How have you been? It's been nearly a year since I saw you last in Rome," Bernley said.

"Yes, it's been a very busy year. But what are you two doing here? I didn't expect a greeting party."

"Well," answered Bernley, "when we heard you were coming in, it just didn't seem right that you should have no one to greet you but a driver."

Christopher smiled. "I'm so glad to see you both. Thank you for making the effort."

"Besides," added Milner, now getting to an additional reason for the airport reception, "there are some things we need to discuss before your arrival at the UN."

Christopher looked curious.

"We'll discuss it in the car, where we can talk more freely."

Once in the car, Alice Bernley reached for the switch that

closed the tinted glass barrier between them and the driver. With their privacy ensured, Milner wasted no time getting to the matter at hand. "Christopher, it is the double curse of wars and politics that when a great leader falls, those who mourn most his loss must, at that very moment, also be most vigilant to defend against the encroachment of those who have lost the least and who see in our adversity an opportunity for their own gain. So it is, even at *this* moment of loss."

"It's started so soon?" Christopher asked.

"It has," Milner said. "There is more power up for grabs at this moment than at any single moment in world history. The first order of business for the UN will be for Europe and India to elect new members of the Security Council to replace the ambassadors who died with Hansen in the crash. In India there are two strong contenders, including the current alternate, Rajiv Advani, and the Indian prime minister, Nikhil Gandhi. Gandhi, who, as you know, is half Italian and was educated in the United States, is clearly more reasonable and would be easier to work with than Advani. But if Gandhi wins, which appears quite likely, Advani plans to return to India to run for prime minister. I don't know how familiar you are with Indian politics, but polls indicate that without Nikhil Gandhi to head it, the Congress Party's coalition will not be able to hold power. If the polls are right, Advani's Bharatiya Janata Party could win enough of a plurality of the 545 seats in the Indian parliament to easily form a solid coalition with a few of the minority parties. The Bharatiya Janata Party is a Hindu revivalist party that appeals to Hindu pride and has as one of its goals to revoke all rights of the Muslim minority.

"So while we would welcome Nikhil Gandhi's election as a member of the Security Council, if it results in the election of Rajiv Advani as India's prime minister, it will have come at a very expensive price. There can be no doubt that the hostilities between Hindus and Muslims in India will sharply increase under Advani, and the border tensions with Pakistan will grow even worse.

"In Europe the most likely candidates are Ambassador Valasquez of Spain and, of course, Ambassador Albert Faure of

France. It's my guess that Faure has his eyes on something much bigger."

"Secretary-general?" Christopher asked. It was a rhetorical question; there was only one position more powerful than that of primary member of the Security Council.

"Exactly," Milner answered.

"That's quite a jump from being an alternate member of the Security Council." Christopher said. "He can't possibly think the Security Council is going to vote for a second consecutive secretary-general from Europe."

"I didn't say it was likely he could win, just that that's what he's after . . . along with half a dozen other people, I should add."

Alice Bernley had been sitting quietly but it seemed to her that the conversation was getting off track.

Milner continued, "Before the new secretary-general is elected, there will be an election to replace the alternate from North America. And if either of the alternates from India or Europe are elected to become primary members, then there will be an election to replace them as well.

"Christopher," Milner said, growing even more serious, "Ambassador Faure has asked me to support his candidacy to replace the late Ambassador Heineman as the primary member from Europe."

"You refused, of course."

"I told him I would."

"What? But why?" Christopher blurted. "Isn't Faure the very person you were talking about when you said we needed to defend against the encroachment of those who least mourned the loss of Secretary-General Hansen?"

"Yes, he is. But there is more to this than you may realize. As unfortunate as it may seem, Ambassador Faure will succeed in his bid to replace Ambassador Heineman on the Security Council; there is no way for us to prevent it."

"But why?"

"Two reasons. First, as I said, the only other candidate capable of getting enough votes is Ambassador Valasquez of Spain. No one else has nearly enough support. Frankly, Valasquez is a fool to run against Faure. His closet is so full of skeletons that it's a miracle none of them has fallen out before this. As soon as Faure's people get around to investigating Valasquez's background, they're bound to start uncovering something embarrassing. If they're smart, they'll wait until the last minute and then get Valasquez to pull out in exchange for not releasing the information to the press. At that late date, no one else will be able to mount a serious candidacy. The second reason is that, as you know, Alice has certain abilities, certain insights into the future, that come to her through her spirit guide, Master Djwlij Kajm."

Alice Bernley took this as her cue. "I am absolutely certain Ambassador Faure will be elected as the primary member from Europe to the Security Council. However, we must view this not as a loss, but as a short-term setback."

"And we must make the most of the situation and find a way to use it to our ultimate advantage," Milner added. "Since we know Faure will be elected with or without my support, it is best that I offer him my support in exchange for something we want. That's where you come in, Christopher."

Christopher seemed a little unsure of the whole situation, but he was always quick to recover. "Whatever I can do to help, just let me know."

"Good," said Milner. "I was sure you'd have that attitude. Now, instead of going directly to the UN you will go first to the Italian Mission."

"As an Italian citizen, assigned to the UN, I would do that anyway, as a courtesy to Ambassador Niccoli."

"Good. When you arrive at the Italian Mission you will be informed that three hours ago Ambassador Niccoli resigned his position as the Italian ambassador to the United Nations in order to pursue other interests."

"What? What other interests?" interrupted Christopher.

"A very well-paid position as a director of the Banque of Rome. A bank in which, not coincidentally, David Bragford owns a twenty-two percent interest. But as I was saying," Milner continued, "at the Italian Mission you will be given a sealed packet and a message to immediately call the Italian president on their secure line. When you reach President Sabetini, he will direct you to open the packet. Inside you will find documents to be presented to the UN Credentials Committee naming *you* as the new Italian ambassador to the United Nations."

Christopher stared at Milner and then at Bernley. Bernley smiled, but for a moment no one spoke. Finally Christopher held his hands out in front of him, gesturing for them to stop. "Hold it a second," he said. "Could you repeat the last part of that last sentence?"

"You heard me right, Christopher. You are going to be named the new Italian ambassador to the United Nations, assuming, of course, you're willing."

"But this is crazy. I've only been an Italian citizen for five years."

"And for much of those five years," Milner answered, "I have devoted myself to preparing you and the people of Italy for this moment. That's why I urged you to become an Italian citizen in the first place."

"But how could you have known?"

"We did not know the specifics," Bernley answered. "Obviously, if we had known that Secretary-General Hansen was going to die, we would have tried to prevent it. But what I know and don't know about the future is not something I get to pick and choose."

"It did not take Alice's clairvoyance," Milner interjected, "to know that one day Hansen would step down. And when he did, we knew we would have to be prepared to preserve the advances he had made."

"I'm sorry," Christopher said, "but I still don't understand. Why would President Sabetini name me as the new ambassador? And why would the priministro agree?"

"There are several reasons," Milner said. "No doubt they like you and trust you. They believe you care about Italy and the Italian people. As for the president, my guess is he's hoping you will someday become his son-in-law."

"His son-in-law?! Why do people keep saying that? Tina and I are just friends," Christopher said emphatically.

"That's fine, Christopher. I'm just listing a few possible reasons. But, doubtless, the biggest reason the president would name you as ambassador and that the prime minister would back his decision, is that Italy wants a voice on the Security Council."

"Hold it," Christopher said. "I think I've missed something. How does *my* becoming the Italian ambassador give Italy a voice on the Security Council?"

"That's why I have agreed to support Ambassador Faure's election as Europe's primary," Milner answered. "Presently, thirteen European nations have committed their support to him. For my part, I am to provide him with the five additional votes he'll need to be elected as primary. In exchange for these five votes, Ambassador Faure will support my candidate to replace him as alternate member. You, Christopher, will be my candidate. And that will give Italy its representation on the Security Council."

Christopher took a deep breath and shook his head in wonderment. "But how can you promise the votes of five countries?"

"Well, one of those votes will come from Italy; that is, from you," Milner answered.

"And the other four?"

"Christopher, Alice and I are not without some influence among the members of the UN. I've quite a large number of chits I may call in. And Alice, well, let's just say that there are many people in the United Nations who greatly value her opinions."

They rode in silence for the next few minutes, but as they pulled up to Two United Nations Plaza where the Italian Mission is located, across the street from the UN, Secretary Milner sought to reassure Christopher. "Christopher, I don't know what you're feeling right now, but let me assure you, you should not for a moment feel like this position was bought. In very few countries can ambassadorships still be bought and sold. Instead, *you* have been sold to the Italian president as the best person for the position and for Italy."

"Thank you, Mr. Secretary. I'm glad you put it that way. I just keep expecting to wake up and find out this whole conversation has been a dream, or maybe for someone to yell 'Surprise!' and tell me this is all a practical joke."

Milner knew Christopher well enough to know that no response was necessary, but Alice Bernley answered, "It's no joke, Christopher."

As Christopher got out of the car, he had one more thought, "I'm supposed to meet Decker in his office."

"I'll call and let him know you'll be late," Milner volunteered.

"Yeah, thanks, I'd appreciate that. But that's not what I'm thinking about. I'm wondering how I'm going to explain *why* I'm late."

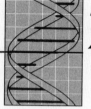

Simple Arithmetic

```
Three weeks later
New York, New York
```

AMBASSADOR LEE YUN-MAI of China called to order the session of the United Nations Security Council and welcomed each of the new members and alternates on behalf of the whole Council. The position of Security Council president rotated among the ten primary members on a monthly basis. It was not a particularly cherished position, but in the absence of a secretary-general it provided the only point of focus for the press. Ambassador Lee was one of the most experienced members of the Council. Now in her seventies and with more than thirty years of diplomatic service, she had served during all but three of the years during which Hansen had been secretary-general. As much as anyone, she hoped to limit the spectacle of the event that was about to unfold, but the election of the first Secretary-General since Jon Hansen would not be without its drama. In much of the world the proceedings were being carried live, with an expected total audience of a half billion listeners and viewers. Under the circumstances, it was unrealistic to hope for total abstinence from grand-standing by the members.

Italian Ambassador Christopher Goodman sat quietly at the C-shaped table in the place assigned to the European alternate member of the Security Council. There was little for him to do but watch; as an alternate he had no power to nominate, second, or even vote on the election of the new secretary-general. On most matters, alternates could speak when the floor was open for debate, but for the election of the secretary-general there would be no debate, only nominations, seconds, and votes.

If Christopher had needed any distraction, there were many other pressing matters to think about. Secretary Milner's projections about India had been right on target; Nikhil Gandhi, the former Indian prime minister, had won the seat as primary from India, and, as expected, Rajiv Advani was now seeking to replace Gandhi as India's prime minister. Even more pressing was the famine in Pakistan and Northern India. With Hansen's death, the relief work had come to a virtual standstill. Christopher's replacement at FAO, along with ECOSOC's Executive Director Louis Colleta, were doing all they could with the resources available, but the matter was now stalled, awaiting debate by the Security Council. Even if it did finally come to the floor for a vote, without the driving force of Hansen there was little hope that the food-producing regions would contribute sufficient relief.

Christopher was in no position to help. As the alternate from Europe, he had replaced Faure as chairman of the World Peace Organization (WPO). While Christopher's experience would have better suited him to work as the alternate in charge of ECOSOC, that position had been held for the last two years by the ambassador from Australia. Under current world conditions, ECOSOC offered far greater visibility and hence the Australian ambassador had no interest in giving it up.

With Pakistani refugee camps growing ever more crowded, those who could were attempting to cross the border into India. Many were intercepted and returned to Pakistan by the United Nations Military Observer Group in India and Pakistan (UNMOGIP), which had monitored the border between the two countries since 1949. But with sixteen hundred miles of border, half of which are traversable (the other half lying in the Great Indian Desert), the number of refugees pouring into India was greater than the UN forces could handle.

The Indian government, while expressing sympathy for the plight of the refugees, had responded to the attempted migration by sending its military to protect its borders against "invasion." India had its own problems with famine and had no interest in allowing any additional mouths at its meager table. So far the Indian military had shown restraint, choosing simply to escort refugees back across the border with a stern warning. There had been a few dozen shootings and beatings, but these were the exceptions. Whether the policy of restraint would continue under Rajiv Advani remained to be seen. Despite efforts to stop the migration, UNMOGIP estimated that hundreds of refugees eluded capture daily. There was no telling how long the Indian government would allow this before resorting to unrestrained military force.

Refugees who made it into India soon found their efforts to be futile. Although food was not as scarce as in Pakistan, it was impossible to purchase and nearly impossible to beg or steal. Even when the refugees had money, the Hindu merchants chose to sell what little they had to their own people, unless a sufficient premium could be paid to convince them to do otherwise. Added to the refugees' problems were the cultural and religious differences between Pakistanis, who are nearly all Muslims, and Indians, who are predominantly Hindu.

At ECOSOC, Christopher might have been able to help. As chairman of WPO, his job had the wholly different focus of keeping refugees from pouring across the border and minimizing the need for India's military intervention.

At the Pakistani/Indian border, more than just countries and cultures met. It was also the demarcation between the UN regions of India and the Middle East and between Muslims and Hindus. Adding a third element to the amalgam was China, which shares a border with both India and Pakistan. For decades, even with the easing of tensions that had occurred under Hansen, the Indian government had provided covert support to the Tibetan Buddhist followers of the Dalai Lama who sought the separation of Tibet from China. China, meanwhile, maintained a very strong relationship with Pakistan.

Were this not enough to distract Christopher from the Security Council proceedings, there was another matter as well. Christopher's predecessor at WPO, Albert Faure, had left numerous unfinished matters. Among them was a UN treaty with Israel to formally extend expired diplomatic agreements, ensure the exchange and safe delivery of diplomatic packets, and provide diplomatic immunity for visiting officials. The treaty had very little to do with military issues, but after being shuffled around the other agencies for two and a half years because no one could convince the Israelis it was in their interest to sign it, someone had decided it should go to WPO because one of the more obscure provisions was a mutual agreement of nonaggression.

Now, appropriately or not, the treaty lay at Christopher's doorstep, and his success in negotiating with the Israelis was seen as the first measure of this untried ambassador's abilities. It was ironic that such a treaty was even necessary, but Israel—which had become a nation as a result of a vote by the United Nations General Assembly—had later resigned its membership because of the reorganization of the Security Council and was now the only country in the world that refused membership in that body.

As far as the Israelis were concerned, the old agreements with the UN could stand just the way they were. They saw no reason to renegotiate and were reluctant to open themselves up to new demands. The Israeli resignation from the United Nations had originally been viewed by her Arab neighbors as an opportunity to isolate Israel from the rest of the world. They had sought a complete and immediate halt of all trade with Israel, but that attempt was doomed from the start. Ultimately, a nonbinding resolution and statement of principles was adopted by the General Assembly that prohibited sales of advanced weapons to Israel, but the resolution had exactly the opposite effect than was hoped for by Israel's opponents. For the first seven years after their war with the Arab states and then with the Russian Federation, Israel's defensive arsenal had consisted primarily of the huge weapons caches left behind by the Russians. Most of the Russian weapons were inferior to those Israel possessed prior to the war, but with modifications they were made workable. Since that time, while most countries' military budgets were being cut back, Israel had maintained a constantly increasing defense budget. The upshot was that while her Muslim neighbors grumbled loudly, there was no real possibility they'd attack Israel again anytime in the foreseeable future. Israel could afford to be a little smug.

Albert Faure, who had never expended much effort on his responsibilities as chairman of WPO, had not even tried to get the new treaty with Israel signed. There was evidence he had let slide or mismanaged a number of other duties as well. The one thing he did seem to do well was to appoint his friends to positions in WPO's administration.

With the formalities behind them, Ambassador Lee opened the floor to nominations for secretary-general. One of the perhaps less democratic holdovers from the days before the reorganization of the Security Council was the manner in which the secretary-general was elected, which required unanimous approval of a candidate by the Security Council followed by a full vote of the General Assembly.[54] During the years of Secretary-General Hansen, this procedure had not been an issue; Hansen had proven during his first five-year term that he placed no region over any other, not even his own. At the conclusion of each of his first two terms Hansen had been renominated by the Security Council and approved by the General Assembly. It was assumed by most that the same would be true at the end of his third term. With his death, the Security Council was faced with the sticky problem of finding a candidate who was satisfactory to all ten primary members. The disapproval of any one of the members would, in effect, veto the nomination. The net result was that everyone knew from the outset this meeting would produce no consensus on the selection of a candidate.

First to be recognized by the chair was Ambassador Yuri Kruszkegin of the Republic of Khakassia, representing Northern Asia. Following the devastation of the Russian Federation, Kruszkegin had left the United Nations to help form the new gov-

[54]The dominance the "Big Five" permanent members of the Security Council demanded when they established the United Nations in 1945 included the assurance that the secretary-general would be acceptable to all five. Since no one with ties to any of the five would be considered unbiased, it was agreed that the secretary-general would be from a nonaligned country. The Security Council would select a mutually acceptable candidate who would then be presented to the General Assembly for approval.

ernment of his home province of Khakassia, but had returned to
the UN five years later. His election to represent Northern Asia on
the Security Council had been unanimous by the members of that
region. Kruszkegin rose and nominated Ambassador Tanaka of
Japan, representing the Pacific Basin. Japan had been very supportive of the countries of Northern Asia in their efforts to rebuild
after the war with Israel. Even before the United Nations voted to
eliminate trade barriers, Japan dropped many of the trade imped-
iments between itself and the nations of Northern Asia. These
steps had been very important to the reconstruction of that region
and Kruszkegin was repaying the debt. The nomination was seconded by Ambassador Albert Faure of France, representing
Europe. Faure's reasons for seconding the nomination were far
from clear. The best guess of most observers was that Faure was
hoping for something in return.

The chair opened the floor for additional nominations and recognized the ambassador from Ecuador representing South
America, who nominated Jackson Clark, the ambassador from the
United States. The nomination was seconded by American-
educated Ambassador Nikhil Gandhi of India. Most observers
had expected the American to be nominated, but weren't sure
how it would play out. Ambassador Clark had only recently
resigned as the U.S. president in order to replace Walter Bishop,
who had died in the crash along with Hansen. The nomination
made it clear just what Clark had in mind when he resigned the
presidency: He wanted to be secretary-general. The primary
member from North America, Canadian Ambassador Howell—
still in poor health but delaying his resignation—was expected to
provide a third vote for his southern neighbor.

Again the floor was opened for nominations, and the chair recognized Ambassador Ngordon of Chad, representing West Africa,
who nominated Ambassador Fahd of Saudi Arabia. The nomination was seconded by the ambassador from Tanzania, representing East Africa. The basis for this final coalition was easily
recognizable as one of common religion and proximity.

The vote was as split as it could possibly be. Since no one
could be nominated without the support of at least two regions,

and no region could nominate or second anyone from their own region, the maximum number of nominations possible was three. Only China had abstained; all other votes were committed. Whoever would eventually be chosen would need the approval of all ten regions and that appeared to be a long way off. For now there was nothing to do but to go on to other business.

Jerusalem, Israel

Scott Rosen was lost in thought as he walked out across the crowded outer courtyard that surrounded the newly reconstructed Jewish Temple. As it had been in ancient days, this nearly square courtyard, called the Court of the Gentiles, was as close to the holy places of the Temple as non-Jews were allowed to come. The mood here had much more an air of carnival than of worship or reverence. Nowhere was this more inescapable than in the column-lined covered portico encircling the perimeter of the Court of the Gentiles. Here, housed in haphazardly misarranged booths and stalls, temple money changers dickered rates of exchange with worshipers to convert various currencies into newly minted shekels—the only currency acceptable for temple offerings. Nearby traders offered pigeons, doves, lambs, rams, and bulls for purchase as sacrifices.

Scott paid no attention to the cacophony. His mind kept going back to a conversation he had had the day before. It had started out as a perfect day. The weather had been beautiful, the traffic was light. A meeting he wanted to avoid and for which he hadn't prepared was indefinitely postponed. The extra time allowed him to tackle some interesting and important work and within two hours he had come up with a way to solve a major problem that had seemed unsolvable to everyone else who had looked at it. An overdue rent check for the house that had belonged to his parents arrived in the morning mail. Sol, the proprietor at the kosher deli he frequented, had added an extra scoop of tuna to his sandwich and had given him the biggest dill pickle Scott had ever seen.

That's when the day began to sour.

Sol came over to talk with Scott while he ate and Scott invited him to sit down. It had started innocently enough: They talked about politics and rising prices and discussed religious issues and the latest gossip from around the Temple—all topics they had discussed before and upon which they almost always agreed. Then Sol mentioned he had been reading his Bible in the ninth chapter of the book of Daniel.

"The prophecy at the end of the chapter says that King Messiah was supposed to come before the second Temple was destroyed!" Sol declared. "That happened in 70 C.E.[55], so he must have already come!"

"Sol, that's crazy!" Scott corrected sharply. "If King Messiah had come we would surely have known."

But Sol didn't yield. "According to Daniel's prophecy, King Messiah was to come 483 years after the decree to rebuild the city of Jerusalem, after it had been destroyed by the Babylonians. Based on Ezra chapter 7[56], the date of that decree can be determined as 457 B.C.E.[57] And when you take into account that there was no year zero, that means King Messiah came in the year 27 C.E.!" Sol pulled out a calculator to show Scott how it all worked but Scott stopped him.

"Sol, what you are doing is very serious. It is forbidden by the Talmud."

"What?" asked Sol in surprise.

"Calculating the time of King Messiah's coming based on the ninth chapter of Daniel is forbidden," Scott answered authoritatively.

"But—"

"In the Talmud, Rabbi Jonathan put a curse on anyone who calculates the time of the Messiah based on Daniel's prophecies," Scott declared.[58]

Sol mulled this over for a moment. Scott, confident he had set-

---

[55]Current Era, or A.D.

[56]Ezra 7:6-7.

[57]Before Current Era, or B.C.

[58]Sanhedrin, Tractate 976, Nezikin Vol. 3, Rabbi Samuel B. Nahmani speaking in the name of Rabbi Jonathan.

tled the question, took another bite of his sandwich. Taking advantage of Scott's full mouth, Sol rejoined the exchange. "But that can't be right," he said, to Scott's sandwich-strained chagrin. "Why would the Talmud not want us to know when Daniel said King Messiah would come?"

Scott forced down his food. "Sol, prophecy is hard to understand. You can't just pull out a calculator and figure out what a prophecy means."

"Why not? That's what Daniel did to interpret the prophecy of the prophet Jeremiah. And that's in the ninth chapter of Daniel, too—the same chapter as the prophecy of when King Messiah would come. Of course Daniel didn't have a calculator, but it's still simple arithmetic."

"Look, Sol, you're dealing with things you don't understand."

But Sol wasn't ready to quit. "Don't you see, Scott? If the Messiah came in 27 C.E., then we did not recognize him. Don't you get it? 27 C.E.! There's only one person who fits the description!"

"Stop it, Sol! I don't know what's gotten into you, but this is wrong, and I won't listen to it. If you fear *HaShem,* you'll be at the Temple tomorrow with your sin offering asking forgiveness." Ever dutiful, Scott used the orthodox method of referring to God as *HaShem,* meaning "the name," rather than *Yahweh* or even *God,* in order to avoid any possibility of blasphemy.

Sol didn't say any more but it was clear he felt no guilt that would warrant an offering at the Temple. Scott grabbed the rest of his sandwich and pickle and left. *Sol just didn't realize what he was saying,* Scott thought. *If he does that sort of thing with his other customers, he won't have any business left.*

❑

Outside the Temple on the broad steps leading down to the street, Scott was distracted from his recollections by someone calling his name. The voice had come from the direction of a large group of tourists, recognizable by their cameras and paper yarmulkes, so he assumed the call had been for some other Scott.

"Scott," came the call again, but this time he spotted its source coming toward him at a brisk pace.

"Joel," he called back to his friend and professional colleague of many years. Joel Felsberg had been a part of the team with Scott fifteen years before, during the Russian invasion. "What brings you to the Temple?"

Unlike Scott Rosen, Joel Felsberg had never spent much time on matters of religion. The only times he came to the Temple were with relatives or friends who were visiting from the United States. "Scott," he said again, out of breath and ignoring Scott's question. "I've found him! I mean he's found me."

"Slow down, Joel," Scott said. "Who have you found? What are you talking about?"

Joel, who was of average build and just under five feet seven inches tall, leaned close to the much larger Scott Rosen and whispered, "The Messiah."

Scott Rosen looked around quickly to see if anyone else had heard, then grabbed Joel's arm and walked quickly down the Temple Mount through another crowd of tourists. The smaller Felsberg, who was easily eighty pounds lighter than Rosen, had no choice but to accompany him. "I've found him," Joel said again as he tried desperately to keep up.

"Be quiet!" Scott warned as he pulled Joel along.

When they reached the parking lot some hundred and fifty yards away, they stopped next to Scott's van. He looked around to be sure no one was within earshot and finally spoke, "Are you crazy?! That's nothing to joke about. And of all places—right on the steps of the Temple! Maybe you don't take your religion or your heritage seriously but some of us do. If anyone had heard you—"

"No, Scott. I'm not joking. I've seen the Messiah. I've seen him," Joel interrupted.

"Shut up, Joel! You didn't see anybody. So just shut up!"

"But—"

"Shut up!" Scott said again, this time grabbing Joel's shirt and shaking his fist in his face. Joel fell silent but the maelstrom was still in Scott's eyes. Scott dropped his fist and began to release his grip. "Is the whole world going mad?" he asked. "First Sol and now you!"

"But—" Joel said again. Scott took hold of Joel's shirt with both hands now, lifting him onto his tiptoes, and brought his face to within inches of his own until they were eye to eye.

"If you say one more word," he said through his teeth, "I swear by the Temple of HaShem that I will—" Scott caught himself. Swearing by the Temple was serious business; next to swearing by God himself, there was no more powerful and binding an oath. It was not to be made in anger or haste. Scott released his grip and pushed Joel, who stumbled back into the side of a car. "Just get away from me until you've come to your senses."

Joel picked himself up and looked into Scott's eyes with a sincerity that even Scott could not doubt. "I really have seen him," Joel insisted.

There was nothing else to do. Scott couldn't bring himself to actually hit his old friend. They had been through too much together. They had fought side by side to save Israel those fifteen years ago, there in that bunker beneath the streets of Tel Aviv. They had been heroes together. There was nothing left for Scott to do but ask the obvious question. "Where?! Where have you seen him?" he demanded, finally resigning himself to having this conversation.

"In a dream."

For a moment Scott just stared, dumbfounded. From the beginning, Joel had known how weak that answer was going to sound but it was the only one he had, and to his mind, that was what God had given him to say.

"And he's coming to establish his kingdom," Joel added finally.

Suddenly Scott's anger changed to concern. He had been wrong to be so brutal. Joel was obviously delusional. Scott had dreams from time to time that felt so real they seemed real even in the waking world. Apparently, Joel couldn't separate dream from reality. "Joel," he said sympathetically, "It was just a dream."

"But it wasn't just a dream."

"I know, Joel," Scott said in the most consoling tone he could muster. "It must have seemed very real to you. But it *was* just a dream."

"No, Scott. Don't you see? I've been wrong all these years. And so have you."

The conversation was taking an unexpected turn. "What do you mean?" Scott asked.

"We've been wrong all this time. My sister Rhoda and her rabbi have been right all along. Don't you see, Scott? Yeshua really is the Messiah!" And then just to be sure Scott fully understood what he had said, Joel used the English version of the name, "Jesus is the Messiah!"

That was the last straw. Scott Rosen's eyes filled with rage. He didn't care whether Joel was delusional or not; this was too much. He grabbed Joel by the shoulders and shook him. "You and that traitor rabbi, you're both *meshummadim!*" he said, using the Hebrew word for traitors. Scott violently threw him to the ground. Joel's left wrist and forefinger snapped as he tried to break his fall.

"I don't know you!" Scott screamed. "I never knew you! You're dead! You never existed! If you ever talk to me again, I'll kill you!"

Scott got in his van and drove off, leaving Joel to nurse his wounds.

23

Offering

New York, New York

ALICE BERNLEY AND ROBERT MILNER strolled slowly past the huge wall of ivy along Raoul Wallenberg Walk, their pace giving no hint of the excitement they felt as they talked of the events of the past few weeks. "It's all coming together; I can feel it," Alice said. "Even if I weren't here to see it for myself, I think I would still feel it. I think," she said, after a moment, "I could be on the moon and I'd still know."

Milner smiled. He did not doubt her supposition for a moment. He could feel it too.

"I've gotten calls and letters, e-mail and faxes from people all over the world. They can sense we're on the very brink of the New Age," Bernley continued.

"Yes. Some of that concerns me, though. I'm afraid there are those who would like to rush its advent. We cannot allow that."

"No one else knows about Christopher?" she asked, her voice laced with concern.

"No. At least not that I know of. If our friends on the Security Council knew, they'd try to make him secretary-general right now." Milner was speaking hypothetically, but Bernley took him seriously.

"We can't allow that," she said.

"No, of course not. The time simply isn't right. No, I don't think anyone else knows about Christopher. At least not yet. But many obviously do know that you and I know something."

"Yes," Bernley said, her mood shifting back to enthusiasm. "I've gotten calls from people and groups I've never even heard of. All of them want to know what they should do."

"And what do you tell them?"

"I tell them to organize, add to their number, spread the word that the arrival of the New Age is near. And to wait."

"Good advice," said Milner.

Ahead of them on the walk stood a tall thin man with graying hair, wearing a tailor-cut European suit. He was flanked by two very large men, both easily twice his weight. The eyes of the larger men were hidden by sunglasses, but the thin man stared directly at them. Had Milner and Bernley not been so involved in their conversation they would have noticed the men long before. Their combined swath blocked nearly the whole walk. They did not seem menacing, but they did appear determined.

"Secretary Milner?" the thin man asked.

"Yes."

"Ms. Alice Bernley?"

"Yes."

"I have a letter for you," the man said as he handed an envelope to Bernley. The man had spoken only a few words, but Milner, who had traveled to every corner of the world, recognized his accent at once. Most would have guessed French, but there was more. It was rougher, more guttural than a true French accent. There were also strong traces of German. The man was obviously a native of Alsace-Lorraine, the region of France that from 1870 to 1945 had traded hands between the French and Germans five times. Milner wasn't sure, but he could think of only one item of business that would bring this man of Alsace-Lorraine to this meeting in the park.

Bernley opened the envelope and began to read the letter inside. "Bob, look!" she said, holding up the letter for him to see as she continued to read.

Milner read. It was as he had suspected, but it was important not to appear too eager. Impressions could be critical. "Please convey our appreciation," Milner said as soon as he was sure of the letter's content, but without reading it in its entirety. He knew Alice could be very excitable and he wanted to be the first to speak.

"You will take delivery of the package, then?" the thin man asked.

"Yes," Milner answered calmly.

"Yes, of course we will," Bernley said, in a much more animated tone. "We would be delighted to . . ." From the corner of her eye she caught the disturbed look on Robert Milner's face, and let her sentence trail off. She recognized it at once as the look he gave when he thought she was getting too ardent. Not that he wasn't just as excited as she; it just wasn't always prudent to show it.

"Where would you like it delivered?"

Milner thought quickly and answered with the most obvious place: "The Lucius Trust at the UN Plaz—" Milner stopped himself. It didn't make sense to ship it across the Atlantic only to ship it back for its final delivery. "No," he said. "Have it delivered to the Italian Embassy in Tel Aviv."

"We will need some assistance getting it through customs," the man said.

"Of course," Milner answered.

"You can expect delivery in one week, if that is acceptable to you."

"Yes, that would be fine," said Milner.

The man reached into his pocket and retrieved a key ring with four keys. "You will be needing these," he said without further explanation. "Ms. Bernley. Secretary Milner." He nodded in farewell, and without another word the three men walked away. Milner now looked at the letter more closely.

> We believe that a certain item, in our possession for a number of years, may prove useful to your current enterprise. At your request, we would be most gratified to surrender the item to you to use at your discretion.

The letter went on to give specifics on the delivery of the item and to note that there were certain precautions to be observed in its transport and handling, of which the writer was sure they would be aware.

Bernley had been right: It was all coming together. "I knew they would contact us," said Milner. "It was just a matter of time."

Tiviarius, Israel

"So, what is it you wanted to talk about?" Rabbi Eleazar ben David asked Scott Rosen as he sat down in his favorite chair. The rabbi's study was a little darker than Scott liked; one of the bulbs was out and there was no natural lighting because the room's only window, like every other wall in the room, was hidden by tightly packed bookshelves. It was quite an impressive collection of books, some in each of the three languages the rabbi spoke fluently.

"I'm concerned about Joel," Scott began.

"Joel Felsberg?" Rabbi ben David interrupted.

"Yes," Scott confirmed.

"I haven't seen Joel since the last time the three of us went to the Jerusalem Symphony. How is he? Is there anything wrong?"

"That's why I'm here. He came up to the Temple yesterday to find me. He was running and waving his arms," Scott exaggerated, "and yelling 'I've found him! I've found him!' I told him to calm down and asked what he was talking about, and he said he had seen the Messiah."

The rabbi raised an eyebrow at this, but the reaction seemed more to convey introspection than trepidation. The rabbi's expression gave Scott the impression he hadn't been listening. "Rabbi?" he said, seeking confirmation that the rabbi had heard what he was saying.

"The Messiah?" he asked after a moment.

"Yes."

"Did he say where he had seen him?"

"In a dream, but he's convinced it was more than that. I guess he thinks it was some kind of vision."

"Hmm," the rabbi said with the same look of introspection. He paused for several seconds and then asked, "Can we be sure it wasn't?"

"Yes. Absolutely."

"Why?" asked the rabbi.

Scott frowned, pained to have to answer. "I hate to even say it," he said. Rabbi ben David waited. "Apparently, whatever he saw in his dream has convinced him that Jesus, or 'Yeshua' as he called him, was the Messiah."

This time the rabbi both raised his eyebrows and pushed out his lower lip. Clearly he was surprised, but there was no indication that he was appalled. Scott had expected a much stronger, or at least quicker, response. The rabbi seemed lost in thought. Obviously, he had something on his mind. Another man might have asked him about his distraction, but not Scott. He had never been one to openly show concern about other people. He was much happier with a room full of computers than a room full of people. The fact that he was here showing concern for Joel Felsberg gave witness to how close the two men were.

"Well, what should I do?" Scott asked, waving his hands to make his point and hoping to draw the rabbi's attention back to the subject.

"About what?"

"About Joel," Scott said, still waving his hands, this time out of frustration.

"I don't think there's anything you can do. If it was just a dream, he'll get over it. Just try to be patient with him."

"What do you mean *if* it was just a dream?" Scott asked in disbelief.

The rabbi scooted forward in his seat. "Well, it's interesting that he should have this dream at this particular time." Scott was still too surprised to notice, but the rabbi no longer seemed distracted. "My studies have recently brought me to a rather interesting passage. Let me read it to you." The rabbi took his reading glasses and a book from the coffee table beside his chair and opened to a place he had bookmarked. Then he began:

Who can believe what we have heard?
Upon whom has the arm of the Lord been revealed?
For he has grown, by His favor, like a tree-crown,
Like a tree-trunk out of arid ground.
He had no form or beauty, that we should look at him:
No charm, that we should find him pleasing.
He was despised, shunned by men,
A man of suffering, familiar with disease.
As one who hid his face from us,
He was despised, we held him of no account.
Yet it was our sickness that he was bearing,
Our suffering that he endured.
We accounted him plagued,
Smitten and afflicted by God;
But he was wounded because of our sins,
Crushed because of our iniquities.
He bore the chastisement that made us whole,
And by his bruises we were healed.
We all went astray like sheep,
Each going his own way;
And the Lord visited upon him
The guilt of all of us.[59]

"Rabbi," Scott interrupted, "why are you reading me this?"

"Just listen," the rabbi answered. Scott did not understand why a rabbi would be reading what was obviously a passage from the Christian New Testament, but he had more respect than to challenge him just yet. The rabbi continued:

He was maltreated, yet he was submissive,
He did not open his mouth;
Like a sheep being led to slaughter,
Like a ewe, dumb before those who shear her,

---

[59]Isaiah 53, *The Prophets Nevi'im*, A new translation of the Holy Scriptures according to the Masoretic text, second section (Philadelphia: The Jewish Publication Society of America, 1978), 477-478.

He did not open his mouth.
By oppressive judgment he was taken away,
Who could describe his abode?
For he was cut off from the land of the living
Through the sin of My people, who deserved the punishment.
And his grave was set among the wicked,
And with the rich, in his death —
Though he had done no injustice
And had spoken no falsehood.
But the Lord chose to crush him by disease,
That, if he made himself an offering for guilt,
He might see offspring and have long life,
And that through him the Lord's purpose might prosper.
Out of his anguish he shall see it;
He shall enjoy it to the full through his devotion.

My righteous servant makes the many righteous,
It is their punishment that he bears;
Assuredly, I will give him the many as his portion,
He shall receive the multitude as his spoil.
For he exposed himself to death
And was numbered among the sinners,
Whereas he bore the guilt of the many
And made intercession for sinners.[60]

Scott wasn't sure whether the rabbi was finished, but he had no desire to hear any more. "Why have you read this to me?" he asked.

"What do you think?" the rabbi asked in return, ignoring Scott's question for the moment.

"I think the Christian writers do a poor job of imitating the style of the Jewish prophets."

The rabbi smiled broadly. It wasn't exactly the answer he had expected but it made the point. "Why do you assume that these are Christian Scriptures?"

[60]Ibid.

Scott still wasn't sure what the rabbi was up to but the question-and-answer teaching style reminded him of his days in Hebrew school. *The rabbi must be using this to make some point about Joel's delusion,* he thought. "Well," Scott answered, as if he were in a classroom, "there are two reasons. First of all, the writer is obviously writing about Jesus: all that business about being wounded because of our sins and crushed because of our iniquities. That's a Christian belief—that Jesus was a substitutionary sacrifice for the sins of mankind. It is obvious this is one of their Scriptures trying to convince the reader that Jesus was the Messiah."

"Is that what it is saying?" the rabbi asked before Scott could get to his second point.

"Of course. It's obvious. It could be nothing else."

"And the second reason?"

"Second," said Scott, "is that I have never heard nor read that passage before. If it was from the prophets, I would have heard it read in synagogue."

Rabbi ben David leaned forward and handed the still-opened book to Scott. Sitting back again in his chair, he crossed his hands on his stomach and exhaled audibly through his thick gray beard. Scott found the passage quickly; it was well marked. Then he looked at the top of the page. It read "Isaiah."

Suddenly his eyes filled with rage. "Were the Christians not satisfied to add their writings to the back of our Bible with their so-called 'New' Testament?" he roared. "Have they now begun inserting their lies into the very text of the Tenach? Where did you purchase this? We must put a stop to it immediately before others are deceived!"

"As you can see," the rabbi said, flipping to the title page, "this is translated according to Masoretic text and was published by the Jewish Publication Society of America. What I read you is in your Bible, too, Scott. You can go home and look."

"That's impossible. My Bible was given to me by my grandfather. The Christians could not have—"

"Those *are* the words of the prophet Isaiah, Scott."

Scott's eyes grew wide with bewilderment. "But why have I never heard this before?"

"You have never heard it because that passage is never read in the synagogue. It does not appear in any rabbinic anthology of synagogue readings for the Sabbath. It is always passed over."

"But who can the prophet be talking about?"

The scrutiny of the rabbi's stare turned Scott's question back to him.

"But it can't be. The prophet must be speaking in allegory."

"Perhaps. In rabbinic school, when I was young and believed everything I was told, they covered this passage briefly and they taught us that Isaiah was speaking allegorically of Israel. But if the 'he' the prophecy speaks of is Israel, who then is the 'we'? Clearly there are two parties spoken of. And if the 'he' is Israel, then whose sins—whose iniquities—have we borne? Who is it who was healed by our wounds?

"'*He* was cut off from the land of the living through the sins of *My* people,'" the rabbi continued, reciting a piece of what he had just read. "Is it not Israel who are God's people? And if Israel is God's people, and 'he' was cut off from the land of the living through our sins, who is the 'he'?" Rabbi ben David frowned and concluded: "So we are back to the same question: To whom does the prophet refer?"

"But what about the part about dying from disease? Jesus was supposed to have been crucified," said Scott.

"In truth," Rabbi ben David answered, "that wording is a very selective translation. You can see right here," he said, pointing to the editor's note at the bottom of the page[61] from which he had just read, "the meaning of the original Hebrew is uncertain. 'Disease' was just a guess. But even with that, who can miss what the prophet is saying?"

Scott did not answer.

The rabbi sighed. "So there is the reason for my distraction," he said, "and the reason I find Joel's dream, or at least the timing of it, so curious. You see, it was because of a dream that I recently read that portion of Isaiah. It was not so colorful a dream as the one Joel described. I'm not even sure I was asleep. I just kept

[61]Ibid., 477.

hearing a voice calling my name and telling me to read the fifty-third chapter of Isaiah. I was as astounded as you when I read it. I could not understand how I could have so long ignored what you have just said is so obvious; allegory simply cannot explain the striking similarity. If ever a prophecy were exactly fulfilled, then this . . ." The rabbi stopped himself from saying more. "Well," he continued, "so now I find myself in a dilemma. As you have said, it is obvious of whom the prophet seems to be speaking, and yet I cannot allow myself to admit it. But," he said, and then paused, "neither can I bring myself to deny it."

New York, New York

The Security Council was called to order to assess the progress toward reaching a compromise on a new secretary-general. Although there was still a long way to go before a decision, substantial movement had occurred. The first major change was the withdrawal of the candidacy of the ambassador from Saudi Arabia. It quickly became clear that certain other regional representatives, particularly India, simply would not accept an Islamic secretary-general and since the selection had to be unanimous, the Saudi ambassador had bowed out. In doing so, he made it clear that whoever was ultimately chosen would have to pay a price for the Islamic region's spirit of compromise and cooperation. The representatives of East and West Africa who had supported the Saudi were then approached by the American and the Japanese ambassadors for their support, but both were reluctant to support either.

After some late-night deliberations between the supporters of Japanese Ambassador Tanaka and the Africans, French Ambassador Albert Faure, who more and more seemed to be filling the role of impartial facilitator, had asked the representative of West Africa whom he *could* support. An hour later, after private discussions between the East and West Africans, they answered that they could support the representative of Northern Asia, Ambassador Yuri Kruszkegin. Faure relayed the information, and the next morning Tanaka withdrew and threw his support to Kruszkegin.

In the meantime, however, the Saudi, who represented the Middle East, had agreed to support Ambassador Clark of the United States. When the Security Council adjourned, the vote was five for Kruszkegin, four for the American Clark, and as before, China abstained. The issue was tabled for seven more days.

Ten days later
Jerusalem, Israel

The black stretch limousine of the Italian ambassador to Israel, Paulo D'Agostino, pulled past the security barriers and stopped outside the front entrance of the Israeli Knesset. Accompanying D'Agostino were Christopher Goodman, Robert Milner, and Milner's guest, Alice Bernley. Close behind the limo, security personnel from the Italian embassy followed in an armored truck carrying a large wooden crate that had recently been delivered to the embassy from Alsace-Lorraine, France.

Inside the Knesset building, in the office of the prime minister, Israel's High Priest Chaim Levin and two Levite attendants had just arrived and were exchanging pleasantries with the prime minister and the minister of foreign affairs while they awaited the arrival of their guests.

"Thank you very much for coming, Rabbi," the prime minister told the high priest.

"I am always willing to be of service to Israel," the New York-born high priest answered. "But tell me, have they still not said why it was so important that I attend this meeting? And why of all days, it had to be today?"

"No, Rabbi. The purpose of the meeting is to allow the new Italian ambassador to the United Nations an opportunity to present arguments for renegotiating our treaty with the UN—nothing that should concern you and, I might add, nothing that really concerns me. The old treaty has lapsed and, while I admit it has a few flaws, I am reluctant to agree to any new negotiations. I would have refused this meeting altogether but for the fact that it was requested by former Assistant Secretary-General Milner, a man of some influence with ties to American bankers. As for why he asked that you be invited and why it had to be on this day, I do not know. He said only that they will be bringing something with them that you will want to see."

The meeting was soon under way and Christopher began to address those assembled. Alice Bernley was the only woman in the room. It was a little awkward explaining her attendance in an official meeting of state, but there was no way Bernley would have allowed this moment to pass without her. Christopher would be brief and to the point; all of the arguments he would make about the treaty had been made before. But that was not the real reason for this meeting anyway. Still, it was necessary that Christopher offer a clear explanation of the treaty's purpose and the reasons the UN believed that a new treaty—not just an extension of the old one—was required. The duration of the proposed treaty would be seven years, and would allow the parties, upon their mutual agreement, to extend its effect for three additional periods of seven years each. There was nothing particularly remarkable about the treaty; it was just typical matters of state. The only thing of even passing interest was a provision for a mutual agreement of nonaggression. Even this was included primarily as a diplomatic formality. Israel certainly had no intention of attacking anyone. After so many years as a nation under constant threat of war, while it still had problems with terrorism, it had established itself militarily as a nation which none of its neighbors would consider attacking.

Christopher's summary presentation lasted only about fifteen minutes. He offered to answer any questions, but none were asked. Apparently the prime minister wanted to get through this as quickly as possible.

"Ambassador Goodman," the prime minister said as soon as it was clear there were no questions, "I am sometimes praised for speaking candidly and other times criticized for being too blunt. Either way, it is the way I am. I hope you will not take offense.

What you have said, though eloquent and well reasoned, has all been said before. And what was lacking before is still lacking, which is to say an apple will always lack the qualities that would make it an orange. You offer us an apple and make guarantees that we will like it as much as an orange. We, on the other hand, are happy with the orange we have. We do not seek guarantees that we will come away from the conference table satisfied with the agreements contained in a new treaty; we are satisfied with the old one. We find no compelling cause to alter that position."

"I appreciate your position," Christopher answered, "and your frank response. I hope that you also appreciate frankness." Christopher spoke quickly, allowing no opportunity for interruption. He was about to get to the real reason for this meeting. "What separates us on this issue is not the need for formal extension of agreements in the old treaty. I'm sure we both recognize the importance of the formalization of agreements for the protection of all concerned. Neither is there disagreement on the issues involved. Diplomatic immunity, transport of diplomatic packages without interference, and mutually held agreements of non-aggression are hardly controversial issues. What separates us, Mr. Prime Minister, is trust.

"In ancient times," Christopher continued, "such diplomatic logjams were broken by an exchange of gifts. I would not be so naive as to believe that your assent could be bought in such a manner, and yet I recognize the precedent and so come bearing gifts." Christopher, who was already standing, walked to the room's entrance and opened the large double doors in a bit of grand display, which was certain to be excused when it was learned what he had brought.

In the hallway outside, four unarmed Italian security guards stood watch around a wooden crate about the size of a small freezer that sat about three feet above the ground on a very sturdy-looking metal table with wheels. Christopher signaled to the one in charge, and the four men rolled the table and crate into the room and then left, closing the double doors behind them.

The crate was built of cedar and was itself a work of art, more a display case than a simple crate. The four sides were hinged at the bottom to allow the sides to fold down to display the contents. At the top middle of each side was a locking mechanism that held the sides securely shut. From his pocket Christopher took a set of four keys. "I do not ask for anything in return," he said, "for with the giving of this gift I gain as well. *What* I gain is hope. Hope that the level of trust between us may grow and that we may, through that trust, come to achieve those things that of necessity governments must accomplish in order to conduct themselves in a manner consistent with the rule of law."

Christopher's appeal could be viewed in either of two ways: as an eloquent plea for something no reasonable person could refuse to grant, or as a bunch of flowery tripe. Either way, it gave Christopher a chance to state again what he was after. For if anything he had said thus far *was* tripe, it was that he was not asking anything in return for this gift. And if his last words were counted as tripe as well, it made no difference; what they were about to see was of such importance to the people of Israel that nothing the prime minister might possibly concede in a new treaty could compare to what they had gained here.

Christopher took the keys and moved quickly to each of the four locks, opening each in the order directed in the letter that had been delivered to Alice Bernley and Robert Milner. As he opened the last lock, he moved back and it became clear just how special this crate really was. On a three-second delay after the opening of the fourth lock, eight pistons simultaneously slid through hydraulic cylinders, allowing the four sides of the crate to drop slowly open. The top was supported by the frame against which the four sides had been sealed. Except for Christopher, who was already standing, and Alice Bernley, who knew what was inside and so stood to get a better look, everyone else in the room was seated and it was not until the sides were about halfway open that anyone caught a glimpse of what was inside. As they did, their eyes grew wide, and all rose to their feet. For a moment no one spoke. Each just stood and stared in awe. And then there was a sound, almost a shriek from the back of the room. The younger of the high priest's two Levite attendants raised his hands as if to shield himself and ran from the room screaming something in Hebrew.

The reaction of the Levite made the prime minister catch himself. For a moment he had almost believed it to be real. Now he was sure he knew better. "It is a very nice reproduction, Mr. Ambassador," the prime minister said to Christopher as he sat back down. He spoke very loudly, casting his voice in the direction of his foreign minister and the high priest with the intent of bringing them back to reality. "I'm sure one of our *museums* will be very glad to accept it. It must have cost someone a good deal of money."

The prime minister's words had the effect he hoped for. The foreign minister, the high priest, and finally the high priest's remaining attendant all came to realize this must be a reproduction. There was certainly no possibility it was the real Ark of the Covenant. It couldn't be. The Ark had not been seen for thousands of years. Still, it seemed a singularly impressive reproduction. The craftsmanship and care that had gone into its creation were astonishing.

"I assure you, Mr. Prime Minister, it is indeed the Ark of the Covenant." The speaker was Alice Bernley. Her voice was very confident and her words matter-of-fact. It was the first time she had spoken since the introductions. She knew her presence at the meeting was inappropriate; she represented no government, she was simply an observer, and now she was no longer an unobtrusive one. She didn't wait for an answer. She didn't really care what the prime minister thought. Her only interest was in seeing the Ark and she moved closer to get a better look.

"Alice is correct, Mr. Prime Minister," Milner said.

The prime minister laughed. "Mr. Milner, I don't doubt your sincerity and I appreciate whatever effort you went to in order to procure this for us, but this simply cannot be the true Ark of the Covenant."

Christopher had let the conversation go on without him long enough. "Mr. Prime Minister, I am well aware of the significance of this day in your nation's history. It is Tisha B'Av, a day of fasting, the day history records that both your first and second Temples were destroyed. It was no accident that I chose today for this meeting. I chose it to offer your people a sign and symbol of hope for the future—that on this day of all days there is hope for all the people of the earth, if only we will cooperate and work together. What you see here, Mr. Prime Minister," Christopher concluded, pointing with his open hand to the Ark, "is the Ark of the Covenant. It is *not* a reproduction. It is *not* an imitation. It is real!"

"Mr. Ambassador!" the prime minister said, raising his voice, "Do you take us for fools?"

"We can prove it's authentic," Christopher answered emphatically, but without raising his voice.

"How?" demanded the prime minister.

"By the Ark's contents."

Suddenly the prime minister fell silent. The suggestion surprised him. Of course. They could look inside. The validation process would be so simple. So simple, in fact, that maybe there was something to the Italian ambassador's claim after all. "Okay," he said. "Let's look inside." Almost as soon as he said it, the prime minister realized that if this were the real Ark, it wouldn't be proper to do that.

"Oh no, Mr. Prime Minister," Christopher said. "That's not exactly what I meant. The Ark must be handled with great care. It would not be wise for just anyone to open it. According to the Scriptures, many have died for mishandling the Ark."[62]

"Well, then how shall we see inside?" he asked.

"I would urge that only the high priest should open it." The prime minister looked at the high priest, who nodded, indicating that at least in general, Christopher was right.

"It does pose some problems," the high priest began in response to the question on the prime minister's face. He moved closer to the prime minister, Christopher, and Milner; leaving Bernley to examine the Ark unnoticed. It was all the same to her; she had no interest in what was being said. "If it truly is the Ark," the high priest continued, "then it should be opened only in the

---

[62]According to 1 Samuel 6:19, because the men of the city of Beth Shemesh looked into the Ark, seventy died (most Hebrew manuscripts and the Septuagint put the number at 50,070). For another example, see 2 Samuel 6:6.

Temple. And yet if it is not the Ark, then it would be an abomination to place it in the Holy of Holies to be opened, especially since we're not sure what's inside. Perhaps it could be brought inside the Temple but not—"

Suddenly a brief but blood-curdling scream filled the room. Behind them Alice Bernley's lifeless body crumpled and fell, her head hitting the carpeted floor with a muffled thud.

"Alice!" Milner cried as he ran to her.

"What happened?" shouted the prime minister.

The remaining attendant of the high priest, who had seen what happened, looked as if he were in shock. "She . . . she touched the Ark," he answered.

The Italian ambassador to Israel, Paulo D'Agostino, who had stayed quiet until this point, ran to the door and shouted for someone to call a doctor.

Robert Milner, finding no pulse, desperately began CPR. A state doctor assigned to the Knesset was there within seconds. He began emergency procedures even as Bernley was being put on a stretcher to be taken by ambulance to the nearest hospital. It would be another twenty minutes before she was officially pronounced dead.

As her body was taken from the room, followed by a weeping Robert Milner, High Priest Chaim Levin quoted from the Bible: "The Lord's anger burned against Uzzah, and he struck him down because he had put his hand on the ark."[63]

The prime minister looked back and forth from the high priest to the Ark and then to the others in the room. The Levite read madly through his Siddur, the traditional prayer book containing prayers for almost every imaginable occasion. He could find nothing for this moment. Christopher went to the Ark and carefully closed up the sides of the wooden crate to prevent anyone else from suffering Bernley's fate.

Finally, the prime minister spoke, "The high priest will examine your Ark, Mr. Goodman. And if it is, in fact, the Ark of the Lord, you shall have your treaty and the gratitude of the people of Israel."

[63] 1 Chronicles 13:10.

24

The Elect

New York, New York

OVER DINNER IN DECKER'S APARTMENT Christopher brought Decker up to date on his trip to Israel and the events surrounding the death of Alice Bernley. Robert Milner had stayed behind in Israel to take care of the arrangements for Alice's body. Christopher explained that though there were still a few fine points to be ironed out, he was hopeful the treaty with Israel would be signed in mid-September and would go into effect by the end of the month to coincide with Rosh Hashana, the Jewish New Year. Afterward Decker gave Christopher a detailed rundown of the efforts to choose a new secretary-general. The two candidates, Kruszkegin from Northern Asia and Clark of North America, had each tried to add to their support but without any success.

It was a very strange dance to watch. Since whoever was ultimately chosen would need the approval of every other member, neither man wanted to risk stepping on the other's toes as they climbed over the other, hoping to get to the top. Two days had passed with no change among the Security Council members. Then Ambassador Lee of China, who had thus far abstained, decided she could not support either candidate despite her personal friendship with Kruszkegin. Acting quickly, the members who had originally nominated the ambassador from the Pacific

Basin and then had substituted Kruszkegin to secure the votes of East and West Africa, again made a switch.

Their new candidate was the Frenchman Albert Faure. Faure held the votes of those who had previously supported Kruszkegin and had added China, which considered the European the least objectionable candidate. India, which had originally supported Jackson Clark of the U.S., when faced with a choice between the American and the European, had decided to abstain. So as far as anyone could tell, the vote was now six to three in favor of Faure.

Decker waited until after they ate before getting to the part about Faure. There was no reason to ruin Christopher's appetite.

Just then the phone rang. Decker answered and heard a familiar voice. It was Jackie Hansen from Christopher's office at the UN. After her father's death Christopher had hired Jackie as his chief administrative assistant. The reason for the call was an unexpected request for an appointment early the next morning. Normally, Christopher got in at about 7:30, but he had planned to go in late the next day so he could catch up on some lost sleep. The circumstances of the request made him put his other plans on hold. Two of the top generals from the World Peace Organization, Lieutenant General Robert McCoid, commanding general of the United Nations Military Observer Group in India and Pakistan (UNMOGIP), and Major General Alexander Duggan, recently assigned to WPO military headquarters in Brussels, Belgium, had arrived in New York without any advance notice and had asked to meet with Christopher as early as possible. Such a request was quite unusual and for that very reason Christopher quickly agreed to meet them in his office at 6:45 the next morning.

❑

The two men were hardly noticed the next morning when they arrived to meet with Christopher, which was the way they wanted it. Jackie Hansen had arrived early to give the office the illusion of activity at the early hour; the rest of the staff would not arrive for at least an hour, and it didn't seem right to have the generals greeted by an empty office. Christopher and Jackie were both in the reception area when their visitors arrived.

As a rule generals can be very serious people but these two had something particularly sobering on their minds. They would have preferred to get right to the heart of the matter, but an issue of this magnitude had to be approached with great care.

'En Kerem, Israel

Scott Rosen sat alone at his kitchen table eating his dinner. Outside, as the evening drew near, he could hear the voice of a neighbor calling her children in from their play. For a moment he thought back to his own childhood and the times he had spent playing with the children in his neighborhood. Often his grandfather, who had lived with them, would come out and throw a softball with him, or they would take a walk together through a nearby park and talk about what Scott was learning in Hebrew school or about the weather. Sometimes his grandfather would talk about his wife. Scott had never known his grandmother and he could listen for hours to his grandfather talk about her.

The steam from Scott's chicken soup—his mother's recipe—rose before him and brought him back to the present, but as he looked around he became aware he was not where he thought he was. This was his parents' house—the one they had owned in the United States when he was a boy. Before him the table was set for five. Near his father's place sat a large brass plate with sprigs of parsley, a small dollop of horseradish, a larger dollop of an apple mixture called *charoseth*, the shank bone of a lamb, and a roasted egg. Next to it was another plate stacked with matzah. The table was obviously set for *pesach*—the Passover. Four of the five places were set for Scott, his parents, and his grandfather. The extra place, in accordance with tradition, was set for the prophet Elijah, should he choose to return from heaven and grace their table with his presence.

Scott gave his head a quick shake and when that failed to have any effect on his circumstances, he tried rubbing his eyes. "Scott, come in here and help your mother," said a woman's voice from the kitchen. It was his mother, Ilana Rosen. As he heard the voice, it was as though the memory of his adult life had been but a dream. He tried to recall what he had been thinking, but the memory was fading too fast. All he could latch onto were a few, small, disassociated parts. He remembered that in the dream of his future there was something about his grandfather dying and him going to Israel, about his parents coming to live in Israel and him telling the authorities that they . . . But the rest of that memory was gone . . . about his parents dying . . . about a war with Russia . . . and . . . Scott brushed the thoughts away as the meaningless vestiges of a daydream and ran in to help his mother in the kitchen.

"Your father and grandfather will be home soon," Scott's mother said when he came into the kitchen. "We need to hurry with the preparations for Passover." Outside the sun was setting, marking the beginning of the Passover *Shabbat,* or Sabbath. Ilana Rosen worked at the cork in the bottle of red wine. "Here," she said as she handed the bottle to Scott, "see what you can do with it." Scott gripped the bottle firmly and gave it a tug. The already-loosened cork came out easily. "Wonderful!" Ilana said as she clapped her hands. "Now take it to the table but be careful not to spill any when you fill the glasses."

Scott poured the wine into the glasses for his parents and grandfather, gave himself half a glass, and then very carefully poured Elijah's cup. This was a very special wine glass, made of hand-cut leaded crystal—though this had always seemed strange to Scott because the glass was clear and he could see no lead in it. Still, it was a very special glass, taken out only for the Passover. For just an instant Scott seemed to have a memory of having broken this glass as he took it from the cupboard when he was fifteen. But that was silly; Scott was only eleven.

Behind him, Scott heard the front door open and turned to see his father and grandfather. Scott stopped what he was doing, ran over to his grandfather, and hugged him with all his might. How wonderful, he thought, to hug his grandfather again. As this thought occurred to him he remembered a part of his daydream:

His grandfather had died, a thought that made him shudder. But that was all a dream. Still, he took tremendous pleasure in feeling his grandfather's arms around him again.

Soon the Passover meal, or *Seder*, began and progressed through each step as directed by the Haggadah, which serves as a sort of a Passover guide book with descriptions, recitations, and the words to songs sung at points during the meal. First was the *brechat haner*, or kindling of candles. Then came the *kiddush*, the first cup, which is the cup of blessing; the *urchatz*, which is the first of two ceremonial washings of hands; and the *karpas*, when parsley is dipped in saltwater to represent the tears Israel shed while slaves in Egypt and the saltwater of the Red Sea. Next was the *yachutz*, when the father takes the middle of three matzahs from a white cloth pouch called the *echad* (meaning unity, or one), breaks the matzah in half, places one half back in the echad and the other half in a separate linen covering. Later, as directed by the Haggadah, the father hides the broken piece of matzah, called the *Afikomen* (a Greek word meaning "I have come") somewhere at the table. The youngest member of the family then must search until he finds it. When he does, he takes the Afikomen to his father to be redeemed for a gift or money. This had always been Scott's favorite part of the Seder. But he would have to wait until later in the dinner for that.

After the breaking of the middle piece of matzah came the *maggid*, the retelling of the story of Moses and the Passover, and then the *ma-nishtanah*, or four questions. Scott, as the youngest member of the family, would in his best Hebrew recite four questions about the Passover, each of which was answered in turn by his father. Then came the recitation of the ten plagues that had befallen the Egyptians. This part had always been funny to Scott because the Haggadah directs that, as each plague is named, those at the table are to stick a finger in their wine and sprinkle a drop on their plate.

Everything was the same as it had been every other year until the family sang one of the traditional Passover songs called "*Dayenu*," which means, "We would have been satisfied." The song is a happy, upbeat piece sung in Hebrew, which names some of the things God did for the people of Israel. After each verse is the chorus, which consists entirely of repeating the one word, *dayenu*. In English the words to the song would be:

> *If He had merely rescued us from Egypt, but had not*
> *punished the Egyptians,*
> > *Dayenu (we would have been satisfied)*
> *If He had merely punished the Egyptians, but had not*
> *destroyed their gods,*
> > *Dayenu*
> *If He had merely destroyed their gods, but had not*
> *slain their first born,*
> > *Dayenu*

And so the song continues, each time stating that if God had only done what was mentioned in the previous verse and not done the next additional things, the singers—representing all of Israel—would have been satisfied.

As they sang the last verse, which speaks of the Temple, Scott's grandfather suddenly stopped singing and shouted, "No!" Scott looked at him confused. "It's not true," his grandfather said. "Dayenu is a lie! We only fool ourselves."

"We only fool ourselves!" agreed Scott's parents.

This was not in the Haggadah. Something was wrong. And then without a sound, immediately there was another presence at the table. A man reached across the table in front of Scott and took the Afikomen, which had not yet been hidden, from beside Scott's father's plate. The man was sitting at the place set for Elijah. Scott recognized him at once as Rabbi Saul Cohen. But this made no sense at all. Scott didn't know anyone named Saul Cohen, except . . . except perhaps in that strange dream. How could he be here in Scott's home, sitting in the place of Elijah and drinking from Elijah's cup—the special cup that Scott's parents kept only for the Seder and from which no one was allowed to drink?

"Let us fool ourselves no longer," Cohen said.

❏

It was nearly midnight when Scott found himself once again an adult and in his home in a suburb outside of Jerusalem. His soup was now hours cold and the only light was from a digital clock and a streetlight outside. He was exhausted. For a few moments he just sat there. If he had any thoughts that the events of the past few hours in his childhood home had all been a dream, they were quickly dispelled. Near him at the table, in the position that had been Elijah's place in his dream or vision, where he had seen Cohen, was a three-quarters-empty glass of wine. It was Elijah's cup, the one that had irreparably shattered into a hundred pieces when he took it from the cupboard when he was fifteen. Even in the subdued light he recognized it. Scott sat back into his chair and noticed the plate beneath his bowl sitting askew on the table before him. There was something under it. He raised the plate and found underneath it the Afikomen, hidden for him to find and redeem.

New York, New York

French Ambassador Albert Faure's secretary showed Christopher Goodman into the office where Faure and his chief of staff awaited his arrival. "Good morning, Mr. Ambassador," Faure said, addressing Christopher. "Please come in."

"Thank you, Mr. Ambassador," Christopher responded. "I appreciate your seeing me on such short notice. I know how busy you must be."

"Well, you said it was urgent."

"It is."

"You know my chief of staff, Mr. Poupardin?"

"Yes, we've met," answered Christopher as he extended his hand.

"Now, to business. Your message said this has to do with the World Peace Organization."

"Yes, sir. As you know the situation in Pakistan has become critical. Voluntary relief supplies simply aren't sufficient. And much of what is sent is not reaching those who need it the most. Hundreds are dying of starvation every day and thousands of others become candidates for starvation. Cholera is claiming thousands more. Unless the United Nations responds quickly with sufficient quantities of food and medicine and the personnel to administer their distribution, this could result in the death of millions."

As Christopher spoke, Faure and Poupardin exchanged a puzzled look. The look remained on Faure's face as he began to speak. "Let me assure you, Mr. Ambassador, that I am as concerned as you with the problems in that region. In fact, I met with the new ambassador from Pakistan on that matter just two weeks ago, along with Ambassador Gandhi. It is my sincere hope that more will be done, and soon. But," Faure continued as he wrinkled his brow still further in puzzlement, "isn't this an issue for ECOSOC and the Food and Agriculture Organization? I thought you wanted to see me about the WPO."

"The matter of supplying food to the region is, indeed, a matter for the FAO," Christopher responded, "but the unrest that *results* from the food shortages is an issue that concerns the WPO." Faure let Christopher continue without responding. "As the previous chairman of the WPO, you are no doubt aware of the problems that have plagued WPO's supply lines over the last two years: $36 million worth of weapons and equipment lost in warehouse thefts; $14 million lost and two people killed in hijacked shipments; and another $141 million worth of equipment simply listed as unaccounted for."

Faure and Poupardin looked at each other in surprise. Faure had no idea losses had been that high. He didn't want to let on just how little he had kept track of such matters when he was chairman of WPO, but he had to ask. "Just a question of clarification," he began. "What percentages of those losses occurred during the time I was chairman; and how much has been reported in the last three and a half weeks, since you've been in charge?"

"Those figures reflect the losses as of six weeks *before* I took over as chairman of WPO."

"Oh," Faure responded. "I had no idea they were so high." Better to openly admit ignorance than acknowledge negligence, he concluded. Christopher's expression showed neither surprise nor anger at Faure's admission.

"So, how does the situation in Pakistan fit into this?" Faure asked, wanting to move from the issue of his negligence as quickly as possible.

"In the last twenty-four hours I have been presented with what I believe to be incontrovertible evidence that the director of the WPO, General Brooks, is personally responsible for at least 95 percent of the weapons and equipment missing from WPO."

Faure and his chief of staff looked at each other again. It was beginning to appear as if they had some nonverbal means of communication and that neither would speak without first checking with his counterpart. "But why would General Brooks be stealing his own weapons?" Faure's chief of staff asked.

Christopher ignored the naiveté of the question. "Apparently he has been selling the weapons to insurgent groups, sometimes for cash and other times in exchange for drugs that are in turn sold for cash."

"That's a very serious charge," said Poupardin, this time without stopping to check with Faure. "I assume you have evidence to back it up."

"I would not make such a charge unless I was sure I could prove it."

Faure and Poupardin mulled this over for a moment, still without words. "Well," said Faure finally, "I suppose you'll be initiating an investigation."

"Yes. Time is of the essence, but I don't believe it's possible to carry out a full and complete investigation so long as General Brooks remains in command. That's why I came to you. I intend to ask the Security Council for approval to immediately place General Brooks on suspension, putting Lieutenant General McCoid in temporary command and granting me full authority over the agency until the matter is resolved. Before I do so, I thought that, as I have so recently taken over from you as chairman of WPO, professional courtesy required that I first inform you of my intentions and that I make you aware of the reasons for my actions."

Faure thought fast. The look on his face said that something about Christopher's plans did not go well at all with his own.

"Well, I appreciate that," Faure said. "Actually, it's a very good thing you talked to me first." Suddenly Faure had become very friendly. "I'm afraid this might be the worst possible time for you to broach this subject with the Security Council."

"I don't believe putting it off is an option," answered Christopher. "The situation on the Indian-Pakistani border requires immediate action."

"I understand your concern, but . . . Well, let me bring you up to date on a few things." Faure got up and walked around his desk, still sounding as though he had nothing but everyone's best interest at heart. "As you know, the selection process for a new secretary-general has been going on for several weeks now. And I'm sure it's no surprise to you that right now the choice seems to be between myself and Ambassador Clark of the United States. At the last vote six regions voted for me, three voted for Ambassador Clark, and India abstained. The next vote is scheduled for Monday, four days from now. Nobody else knows it yet, but I've gotten a firm commitment from Ambassador Fahd to support me on the next vote and we're very close to reaching an agreement with India. That will leave Ambassador Clark with only two votes: North and South America. With that kind of majority Clark will be forced to concede.

"Now, you're a reasonable man," Faure continued. "You obviously realize that if you're right about what General Brooks has been doing with WPO resources, I had nothing to do with it. But some people might not see it that way." Faure's was at least a sin of omission; he had almost entirely ignored his responsibilities when he was chairman of the WPO and had handpicked Brooks when the previous commanding general retired. Brooks and Faure were old allies.

"They might try to blame me for Brooks' actions," Faure said.

"If this comes out right now, the American is sure to try to use it to ruin my candidacy for secretary-general." Christopher was about to interrupt, but Faure held up his hand to stop him. "Now, I understand," Faure continued, "the urgency of getting to the bottom of this, but there must be some other way for you to conduct your investigation without bringing the matter to the Security Council just yet."

"Mr. Ambassador," Christopher responded, "anything less than a direct route will cost time that I do not think we have to spare. Even if the Security Council grants my request immediately, it will take six to eight weeks to make the needed changes in personnel and to ensure that adequate equipment and supplies reach our troops on the Indian-Pakistani Border."

"Now the last thing I want to do is to prevent you from doing something you feel that you have to," Faure answered. "That's not the way I operate. And, besides, if I *should* be chosen as the nominee for secretary-general, and if I am approved by the General Assembly, well, then, of course no one can be sure, but you could very possibly replace me as primary on the Security Council." Faure wanted to point that out, just in case the possibility had escaped Christopher's attention. "The last thing I want is to cast a shadow on our future relationship. However," Faure paused, "with so much riding on this, for both of us and for the whole world, I suggest you explore every possible option before you do anything imprudent."

Christopher's response was terse, but his voice showed no anger. "I *have* explored every possible option."

"And you feel this is your only course?"

"Yes."

Faure's frustration was growing harder for him to conceal. "Can you wait at least four days?" he urged.

"No, I don't believe I can."

Faure looked at his chief of staff and shook his head. "I think he's in league with the American ambassador," Poupardin interjected. "He may be an Italian citizen now, but he was born in America." Then Poupardin addressed Christopher directly. "Why else would you be so inflexible?"

"Gerard!" Faure said sternly, calling his chief of staff to heel.

"Please, forgive me, Mr. Ambassador," Poupardin sputtered with a well-trained show of remorse.

"I, too, ask your forgiveness for Gerard's injudicious response," Faure said. "But you must realize that many in Europe may see this the same way." Faure was getting desperate. Poupardin had intentionally made the charge the way he did so Faure could call him down and then make essentially the same charge while seeming entirely proper about it because the subject had already been broached. It was an effective ploy, and it was not the first time they had used it.

"Consider this," Faure said. "Within a week I could be secretary-general and you could be the new primary member representing Europe. While General Brooks' actions are reprehensible—if indeed he is guilty as you charge—his removal will have little immediate impact on the problem. You said yourself, it will take six to eight weeks to make all the changes you want to make. And, in truth, even if you make all of these changes, it will have only limited impact on the delivery of food to the starving, and that, after all, is what all of us really want. Now, if you will delay your action until after the vote, you have my word that I will apply the full influence and power of the position of secretary-general both to speed the changes you feel are necessary for WPO and to ensure that adequate distribution of food reaches those who need it."

Christopher considered Faure's argument. It had merit. Finally he yielded.

"Excellent!" Faure said.

"But," Christopher added, "in exchange, I want your assurance that whatever the outcome of the vote on Monday, you will help get my request approved by the Security Council."

"Of course," Faure promised.

Poupardin apologized again for his comment and Christopher was soon on his way.

❑

"That man could be dangerous," Poupardin said as soon as Christopher was gone. "What would you have done if he had refused to wait?"

"Gerard, it is my destiny to be secretary-general. I would have done whatever was necessary." Poupardin smiled to himself and walked around behind Faure's chair, and began to massage his shoulders.

"It seems the price of Robert Milner's support for my election to the Security Council may be higher than we first anticipated," Faure said. "We will have to keep a very close eye on that young man."

"Shall I call General Brooks?" Poupardin asked.

Faure took a deep breath and held it as he thought. "Yes, I suppose we should," he said as he exhaled. "Tell him he had better get his house in order, and quickly, if he wants to keep his job. But don't take too long with Brooks; we've got other things to worry about. We have to get a commitment from Ambassador Gandhi and try to soften up South America's support for Ambassador Clark. I think we have to assume that our friend Mr. Goodman will not wait, should another vote be required."

❑

Conditions on the Indian-Pakistani border did not improve over the next four days; relief shipments were too few and too slow and the number of refugees attempting to cross the border continued to swell. To stem the tide, the Indian government increased their border guard sixfold. Reports spread of abusive treatment, torture, and summary execution of refugees who crossed into India. The government of Pakistan, in response to the Indian buildup, had significantly increased the number of its own troops along the border.

In New York it was the day the Security Council would again try to choose a new secretary-general. It was also the end of the period Christopher had promised to wait before requesting emergency authority over the World Peace Organization. In a corner of the anteroom outside the Security Council chamber, prior to the meeting, Christopher Goodman stood talking with Ambassador Gandhi about the situation in Pakistan. He had met with the Pakistani ambassador the previous evening, along with Saudi Ambassador Fahd, who was the primary from the Middle East on the Security Council.

Inside the chamber, Albert Faure and Gerard Poupardin went over a few last-minute preparations. At the outset, four days had seemed like plenty of time to get India's vote in line. As it turned out, Ambassador Gandhi had held on for a number of specific guarantees before he agreed to support Faure.

"I just wish I felt better about Gandhi's vote," commented Poupardin. "I'm not sure we can trust him."

"Oh, I wouldn't worry about the Indian," Faure responded confidently. "He knows he'll never get anyone else to agree to the kinds of guarantees I've made."

"I just saw him talking to Ambassador Goodman outside the chamber on my way in."

"Did you hear what they were talking about?"

"No, I didn't want to be too obvious."

"Well, it was probably nothing."

"Probably, but Goodman was also seen last night with Ambassador Fahd."

A disquieted look flashed across Faure's face. "Why was I not told of this before?" he asked.

"I only just heard of it myself."

Faure's mood became more pensive than concerned. "Why don't you go out there and see if you can hear what they're talking about. If you have to, just go up and join in. If they seem uncomfortable with you being there or if they change the subject, get back in here and let me know right away."

Poupardin got up to leave, but it was too late—the Indian ambassador and Christopher were just entering the room to take their places for the meeting. Ambassador Lee Yun-Mai of China called the meeting to order and soon the issue of the selection of the new secretary-general was brought to the floor. As expected, the nominees were Ambassador Jackson Clark of the United

States and Ambassador Albert Faure of France. The vote was taken in the customary manner by a show of hands. Ambassador Lee called first for those supporting the nomination of Ambassador Clark. Immediately the Canadian Ambassador, representing the North American region, and the Ecuadorian Ambassador, representing the South American region raised their hands. It was just as Faure had planned; he could almost taste the victory he longed for. Then, slowly, without allowing his eyes to meet the stunned gape of Faure, the Saudi slipped his hand upward. From the corner of his eye, Faure's attention was drawn by his chief of staff, Gerard Poupardin. Even across the room the single word on his lips was as clear as a shout: "Goodman," he said, under his breath.

Faure muttered an epithet.

From Faure's left, the door to the Security Council chamber flew open and a tall blond woman in her early forties rushed in. Undistracted, Ambassador Lee noted the count of hands: Three regions supported the ambassador from the United States. Without pause she called for those supporting Ambassador Faure. What Faure saw only intensified his despondence. Including his own, only five hands were raised: Ambassadors Kruszkegin of Northern Asia and Lee of China had chosen to abstain. Unlike Ambassador Fahd, Kruszkegin looked directly at Faure while Lee counted. Filled with rage, Faure turned to face Christopher, but Christopher was not there.

Quickly Faure's eyes scanned the room for Christopher, to no avail. He looked back at Poupardin, his eyes asking the question of Christopher's whereabouts. Poupardin pointed. In a corner of the great room, Christopher stood talking with Jackie Hansen, who had arrived during the vote with an urgent message. Faure's rage went unnoticed or at least unacknowledged by Christopher, who was listening to Jackie and quickly scanning the contents of the message she carried. Even as he read the dispatch, he began to move resolutely toward Ambassador Lee.

Contrary to Faure's assumption, the actual reason for the shift in votes was that Ambassadors Fahd, Kruszkegin, and Lee had learned of the promises Faure had made in order to get the vote of the Indian ambassador. They felt it was not in their interest to have a secretary-general who was under the obligations Faure had placed himself. Lee and Kruszkegin's response was to abstain; Fahd chose instead to support the American for whom he had voted earlier. None of this would ever be known by Faure. And what was about to unfold would make him absolutely certain that the whole situation had been Christopher's doing.

Christopher finished reading the note and proceeded directly across the room to Ambassador Lee. Handing her the dispatch, he whispered something and she began reading. As she did, Christopher went back to his seat and stood in order to be formally recognized. All eyes watched as she read. When she finished she struck her gavel and declared that no consensus had yet been reached, and the selection of a new secretary-general would be postponed for two weeks. She then turned her eyes toward Christopher and said, "The chair recognizes the ambassador from Italy."

"Madam President," Christopher began, addressing Ambassador Lee, "as you have just read in the dispatch, within the last hour a contingent of approximately twenty-seven thousand Indian infantry have crossed their mutual border with Pakistan in apparent response to continued border crossings by Pakistani refugees seeking food. They appear to be headed toward the three UN relief camps. In response to the incursion, United Nations forces under the direction of Lieutenant General Robert McCoid have engaged the Indian forces."

The room erupted. Members of the media tried to move to get a better shot of Christopher as he spoke; several staff personnel hurried from the room. Both the ambassador from Saudi Arabia, representing the Middle East, and the ambassador from India attempted to be recognized by the chair. But Ambassador Lee refused to recognize anyone and Christopher continued. "No report of casualties is yet available, but Indian troops in the area outnumber UN forces by six to one. General McCoid has ordered reinforcements into the area, but their arrival is not expected for several hours and the General warns that such movement will weaken UN strength at other points along the border."

Christopher completed his report to the Security Council and then, exercising his right as an alternate member, proceeded to make his request to remove General Brooks and to take emergency authority over the WPO. It probably would not have made any difference if he had made the request four days earlier. Still, these new events would make it much more complex and difficult to correct the problems.

Near Capernaum, Israel

Scott Rosen was not sure how he knew it, but there was no doubt in his mind he was supposed to be here. On a grassy hill on the northern shore of the sea of Galilee near Capernaum, he sat and waited, though not at all sure of what it was he was waiting for. He had been there for nearly an hour, just sitting and waiting, and now the sun was beginning to set. The terrain around him formed a natural amphitheater with acoustic qualities that allowed a person on the hillside to clearly hear someone speaking at the bottom of the hill. According to the local tour guides, this was the spot where Jesus had taught his followers.

When Scott had arrived, there had been tourists walking the slopes around him. But as evening set in he had briefly been left nearly alone. Now, over the last fifteen minutes, a steady flow of people, all men, had begun to fill the hillside. But these were not tourists; there were no cameras, no binoculars, no yapping tour guides. In fact, though their number grew into the hundreds, and then thousands, no one spoke at all. Each man simply found what seemed like a good place and sat down.

Over the next few minutes the trickle became a flood; now thousands arrived every minute. And still not an utterance was heard. Scott saw several people he knew. The first was Rabbi Eleazar ben David, to whom he had talked a few days earlier about Joel. Then he saw Joel—his hand and wrist in a cast, the result of their last meeting. Joel searched Scott out from among all the men on the hill and smiled broadly when he found him. Scott returned an anxious smile, and Joel sat down nearby. Neither said anything.

At the end of an hour there were more than a hundred thousand, and still no one spoke. Soon there were no more arrivals and the crowd's attention turned toward some movement at the bottom of the hill. Two men stood up and one of them began to speak. His voice was deep and rich and measured. Scott was too far away to see him clearly, but he could be heard by all. Scott recognized the voice at once. It was Saul Cohen.

Standing at Cohen's side, the other man remained silent as he looked up at the crowd and thought back to that pivotal summer day when he and his brother and father had fished these very waters two thousand years before.

25

Old Enemy, Old Friend

```
Sixteen months later
Somewhere in northern Israel
```

THE FRIGID, RAIN-STARVED GROUND cracked beneath the old man's weight as he walked along at a steady, purposeful pace toward the west. Even his gaunt appearance and wind-dried skin did not reveal the man's true age, which was thirty years beyond what anyone might have guessed. As he crested the top of a small hill, he could see, still some miles distant, the silhouette of the gold-domed Bahá'í temple above the terraced city of Haifa, which marked the end of his trek. After fourteen days in the Galilean wilderness he looked forward to a few days of regular meals, human contact, and a much-needed bath. The nearly empty pack on his back had been overstuffed with dried fruits and nuts when he started. His canteens, now empty, had added quite a bit of weight to his initial load two weeks earlier.

Normally, after a brief stay at the temple, he would be off again for another week or two in the wilderness, but this time there were other tasks that required his attention. For more than a year, since the cremation of his close friend and confidante Alice Bernley, Robert Milner, the former assistant secretary-general of the United Nations, had lived the life of a monk, going off into the wilderness of Israel for up to three weeks at a time before returning to the civilization of the Bahá'í temple. His only companion on these journeys was Tibetan Master Djwlij Kajm, Alice

Bernley's former spirit guide. During Bernley's cremation Djwlij Kajm had come to Milner and spoken to him in Bernley's voice. Up until that time Milner had known the Tibetan only through Alice, his channel to the physical world. Now Milner knew him in a much more intimate way. Over the last sixteen months, Master Djwlij Kajm had taught and trained Milner for the work to be done. Finally, on this most recent journey, Milner had completed his spiritual apprenticeship and had received into himself a guiding spirit who united with his own, the two becoming one.

The mission that called Robert Milner out of the wilderness at this time would take him in a few days to the city of Jerusalem, where he would await the arrival of Christopher Goodman and Decker Hawthorne.

New York, New York

"We cannot afford to compound our mistake by letting this go on any longer!" French Ambassador Albert Faure declared as he brought his fist down on the table before him. Nearby, Faure's chief of staff, Gerard Poupardin silently surveyed the reactions of the other Security Council members. From his perspective, the address seemed to be going well.

"It has been nearly sixteen months since this body voted to give emergency authority to the ambassador from Italy to personally direct the operations of the World Peace Organization. At that time we were assured by the ambassador that he had substantial evidence to corroborate his charges of corruption by the WPO's commanding general. No doubt the decision of this body came in part as a result of the incursion of Indian forces into Pakistan and in part because of our shared concern for the plight of the Pakistani refugees. And yet now, sixteen months later, we have still been given no concrete evidence of any complicity in, nor culpability for, any wrongdoing of any sort by General Brooks. Indeed, while the losses of materiel have dropped dramatically, there is every reason to believe that this has been solely due to new security measures, which General Brooks was in the process of implementing even as Ambassador Goodman stood before this body requesting emergency authority to place General Brooks on administrative leave, and then took direct control of the WPO into his own, far less experienced hands.

"And is it possible that a more pernicious hour could have been chosen by the Italian ambassador for making his charges, than at the very moment the incursion into Pakistan had begun? Charges whose only result was to undermine the structure of authority, incite derision, and weaken the *esprit de corps* of our forces when the leadership and guidance of General Brooks was most critically needed?

"And so, what began with the incursion of a few thousand troops has grown into what must be considered a full-fledged war between two peace-loving regions that threatens the borders of a third, China. And ironically, though the drought that led to the war has now lessened, still the war goes on, prolonging the famine by diverting resources and energy into fighting instead of into planting crops."

For twenty-five minutes this went on. Faure held nothing back. His intent was to ascribe to Christopher as much responsibility for the war as he possibly could. All of his charges hinged on Christopher's inability to produce conclusive evidence proving General Brooks was responsible for the losses of equipment and supplies incurred by the WPO. In the four days Faure had bought for him, Brooks had done an excellent job of covering his tracks beneath heaps of shredded documents. As for Faure's charges that Christopher was responsible for the continued hostilities in the region, history proved this a dubious conclusion. Since 1947, when Pakistan was carved out of what had been northern India, the two countries had been at war four times and at the brink of war on a dozen other occasions. That a war, once started, would continue and expand was no more surprising than that a brush fire, once lit, would continue until it has consumed everything around it. And if there was a threat to China, it was a well-deserved one, for China's arms merchants had very quickly accepted the offers of hard currency from the Pakistani government. Even Faure's charge that Christopher had taken control of the WPO into his own hands had only a little more than a trace of truth. Although Christopher was consulted regularly on the WPO's efforts, from the outset he had placed Lieutenant General Robert McCoid in charge of operations.

Still, Faure was making his point convincingly. And it was an address for which much preparation had been made. In the weeks prior, General Brooks' supporters and later Brooks himself had heavily lobbied members of the Security Council and other influential UN members. Faure's goal was clearly not just to force a vote to restore General Brooks to power, but to so humiliate Christopher that he would not be able to maintain his position as Europe's alternate to the Security Council. Key to the plan's success was that those who had engineered Christopher's election were apparently no longer a factor: Alice Bernley was dead and Robert Milner had not been seen since her funeral. But removing Christopher was just one part of Faure's plan.

In the months following Faure's unsuccessful bid to become secretary-general, every other imaginable candidate had been considered, but none could muster the unanimous support of the Security Council. Faure had seen to that. As the possibility of a consensus lessened, the frequency of the attempts also decreased, and the rotating position of Security Council president had come to be treated as acting secretary-general. It was Faure's intent that it remain that way until he could make a renewed bid for the office himself. But it would have to come soon, and Faure knew it. If the status quo remained for much longer the Security Council might decide to make it a permanent arrangement. In preparation for the renewed bid, Faure was doing favors wherever he could, trying to appear as fair and as diplomatic as possible. Except, of course, to those who got in his way. Faure considered Christopher to be in the latter category.

In a slightly different category was Nikhil Gandhi. He was not inflexible, but so far Faure had found his price to be too high. Giving him what he wanted would mean alienating others. Faure would have preferred the election of Gandhi's chief rival, Rajiv Advani, as primary to the Security Council. Advani and Faure had gotten along well as alternate members. Advani was now India's prime minister, but Faure had no doubt that he would prefer being India's primary . . . should anything unfortunate happen to Nikhil Gandhi.

Kruszkegin and Lee presented a bigger problem for Faure. Both had served many years with Secretary-General Jon Hansen, and both had grown to distrust Faure in the last year. Lee and Kruszkegin talked frequently, and both had come to the conclusion that Faure must never become secretary-general. If Faure was patient, he could hope that Lee would retire soon. Kruszkegin, however, could be expected to be around for at least five or six more years. And Faure was not that patient.

❏

When the vote came, it was a humiliating loss for Christopher. He had defended himself well when it came his turn to speak, but in the end only Lee, Kruszkegin, and Ruiz of South America voted to sustain Christopher's emergency powers over the WPO. Christopher remained as chairman and titular head of WPO, but General Brooks was restored to his position as commander of the actual forces.

Decker Hawthorne watched the vote on closed-circuit from his office in the UN Secretariat building, then hurried across the street to Christopher's office at the Italian Mission to be there when he arrived. Christopher was obviously angry and frustrated—two emotions he almost never displayed.

"Well, did you see it?" Christopher asked in a sickened tone as soon as Decker walked in.

"I saw," Decker answered, the anger in his own voice tempered by a desire to be as comforting as possible.

"The worst part is that it's my own fault!"

"Don't be so hard on yourself," Decker said consolingly. "Faure has been at this game a lot longer than you."

Christopher didn't seem to take much consolation in that. "How could I have been so stupid as to have gone to Faure and told him I was going to launch an investigation of General Brooks? I must have been out of my mind!" Christopher paced as he spoke.

"It may not have been the *smartest* thing, but I'm sure your intention was to do the *right* thing. You simply gave Faure the benefit of the doubt," said Decker.

"I gave him a lot more than that!" Christopher fumed. "I gave him four days of warning. It's no wonder I couldn't prove anything: General Brooks had four full days to destroy the evidence. I made a total fool of myself." Christopher shook his head introspectively. "It's no wonder Gandhi and Fahd voted against me, but Tanaka and Howell?" he said, referring to the ambassadors from Japan and Canada, respectively. "Are they blind? Don't they see what Faure is? He'd bring the whole world down around him if he thought that when it was all over he could stand at the top of the heap of rubble and declare himself king!

"You know, it never made sense to me that when the voting on a new secretary-general first began, Faure seconded the nomination of Ambassador Tanaka. And then later, when the West Africans rejected Tanaka, Faure was there to suggest Kruszkegin as a compromise candidate. It seemed so out of character for Faure to be promoting anyone but himself. I thought maybe I had been wrong about him: Kruszkegin would have made a great secretary-general. So when things worked out that Faure was nominated, it worried me at first but then I almost got used to the idea. Well, it took me a long time to realize it, but I'm convinced the only reason Faure seconded the nomination of the Japanese ambassador and later supported Kruszkegin was to build a base for his own nomination. I don't think he had any intention of helping Kruszkegin or Tanaka. It was all part of his plan to be elected secretary-general himself."

Anger burned in Christopher's eyes. He stopped and stared out his window. Outside, freezing rain fell on the street-blackened remains of the snow that had fallen three days earlier. "I've got to get away from here for a while," Christopher said.

"Why don't you take a few days and go stay at the house in

Maryland? In fact, if you don't mind the company, I'll go along with you." It had been nearly six months since Decker had visited the house in Derwood. He wanted to make sure that it, and more importantly the grave of Elizabeth, Hope, and Louisa, had been well cared for by the agency he had hired to see to the property.

"Thanks, Decker, but I'd like to get as far away from the UN as possible. Normally I'd go to Rome, but if I go there, the reporters will be on me about this vote before I've even hit the ground. And frankly, I'd rather not face President Sabetini right now."

Decker started to make another suggestion, but decided it was probably best to stay quiet and let Christopher think. Christopher stared out the window. Decker had never seen him look so distraught. It seemed there must be more to this than Christopher was saying.

"Christopher," Decker asked after a moment, "is there something you're not telling me?"

Christopher looked at Decker, his face filled with anxiety and trepidation. It was as though Decker had seen something Christopher himself did not want to admit but could no longer deny. "I have this feeling," Christopher began uncomfortably as he shook his head again, apparently unsure of what the feeling meant, "that something is about to go terribly wrong, that this is just the beginning, that Faure and Brooks are going to be responsible for some terrible tragedy. And I am helpless to try to stop it." Christopher paused, but Decker had nothing to say. "Am I wrong to want to get away?" Christopher continued. "To leave it behind me for a while?"

"No, of course not," Decker answered reassuringly. "We all have to get away sometimes to think."

"Maybe I'm just spoiled. I've never really faced a problem I couldn't handle. For the first time in my life I have no idea what to do."

Decker started to say, "Welcome to the human race," but decided it was better left unsaid.

"I know this is going to sound strange," Christopher said

finally, "and I really can't explain why, but for some reason I feel I need to go to Israel."

"Israel?" Decker echoed in surprise.

Christopher shrugged his shoulders. "I just have a feeling that maybe I'll find some answers there."

26

The Reason for It All

Tel Aviv, Israel

THE COLD, ARID, MORNING air of Tel Aviv quickly absorbed their moist breath as Decker and Christopher left the terminal at David Ben Gurion Airport and hailed a cab. With his attention on the taxi, Decker did not even notice the two uniformed police officers who ran out the door of the terminal behind them; nor did he notice the young man who stood off to their right talking to an older couple. Suddenly, though, it became impossible not to notice them. The young man, seeing the police, quickly broke and ran along the edge of the sidewalk between the taxi that had just pulled up and where Decker and Christopher stood. He got no farther. One of the policemen, anticipating his attempted route of escape, grabbed him and wrestled him to the ground right at the feet of Decker and Christopher. That's when Decker noticed the strange blood-red marks on the young man's forehead. For a moment Decker thought the man must be bleeding; as he looked more closely he realized it was writing, almost like finger painting, in Hebrew characters.

There was little time to think about it as the Palestinian taxi driver jumped smartly from his car, took their luggage, and threw it quickly into the trunk. He didn't even seem to notice the police or their struggling captive.

"I wonder what that was all about," Decker said, still watching the action through the window as he and Christopher settled into the cab.

"Oh, you mean the man the police were arresting?" volunteered the driver as he pulled away from the curb.

"Uh . . . yes," Decker answered, a little surprised. He had really just been thinking out loud and didn't expect an answer. "Did you see what happened?" Decker asked. "He was just talking to some people there in front of the terminal."

"Yes," the driver replied. "He was KDP." The reference meant nothing to Decker. "That's what they do: talk to people. It's *what* they talk about that's the problem. They're very odd. They know things about people; things that people don't want others to know."

The driver seemed to be a rational person, but Decker found it difficult to believe what he was saying.

"I think they're psychic," the driver continued, as he turned onto the highway. "They're not supposed to be around the airport or any of the tourist spots: It's bad for business. But that doesn't stop them."

"You said he was 'KDP.' What does that mean?" Decker asked.

"Well, that's the English. In Hebrew the letters are *Koof Dalet Pay*. The English is shorter to say than the Hebrew, so most people just call them KDP. Did you see the writing on his forehead?"

"Yes, I was wondering about that. What was it?"

"I didn't get a good look but it was the Hebrew characters for either Yahweh or Yeshua. Yahweh is the Jewish name for God, and Yeshua is Hebrew for Jesus. All of the members of the KDP have either one or the other."

"So, are they Christians or Jews?" Decker asked.

"They say they're both," the driver answered. "Of course the other Jews won't claim them, but many KDP used to be very respected Jews. Some of them were even rabbis, and I heard that one of them used to be an attendant of Israel's high priest."

"What about the writing? It looked like smeared blood. It appeared to be still wet."

"Well, they say it's lambs' blood from the sacrificial lambs at the

Jewish Temple. But whatever it is, it won't wash off. It's like a tattoo. I think it's some kind of permanent dye."

"Are you saying the Israeli government put the mark on the KDP members so that they could keep track of them?" Decker asked.

"Oh, no! The Jews won't even say 'God,' much less write his name. They hate the KDP because they have his name written on their foreheads. What makes it worse is that the Jews say that since the other half of the KDP have Yeshua written on their heads, it's like they're making Jesus out to be equal to God. They tried to get the government to deport all the KDP but no one else wants them either."

"So the KDP marked their own foreheads?"

"Yes. Well, they claim it was put on them by angels."

Decker let out a *hmm*.

"It seems stupid to me to put something like that on your forehead. It just makes it easy for the police to spot them."

"What will the police do to the one at the airport?" Decker asked.

"Oh, they'll probably hold him for a few days and then let him go. They can't do very much. There's just too many of them. If they arrested all of them, there'd be no room left in their jails for us Palestinians," he added sarcastically.

"How many KDP are there?"

"They say there's exactly one hundred and forty-four thousand, but I don't think anyone has actually counted them."

"A hundred and forty-four *thousand?*" Decker gasped.

"It was very mysterious. It all happened about a year ago. One day nobody had even heard of the KDP and the next day they were all over the place."

"That's incredible."

"That's how they got their name."

"I wanted to ask you more about that." By now Decker was leaning forward, his head partway over the back of the front seat to facilitate the conversation.

"Well, in Hebrew the same characters are used for letters and numbers," explained the driver. "For example, the letter *tav* is also the number nine. So you can add the numbers of the letters in a word. Say you added the letters in the Hebrew word for *bread;* that would equal seventy-eight. You can add up the letters in any word. The Jews call it *gematria.* Some of the Orthodox Jews use it as a way to make decisions, almost like most people in the rest of the world use astrological signs and horoscopes. For instance, some rabbis say that to memorize something you should repeat it one hundred and one times, because when you subtract the value of the Hebrew word for *remember* from the value of the Hebrew word *forget* the remainder is one hundred and one. But I think they make up the rules as they go along because a lot of times it doesn't make any sense. Anyway, sometimes a number will also be a word. Like, uh . . ." The driver tried to think of an example. "Okay," he said after a moment, "the characters used to write the number fourteen spell out the Hebrew word for *hand.* Of course Hebrew doesn't have any vowels like in English, so you have to use your imagination a little. Anyway, as it turns out, the characters used to write the number one hundred and forty-four thousand also spell the words *Koum Damah Patar*—KDP for short."

"What does that mean in English?" Decker asked.

"Oh just nonsense. Literally it means 'Arise, shed tears, and be free,'" the driver answered. "It's just an easy name for them, I guess. Actually, they can be pretty nice people when they're not preaching at you or telling you about the things you've done that you wish they didn't know about and maybe would rather not think about yourself."

"Have you ever talked with one of them?" Decker asked.

"Oh, yes. It's probably happened to everyone in Israel at least once. One day I was fixing a flat tire. I had burned my hand the day before and had it bandaged so I was having some trouble. This guy came up, and without asking just started helping me. When I looked up I saw he was KDP. I was surprised but he just kept working."

"He helped you change the tire?"

"Yes. Like I said, they're very strange. Sometimes they start out by doing you a favor, and they never take any pay. After we finished with the tire, out of the blue he told me how I had burned my hand and he said that the reason I had burned it was so that he'd be able to help me and then I'd listen to what he had to say. I don't know how he knew about my hand, but then he started telling me other things."

"Like what?" asked Decker.

"Well, personal things. Like I was saying, things that people would rather not talk about."

"Oh," Decker said. He hadn't meant to pry. "You said that *sometimes* they start out by doing you a favor. What about the rest of the time?"

"Well, my neighbor's wife decided to follow one of the KDP around, hoping to hear what he was saying to other people. But he turned around and called her by name and said she was a gossip and a liar and she had stolen from her employer. He went on and on. She ran away, but he followed her. The farther she ran, the louder he yelled and the more people that heard. It was like he was reading a list of everything she had ever done wrong. Finally, she begged him to stop and he told her she should repent of her sins and follow Yeshua and that if she did, God would forgive her for everything."

Decker shook his head in wonderment.

"There's one other strange thing about them," the driver added after a moment. "They claim one of their leaders is the Christian apostle John."

Decker was about to ask the driver to explain when Christopher, who until this point had remained silent and distracted, suddenly jumped as if he had received an electric shock. "What?" Christopher asked the driver, his voice full of both surprise and dread.

"Yes, pretty crazy, huh?"

Christopher's brow seemed to furrow in pain. His eyes moved slowly but erratically, as though there was a very unpleasant scene running through his memory over and over again.

"Christopher, are you all right?" Decker whispered. Christopher didn't answer. For the next several minutes they rode in silence, but Decker could see that inside Christopher's mind there was a battle raging. After a few more minutes Christopher seemed to slowly resign himself to whatever was bothering him. Finally he spoke.

"I'm sorry for not answering you earlier," he told Decker. "I've just remembered something." Decker remained silent, though it was obvious he wanted to know more. But this was not the place; it would have to wait until they reached the hotel.

A half hour later the driver pulled up to the front door of the Ramada Renaissance Hotel. It was Decker's choice. It was the same hotel that he and Tom Donafin had stayed in twenty years earlier. He had even tried to get the same rooms but they were unavailable. As they got out of the car, Decker's thoughts were torn between his own memories of this place and wanting to know what Christopher had remembered in the cab. The pain had passed from Christopher's eyes. Now he was just deep in thought.

❏

About forty yards away on the other side of the street, two men watched. On the forehead of one was the mark of the KDP.

"There they are," the smaller of the two men said.

"I see them," answered the one with the mark.

"So, let's do what we came for."

The one with the mark hesitated. "Maybe we should wait until they're separated."

"You're not changing your mind, are you, Scott?" the smaller one asked.

"No . . . I mean . . . I don't know; maybe I am, Joel. It all made so much sense before, but now that we're here"—Scott Rosen shook his head—"all of a sudden I'm not so sure we should do it."

❏

Decker tipped the bellman who brought the luggage to their adjoining rooms and then closed the door. Finally, he and Christopher could talk openly. "What did you remember in the car?" he asked, not wanting to waste any time.

Christopher seemed to be searching for words. "It's about the crucifixion. It's . . ." Christopher paused, and then started again, "Somehow, what the driver said about the Apostle John brought back a memory that . . . I don't know, maybe I've suppressed it. Maybe I don't want to remember."

"What?" Decker prodded.

"The Bible says that it was Judas who betrayed Jesus." Christopher shook his head. "He has always been blamed, but Judas is not the one who betrayed me.[64] He had a part in it, but he was deceived. The one who put him up to it was John. I remember it clearly," Christopher continued, "but I still don't understand why he did it. John was one of my closest friends. And yet he betrayed me. He got Judas to do the dirty work and then blamed it all on him. But John planned it. Somehow he convinced Judas it was necessary to turn me over to the *Sanhedrin*—the Jewish officials—in order to fulfill an Old Testament prophecy. He told Judas that when the prophecy was fulfilled, I would call down the armies of God to defeat the Roman legions who occupied Israel and I would bring about a Jewish kingdom that would be like heaven on earth.

"I can see it like it was yesterday. As I hung there on the cross, of all of the disciples, John was the only one who came.[65] I knew what he had done. When I saw him there, I thought he had come to ask forgiveness. I called to him to come closer so I could speak with him. I told him I knew what he had done. To my surprise, he admitted it freely, but without remorse; he almost seemed to boast about it. Yet to everyone else, he let the blame fall on Judas. And poor Judas, overcome by his undeserved guilt, hanged himself.[66]

"I tried to reason with John. I told him that if he would just ask, he would be forgiven. I would forgive him and I was sure the others would as well. But he refused. He bragged that forever-

[64]Readers are reminded of the *Important Note from the Author* at the beginning of this book.

[65]John 19:25-27.

[66]Matthew 27:5.

more Judas would be known as the betrayer of the Messiah, and then he laughed and said that he would be remembered as 'John the beloved.'

"I told him that despite his lack of repentance, I forgave him for what he had done to me, but I could not forgive him for what he had done to Judas."

"But that was two thousand years ago," Decker argued. "How could John still be alive?"

"I don't know," Christopher answered. "But I know it's him. I can feel it."

Decker realized he was just going to have to trust that Christopher knew what he was talking about, no matter how fantastic it sounded.

"Do you think he knows about you?" Decker asked.

"I don't think so."

"Maybe coming to Israel was a mistake. If John really has a hundred and forty-four thousand followers it may not be safe for you to be here."

"I don't think we need to worry, Decker. There's no way he could know about me. I just wish I could understand why he betrayed me."

❑

Decker and Christopher decided to nap for a few hours before going out for the afternoon. Decker had not seen the Temple since it was completed and Christopher, who was well known in Israel as the man who had returned the Ark, had an open invitation from the high priest for a personal tour. Much of the Temple was forbidden to non-Jews, so they would not be able to see all of it, but they would see more than most.

When Decker awoke he looked at the clock and realized he had overslept by several hours. It was almost three-thirty. This would make it much harder for him to adjust to Israeli time, but he thought the extra sleep would be good for Christopher. He got dressed quickly and knocked at the door between their two rooms to wake Christopher, but there was no answer. He knocked again and then opened the door. Christopher was not there. Taped to the mirror in his room was a note in Christopher's handwriting.

> I knocked on your door, but you didn't answer. I decided
> to let you sleep. I'm just going to wander around the old
> city for a while. I need some time to think. Don't wait up
> if I'm late.

Decker decided he'd do the same. The old city wasn't that big—maybe he'd run into Christopher along the way.

❑

As Decker walked down the narrow streets and still narrower alleyways of the city, he thought back to the time he had been here with Tom Donafin. Tom had done all the sightseeing then; Decker just looked at the brochures and picture postcards Tom brought back. He had been saving most of his sightseeing for when Elizabeth and the girls arrived for Christmas vacation. But that had never happened. Decker sighed. Even after all these years, he thought of them every day and still missed them terribly.

By five o'clock the sun had begun to set and Decker found a small restaurant down a side alley where he had dinner. Afterward he headed back to the hotel. Christopher still had not returned, so Decker left the door between their rooms open and watched a movie until he fell asleep. When he awoke it was still dark outside and he assumed he had slept for a couple of hours. He went to Christopher's room and found it just as it was before; the note still hung on the mirror. Decker went back in his room to turn off the television and saw that the clock on his night table said it was nearly six; Christopher had been gone all night. Decker ran back into Christopher's room as if that might make some difference. It made none.

Decker called the number for Christopher's phone and then realized when he heard the ringing from Christopher's suitcase that he had not taken it with him. He called the front desk, but the night desk clerk had not seen him. He called the hotel restaurant, but it was closed. He called the hotel bar, but it too was closed. Reluctantly, he called Jackie Hansen, who was just getting ready for bed in New York, but she had not heard from him. Finally, he called the Italian embassy in Tel Aviv. Decker identified himself to the person in charge and at his insistence, the ambassador was roused from his sleep. The ambassador, who didn't really appreciate being awakened, said he had not heard from Christopher and was not even aware that he was in the country. He took advantage of the opportunity to point out to Decker that it was proper protocol to notify the embassy whenever a visiting ambassador was in the country. The ambassador recommended calling the police, but Decker said he wanted to wait just a little longer for Christopher to show up before doing that. The ambassador didn't argue.

Decker went down to the hotel lobby to wait and let the desk clerk know where he was in case any calls came in. Time went by very slowly, but Decker felt he should wait until at least eight o'clock before calling the police. He checked his watch frequently and as soon as eight o'clock came he crossed the lobby to make the call. As he reached into his pocket for the correct change he suddenly felt a presence near him and looked up. Standing there not two feet away was a familiar face he had not seen in more than a year. He was quite a bit thinner than the last time he had seen him, but Decker recognized him immediately. "Secretary Milner?" Decker said, surprised to see him there.

"Hello, Decker," Milner answered.

"What are you doing here?" Decker asked as he hung up the phone. "Have you seen Christopher?"

"Christopher is safe," Milner said, not directly answering the question.

"Thank God! Where is he? I thought he might have been taken hostage by the—" Decker stopped himself.

Milner finished his sentence for him. "By the KDP?" Decker did not respond, though he was surprised that Milner knew what he was thinking. "No," Milner continued, "I have no doubt they'd love to do just that, but Christopher is safe."

"Well, where is he?"

Milner reached out and touched Decker's shoulder "Look," he said. Decker sensed a power flowing from Milner's hand and suddenly in his mind's eye, he could see Christopher. The scene was as clear to him as the room around him. Christopher was sitting on a large stone near the mouth of a cave. He was alone and in a mountainous area that could best be described as wilderness. "Is he all right?" asked Decker.

"He's fine, though by now he's beginning to grow hungry." Milner removed his hand from Decker's shoulder and instantly the vision vanished.

"If you know where he is, take me to him."

"That's not possible," Milner answered. "He must be left alone. This is his time of preparation."

"Preparation for *what?*" Decker demanded.

"Mr. Hawthorne, the world is about to undergo a time such as it has never known before. A time so dark and bleak that the destruction of the Russian Federation and what we call the Disaster will seem mild by comparison. Unfortunately there is nothing we can do to prevent its occurrence. But if we as a species are to emerge from it and to go on to our ultimate destiny, it will happen only under Christopher's leadership. Without that leadership, the world as we know it will utterly perish. I have known this since years before I first saw him, and now you know it as well. What Christopher goes through now will prepare him for that hour."

Decker was too stunned to respond right away. In the back of his mind he had always wondered if there wasn't some greater purpose to Christopher's birth than simply being the product of Harry Goodman's experiment. After a moment he managed to ask, "What about the KDP?"

"They shall not harm him, though they would relish an opportunity to do so."

"Who are they?" Decker asked. "Are they a part of this?"

"They are. As you know, when Alice Bernley was alive she headed the Lucius Trust near the UN. That location was not an accident. For years the Trust has been a sort of clearinghouse for thousands of what we call New Age groups from all around the world." Decker started to speak, but Milner anticipated his response and continued. "The New Age is not just some fad, some passing fancy. It is the result of a maturing, a ripening of the human species in preparation for the final and most glorious step in its evolution. Humanity is on the very threshold of an evolutionary stride that shall place us as far above our present state as we are now above the ants on the forest floor.

"The KDP were to have been the spearhead of that," Milner continued. "Unfortunately, at the very moment of their inception their course was subverted by the two men who are now their leaders."

"One of whom is the Apostle John?" Decker asked.

"Yes." Milner did not appear at all surprised that Decker should know this. "You have heard of the strange ability of the KDP to look into a person's past?"

"Yes."

"Such an ability is only a faint precursor of what is to come. Soon that ability shall seem as no more than a firefly in the blazing sun. Such powers should be used to look into the hearts of others, to find those places where compassion is so desperately needed and to offer comfort. Instead, under the leadership of John and another man named Saul Cohen, they use their gift to dredge up what would be better left forgotten and to savagely claw open old wounds and call attention to human frailties. And yet, that is the least of their monstrous inhumanity. Their powers for evil are far greater than anything any sane mind could imagine. This drought Israel has suffered these sixteen months is their work. And they shall do far worse before it is over."

"What can be done to stop them?"

"By ourselves we can do nothing. The fate of the world and of humankind rests squarely on the shoulders of the one you have raised as your own son. The conclusion is by no means foreordained. Let us hope that he is equal to the task."

For a moment both men were silent. It took Decker a moment to even begin to comprehend the magnitude of what Milner had just told him.

"How long will Christopher have to stay out there?" Decker asked, finally breaking the silence.

"Forty days."

"Forty days!" Decker blurted out, loud enough for anyone in the lobby to hear him.

"There is no other way," Milner answered, exaggerating his whisper to quiet Decker.

"But if he doesn't freeze or die of thirst first, he'll starve!"

"He will do neither, though the preparation will certainly be brutal and unmerciful. Still, he is there by his own choice. No one could force this upon him. He has chosen it for himself. If he wishes, he may withdraw from the preparation at any time."

"Then I'll stay here and wait for him," Decker said.

"You too must choose of your own will," Milner said. "But you can do nothing here. If you return to New York you may be able to provide essential information to Christopher upon his return, which will help him in the decisions he must make."

Obviously there was no real choice; Decker had to return to New York. But just as obvious was his concern about leaving Christopher. He was sure Milner would never let any harm come to him; next to Decker no one was closer to Christopher, and in some respects Milner was probably closer. Still, this could be a matter of life and death. Milner could see the worry in Decker's eyes and so once more placed his hand on Decker's shoulder. Suddenly, a peace such as he had never known swept over Decker and his anxiety just seemed to vanish.

"Will you stay here?" Decker asked.

"Yes. I cannot go to him, but I will stay as close to him as I can."

Decker nodded his approval. "I'll leave on the next available flight, but I'll be back in thirty-eight days, before Christopher returns."

"Good," Milner said. "And now I must leave." Decker shook Milner's hand firmly and Milner turned to leave, but stopped before he had gone two steps. "Oh, Decker," he said as he turned halfway back around, "be particularly careful of Ambassador Faure."

"Is he a part of this somehow?"

"Not exactly," said Milner. "He's just a very ambitious man who will stop at nothing to become secretary-general. The forces who oppose us seek out such men as surrogates to accomplish their goals for them."

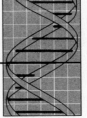

27

Stopping at Nothing

New York, New York

"BACK SO SOON?" Jackie Hansen asked as Decker arrived at the Italian Mission in New York. "I expected you two to be gone for at least a week." Decker showed himself into Christopher's office and signaled without speaking for Jackie to follow. "What's up?" she asked after she closed the door. "Where's Christopher?"

"He's still in Israel," Decker answered. "He's going to be there for about a month and a half." Decker was hoping to make this explanation as simple as possible, but it wasn't going to be easy.

"A month and a half!" Jackie exploded. "He can't do that! He's got things to do, meetings to attend, speaking engagements." Decker held up his hands to stop Jackie so he could continue his explanation, but she had never yielded to that ploy in the past, and she wouldn't now. "I'll just give him a call and point out a few things to him! What's the number at his hotel?"

"He's not at a hotel—"

"Fine. What's the number where he's staying?"

"Jackie, it's just not possible to reach him."

"Well, I'll just call him on his private number."

"Jackie, stop! He doesn't have his phone with him. Please, just wait a minute." Jackie crossed her arms and stopped talking. For a moment at least, she was listening. Decker quickly seized the opportunity. "We found Robert Milner."

Jackie dropped back against the edge of Christopher's desk. "Is he all right? Is he alive?" she asked. After being missing for sixteen months, nothing could be taken for granted.

"He's fine. He looks just fine." The news of Milner had the disarming effect on Jackie that Decker was hoping for. Now perhaps he could try to explain without Jackie interrupting. "Christopher is with him," he said. It was a little less than the truth, but a lot easier to explain.

"Well, they must be staying somewhere," Jackie said, getting back to her previous track.

"Yes, of course. But there's no phone and there's no way to reach them."

This understandably made no sense to Jackie. "You mean they're camping out or something?" she asked, offering the only suggestion she could think of.

"Well, yes. In a manner of speaking, I guess you could put it that way."

"But it's the middle of winter. They'll freeze!"

Decker had run out of simple explanations. "Look. they'll be fine. You know how I feel about Christopher; he's like my own son, the only family I've had since the Disaster. I wouldn't leave him there unless I was sure he'd be all right." As he finished he realized his words had been as much to reassure himself that he'd made the right decision as they were to convince Jackie.

"But why didn't he at least call?"

"I know it sounds crazy," Decker said, "but there just wasn't an opportunity." Jackie's expression told him that the part about it sounding crazy had been a correct assessment. "Look, I don't really understand it either. Milner said it all had to do with some New Age stuff."

"Oh," Jackie said, not as though she now understood, but rather as though suddenly she no longer needed to. "Well, uh . . . then I guess I'd better get to work canceling Christopher's appointments."

Decker was dumbfounded by Jackie's sudden change of attitude but was glad he didn't need to explain Christopher's absence any further. Now he could concentrate on his own anxiety about leaving Christopher in Israel in the first place—not a very comforting accomplishment, he realized.

"Jackie, there's one other thing," Decker added, "something I need your help with. When Milner and Christopher are finished with whatever it is they're doing in Israel, I'm supposed to meet them there and brief Christopher on everything that's happened at the UN while he's been gone—not just things that concern Italy or Europe, but everything. I'll have someone in my office compile and index every press release that goes out of the UN Printing Office. I'll take care of any reports, studies, speeches, white papers, etc. Christopher is especially interested in any information on Ambassador Faure's activities. I know you've got friends in nearly every office—"

"Not in Faure's office," Jackie interrupted.

"What about through the Lucius Trust?" Decker suggested.

"Faure doesn't let anyone from his office associate with the Trust."

"You're kidding! Barring free association of employees is against international human rights and labor laws."

"Well, he doesn't exactly prohibit it. It's more a matter of very careful hiring. Secretary Milner looked into it a few years back and apparently didn't think we could prove anything."

"Too bad," Decker said.

"Maybe somebody I know knows someone in Faure's office," Jackie suggested. "I'll try to find out."

"Great," Decker said. "But you need to be very careful in how you go about it. It could be very damaging if any of this gets back to Faure."

"Of course," Jackie answered.

❑

Two days later Jackie Hansen came up with a contact, a friend from the Lucius Trust who had a friend who was a low-level staffer in Faure's office. This meant that any information the staffer provided would be limited to what was said around the office, and then further limited by what he remembered and how well he remembered it, and then by what he was willing to tell Jackie's friend. Finally, it would be passed to Jackie, who would commit it all to paper for Decker. By the time the information reached Decker, it would be in at least its fourth telling. Still, it might help fill in some holes along the way and, as Decker well knew from his days in the press, any bit of information could be important.

The first piece of information to emerge was simply a vague indication that Faure was leaning hard on General Brooks to end the war as swiftly as possible—hardly a major news item. But it did help explain Brooks' action a week later when he issued an ultimatum to Chinese arms merchants to immediately cease sales to the combatants. The move did not set well with Ambassador Fahd, the Middle East Security Council Primary. The arms from China were not going in the generic sense to the "combatants," as Brooks described them, but rather to only one of the combatants: Pakistan, a country in Fahd's region. Stopping the sale of Chinese weapons would only benefit India. And Pakistan was not the only Middle East country with an interest; the Chinese arms were being purchased with oil money.

Fahd attempted to get the Security Council to condemn Brooks' ultimatum but was supported only by the West African representative. The Security Council was reluctant to interfere with the specific actions of the World Peace Organization. They saw their role as one of setting policy, not regulating tactics. As long as General Brooks' actions stayed within the conventions established in the WPO charter, the Security Council could be expected not to interfere.

China abstained from the vote. Ambassador Lee felt that voting to condemn General Brooks would be seen as tentative approval of the arms sales from her country. China's official position had always been that while it opposed the sales of weapons, it was not willing to interfere with the free trade of its citizens. Ambassador Lee, however, did proceed quickly and quite forcefully to prohibit Brooks from crossing into Chinese territory to enforce his ulti-matum. Any efforts to interdict the flow of arms from China would have to be at the border with Pakistan. Her motion passed nine to one, with only India opposing the directive.

Coincidentally, it was to be one of Ambassador Lee's final acts as a member of the Security Council. Two days later, while taking her regular early morning walk, Ambassador Lee was struck by a hit-and-run driver and died on the way to the hospital. Following her death, the Security Council voted to take a two-week recess to allow China to select a replacement. A memorial service was held for Lee in the Hall of the General Assembly before her body was returned to China for burial.

Two weeks later

"Welcome back, Mr. Ambassador."

"Thank you, Gerard," Ambassador Faure responded as he hung up his overcoat.

"How was your flight?"

"Too long. We sat at DeGaulle Airport for more than an hour before we even got off the ground." Faure sat down at his desk and began flipping through a short, neatly stacked pile of papers. "What's the news from General Brooks?" he asked his chief of staff without looking up.

"Things appear to be going well. As you predicted, the interdiction of Chinese arms into Pakistan has resulted in a distinct advantage for the Indian forces. General Brooks estimates that it will probably take another few weeks before we see the full effect, but I think we can look forward to a swift resolution of the conflict and, more important, to India's support on your next bid to become secretary-general. I think Ambassador Gandhi will find it difficult indeed to vote against you under the circumstances."

"Good. And our relations with Ambassador Fahd? Anything new there?"

"No. You're scheduled to have lunch with him tomorrow, so you should get a clear reading on his thoughts then. So far there has been no indication that he holds you personally responsible for General Brooks' actions. I think your support for Ambassador Lee's motion to prohibit UN forces from entering Chinese territory helped delineate you from Brooks in the minds of most of the Security Council."

Faure didn't respond; he was distracted from the conversation by one of the documents in the stack of papers. Poupardin knew the look and waited silently as Faure examined it. After a moment, Faure began to glance through the rest of the accumulated stack and picked up the conversation exactly where it had left off. "Yes," he said, smiling. "That couldn't have worked better if I had planned it."

"A few more fortuitous circumstances like that and you might have gotten China's support without having to—"

"Fortune is a very uncertain ally, Gerard," Faure chided. "Besides, we do not have the luxury of waiting for fortune to strike. Mark my words, if a new secretary-general is not chosen within the next six months, I'm convinced that the Security Council will vote to do away with the position altogether and have the responsibilities permanently rotate among the Council members. We must make our own fortunes." Poupardin nodded in agreement. "What about the Chinese situation?" Faure asked.

"You're scheduled for dinner with the new Chinese ambassador tomorrow night. I've prepared a briefing packet for you." Poupardin handed the packet to Faure. "I don't think you'll find anything outrageous there. Our intelligence on him indicates he's basically a reasonable man. He doesn't expect any promises. His main criterion in selecting a new secretary-general is simply that the candidate be willing to give a fair hearing to China's position."

"Well, I think I can convince him that I'll be all ears," Faure smiled.

"Of course," Poupardin continued, "since he's not asking for anything, we can't really count on his support. But if you can convince him you'd be the kind of secretary-general who's willing to listen, I think you can at least count on him not to oppose you."

"Excellent," Faure said, as he put the papers back in a pile on his desk. "Then I'd say we made a pretty good trade for Ambassador Lee."

"Yes, sir."

"What about Kruszkegin?"

"We're watching his schedule closely for the right opportunity."

"Be sure you clear it with me before you authorize any specific action. We can't afford any mistakes."

"Yes, sir."

"Well, if there is no more pressing news," Faure said, as he opened his brief case, "I picked up a few videos for you while I was in Paris. They came very highly rated."

"These look great," Poupardin said, as he took the disks from Faure and eagerly examined the photo collage on the cover of one of the disks. "We can watch these when you come over tonight."

"It sounds like fun, Gerard, but I promised Suzanne and Betty I'd take them to dinner when I got back," Faure said, referring to his wife and daughter. Poupardin was obviously disappointed. "I'm sorry, Gerard," he said, and then looked at his watch. "I suppose we have a few minutes right now, if you'd like."

Poupardin smiled and went to lock the door.

❑

Ambassador Lee's replacement was a much younger man in his early fifties. His stamina for the responsibilities of his new office would soon be tested. As the Security Council reconvened, they tasted the first bitter fruits of General Brooks' ultimatum and the resulting blockade at the Pakistan-China border. Forced to take up fixed positions to enforce the blockade, UN troops had quickly become the targets of sniper fire and guerrilla attacks by Pakistani forces. The Pakistani government officially condemned the attacks, stating that the attackers were independents, not associated with the Pakistani army. They also took the opportunity to reiterate their position that since the blockade was not in the host country's interest, the UN forces were not acting within their charter or in accordance with the original invitation from Pakistan for the placement of troops within its borders. They went on to explain that since all available Pakistani forces were engaged elsewhere, there was really very little they could do about the guerrilla attacks.

Far worse than all of this, however, were the threats of a rogue

Pakistani militia called the Pakistani Islamic Guard. According to the reports, the Islamic Guard, fearing that the war would soon swing in India's favor, had planted nuclear devices in eight major Indian cities. Though it seemed unlikely the Guard could have acquired nuclear weapons, the magnitude of the threat compelled the Security Council to take them seriously. The Guard's demands were straightforward enough. First, all UN and Indian forces must leave Pakistan, and second, for good measure, India must surrender the long-disputed Jammu-Kashmir province to Pakistani control. Prime Minister Rajiv Advani would consider neither demand, and thus far was satisfied to hurl insults and counterthreats.

28

The Power Within Him—
The Power Within Us All

The wilderness of Israel

IT WAS JUST AFTER DAWN. Robert Milner acted as navigator while Decker Hawthorne drove the rented Jeep through the mountain pass on their way to meet Christopher. In the Jeep Decker had brought food, bottled water, and a first-aid kit. His thoughts alternated between worry about the condition in which they would find Christopher and anticipation of what Robert Milner had told him in the lobby of the Ramada Renaissance forty days earlier. The barren countryside brought back memories of Decker's own wilderness experience eighteen years earlier, when he and Tom Donafin had made their way through Lebanon toward Israel before being rescued by Jon Hansen. He recalled the powerful shift of his emotions in that moment as he lay on the ground, tangled in barbed wire, with three rifles pointed at his head, expecting to be shot, and then suddenly recognizing the UN emblems on the soldiers' helmets and realizing that he and Tom were safe.

In the past, when Decker had recalled that moment, he'd thought of it as just another case of being in the right place at the right time. Now he could not help but believe it was much more. Had it not happened, he would not have met Jon Hansen, and he surely would never have become his press secretary. And had Decker not worked for Hansen, who later became secretary-general, then Christopher would not have had the opportunities he did to work in the UN and later to head a major UN agency and then become a UN ambassador serving on the Security Council. Surely this was more than chance.

It occurred to him that this chain of events had not just started on that road in Lebanon. There was the destruction of the Wailing Wall, and then he and Tom were taken hostage; and before that, there were the events that had allowed him to go to Turin, Italy, in the first place. Had he not gone to Turin, he certainly never would have been called by Professor Harry Goodman on that cold November night to come to Los Angeles to see what Goodman had discovered on the Shroud.

As he continued to think through the chain of circumstances that had brought him to this point, he tried to find the single weakest link in the chain, the seemingly least important event that, had it not occurred, would have averted any of the later events.

"Some things we must assign to fate," Robert Milner said, breaking the silence. It was as though he had been listening to Decker's thoughts.

"Uh . . . yeah, I guess so," Decker answered.

The days leading up to his return to Israel to find Christopher had been some of the most anxious of Decker's life. At times he could barely concentrate on his work as he counted the days until Christopher's return and anticipated what would follow. Milner had talked about a time so dark and bleak that the destruction of the Russian Federation and the Disaster would seem mild by comparison. Somehow the horror that might otherwise have consumed Decker at such a thought was mitigated by the hope that Milner also foresaw. Certainly, to this point, nothing cataclysmic had occurred, though the unrest in India and Pakistan might well foreshadow such events. Decker realized he would have to accept the bad along with the good. He just didn't want to dwell on it, especially if, as Milner indicated, such events were inevitable.

Ahead on the trail, a shapeless form began to take on definition. Had Decker noticed it before, he would have thought it was a bush or a tree stump or perhaps an animal, but until this moment it had blended so well into the background that it seemed an inseparable part of its surroundings. "There he is," said Milner.

Decker pressed a little harder on the gas pedal. As they got closer, he began to wonder again in what condition they would find Christopher. The last time they were together, Christopher had told Decker he was beginning to wonder whether in the final analysis his life had been a mistake. Now, forty days later, he was—according to Milner—the man who would lead mankind into "the final and most glorious step in its evolution."

In another moment they could see him clearly. His coat and clothes were dirty and tattered. He looked thin but strong. Over the forty days his hair had grown over his ears and he now had a full beard. When Decker saw his face, he was startled for a moment by the astounding resemblance to the face on the Shroud. One thing, however, was very obviously different. The face on the Shroud was peaceful and accepting in death. On Christopher's face was the look of a man driven to achieve his mission.

Milner was the first one out of the Jeep. He ran to Christopher and embraced him. Patting Christopher on the back caused a small cloud of dust to rise from his clothes. Christopher then went to Decker, who reached out his hand. Christopher refused it and instead hugged him as well. He smelled awful, but Decker held him for a long time anyway.

"Are you all right?" Decker asked. "I've been worried about you."

"Yes, yes. I'm fine." Then turning slightly to address both Decker and Milner, he continued. "It's all clear now. It was all part of the plan."

"What plan?" asked Decker.

"I've spoken with my father. He wants me to finish the task."

"You mean . . . God? You talked with God?"

Christopher nodded. "Yes," he said quietly. "He wants me to complete the mission I began two thousand years ago. And I need your help, both of you."

Decker felt as though he was standing on the crest of a tidal wave. Suddenly his life held more meaning than he'd ever imagined possible. He believed what Milner had told him about Christopher's destiny; if he hadn't, he never would have left Christopher alone in the desert. But then it had all been cerebral. Now he was hearing it from Christopher's own lips. This was a turning point, not only in the lives of these three men, but of time itself. Just as the coming of Christ had divided time between B.C. and A.D., this too would be a line of demarcation from which all else would be measured. This undoubtedly *was* the birth of a New Age. Decker wished Elizabeth were alive to share it with him.

"What can we do?" Decker managed.

"We must return to New York immediately," Christopher answered. "Millions of lives are at stake."

❏

Before leaving New York, Decker had arranged for the loan of a private jet from David Bragford, telling him it was for Milner. As planned, the jet and crew were waiting at Ben Gurion Airport when Decker, Christopher, and Milner arrived. Decker had brought clothes and a shaving kit from home for Christopher, but though he eagerly took advantage of the shower on Bragford's plane and welcomed the clean clothes, Christopher decided to forego the razor and keep the beard.

As Christopher ate his first meal in forty days, Decker briefed him on events at the UN. Afterward Christopher began to pore over the reams of documents Decker had brought for him to review.

❏

Three hours into the flight, one of the crew members came into the cabin, obviously very concerned about something. "What is it?" Decker asked.

"Sir," he said, "the captain has just picked up a report on the radio. Apparently, the war in India has just gone nuclear."

"We're too late," Christopher whispered to himself as he let his head fall into his open hands.

The crewman continued, "The Pakistani Islamic Guard have detonated two nuclear bombs in New Delhi. Millions are dead."

For a long moment they sat in stunned silence, then Decker turned to Milner. "This is what you were talking about in Jerusalem, isn't it?"

"Only the beginning," Milner said as he reached over and hit the remote control to turn on the satellite television.

Immediately the screen showed the mushroom cloud of the first atomic bomb set off in New Delhi. The billowing cloud of debris seemed to roll back the sky like an immense scroll of ancient tattered parchment. Two days after the Pakistani Guard first warned of hidden nuclear weapons, the television network had set up remote cameras to run twenty-four hours a day outside the targeted cities just in case the Guard carried out its threats. Even from ten miles away, the camera began to shake violently as the earth trembled from the blast's awesome shock wave. Several hundred yards in front of the camera a small two-story building vibrated with the quake and then collapsed. An instant later a bright flash on the screen marked the second explosion.

"That was the scene approximately one hour ago," the network commentator said, his voice registering his horror, "as two atomic blasts, set off by the Pakistani Islamic Guard, rocked the Indian subcontinent. It is believed that the action came in response to the successful interdiction of weapons into Pakistan from China and a new ultimatum issued by General Brooks, commander of UN forces in the region. According to sources close to the Pakistani Islamic Guard, leaders of the Guard were convinced that UN special forces were close to locating the bombs, which would have left little to prevent India from invading Pakistan.

"Within minutes of the explosions the Pakistani government strongly condemned the action by the Guard who, they repeated, are rogue forces *not* associated with the Pakistani government. But by then India had already retaliated, launching two nuclear-tipped missiles on Pakistan. Apparently prepared for such a response from India, China immediately launched interceptors, which successfully brought down the Indian missiles before they could reach their targets.

"Prior to that launch, China had attempted to maintain a neutral position in the long-running conflict between its neighbors. That neutrality was frequently called into question, however, because of the Chinese arms merchants who served as the main source of weapons for Pakistan."

As Christopher, Decker, and Milner watched, new information poured in at an incredible rate. In a matter of only a few hours, the entire war was unfolding. In response to China's action, India launched a conventional attack on the Chinese interceptor bases, while simultaneously launching five additional missiles on Pakistan. Three were intercepted; two reached their targets.

Pakistan then responded to India's attack by launching a volley of its own nuclear weapons and within minutes the Pakistani Islamic Guard set off the remaining bombs they had planted in Indian cities.

In a temporary lull in the action, the scene on television switched to a satellite feed from a camera mounted on the top of a remotely controlled all-terrain rover, which showed the first horrifying scenes from the suburban areas of New Delhi. Fire was everywhere. Rubble filled the streets. The sky was filled with thick black smoke from the fires and radioactive fallout, which blocked out the setting sun as though it were covered by a loosely woven black cloth. Scattered around the landscape were hundreds of people, dead and dying. Immediately in front of the vehicle, the mostly nude body of a young Indian woman lay sprawled in the street. All but a few scraps of her clothing had been burned away. On the less charred parts of her body, where some skin remained, the flowered pattern of the sari she had been wearing was seared into her flesh like a tattoo.

Sitting on the street beside the woman's body, a startled young girl, three or four years old, looked up at the rover and began screaming. The bombs had not been so merciful to her as to her mother; she might languish two or three days before life fully released its grip on her. For a moment the camera dwelled on her. Her skin was covered with numerous open blisters.

Christopher turned away from the screen. "I could have prevented this," he said. It took a moment for the statement to sink through the horror and register with Decker.

"Christopher, there's nothing you could have done," Decker answered. "It's useless to blame yourself."

"But there *is* something I could have done. I told you before we left New York that I felt Faure was going to do something that would lead to catastrophe, and that there was nothing I could do to stop it. But it wasn't true. There was *one* thing I could have done. And now, because I hesitated, millions have been killed and millions more will die. Even after the war is over there will be untold deaths from fallout and radiation poisoning. And unless the UN acts to provide immediate relief, millions more will die of starvation and disease."

"But it's crazy to blame yourself for this. If this is the result of something Faure did, then the responsibility rests with him alone."

"Oh, the responsibility does indeed rest with Faure. It was he who put General Brooks back in control, and it was he who directed Brooks to issue the two ultimatums. With the first, Faure was hoping to bring the war to a quick close in India's favor. In return, he expected to gain Nikhil Gandhi's support for his bid to become secretary-general. With the second ultimatum, Faure believed he could force the hand of the Islamic Guard. General Brooks assured him that the Guard didn't really have nuclear devices planted in India, but Faure knew the risk he was taking! If there were no bombs, then the ultimatum would call the Islamic Guard's bluff. On the other hand, if the threat was real, Faure knew that a war would destabilize India to the point that Gandhi would likely return to rebuild India and Rajiv Advani would replace him as primary on the Security Council. Either way, Faure calculated that he would benefit."

"Are you sure about all this?" Decker asked, unable to believe that Faure would sacrifice so many lives to become secretary-general.

"I am," Christopher answered. "I'm not saying Faure intended to start a nuclear war. But through his ceaseless quest for power, his neglect of the WPO, and his appointment of corrupt men, Faure first created the environment where war could happen. Then, in his desperation to become secretary-general, he pushed the combatants over the edge."

"Christopher is correct," Milner said with certainty.

"Faure is also responsible for the murder of Ambassador Lee," Christopher added. "And he is planning the assassination of Yuri Kruszkegin. There is nothing he will not do to achieve his goals. I must stop him now, before he can do any more."

"Why didn't Faure just kill Gandhi, instead of risking the lives of so many?" Decker asked, still struggling to believe the magnitude of Faure's malevolence.

"The death of Ambassador Lee was believed to be an accident," Milner answered. "If Kruszkegin died, most would assume it was coincidence. But no one would believe that the death of three primary members was just a fluke, especially if soon after that Faure became secretary-general precisely because of the replacement of those three members. Besides, killing Gandhi would still leave him the problems in India and Pakistan to deal with as secretary-general. Better to try to end the war quickly in India's favor and ingratiate himself to Gandhi, rather than bring suspicion on himself with three untimely deaths."

"What are you going to do?" Decker asked Christopher.

"In the third chapter of Ecclesiastes," Christopher answered, "King Solomon wrote, 'There is a time for everything: a time to be born and a time to die, a time to plant and a time to reap; a time to heal and a time to kill.'"

Decker looked back and forth from Christopher to Milner and then back to the television screen. As the camera panned the devastation, in the distance, where the smoke and radioactive cloud had not yet entirely shrouded the earth, the moon rose above the horizon, glowing blood red through the desecrated sky.

❑

It was another two hours before their plane landed in New York. They went directly to the United Nations, where the Security

Council was meeting in closed session. As night fell in the east, the war continued to spread. Nuclear warheads dropped like overripe fruit, appearing as falling stars in the night sky. The destruction spread six hundred miles into China and to the south nearly as far as Hyderābād, India. West and north of Pakistan, the people of Afghanistan, southeastern Iran, and southern Tajikstan gathered their families and all they could carry on their backs, and beat a hurried path away from the war. In just days the local weather patterns would fill their fields, rivers, and streams with toxic fallout.

Pakistan was little more than an open grave. India's arsenal was completely spent. What was left of its army survived in small clusters that were cut off from all command and control. Most would die soon from radiation. China was the only participant still in control of its military and it had no interest in going any further with the war.

In the few hours it had taken them to fly from Israel and arrive at the UN, the war had begun and ended. The final estimate of the number killed would exceed four hundred and twenty million. There were no winners.

❑

Christopher reached the door of the Security Council Chamber and burst through, followed closely by Decker and Milner. For a moment the members stared at the intruders. Everyone knew Decker, but they had not seen Milner in a year and a half and the change in Christopher was more than the hair and the beard; his whole demeanor had changed. When he recognized Christopher, Gerard Poupardin, who sat some distance from Faure, looked over at another staffer and laughed, "Who does he think he is? Jesus Christ?"

Christopher seized the opportunity provided by the startled silence. "Mr. President," Christopher said, addressing the Canadian ambassador who sat in the position designated for the president of the Security Council. "Though I have no desire to disrupt the urgent business of this body in its goal of providing relief to the peoples of India, Pakistan, China, and the surrounding countries, there is one among us who is not fit even to cast his vote among an assembly of thieves, much less this august body!"

"You're out of order!" Faure shouted as he jumped to his feet. "Mr. President, the alternate from Europe is out of order." The Canadian ambassador reached for his gavel but froze at the sheer power of Christopher's glance.

"Gentlemen of the Security Council," Christopher continued.

"You're out of order!" Faure shouted again. Christopher looked at Faure, and suddenly and inexplicably Faure fell back into his chair, silent.

Christopher continued. "Gentlemen of the Security Council, seldom in history can the cause of a war be traced to one man. On this occasion, it can be. One man sitting among you bears nearly the total burden of guilt for this senseless war. That man is the ambassador from France, Albert Faure."

Faure struggled to his feet. "That's a lie!" he shouted.

Christopher stated the charges against Faure.

"Lies! All lies!" Faure shouted. "Mr. President, this outrage has gone on long enough. Ambassador Goodman has obviously gone completely mad." Faure could feel his strength returning. "I insist that he be restrained and removed from this chamber and that . . ." Faure once again fell silent as Christopher turned and pointed, his arm fully extended toward him.

"Confess," Christopher said in a quiet but powerful voice.

Faure stared at Christopher in disbelief and began to laugh out loud.

"Confess!" Christopher said again, this time a little louder.

Abruptly, Faure's laughter ceased. The panic in his eyes could not begin to reveal the magnitude of his torment. Without warning he felt as though his blood were turning to acid as it coursed through his veins. His whole body felt as if he were on fire from the inside.

"Confess!" Christopher said a third time, now shouting his demand.

Faure looked in Christopher's eyes and what he saw there left no doubt as to the source of his sudden anguish. He stumbled in pain and caught himself on the table in front of him. Blood began to trickle from his mouth and down his chin as he bit through the tender flesh of his lower lip; his jaw clenched uncontrollably like a vice under the unbearable agony. Gerard Poupardin ran toward Faure as those near him helped him to his seat.

The pain grew steadily worse. There was no way out. "Yes! Yes!" he cried suddenly in excruciating anguish, as he pulled free of the grip of those helping him. "It's all true! Everything he has said is true! The war, Ambassador Lee's death, the plan to kill Kruszkegin, all of it!"

Everyone in the room stared wide-eyed in disbelief. No one understood what was happening, least of all Gerard Poupardin. But everyone heard him—Faure had clearly confessed.

Faure hoped only that his confession would bring relief from his torment, and in that he was not disappointed. No sooner had he finished his confession than he fell to the floor, dead.

Someone ran for a doctor and for about fifteen minutes the chamber was filled with confusion, until finally Faure's lifeless body was taken from the room.

"Gentlemen," came a somber voice from near the spot where Faure had fallen. It was Christopher. "A quarter of the world's population is dead or threatened by death in China, India, and the eastern portions of the Middle East. There is so much that must be done, and it must be done quickly. As indelicate as it may seem: With the death of Ambassador Faure, until France can send a new ambassador and the nations of Europe can elect a new primary, as alternate from Europe, I am now that region's acting primary representative. Gentlemen, let us get to the business at hand."

❑

The coroner's report would find that Albert Faure died of a massive heart attack, brought on, it seemed, by the tremendous burden of guilt for what he had done. For Decker, no explanation was necessary: Christopher had begun to exercise the unexplored powers within him. He could only hope and pray that these powers would be equal to the challenges the world would soon face as Christopher led mankind into the final stage of its evolution and into the dawn of the New Age of humankind.